Half-Bead of Fundy

A Native American Mystery

PHYLLIS A. FAST

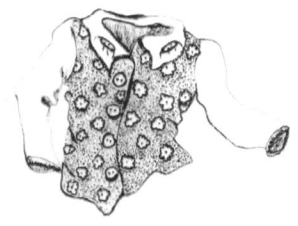

Half-Bead of Fundy: A Native American Mystery
First in a series

Fast, Phyllis A.
ISBN: 978-1523940349 (Library edition)
ISBN: 978-0-9974977-2-4 (trade paperback)
ISBN: 978-0-9974977-0-0 (ebook)

This book is a work of fiction. All of the characters, organizations, and events portrayed in this novel are either the products of the author's imagination or are used fictitiously.

Keywords:
1. Fiction—mystery. 2. Native American—fiction. 3. Alaska Native—fiction.
4. Artists—fiction.

Denaakk'e words are in the Koyukon Athabascan Dictionary (2000) by Jules Jetté and Eliza Jones. The editor-in-chief was Dr. James Kari, linguist. It was published by the University of Alaska Fairbanks. Significant linguist sources are Dr. Elisa Peter Jones of Koyukuk. Alaska and her daughter, Susan Paskvan of Huslia, Alaska.

Cover painting 'Pocohontas Lips' by Phyllis A. Fast, oil, 2003.

Book design and prepress services by Kate Weisel (weiselcreative.com)

PRAISE FOR
HALF-BEAD OF FUNDY

Half-Bead of Fundy — Native American Paranormal
5 stars (Amazon)

"A 5-star blend of cultural interfaces driven around in a used Passat by a young Native American woman who hears a 'voice'. The 'voice' belongs to Deloo's metaphysical spirit guide Baasee'. Then there is the Chinese connection, the Cuban spirit healing, the Canadians, the Boston Brahmins and the Harvard alums. All told with a Native American curved story line involving murder, cross country chases and scaling tall buildings while dodging bullets. It would take a Native American anthropologist with a Harvard PhD to make it work. So it does.

"For readers interested in Alaskan Native American culture there are words, references and philosophy that all add to the telling. The most intriguing part, for me, was the relationship and machinations between Spirit Guide and guided mortal. Is this the author's vivid imagination or does she have a special connection? Is a chance meeting a coincidence or a connection? We may find out if there are sequels.

"While the author avoids any form of clichéd cliff hanger there are hints of further adventures of Deloo and Baasee, perhaps on the metaphysical side. I've read several other 'paranormal mysteries' but this is the first that provided me with more than just a glimpse of how paranormal may work. I look forward to future, hopefully far reaching, adventures of Deloo and Bassee." –DL, 2016

Half-Bead of Fundy
5 stars (Amazon)

"A must read Mystery. Entertaining and elegantly written. The story races along with passion between the mystical spirit world of Baasee and the Koyukon Athabascan, Deloo, to unravel the twists and turns of this thriller!" – JH, 2016

Half-Bead of Fundy
5 stars (Amazon)

"Fast has created an engaging mixture of mystery and humor. The narrative, told from the viewpoint of Deloo's spirit guide, swings through maritime Canada to Boston as the young Athabaskan solves the mysterious death of an innkeeper." – JKR, 2016

DEDICATION

To my mother, Elsie Feodosia Harper Fast

ACKNOWLEDGEMENTS

Like all stories, there is a grain of truth to them. That grain in this novel is the inn on the eastern side of Nova Scotia. Years ago I happened upon such an inn. Unlike in that of Deloo's story, I didn't call ahead and the inn was full. When I returned a couple of years later, I tried to find it, but couldn't. Moreover, none of the many people I asked had ever heard of it.

Many people helped me in varying capacities. My friend and colleague, Jane Harper, tops that list. Not only is she a resourceful copyeditor and brilliant writer, as well as a lifelong friend. I am grateful to Jan Harper Haines, author of *Cold River Spirits*, for providing constant reminders of the essence of good writing. Dr. Gerald Kovacich, author of many books on global information warfare, offered me sound advice on how to organize my writing for publication.

Two of my colleagues at the University of Alaska Anchorage were steadfast mentors about the lessons that we get from the fields of sociology and cultural anthropology. They are Dr. Ann Jache, a sociologist, and Dr. Kerry Feldman, an anthropologist and writer himself.

Many others have read parts of the novel. Many of them are in my family and include Esther Fast and Richard Fast, Johanna Harper, and Michael Harper. I am also grateful to my niece, Ariel Myers in Hawaii, and my niece, Lisa Meyers in Alaska. I also thank Darryl Lundahl and Barbara Haury of Luebeck Germany for their constant encouragement.

LIST OF CHARACTERS

Deloo Dena Goode   The protagonist is an Alaska Native woman, age 21, whose mother (Taale) is Tleeyegg'e hut'aane (also known as Koyukon Athabascan), Athabascans who live on the lower Yukon River in Alaska. Since people of the Tleeyegg'e nation follow the mother's line by cultural custom, therefore so is Deloo. Deloo's father is a deceased white American whom she never knew. Deloo (pronounced *duh-LOO*) is short for Delookeełt'aa, and means she's cute in Denaakk'e (the language of the Tleeyegg'e nation).

Baasee'   Spirit guide for Deloo. The storyteller is both telling as well as playing very active trickster-like role. In Denaakk'e her name means 'Thank You'. The name is pronounced *bah-SEE*). It rhymes with bossy. She is proud of her fourteen thousand plus years of life and afterlife.

Taale Dena   An Alaska Native who is Tleeyegg'e hut'aane (also known as Koyukon Athabascan), Athabascans who live on the lower Yukon River in Alaska. People of the Tleeyegg'e nation follow the mother's line by cultural custom.

Prize Woman   Also called Ming Liu Wu, is half Chinese and half Inuit of Canada. She is fluent in Inuttitut of northern Québec (her first language), Inuktitut (spoken in other parts of Canada), English, French, and Mandarin.

Chuan Wu   Ming's husband. He is Chinese, speaks Mandarin and English, and several computer languages.

Brent Clerick   Archaeologist. He is a white man from Alaska.

Howard Lee   Banker. He is both white with heritage in Canada and the United State as well as Chinese

Luisa Lee   Howard's wife. She a Cuban curandera (healer) from Florida, United States

Harold (HayJay) Johnson   Deceased, nephew and best friend of Howard Lee

Rosemoira Keilleher   Innkeeper of the Secret Spirit Inn in Nova Scotia

Qanik   Deceased, he is the fiancé of the little ghost

Little Ghost   Deceased, she is Ming Liu's twin sister and Qanik's fiancée.

Woody (Woodrow) Morrow   The late Arthur Goode's best friend

Arthur Goode   Deceased, Deloo's husband. He died five months after they married.

Matty Goode   Arthur's mother

Zachary Goode   Arthur's father

Charlotte Lee   Howard's mother

Lydia   Howard's older sister

DENAAKK'E ATHABASCAN WORDS
(language of Deloo and Taale).

baasee'   thank you, borrowed from French fur traders of the 19th century. Pronounced *bah-SEE*

Denaakk'e   The Athabascan language (one of 11 in Alaska) spoken by the Koyukon people

dotson   common raven. When capitalized, Dotson or Raven refer to the trickster spirit of the raven. Pronounced *dot-SONE*

hutłanee   a warning of bad luck. Pronounced *hoot-LAN-ee*. The ł is called the Indian-L or Bar-L. You can pronounce by pressing your tongue upward against the roof of your mouth and hissing like a cat.

Koyukon   a fabricated name for the Tleeyegg'e hut'aane Athabascans who occupied the area around the Yukon River at the mouth of the Koyukuk River. There are eleven separate nations (once called tribes) of Athabascans in Alaska.

Naagheltaale   the Big Dipper constellation. Pronounced *Nah-rell-TALL-eh*. gh is made by a the twist of sound at the back of the tongue.

Tleeyegg'e hut'aane   the word used in Denaakk'e for their own nation.

More Denaakk'e words are in the *Koyukon Athabascan Dictionary* (2000) by Jules Jetté and Eliza Jones with the mastery of Dr. James Kari, linguist. It was published by the University of Alaska Fairbanks.

CHAPTER ONE

"Why does this silver stuff keep jabbing me?" Deloo twisted her wedding band. Arthur, her late husband, claimed it was Asian. She watched a car pull into the roadside turnout next to her. "Maybe they know. The guy looks Chinese." She shuddered. "Ugh! What kind of racist creep am I now? I'm not the queen of the world. It doesn't matter what he looks like."

Deloo's work-rough hands exposed her brief stint of pinching slim fingers between the killer jaws of pliers and getting in the way of other angry tools. By contrast, the wedding band showed off a smooth dragon carved into green stone and centered by the offending silver filigree. Deloo was rich at last. The kind of fresh-faced widow-rich that I arranged.

I am Baasee', an old spirit guide. Like Deloo, I stem from multiple heritages, and like Deloo, only one of those heritages counts. For me it's Tuudzaado people. For Deloo, it's Tleeyegg'e hut'aane, a nation also called Koyukon Athabascan of the Yukon River in Alaska. Her late husband, Arthur, called her Lulu, but she prefers Deloo. I knew Arthur would die soon. Deloo didn't and grieved. Now I worry about her.

Grandfather Kwaikit observed in our silent way, ~*as usual, you are too bossy. Let Deloo figure things out for herself. Your job is to make sure she stays healthy and successful.*~

I agreed with him, although there's nothing halfway about poverty. Poor half-breeds get lumped in with the other poor Natives. People called Deloo a welfare brat even when her mother rejected food stamps. Deloo hated the way people treated her. I, Baasee', felt it my spirit guide duty to improve Deloo's life. Normally I try to make do with helping Deloo make the best of whatever happens. There was one time, though, when I took matters into my own tendrils. I, Baasee' The Belligerent, knocked a boy right into a snow bank and didn't let him up. He was the first to call her a welfare brat. He thought he'd fallen by accident. He couldn't tell that I, an invisible spirit woman, had shoved him down. Grandfather Kwaikit saved the brat's life by pulling me away from him.

~*Make do with what she's got,*~ he told me over and over again. ~*Making do doesn't mean killing some other poor mortal—or your mortal!*~

Okay, so I have maturity issues and I'm doing better. That was almost seventeen years ago. Deloo still doesn't know I exist. She doesn't believe in spirits, but she does believe in herself. At least there's some justice in the spiritless world. That rotten kid got in with the wrong crowd and now lives in a jail somewhere far away. My little Deloo grew up tough and learned how to fight. Her mother, Taale, taught her that. I decided I should make her rich. Grandfather agreed for once. It helped that Deloo's half-breed green eyes sparkled and that she uses her dimple with sweet innocence. So what if her husband died young? He would have loved her forever, but did not know how important his life insurance was to Deloo's future. He's dead now. So sorry. So sad. I looked around for Grandfather Kwaikit. It wasn't my fault and so far Deloo has handled the first year of grief well enough using Athabascan stoicism.

Enough dithering and time to work with the here and now. A woman hopped out of the newly arrived vehicle in our pullout and ripped off the black and white dress that showed off her glossy hair.

"Huh," Deloo grumbled. "A half-breed dress. No wonder she took it off. No one wants half-breeds, not even half-breed clothes." I sent her an image of Great Aunt Pauline frowning. Deloo snickered at my anonymous humor.

Meanwhile, the stranger flung her offensive dress into the trunk. Smells of rancid fish oil prickled Deloo's nostrils. Something black fell on the ground beside the stranger. The woman ignored it and reached for a second, more colorful dress.

Her companion, the driver, shouted, "Hey! Someone's watching you."

The woman scowled. Her eyebrows formed indignant knotty eyebrows. Reedy as a willow shoot, her dark skin betrayed her own mixed descent. Then she smiled, transforming her face into radiant beauty.

"Prize Woman," Deloo mouthed, plucking a mythical name from memory.

In a fluid motion, Prize Woman hurled the second, very vibrant garment skyward. It soared above her head before spinning downward.

Once the new dress encased her, she dove into her car. The driver squealed onto the road, spraying the side of Deloo's Passat with gravel.

Above us, I spotted a raven heading into a rising current, wings cocked for a dance with an invisible force. The bird folded its left wing and plunged toward Deloo's car. I waited. As I knew it would, the rascal opened its wing just before colliding with us. It pitched a tan cube at Deloo's windshield. Despite the cracking noise, nothing happened to the car or to the tan cube now bouncing on the ground beside Deloo's door. It landed next to whatever Prize Woman had dropped. I saw it was a coin purse. Making a hook at the end of one of my longer tendrils, I reached down to examine it. Sure enough, it held coins. I hefted a coin up to the hood of the car so that Deloo would notice. Since she doesn't see or hear me, I have to do what I can to get her attention. For good measure, I dropped the tan cube on the car too. Both cube and coin wobbled on the hood and then into the gutter of the windshield.

"What on earth?" Deloo sprang out of the car and pried them out of the groove. "This is a Loonie." She referred to the Loonie or the Canadian dollar coin. She was about to discard the cube, but I forced her to keep it. She sniffed at the ordinariness of the tan plastic cube and stuffed it into her jeans pocket. Money speaks louder than anything and Deloo hopped from one to another coin like a bunny. Soon she clutched twelve dollar coins. She got back in her car and tossed them into the empty ashtray near the gear shift.

In case you're wondering, Deloo isn't just another person. She is my mortal—the one I guide. My spirit guide responsibilities are demanding. Usually, if I think of it and Deloo does it, she benefits. She suffers through my not-so-good notions. At the moment I was using tried and true spirit-guide methods to help a widow move out of grief. One of those methods involved teaching her to understand that she had been in poverty and now she's not because of her late husband. That step is in progress.

After a long look at the twelve gold-colored coins, Deloo reached for the small sketchpad and colored pencils she kept wrapped around the sun visor. She flipped to a blank sheet. As always, she used her non-dominant left hand to draw rough, dark lines of the coastline. Her fingers screed across the paper in sudden fury. For ten seconds she felt pure hatred for Arthur for abandoning her by dying. Reaching for his camera, the camera she dangled around her neck, she calmed herself, once again suppressing grief the Athabascan way. The camera, encased

in black and white leather, clamped down on all her ordinary emotional expressions, leaving her room to work artistically. He'd taken photos
with it on the day he died. Deloo hadn't recovered enough emotional
strength to deal with her husband's last views of the world.

Steadied by warm thoughts of Arthur, she drew a simple picture of
Prize Woman backed by the Bay of Fundy. Deloo had ten other sketch-
pads of that size. Nine of them were still blank. I've known Deloo since
she scribbled her first artwork onto her mother's dining room wall. Now,
two decades later, she had become a freelance artist. She was beginning
her career and on her way back to her mother's house in Alaska.

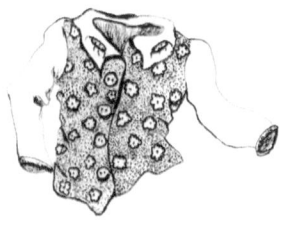

CHAPTER TWO

Deloo added a flourish of deep indigo to indicate the Bay of Fundy behind the figure. She applied a sweep of gold to remind her of Prize Woman's bright smile. One of the Loonies in the ashtray sent a spiral of light through the car. Deloo stared at the ashtray and then felt her hand move of its own volition to the sketchpad. I recognized what was happening. Deloo always welcomed the pull of a myriad of oddball spirits. She drew a second figure on the paper behind Prize Woman. The new woman sat, knees drawn up to her chin, black eyes burning with wrath. One of the woman's hands held something translucent and yellow toward the image of Prize Woman.

Deloo drew long tendrils of gold and copper emanating from the hand. Her breath came in short spasms as if she, Deloo, had been running—or screaming. She stared at the second woman in the drawing and rasped, "Who are you?"

The woman in the drawing, to me a ghost rather than a lovely, full-fledged spirit like myself, didn't answer.

I inspected the stranger—the real ghost beside me in my space rather than the figure in Deloo's drawing. She appeared to be no more than twenty-one or two, meaning she died when she was around Deloo's age. I guessed her chronological age to be forty, suggesting that she was closer in age to the naked woman they'd seen a few minutes ago, the one in the other car. Something violent had killed this little ghost. I nudged the ghost to engage her in dialogue.

She ignored me.

I looked for her mentor. A mature spirit like me should have been with a newish ghost like her, but she was alone and I had my own assignment, Deloo. I sent an alarm message to the Invisible Forces. Orphaned ghosts need to be both guided and protected. As usual, nothing happened. I shrugged.

The ghost grabbed Deloo's drawing hand again. I blocked her. Once is enough. Twice calls for a polite request of the artist's spirit guide—me, Baasee' the Vigilant.

The ghost fired a jagged bolt of raw power that missed me. She didn't miss Deloo, whose vision clouded.

Deloo clutched her eyes. "Ooh."

No one violates my mortal. I put a powerful shield around my innocent Deloo and imprisoned the guilty little ghost in a curl of solid darkness. I'd let her out when a decent ghost mentor came to get her. That could take a while. Feeling slight remorse, I peeked into the dark place I'd stashed her to make sure the little ghost was all right.

She was—still.

Still is better than gone for good. I resealed the dark place and turned back to Deloo. I bathed Deloo's dim eyes in warm, sudsy, healing light. In a few moments she recovered from what I think of as ghost shock. It can happen when an untrained dead person tries to use the body of a live human. They end up maiming our sweet, beloved mortals, and the great, meaning me, Baasee' the Great, can cure our treasured ones. Well, all right. Grandfather Kwaikit would do it better, but you get my drift. Besides, now Deloo and I are going home to Alaska by way of Nova Scotia.

Oh, Deloo's home is not Nova Scotia. It's mine. Sort of.

Ancient Nova Scotia. I am of the Tuudzaado, the Shadow People, and the first people on the edge of the glaciers in northeast North America. We lived through the massive flooding at the end of the Ice Age. We call it Zana. I gazed at Deloo. Making sure she produced excellent results is my job. Going back to my homeland is not.

Just as Deloo's eyes recovered, the driver of a big sedan dallied beside the turnout while he aimed a camera or phone in Deloo's direction. Since Deloo is short, the camera caught only her shiny dark hair, her sunglasses and little else.

Everything about him jangled my warning bells. I shot a bunch of questions to the invisible forces. Sometimes I get answers that make sense. Most of the time I don't. This time it went like this: Was he a sex-crazed maniac? No. At least not sex-crazed. Was he connected to Prize Woman? Yes. How? I got garbled nonsense. Did he intend to harm Deloo? Maybe. If he felt it necessary. Does he know Deloo? No. Who is he? Mangled gobbledygook.

Disgusted with these answers, I turned to what Grandfather Kwaikit terms 'good thinking'. I psyched the stranger: extreme intelligence but ordinary circumstances looked upside down to him. Like what did he photograph? Deloo? He'd aimed too-far downward for that. Maybe he was after her Alaska license plate. I looked at him in my way as well as Deloo's way just in case he showed up again.

Deloo, unaware of my investigation, peered at him too, but saw nothing save his very bright, blue eyes.

He spotted her looking at him and grimaced. I didn't want him around my Deloo. I tried to pry more information out of his thoughts, but he gunned his engine and sped away. In a hurry I flourished magic power to zap the photo from his camera. To put my anxiety about the little ghost woman and the odd strangers out of my mind, I flipped through pages of a dog-eared paper atlas on the front passenger seat. It was time to think about me for a while.

A couple of maps were stuck together. Of course I wanted one of the pages she'd jelly-pasted to the one above it. Irritated at her habit of eating peanut butter and jam sandwiches in the car, I tried several methods to unstick the paper. I became aware of a sweet silence and shot a glance at Deloo.

She gaped at the atlas. I had tackled the jelly by rippling the middle part of the two sheets. Deloo waved a hand in front of the car's air vents above the map.

~The fan's not blowing, Deloo! The car is not running,~ I air-shouted at her unhearing ears. With a final twitch of paper I stopped.

Deloo patted the atlas and noticed the fruit jam. She tugged the guilty pages apart and left the book open to dry. The map I wanted was now on top.

"Weird." Deloo frowned, turned on the ignition and shoved the transmission into drive. Soon we left the New Brunswick side of the Bay of Fundy to enter Nova Scotia. While she drove I pondered the growing list of strangeness about Deloo's short, mixed-descent life. She'd had more than the usual runs of bad luck, but I helped, spirit-guide style. It had been a real challenge, and still needed work—the kind Grandfather taught me to do.

My grandfather discovered my transition after death was in a nose dive when I was in my thousands. He took over my training and taught me how to fix things for mortals, such as how to help a new widow like

Deloo get rich. Solving mortal problems isn't easy if you happen to be dead, invisible and old.

How old?

Well, I did fight with a saber tooth tiger once. Almost bled to death, but I won. Saber tooths died out ten to twenty thousand years back. That makes me very old by any standard. No matter how much I love being able to help other people, though, my first priority is always my current mortal, Deloo.

She chose that moment to grunt. I was amazed to find that we had already reached the Atlantic coastline. Deloo pulled into a huge parking lot and steered her car toward a bookstore. She wanted tourist information. I fanned her mind with notions about the importance of the seabed beside Nova Scotia. Ignoring my needs, she picked out a colorful book advertising museums, casinos and gift shops and stood in line at the counter.

"Is this yours, Miss?"

Deloo glanced at the tiny box-like tan object in the man's hand and gasped when she saw his eyes. Automatically, her right hand clutched at the camera that hung around her neck.

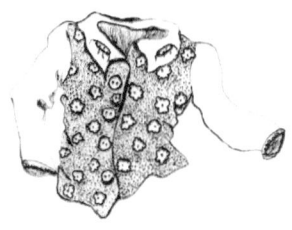

CHAPTER THREE

I, silent and invisible, took note of the man's bright, blue eyes. He was the man who'd photographed her earlier. Then I studied the thing he held out. It resembled the tan cube the raven had released a few miles ago, so I pushed Deloo to check her pocket.

~*Do you still have the one that raven dropped?*~ Deloo doesn't hear me. I'm used to it, but sometimes she acts on my suggestions, and did so this time.

Deloo rooted around in a jeans pocket and felt the one sent to her by Raven, or as she knew it in Denaakk'e, dotson (pronounced dot-SŌN). While she didn't pull it out to look at the color, she could tell it was the same size and that it had etching on one side. So did the stranger's.

"It was on the floor near tourist books," he issued his best lady-killer leer.

Deloo didn't notice. He was old. She glanced toward the bookshelf and frowned at the old guy. Lots of white laced his thinning blond hair. He held the object toward her with a diminished smile.

Deloo recognized his vivid blue eyes. She shook her head.

"It's a bead. It matches your beautiful jacket."

Deloo glanced at the front of her denim jacket just as the clerk waved. She paid for her book and hustled toward the door.

"Are you sure this isn't yours?"

"It's horrible. My mother would never use plastic. Our beads come from nature."

While Deloo flounced out of the bookstore, I watched the man's legs tightened as if to spring at my mortal infant. I sent the gift of fear to Deloo's legs. Always light on her feet, she responded by racing to her car.

He stared through the glass, taking note of the Alaska license plate. He produced a cell phone and tapped it a bunch of times. Then he frowned. The photo he'd taken of Deloo's car a short time earlier turned out to be blurry. I was disappointed that I failed to wipe out the photo. Then, just as Deloo slammed her car door, Blue-Eyes reached his own vehicle.

Deloo shoved her car into reverse and drove several miles before spotting a visitor's information sign. Someone helped her find lodgings and made the call for her. In a few minutes, we were on the road again, this time heading toward Halifax. The volunteer scribbled the inn's name and driving directions about finding it on a sheet of paper that Deloo taped to the front of her visor.

Deloo flipped on the car radio. Céline Dion sang into our small space, "There's no living without loving you." Although a song from her mother's era, Deloo sang along, jutting out her chin in sync with the rhythm. It was a poor choice for a young widow, but it fit Deloo's mood for adventuring into the singer's homeland.

I heard a spirit voice, undetectable by Deloo. The voice crooned, ~*It would be like living without being alive without you.*~ Who was butting in on me and my mortal? Then I recalled the little ghost. Since Deloo didn't hear the little ghost any more than she heard me, I decided to join them with mild pumping vibrations that glided through Deloo's shoulders. Miles disappeared with our enthusiastic rendition of radio songs until Deloo came to an intersection.

"Oh no." Confused, Deloo pulled over to study the directions on the visor as well as a clutter of paper on the seat beside her.

While she studied old maps, I watched a scruffy raven, oops, make that a scruffy dotson drag its wing as it hobbled along the asphalt. Out of nowhere a child's kite tumbled onto the road. As if possessed by a devil, the raven attacked the kite. Someone had painted a dragon on the kite in flamboyant red and gold. Painted smoke curled out of its dragon nostrils. It seemed to snarl. The bird plunged its black beak into the kite fabric and squawked. Soon the dragon image looked more like a dead worm than a symbol of Chinese power. The air trembled.

The dotson squawked, flapped a couple of times and floated to the hood of Deloo's car. It hopped toward the driver's side. The bird snagged the edge of Deloo's window. Ducking into the car, it tweak at the piece of paper on the visor, missed and scratched Deloo's wrist. She cursed, noticing the blood smear the name, Secret Spirit Inn, on the notepaper. The dotson flew away.

Something about the blood on the scrap of paper impelled me, the space-shifting Baasee', toward a fancy apartment near Halifax. A stranger drummed his fingers on a couch. I faux-panted, showing the spirits of the joint how hard I had worked to get there. They didn't notice. Instead, they were scrutinizing an old woman and her forty-something companion. How dull can things get? I parked my elegant underside next to the female and tuned into sheer boredom. Why was I here when my innocent Deloo was being stalked by a guy who looked meaner than a mastodon in rut? I could feel Grandfather Kwaikit's sarcasm telling me to suck it up and find out what was happening in this strange house.

I gathered the man's name was Howard. He smiled at his mother. "It's good to see you here. You don't get back to Canada, let alone your hometown, often enough Mother."

Charlotte got right to the point. "I've been asked some odd questions about my grandson. Lydia told me he wants to apply for a gun license in Montreal. But, now she thinks he's missing again. He's not at the Inn. He's not at the lodge in Cape Breton." Charlotte fluttered pasty-white hands. "I'm eighty-six. Too old for this nonsense."

Howard, drumming his long fingers through thinning blond hair, said. "When he asked about wanting to kill two years ago, I told him that some are allowed to kill, but we are not among them." He slapped the couch cushions and stood up. "I'm going to Montreal in a day or so. I'll see him then."

* * *

Two hours later, Deloo glanced up and caught sight of yet another raven perched on a homemade sign. "That's it! The Secret Spirit Inn." She pointed as if to show me the placard. The raven turned, hopped off the plywood and danced toward her, eyes expectant. When she didn't offer him any food, the raven spat out a rusty croak and lifted away in a graceful arc.

Deloo scoffed, forgetting that it was hutłanee to make fun of Raven. "Dotson! Always lying."

I preened at her use of Denaakk'e. Hutłanee (pronounced hut-LĂN-ee) means bad omen. She peered at the sign. It was more or less as the tourist agent said. "Secret Spirit Inn - 4 km." The sign was illegible. Three more signs, each cruder than the last, marked off the kilometers.

The fourth was a simple arrow. Deloo made the turn with her aura spiking.

I loved it when she dredged up a relic of her tomboy years. Deloo used to race the neighborhood boys to the park where Alaska's scrawny trees invited them to climb to creaky tops. Deloo always scrambled to the highest point, yelping "I made the ascent! I Am The Harper!" She referred to Walter Harper, an Athabascan man; the first person to set foot on Mount Denali's topmost peak.

Today Deloo wasn't on her way to climb mountains. Unbeknownst to her, she was on her way to Zana. It's been thousands of years since I've been home-and that was on the day I died. The road narrowed to a track. Deloo navigated from one puddle to the next. The camera banged against the steering wheel, Deloo's boney chest, and the door. The car rocked too much for her to tuck it under her jacket.

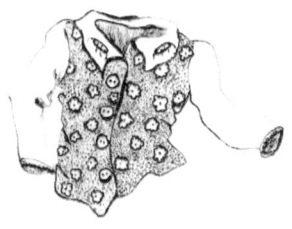

CHAPTER FOUR

To lend Deloo a dose of courage, I helped her invent a conversation with her favorite elder, Great Aunt Pauline (a living woman who ruled all decisions in Deloo's family). I do what I can to keep my connection with Deloo alive, just in case it should come in handy, so I pretended to be Great Aunt Pauline.

"That raven gave me Mad Dotson disease!" Deloo imagined Great Aunt Pauline cackling at her use of Denaakk'e. I pitched her a warning to be respectful of Raven. After a moment of carefree hilarity, Deloo sobered and whispered "Hutłanee. Sorry, Great Aunt Pauline."

Dozens of twists and jarring smacks forced Deloo to focus on the road rather than Great Aunt Pauline. Soon she came upon an elegant nineteenth century manor house now serving as a bed and breakfast. To the left of the building she caught a glimpse of turquoise and magenta spreading across the late afternoon sky and below it a single vehicle, an ancient minivan. Deloo pulled to a stop next to it and a sign that announced "Registration".

Above her, I glanced at the sun. Far past noon. Then I recalled that it was June fourth and glanced at Deloo. Her first wedding anniversary would have been June fifth, had her husband lived. Something tickled my misty backside. I could almost hear Great Aunt Pauline's voice whispering hutłanee. I knew that I had brought Deloo into danger.

The rutted ride had invigorated her. She slid out of her Passat and walked to the rocky beach. The main door cracked open and a woman poked her head out. I kept Deloo's eyes on the world around her. The innkeeper, meanwhile, stepped out onto the porch and waved. Using magic, I kept Deloo's head pointed toward the sky, so the woman's wave went unnoticed. The innkeeper opened her mouth wide and called out, "Can I help you?" The wind whipped the words away and Deloo didn't hear her. Instead, Deloo kept walking toward the sea and let her artist's eyes rove. Boulders glistened through the dark water. The beach was rocky and slick in spots. After a long look at the Atlantic Ocean, Deloo was about to turn toward the manor house when something caught her eye. It was my doing. I peeped with spirit tools through her mortal eyes to get Deloo's perspective. I, rather both of us, saw a tangerine haze transform the turquoise to a darker hue. The orange color, typical of my era, enthralled me but startled Deloo. She blinked hard to clear her eyes. Opening them, she saw a small fishing boat heading toward shore and a lighthouse just beyond. Then, thanks to me, the modern lighthouse vanished. In its place a set of ancient boulders-boulders of my era-appeared to settle on top of the existing stones. Their placement formed two distinct beaches. One belonged to Deloo's era. The other to mine. The orange view had less water than the blue, modern view. Maybe the difference was due to climate change.

Later I would confess to Deloo that I had caused the strange double vision. I used to walk along the coastline near that very spot. I thought that my borrowing her eyes for a moment would give Deloo a sense of me and my world. Instead and to my great sadness she didn't see beauty in Zana at all.

"Are you the woman who called a while ago?"

The unexpected voice combined with the odd visual experience shook Deloo. She spun around. A thin, fortyish woman smiled at her from the porch. From my lofty position above Deloo, I got another unnerving sensation and studied the stranger.

The woman said to Deloo, "Sorry. I didn't mean to frighten you."

Deloo attempted a casual laugh but nothing came out except a squeak. A light breeze cut through her tee shirt and she shivered. Then she cleared her throat and answered, "Yes. Well, someone from the Visitor's Center called for me." She eyed her car and said, "Excuse me while I get a wrap."

"Of course. It's drafty out here."

From the shadows of the inn's gloomy interior a dark figure peered at Deloo's retreating back. I heard the words, but made no effort to figure out who the third person was.

"Is she leaving?"

"Quiet!" The innkeeper shook her head at the other person and maintained her stance on the porch. "Go upstairs before she comes back."

I should have taken that moment to examine the other person. But I was worried about Deloo.

Deloo trotted to her car, and reached in for her jacket. She said, "it's cooler than I thought it would be, and I'm used to the cold." She slipped her arms into the lined and beaded denim jacket her mother had given her for Christmas. It was different from other jackets her mother made. For one thing, it was made of denim instead of moose or caribou hide. Plus, it showed off dozens of bone and ivory heirlooms.

"It's beautiful!" the innkeeper smiled. "Are you from one of the reserves?" Without giving Deloo a chance to answer, the woman turned and walked back to the heavy oak door. She gestured toward Deloo with another welcoming smile. "Come on in. They told me your name, but I didn't write it down. Could you tell me?"

"Deloo Goode." Deloo followed the woman to a small desk. The innkeeper wrote Della. People had done that all of Deloo's short life. She went into auto-speak. "That's D-E-L-O-O."

The woman's smile faded but she appeared to write. Deloo glanced at the registration form. Even from where she stood, Deloo could see that the innkeeper had scratched through "Della" and scrawled "D" without finishing. Looking at the newcomer, the innkeeper asked several questions without waiting for an answer.

Deloo squeezed in answers to some of them, "no, Athabascan. My name means cute or pretty in Denaakk'e, our language." The woman looked interested so Deloo added, "I'm from Alaska."

The innkeeper's eyes darted from her sheet of paper to Deloo and seemed to darken as they traveled across the front of Deloo's beaded jacket. "Where in Alaska?" she asked through tightened lips.

"The interior. I'm from the Tanana River. A town called Fairbanks."

The innkeeper straightened. No friendliness gleamed from frigid eyes. "Are you the woman who came to the Secret Spirit Inn a couple of years ago? Why are you here again? Why didn't you call me yourself?" She stared at Deloo's sleek, dark brown hair. "You've cut your hair. Took years off you."

Deloo took a step back. "You've made a mistake. My hair is always this long and I've never been here before."

The innkeeper didn't answer. Instead, she walked around my girl to examine the jacket from every angle. When she finished, her hand stretched forward.

I tried a dash of psychic intrusion to find out what the innkeeper was thinking. All I got was a jumble of half-formed images, none of them

useful. Using more directive powers, I urged Deloo to leave. As if awaiting my command, Deloo scowled and backed away.

"Come on. Let me see it. It's not your usual style. Why'd you change
the pattern after all these years?" Her fingers curled around a piece of
incised ivory. "I like this better than the chunky plastic beads you've
been using. Not that I blame you. Seventeen jackets in one design with
no changes has got to be boring. Take it off."

"What?!" Deloo slapped the groping hand. "Leave my jacket alone."

The woman jerked away from the blow. Then as if Deloo hadn't
spoken, she grabbed Deloo's lapel. "I told them I don't like anything
but jackets sewn with deer hide." She shrugged her thin shoulders and
grumbled, "not that they ever listen to me."

Deloo stumbled backward across the door jamb. The door swung
outward with no resistance. She escaped into the open air and retorted,
"This is my jacket. Why should I care what you think?"

The woman pursued Deloo onto the porch. "You look so much
younger than I remember. How old are you?"

"I've never seen you before, Lady!" Deloo's tight throat strangled her
bellow down to a mere whisper. She careened off the porch. "You've got
me mixed up with someone else."

"You're from Fairbanks, Alaska. Why else would someone of your
kind drive all the way out here if not to bring me that jacket?"

Deloo, still back-stepping, made her way down the path. "What do
you mean by my kind? A Native woman? A half-breed? Well, it's not for
you. You're crazy." Afire with adrenaline, Deloo turned and galloped to
her car.

"Wait a minute," the woman shouted, "didn't I hear that you'd disappeared?" She squinted at Deloo. "As I remember it . . ."

Deloo didn't stop. She fought with the car door. After a panicky moment she leaped inside as if her legs had developed springs. Realizing
that Deloo had been kicked out of a hotel, I called for my grandfather,
who made an expedient psychic connection. Deloo was ready to race
away. ~*Odd things have happened today.*~ Edgy, I shot him a psychic
report of the tan-cube incident.

~*I'll work on it, Granddaughter. Take care of yourself and that child
of yours. Isn't tomorrow the anniversary of her marriage?*~

~*Good memory. Yes, it is.*~ Deloo's husband, Arthur, died over sev-
en months earlier. She had been numb for the first few weeks afterward.
Deloo still wasn't up to analyzing situations as she'd had done a year

ago. For example, she had not tried to ask the innkeeper more questions about the jackets. I could have made Deloo ask, but didn't see the need for it. I should have. In hindsight, I now realize that something in that inn had hampered me. I didn't believe it had anything to do with being a half-breed. On the other hand, if I had been in full power, I should have seen the figure of someone other than the innkeeper close the bedroom drapery above the door marked Registration. I should have got more psychic data in general.

Deloo was oblivious to me. She fumbled with the ignition. As she did so, the ashtray sawed its way open and one of the Loonies bounced upward. It hit the top of the ashtray and hung in naked air with no more than its own imagination to hold it in place. Its imagination was short lived and it fell back toward its eleven creepy friends.

Angry at yet another being, albeit an inanimate one, blocking her plans, Deloo punched the ashtray lid to force it to close. Nothing happened. She took a breath and tapped it. The lid paused long enough to make a point and then shut itself. Deloo stared at it in silence.

I wondered if it was a sign from the Invisible Forces to investigate the Inn, but I noticed a dark plume arise from the roof of the Secret Spirit Inn and knew it was too late. Too late for the innkeeper. I sent an urgent warning to Grandfather Kwaikit about the plume. It meant someone was going to die soon. Using a spirit guide spell, I made Deloo bring the car to life. Deloo completed a jagged circle. I concentrated on her driving until we both saw a widening in the road. She pulled over and took a deep breath.

"What a horrible experience! Ugh! I hope I can find another hotel pretty soon."

Deloo was never one to pray so I was stunned when she added, "Please, Great Spirit, protect me from that woman and PLEASE take me to a good hotel."

With some misgivings, I added "Great Spirit" to my other name, "Great Aunt Pauline", and thought about the roadways between the Secret Spirit Inn and Halifax. Although her sleeping arrangements were as yet non-existent, Deloo was still in good shape for more driving. I reproached myself. I had been thinking about me rather than Deloo. We were so close to where I used to live; I couldn't help but want to soak it in. The colors, most of them anyway, and the flow of the clouds matched my memories.

Pulling myself together, I communed, ~*this was my favorite beach at sunset.*~

Using commune mode is a standard spirit guide technique. Most mortals don't know that we are talking to them all the time. They think they are the authors of every flickering thought. I had kept up a running commune monologue for years, but Deloo never listened. So now, of all times, she unplugged whatever had stopped her from hearing me before.

Deloo braked the car, head snapping. She looked for the speaker, fearing the ridiculous innkeeper had jumped into her car. Deloo got out of the Passat and examined the backseat. She couldn't see the backseat itself, having crammed it with things that didn't fit into the trunk.

Deloo slid back into the driver's seat and thought about what she'd heard. She had the distinct impression that a woman had spoken. Not male. Not Arthur. Our lives changed in that instant.

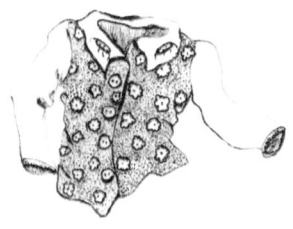

CHAPTER FIVE

Thinking I'd imagined it, I hummed a calming mantra before continuing. Others of my kind chatted up a storm with their mortals, both sides gibbering nonstop. I'd never been so lucky. Why now? I pondered. Deloo both heard me and identified my gender. Moreover, she didn't panic. Well, I was lathering her with love/soothe/keep-breathing feelings to tamp down any aftershocks from the Secret Spirit Inn. I tried to remember my plan. Eons ago, I developed a plan for the moment when Deloo once again noticed me. It included always thinking in English rather than the wordless Eternalese of my immortal fellows. Hmm. That is all that my plan included. Without a stockpile of canned words, I fumbled, *~isn't it beautiful?~*

"Did that batty woman drive me crazy? Did she start me fantasizing about Arthur?"

I tried a distraction. *~Cadmium orange.~*

"What?"

Still not quite believing that she had asked me, I commune-babbled, *~your sky is plain blue. Mine was cadmium orange.~* I admit I was thinking that my old world was superior to this polluted world of the twenty-first century. Well, who wouldn't?

At first Deloo simply sat. Stunned. For several minutes. I got impatient. Annoyed with the slovenly habits of the unchanging, slow-witted human brain. At least we were quicker thinkers back in my time.

Although it was the barest flicker of an attitude on my part, Deloo sensed arrogance. Arthur's kind of arrogance always torched off a burst of fury in Deloo just as a single touch from one of his long fingers could ignite quite another kind of flame.

Without considering the oddness of the exchange, she snapped aloud, "Why? Cadmium is a form of lead. Was there lead poisoning in your air?"

I know she didn't mean to do it since she didn't know me, but she was rude to me, the wise and wonderful Baasee'. Although taken aback, I tried again, *~there are many more poisons in your air than there were in mine, but I was not thinking about poison when I said cadmium orange. Rather, I referred to the color.~*

I thought back to her infancy, trying to conjure up a euphoric mood between us. Like most babies, Deloo used to see me and hear me. We used to laugh and play together for minutes on end. When she stopped, I left messages for her in dreams. As soon as she was old enough to hold a crayon, I would wake her up to draw pictures about my messages before she forgot them. Maybe that's why she has become such a good artist. Did I happen to say that my mortals are always the smartest and most talented beings ever to be born on this planet? Deloo is proof. She is so talented that she has won First Place for artwork in every grade through sixth, and twice when she was in high school. She did well in college, although the recent prizes tended to be called "Honorable Mention". Her highest prize was the "People's Choice Award" that she got because her late husband stuffed the ballot box.

Deloo relaxed, and we sat in silence. As often happens, quiet in one area seems to send shock waves to another.

* * *

"She had the jacket, but she made it wrong."

The innkeeper placed two phones on the kitchen table side-by-side. The black one had its speaker on, the silver phone was on mute. She pushed them closer to each other and pawed through a stack of papers.

Someone came into the room and reached for a phone. She slapped at the hand, and tilted her chin toward the stairway. The visitor shrugged and stepped back to lean against the wall.

"What's the name again?"

"Yes," she poked at the sheet on top of the pile. "It's Gardener or maybe Green. Hmm. I didn't finish writing her first name either. It was something like Donna or Diane. Diane sounds about right. Diane Green."

A garbled sound of interrogation issued from the black phone.

"No. She ran off before I could ask." She repeated at intervals, "No." ... "No." ... "No, I didn't get her phone number. All I know is she's from Fairbanks, Alaska."

A tinny voice rang into the room. The innkeeper's complexion changed from delicate pink to deep purple.

"License plate?" She shouted. "No, I didn't write down her license plate number. The mud was too thick. All I saw were specks of yellow with dark."

"Was it an Alaskan plate?"

"Maybe. I don't know, I tell you."

She paced, then sat. More sounds chopped the air. "She said she was, but she didn't look like a First Nations woman to me, although she has long dark hair. Not like it was when she came by here a couple of years ago. Back then it was easy to see she was a First Nations woman. Back then, her hair was so long, it hung past her hips. She's smartened up a bit, cut her hair, and shows off her eyes better. Green, eh?"

When the other person stopped yelling, she said, "Take it easy." Unwinding herself from the table, she added, "It's that jacket she wore. I told you, I just thought it might be one of yours, eh?"

The voice from the black phone swore at her.

"Mind your tongue. The point is, she knew about us. Why else would she have come out to this edge of nowhere?" She pressed the "end" key and glared at the offending phone. Taking a deep breath, she lifted the silver phone and asked, "Did you get all that?"

"Yes. Thanks. Watch out for yourself. I'll be in touch." The speaker disconnected.

"I didn't know about the jackets," the visitor behind her said. "Tell me about them."

* * *

Using my magnificent oculars, I could see the highway ahead. I had known since her birth that I would have to get her out of one pickle after another. So far, so good. After playing cowboys and Indians with her as a toddler, I'd got used to being The Lone Ranger followed by Tonto-cum-Deloo. Those games filled me with delusions of grandeur about vanquishing evil. At Grandfather Kwaikit's suggestion, I left a piece of myself there, allowing me to monitor Deloo while I listened to the phone call.

"Ow!" the front left tire collided with a rock and Deloo bobbled on the seat. She rubbed the top of her head. The heart shape that housed my emotional vocabulary tingled. Her nose wrinkled.

I communed, ~*Aw, poor baby,*~ and searched for the little song I had composed twenty years ago to soothe her many wounds.

~*Poor little Deloo, don't cry today. Your little head wants to play!*~ I sang the song and vibrated the air around the tiny swelling above her parietal lobe to give her a sense of a warm, loving massage.

Just as she did when she was two, she giggled. "I remember that song! You always sang it when I got hurt."

The heart shape in me wobbled. ~*You remember it?* ~

Have I mentioned that Deloo's the most wonderful mortal I've ever known? I simulated dabbing at the big tears glittering on my imaginary eyelashes. I sighed although sighing without lungs isn't easy.

Something was wrong at Secret Spirit Inn, and I needed to find out if Deloo would suffer because of their problems. Moreover, I was getting information about Deloo from them. It's a good thing I am fluent in ten Asian languages, including Mandarin. My mental in-box was filling with that mangled conversation of an hour ago. I recognized the chaotic irritability of the innkeeper. She had been talking in English to someone who thought in Mandarin and English. Both at once. The other listener, the one whose phone she'd kept on mute, thought in upper-class English and more commonly in another. I love working with complex thinkers. It keeps me on my dainty toes with their fake sparkling toenails.

~*Deloo! Stop. Something's wrong.*~ I kept my commune voice neutral.

Deloo jammed on the brakes. "What is it? What's wrong?"

~*I've picked up something odd from that innkeeper. She called two people about you.*~

"Two!? Who are they?"

~*I need time to work it out. One of them is an angry person who kept shouting at her in English. The background thoughts were in a Chinese language-Mandarin to be exact. I need to go over the conversation again. Find a place to stop.*~

Deloo drove the car deep into a thicket of alder that lined the narrow road. Without warning, a car fishtailed around a curve and into the muddy lane she'd occupied seconds earlier.

"Was that who you meant?"

I paused. The demonic driver was one of the people the innkeeper had phoned. The main thing was to keep Deloo safe. I shout-communed, ~*Yes. Get out of here. Now!*~

At the intersection a few feet away, Deloo turned right toward Halifax. Her rear tires showered the alders with an arc of stones. She reached a shallow pullout near the place we had watched the raven destroy the Chinese kite. A piece of fabric was stuck in a bush. Deloo saw it and stopped.

~*What are you doing? You must leave here at once.*~

Instead of obeying me, Deloo threw the car into reverse and turned around. The car squealed, seeming to agree with me.

~*Deloo,*~ I yapped, ~*where are you going?* ~

"Back!" Deloo barked. "I'm going to find out what they want."

By that time Deloo had raced to a high point in the road that offered a distant view of the inn. The stranger had chosen a parking spot that was not visible to anyone inside the building. An obvious sign of danger. Enough was enough! It was time for an ancient spirit guide to take over the controls. I forced the car engine into a stall. Deloo tried to start the car again. When it didn't she banged on the steering wheel and shouted for help. No one but me heard her.

~*We're not going back to the inn.*~ I intoned.

"You said those people are after me. I'm going to find out why." Deloo pulled on the handle of her car door. The lock flew open and her door opened a crack.

Before Deloo could move, I slammed the door shut and locked it.

"What?! Let me out!"

~*No. My job is to keep you safe and alive. This car is going to move one direction: away from here.*~ My commune voice was firm.

She tried the ignition key. Nothing happened.

"Sheesh!" Deloo waited, tried again, and then caved. "Okay. I'll go just like you said."

I released my hold on the car and Deloo's car burst into life. She turned and drove away, her face gripped in a horrendous frown.

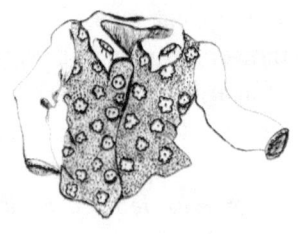

CHAPTER SIX

Rosemoira Keilleher gazed across the familiar cove. It was her favorite time of day, favorite season of the year. The sun was still warm. The tide was in and she could see three small fishing boats in the distance. She stood in the doorway, delaying as long as possible her work in the old-fashioned kitchen where heaps of tableware, pots, and pans covered every surface. She hated the inconvenient location of the single sink and wished the inn's owner would agree to put in a big commercial washing area with three big steel vats and all the new gadgetry that made life easier. About to turn away from the allure of sun and fresh air, she spotted a flicker of lights. She squinted at the road but saw nothing more.

"You should go upstairs before I make you do the pans."

Her unofficial guest laughed and vanished up the stairs without a word. The innkeeper waited until she'd heard the racket of footsteps make it all the way to the top of the steps. Soon the clatter of metal on metal in the sink prevented her from hearing the front door open.

Someone crept through the big sitting room toward the kitchen and paused to watch the innkeeper. She didn't notice. Her chi, as Taoists call it, or life-force as English speakers name it, flowed counter-clockwise in large circles from left to right. The kitchen sink, with its long counter on the left, put her at a disadvantage because she always ended up making an extra half-turn to put the pots down on the right after she rinsed. Never a slacker, Rosemoira scrubbed all of the pots and pans so hard it looked as if she had used sandpaper, just as her mother had done.

The watcher waited until her chi had shifted her body to face the corner, leaving her attention as far away as possible.

"Tell me how you met her." The voice rasped low.

The innkeeper threw her hands up and whirled around. The heavy cast-iron skillet in her left hand struck the newcomer's shoulder. The unexpected weight of the skillet, rather than any additional force from her, knocked the newcomer off balance. As soon as she recognized the visitor, she lowered the skillet.

"What are you doing here?" Her eyes went to the door. No one appeared.

"I asked you to tell me how you met her." The visitor rolled to the right and used the forward movement to leap off the floor without using hands for either balance or strength.

She gaped at her visitor's amazing agility, then an unwieldy paper sack caught her eye.

Her visitor distended thin lips into a garish smile and set the bundle on the table.

"Look," the taut lips relaxed until the smile seemed almost natural. "I brought dinner. I hope you like Chinese. I've got sweet and sour pork. I made it myself. I cook Chinese food better than anyone in Canada."

Rosemoira frowned and sidestepped toward the door that led to the big sitting room. An arm snaked out to stop her. She pushed it away and said, "I'm not hungry." She stared at the counter where she had left the black phone, hoping her visitor wouldn't notice it.

"What's the problem? You need food. Come on. Let's eat while it's still hot." Angling a lean body between her and escape, the visitor opened the paper sack, took out paper plates and palmed a small plastic zipped baggie with dried leaves in it. Reaching into one of the cabinets for a serving spoon, the visitor scooped a large helping of steamed rice onto each paper plate.

Aware of her gaze, the visitor stretched a hand toward her and caught her head in it. When their lips almost touched the other murmured, "You'll like this. This is my best recipe, sweet and sour pork."

The heady aroma reminded her that she hadn't eaten all day. She sniffed. She was, despite the odd arrival, hungry enough to eat whatever it was that wafted around the room. Nervous, she tapped the nearest kitchen chair. "Sure. I'll join you. Have a seat."

Her visitor inclined a gracious head and slid the chair out from under the table with a flourish. "Thank you, Madame. You've been working hard. I'll prepare your plate."

She watched the other, eyes petrified like a mouse watching a cobra. She turned away just long enough to move toward the chair. Her guest used that second to insert the innkeeper's chopsticks into the bag of leaves, snag a fat pinch of dry herb, and watch it flutter into the pork. Then, head canted away, the guest slid the paper plate toward her and opened the drawer where she kept paper napkins, and removed two.

"How do you know where I keep things?"

A hand hovered over the napkins a beat longer than was needed. Without looking at her the other shrugged, "you aren't here all year. Our mutual benefactor sends me to Halifax once in a while and lets me stay here."

Thinking about the possibility of someone else sleeping in her bed caused her to take in a sharp, indignant breath. In the process, she caught a big whiff of sweet and sour sauce. She could tell it had too much garlic in it for her taste, but it smelled good enough.

"Well, I need to be warned about you coming here once in a while. You and I have already talked," she said as she extracted the chopsticks from the food. "I told you I didn't get a good look at her car."

Her visitor straddled the chair instead of sitting with knees under the table, hating to be imprisoned. Stabbing at the pork with practiced ease, the visitor slid the loaded end of the chopsticks into a waiting mouth. After a moment of satisfied chewing, the visitor grinned. "I know. But I wanted to make sure I understood what you meant by having met the Alaskan woman before today. How long ago was that?"

Rosemoira shook her head and struggled with her chopsticks. The pork was easy to stab and lift. She made a big show of enjoying the flavors before answering. She shrugged and pointed to the wall calendar as if it could say it for her. "It was two years ago. That would have made it the fifteenth jacket." She paused as if waiting for an accolade.

The visitor suppressed a rude remark by instead barking out a false laugh. "I have forgotten how long you've been doing this for us. So? Two-and-a-half years ago? I remember that it came at the usual time in December. Where did you meet her? Here?"

The innkeeper coughed. It was a light, dry cough. She touched her throat, wondering if she was coming down with another flu. Her lips felt a little numb, too. Better see the doctor.

"Yes, it was midwinter. A couple of weeks before my vacation. We had a lot of guests that week. The waiting room was packed with new arrivals. I was swamped because I had to do the registration. She showed up without warning carrying the beaded jacket. I asked her to wait in the kitchen, but she wouldn't come in. She just lurked in the lobby the whole time. Said she wanted to meet me. She wanted to know more about how we used them."

She held up a hand, noticing with distant interest how little it moved for all the effort she put into lifting it. As she studied the problem limb, she got a strong whiff of something. It seemed familiar to her. She suspected it was from the food she had ingested. She allowed herself to relax and recall the scent.

Monkshood.

Also called wolfs bane and aconite. She remembered now from her days in the emergency ward. A poison that causes the central nervous system and lungs to fail. Monkshood made lips feel numb, just like hers had done a few seconds ago. Then the throat tightened, making it hard to swallow. What was that called again? Yes. That's it, dysphagia. She guessed she had passed that stage already. She tried to remember other symptoms. Gave up. At least nothing hurt now.

She watched the person who had just killed her. They had known each other a long time. She smiled, or thought she did, and then considered the question again. She said, or thought she said, "We had a great talk together. She spent the afternoon with me. I showed her what I did with the jackets after they arrived. She was curious about why you people had to be the ones who inspected it. After all, none of you are experts in First Nations regalia or anything."

"What did you tell her about us?"

She stared at the visitor without moving.

The visitor realized then that there had been too much wolfs bane in the sweet and sour sauce, and it was affecting her fast. Rosemoira wore two heavy sweaters as she always did. Studying her with new interest, her friend realized how much bulk they added to her figure.

"I guessed wrong. I thought you weighed closer to one-forty. Looks like I was way off."

Rosemoira heard the words and knew she had navigated into a sublime world of pure thought. She continued, forming the ideas in her mind rather than with her now-still mouth.

I wondered why she had the jacket on instead of in the usual box. She said it was cold, and her own coat was not right for Nova Scotia, so she put on the fifteenth jacket instead. She asked me if the management looked for anything in particular. I told her that none of you liked it when I opened the boxes, but they came here to the Secret Spirit Inn. I am alone here most of the time, so I opened them anyway. Beaded jackets. I inspected them to make sure they were sewn right. Customers are getting better and better at spotting problems with First Nations work.

You weren't the usual one to open the boxes, but who was I to argue?

You are one of them. Besides, I was off that week. Qanik was on duty. I stayed here, though, in my room off the kitchen. Qanik had the room at the top of the stairs. You didn't notice me, even when I served you endless cups of coffee. You were oblivious to everything but the beads you pried off the jacket, one at a time. Pop! Pop! Pop!

You were so caught up in what you were doing that you were surprised when Qanik said hello. You were quick to gather everything up and go. You didn't notice that one of the beads fell on the floor. Qanik picked it up. We couldn't figure out what it was. So plain, it couldn't have been worth more than a few pennies. He took it. I didn't want it.

Rosemoira slid off the chair and onto the floor without moving her arms or legs. One eye twitched. The air eddied above her.

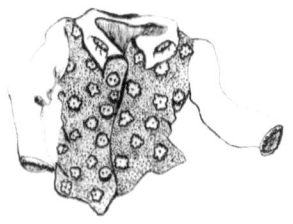

CHAPTER SEVEN

The unofficial guest waited in the small room at the top of the stairs. A half hour passed. The guest opened the door a little more, hoping that Rosemoira would call as soon as the coast was clear. She didn't. Spine prickling, the unofficial guest donned cotton gloves and moved through the small room, wiping all touchable surfaces, killing numerous spiders along the way. By the time the guest had wiped every surface in the tiny bedroom as well as all of the public rooms upstairs, a car engine burst into life. Gravel rattled under a moving vehicle.

The inn's now single living human occupant, its unofficial guest descended to the main floor. There the unofficial guest tiptoed toward the kitchen. A shoe attached to an unmoving ankle told the nasty story. The unofficial guest examined Rosemoira to make sure she had expired. An odd feel to the kitchen sent a flurry of moods juddering through the unofficial guest's body and mind. She was dead, however, so the unofficial guest suppressed the dominant one: fury. Besides, a slight numbness on the unofficial guest's own lips and a faint but familiar odor brought a new realization. Rosemoira had consumed a poison the unofficial guest knew all too well: aconite. The guest went back upstairs to pick up a small case and an even smaller knapsack. The unofficial guest left the inn and entered a tidy out-building. A fragment of colorful fabric fluttered into the building and came to rest in the dirt beside the vehicle. Unaware of it, the unofficial guest pulled out of the storage unit and drove toward the provincial border between Nova Scotia and New Brunswick.

The cloth, still inside the garage, took flight although there were no drafts to assist its peculiar excursion. It made its way to an airshaft and pressed itself against the screening. With no one to protest with scientific tedium, it released its molecular structure and reassembled itself on the other side of the screen. For a fleeting moment it changed shape to something fishlike, perhaps a dragon fish, maybe something more timid, like a cichlid. After swimming like a fish, the rag emerged as a dry, but dirty dragon. The dragon's nostrils seemed to flare with a puff of smoke. A flurry of air whirled the scrap of kite material far away from the inn.

* * *

An individual texted time of arrival at a particular parking lot and tried to get rid of the odd feelings that swirled within. It didn't work. Something, maybe the ancients were right, maybe it was the dead woman's soul, whatever. Something had followed. It was worse than the poison itself. Jittery, the killer put on dirty cotton gloves, got into the stolen car, and drove along the twisted road to the main highway. Less than thirty minutes later a dark car pulled into the parking lot of a small business plaza. The driver parked near a dumpster and tossed the trash bag inside. Leaving the stolen car beside the dumpster, the driver approached the passenger side of a waiting car and got in.

Unseen, off-duty Inspector Al Beamus of the Royal Canadian Mounted Police (RCMP), stepped out of a convenience store across the street and watched the odd activity. Responding to well-trained internal alarms, he called the direct line. In less than five minutes an RCMP officer pulled up beside Al. Together they walked to the dump to retrieve the wadded paper sack.

"I'll have it checked out. Did you get the vehicle's plates?"

"Sorry." Frown lines formed on Al's forehead. "It was too dark and the people were very quick about their business. I couldn't even see if they were men or women.

* * *

A muddy, grey stone did not fit Luisa's skinny butt, however it fit her mood. She rested her head on her knees and allowed the brisk wind to freeze her mind.

"Hola, my beautiful Luisa. What are you doing here so late? It's getting dark."

"I was going to ask you the same thing. I couldn't find you in the room." She could see that he was depressed. His nephew, she supposed. She told him not to try to find HayJay any more. Howard didn't believe her. For reasons that eluded him, he knew he had to meet with his nephew this week. Just being near his nephew drove him crazy. He sank to the dank beach, not aware of the cold air.

Then she smelled the taint of rot and something worse. She recognized both all too well. Each of them had burned full wardrobes over the years to rid themselves of the smell of death and other forms of putrefaction. If they had been closer to home-her homeland of Cuba-she would know what to do to rid him of the stench. Here in Canada she would have to innovate.

She grinned. He hated her innovations. Healers of her mystical background as a curandera of Cuba had to do what was needed.

He seemed too spent to notice her mood. A cool, salty breeze took away the smell but not the feel of an angry soul, a female soul. The curandera drew upon her training to call for spirits. She reached deep into herself to find out which spirit would guide her through a cure for a soul killing.

Her father had taught her how to call upon hundreds of plants and animals to help cure sicknesses. Her father's style was to study the case for hours before selecting the best spirit for the sick person. She had minutes. Her father would have set up his curing area with enchanted tools that worked with the spirit he had chosen. Then he would have sung a magical song to bring forth the healing spirit. Her father's method worked well in Cuba and later in Florida because he could keep all of his tools locked away from others.

His daughter didn't have that luxury because she no longer lived in Cuba or Florida. Instead, she kept her tools sequestered in a secret closet in their house in Massachusetts. Over time, she had learned how to devise new methods. Even so, she always tried to work just as her father had taught her to do, seeking out the spirits of plants and animals, Cuban plants, Cuban animals. That wasn't likely tonight in a world as far north as Nova Scotia. Besides, her patient was failing fast and she had to hurry. Instead of being able to spend hours studying the situation, she had to hope that the right spirit would come to her.

One arrived. She felt a thrill run through her bones when she recognized which spirit had responded. It was the powerful spirit of the spiny dragonfish common in the Caribbean Sea near Cuba. Fitting, considering the kind of man she needed to heal. She had worked with a dragon fish spirit a few years earlier as had her father. She had the right song for it.

As she sang her dragon fish song, the spirit joined her. She bowed her head in humility, grateful to be with this dangerous spirit; knowing it could cure her patient-her husband. Together husband and wife turned to walk the beach toward the motel. It was dark. There were no lights except for a tiny pool of amber at the main office at the far end of the building. Still on the rocks, she stopped singing.

"Take off your clothes," she commanded while she unzipped her jeans and dragged them off her legs. She yanked off her tee in one motion and stared at his unmoving body. "Come on. I know what we need to do. Now! Take off your clothes."

Her extreme thinness gave him the impression that she had no strength, and he was always caught by surprise when she man-handled him without effort. She did so now by sliding her left arm behind him until she found his right hand and torqued his arm up along his back. He stumbled on the indifferent, wet stones, and dropped to his knees.

"Hurry," she breathed into his ear. "I'm getting cold." She put his right hand between her thighs as if to prove her point.

He scrambled to his feet and took off his clothes. And wavered.

"Woman!" He said, hoping to stop her. When she didn't answer, he searched his limited Spanish vocabulary for the word, "Mujer! It's too cold and dark. Let's wait until morning," he whimpered. Much as he needed the benefits of her cures, he hated her Cuban customs.

Ignoring him, she pushed him along the murky beach. "Come with me! The dragon fish will guide us tonight." Tucking his hand against her belly, she led him along a narrow, rocky path. Soon they were stumbling between large rocks along an even rougher trail. She kept on walking until they were both more than knee deep in freezing water. She seemed to glide as if they walked on dry, smooth sand instead of rocks. As they moved, she once again chanted the dragon fish song in a low voice. The eerie sound seemed to envelop him and give him strength.

It was windy, but he didn't feel the cold air or the heat of her body. He felt dizzy and wondered if he had lost his sense of touch when she kicked the back side of his knees. He flopped into the water. He knew he should have felt pain. Keeping his grip on her hand, he made sure she came under with him. They struggled together in a familiar duel that intensified until she pinned him on his back and pulled him deeper under the water. He didn't want to fight.

Listen to me. Listen to the dragon fish.

Her thoughts or her voice, he wasn't sure which, cut through his dull apathy. He felt another woman's presence. She, a woman who'd just died, seemed to press herself against him. Against his will, he recognized the ghost as Rosemoira Keilleher, the innkeeper of the Secret Spirit Inn. Rosemoira's ghost seemed to lean into his groin. Also aware of the ghost, the curandera understood it was the innkeeper who willed her husband to die. She did not ask why.

Then the ghost of Rosemoira evaporated.

He ripped free and stood up, leaving the Cuban woman in the water. Breathless and excited to be alive, he grabbed one of her arms and pulled her upright. Just as he did so, he felt something release its grip on him. He waited, wondering if it was the innkeeper or the Cuban dragon fish that left.

"Give thanks to the dragon fish," she growled. "It saved our lives." She tugged on his arm and guided him back to shore, all the while chanting a song of thanks for helping to fight off an evil spirit. She finished the chant just as she opened the cottage door. The heat of the cottage, albeit set on low, was so intense it seemed to slam against their naked bodies.

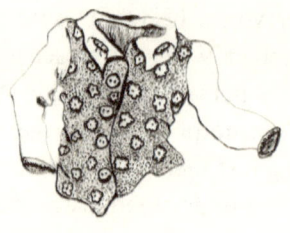

CHAPTER EIGHT

After sliding into a spirit guide mode of sleep, a vision opened. I call it the cliff vision. I'd had this one six other times before Deloo was born. Until now, they'd all been the same.

A man tossed a small tan cube to his companion. Wind ruffled his short hair.

"It was all about these, wasn't it?" the dying man wheezed.

Instead of answering, the other person pocketed the cube and watched for more symptoms of dysphagia. The man sagged onto a waiting tarp. The killer dragged the corpse to the edge of the cliff and almost slid over the edge along with the victim. The body bumped downward and gave itself to icy water.

Since Grandfather Kwaikit expects to know about my visions, I contacted him.

~*What's different?*~ Grandfather's psychic communes were still as curt as always.

~*The victim is wearing cotton jeans. He's always worn various kinds of hide leggings, except the first time, when he was naked.*~

~*Could you make out other features?*~

~*He's always had shaggy black hair. In this one, his hair was black and short. It bristled straight out from the skin like yours did when you cut it too short.*~ Grandfather had always been practical about his hair. Most of the time he plaited it into a single braid, but once something happened and he had to cut it closed to the bone. It looked funny. If we'd had lightweight hats back then, he'd have worn one.

Grandfather Kwaikit considered. ~*Keep me posted.*~ He departed.

* * *

While Deloo drove, I maintained contact with a psychic bug that I left behind at the inn. It fizzled out after an hour. It's the sort of thing I used to watch over Deloo when she was with a crowd. I'd be a fool not to find out more. The killer's thoughts were pictorial and focused on the victim. The innkeeper's thoughts were nonverbal. At the end she focused on snippets rather than the whole killer: An arm, the movement of a slim body, intense eyes. It bothered me that I couldn't see a logical connection between the people at the Secret Spirit Inn and Deloo or her jacket.

Meanwhile, the world darkened. Deloo needed a hotel. Intending to take the first, make that the second, or whatever exit to get back to Halifax, Deloo missed the exact instant to turn the car at each key moment, and thus kept on driving. When she motored past the last turn to Halifax, she continued on. Rain increased the black of night, while her depression filled the car. I spotted a sign displaying the silhouette of an airplane and another welcoming her to the town of Truro. It was nine in the evening. Deloo had been on the road more than thirteen bizarre hours, including the less than blissful reunion with me, her invisible toddler-hood friend.

Deloo inched along the highway, this time determined to turn at any exit for a hotel. Overwhelmed by despair to do such a simple thing, she wailed. At first, it was a formless, loud din. In a while she shaped it into a loud whisper. "I feel like the Blind Man. But there's no loon, no lake, and no light." She referred to a common Athabascan story called the Blind Man and the Loon. In the story, the spirit of a Loon guided the Blind Man to safety and restored his vision.

Happy to be assigned such a role, I invoked the Loon's main line with a simple Commune, ~*Come to me.*~

The Passat swerved a little. I feared Deloo would fight again, but she adapted to me as Loon and intoned, "Okay."

Not an inspired ad-lib, but good enough for me. Soon I helped her see billboards for familiar hotel chains. She spotted a vacancy sign and I helped her right foot know it had to ease off the gas and move over to the brake pedal. She came to a gentle stop in front of a hotel. I helped her take a couple of deep breaths before going inside. She was serene when she entered the lobby. After a brief discussion about the price, the desk clerk checked her in and handed her an electronic key.

Deloo thanked him with a glum smile, took the key card and wheeled her small suitcase to the elevator. Inside the room, She pulled out her phone. While it was past ten at night in Nova Scotia, it was still early evening in Alaska. She called her mother's Fairbanks number and told Taale what had happened.

After a squawking of shock waves, Taale realized that her daughter was all right. Taale relaxed and launched a calming technique. Her method, always the same, was simple. "Deloo, we've lived through bill collectors and survived. You did more than survive today. You fought back and won! Keep it up. You're my champ." Illogical and successful. Deloo laughed and asked how things were going.

Since going to Massachusetts with her in-laws after her husband's funeral, Deloo had yearned for her mother, but the Athabascan in her kept her stoical. She followed her mother in that way. Taale Denaa's legal first name, Naagheltaale (pronounced Nah-rell-TALL-eh), referred to the Big Dipper in the Denaakk'e language. Taale knew of a couple of versions about the way the Big Dipper came to be. In one transcribed by a European priest, the stars that shape the dipper are a man who is befriended for eternity by a raven. In the one I prefer, the stars shaping the Dipper accompany a woman who is pregnant. As in the second version, Dotson (Raven), stays with the Big Dipper for eternity. I like the second because it fits Deloo's Tleeyegg'e hut'aane ancestors who follow the mother's line. The symbol of a pregnant woman makes sense with that background. Taale, like most Athabascan women, thinks of herself as a tough street fighter. That's why Deloo never heard anyone say Taale's full name. Once a classmate called her "Dipstick" (as in Big Dipper-stick). Taale didn't like it and threw a mean punch that knocked the boy out. I have encouraged Deloo to learn to fight the way her mother does.

"Get some sleep and don't waste any money." Taale had scrimped and saved money all of her life and expected Deloo to do the same.

I was once again up to my spangled, yet wise and wonderful eyeballs about death and intrigue, so I didn't notice that Deloo had ended the call. I glanced up when I felt surges of anxiety from the mortal side of the veil. Deloo was scrounging through her carryall when she yelped. She had stabbed her right hand on the sharp spines of the filigree on her wedding band.

~Thank you for taking me home,~ I said to her as I checked the damage her ring caused. Not much. I wondered how to find a jeweler who knew how to resize such a fancy band.

Deloo's tongue on hearing my sudden commune, turned as dry as the pastry, and got in the way of her teeth. The bite sliced a few cells out of her tongue. Tears gushed from her eyes and ran down her nose.

I chanted ~*Poor little Deloo / don't cry tonight. / Your little tongue / will be all right!*~

Despite the pain, Deloo managed a tiny giggle. She slid the camera strap over her head and lifted her late husband's camera to the night-stand as she usually did. She wedged it between the lamp, clock and her pencil case. Then dabbed at the edge of her lips.

I soothed her with a mild pain-killing vibration and offered a sugges-tion, ~*didn't I see some stuff for canker sores in your bag?*~

Deloo rooted around in the carryall and found what she needed. "-oo -ou ha- eyes?"

I knew she was trying to say 'do you have eyes?' without doing more damage to her tongue. I answered, ~*not like yours. Mine are like looking through a camera with thousands of lenses.*~

Deloo blinked with a dragging urge to sleep. It was a natural reaction to shock. ~*Deloo, my dear child, it's time for you to get a good night's rest. Why don't you crawl into that nice, warm bed?*~ I spread a wash of sleep-oriented good feelings around her. It worked. Deloo was asleep before her head reached the pillow.

I, too, relaxed. My trip back to Zana was not what I had expect-ed. Something stirred in me that I hadn't felt in eons. Instead of seeing sights, I was satisfied with a zeal to protect my family (now it's Deloo) and my world, Zana. I dreamed.

A little girl peered around the trunk of a skinny spruce tree. The toddler was so scrawny that when she ducked behind the tree, she dis-appeared. Her titter caressed me like rustling leaves in a gentle breeze. I awoke into the dream. With practiced care I kept my mind still so that the dream might continue. The toddler stepped out from behind the tree trunk and grinned toward someone taller and farther away than me, but still in my general direction. One cheek in the very dark-skinned face had a dimple that flashed in the bright dream light. She waved. I knew she was waving at someone else, but the girl's black eyes seemed to move and connect with mine just before the dream faded.

I struggled to stay in the dream with my cave-baby self. Thousands of years had passed since that moment and yet I still ached for my mother, the person receiving my wave. I knew hundreds of words from dozens of languages, each with haunting methods of expressing love, and not one of them lessened the endless loss I felt for my mother. I writhed, and in my writhing, I found Deloo, enchanting Deloo, writhing as well. I air-wrapped myself around her as I used to do when she was little and sleepless. Just as she did as a little girl, she reached out.

Deloo's left hand felt for the spiral sketchbook she'd placed at her bedside for just such moments. It wasn't there. Her stomach churned with fear. Then she remembered. The hotel nightstand was on the right, not the left. Sitting, she switched on the light and scribbled a few notes, ending with a drawing of the child. Satisfied that she had caught all the details she could remember, Deloo fell asleep with the lamp shining on her face. The open sketchbook lounged across her chest, open to the drawing of little me.

Freelance artist. After closing the sketchbook, I aimed a tendril of light at it. The spiral-bound book floated to the nightstand and nestled into position. I smiled at my dozing girl. Those had been my words for her, "freelance artist." I'd sent them to her through mental and visual channels, through the words of others and through her own emotions.

Deloo wanted a career in art, so she went into the two-year program at the Institute of American Indian Arts, also called IAIA. Even so, she couldn't envision what an artist does for a living until her mother-in-law, Matty, expressed deep satisfaction with Deloo's paintings. Matty reveled even more when Deloo responded to her suggestions.

"Deloo, you should do this for a career. You snatch images from my mind and put them on the canvas just as I see them." Matty was thrilled at the huge portrait Deloo had made of Arthur, her late son and Deloo's deceased husband.

I agreed that Deloo had brought Matty's son back to life with expressionist passion. That was when I inserted the words, 'freelance art' into Deloo's thoughts, but it wouldn't have caught on without Mrs. Goode's enthusiasm. A few days later one of Matty's friends asked Deloo to paint a portrait of her daughter. Deloo's body signals shifted from grief to hope. It let her live up to the three main Athabascan cultural values: independence, self-sufficiency, and family loyalty.

Deloo submitted her first commissioned painting to her client two weeks later. Both thrilled and gratified, she accepted two crisp one hundred dollar bills in payment. Matty's friend beamed while Deloo wrapped the painting in layers of acid-free paper, which she then covered with cardboard.

Nonetheless, Deloo sorrowed on. I take the blame for Deloo's present state of grieving. A year ago I knew at once that Arthur was destined to live a very short life. It's what an old spirit guide like me does. I can size up a potential spouse and make "arrangements" better than any living person. I psych out the real personal and financial situation of the would-be spouse, whereas in mortal-run marriage arrangements, everyone lies about their assets. Spirits like me can override such selfishness and lies. Back in the day when arranged marriages were more common, I often helped by bringing issues out into the light of day-issues that one side or the other would much rather remain hidden. It's even better in the current era where love triumphs over family goals, and young people think they are choosing their own partners instead of allowing others to mess things up for me-oops, I mean them.

When I laid my wraithlike eyes, okay-ocular sensors, on Arthur, who followed her around that first day in a haze-a haze augmented by beer after beer after beer, I ran the usual tests. Every prediction I worked through on him came up with the same results: Arthur was rich and would be dead within two years. How scrumptious is that?

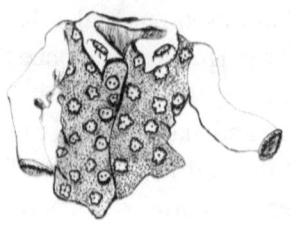

CHAPTER NINE

The insurance policy made everything I wanted for Deloo come true. All I would have to do is ensure he accompanied his good intentions with the necessary legal paperwork stating that my Deloo was his beneficiary on his life insurance policy. When all of that happened, I was a contented spirit guide. Thus, when he was about to fall down drunk on the evening they met, I had her turn, reach out, and hold him up. The rest is history.

Sluggish history. Weeks passed before the money came to Deloo. I became very perturbed. Mr. Goode, Deloo's father-in-law, took it. He had been fiddling with Deloo's money for weeks without giving it to her. Sure, sure. He explained it all to her, but how was I, an old cave girl, supposed to know what a Limited Power of Attorney was? The pall of words alone was enough to bend my twinkling body into knots. So when Zachary Goode asked Deloo to sign the limited power of attorney and a check, I waited for him to return the check to my spic and span, adorable Deloo, but he didn't.

I learned weeks later that he thought all his mumbo-jumbo had accomplished the goal of informing us, er, that is, Deloo about her financial situation.

At first captive to blinding anguish, Deloo didn't catch on about the insurance money. Instead, Deloo worried about money with the same limitations that imprisoned her impoverished mother. Deloo spent each night in her dead husband's childhood bedroom, counting pennies. She decided to make the near three thousand dollars she'd saved last a little longer by camping out on the way back to Alaska. In a tent. Alone!

* * *

Deloo's life, thanks to the Goodes' social contacts in Cambridge, soared. Suddenly an acknowledged artist with prospects, she could return to Alaska with a sense of independence she didn't have either as a single girl or five months as a new widow. Now, a few days after selling her first commissioned painting, Deloo told Matty and Zachary about her travel plans in a shy, rushed voice while I swished invisible electrical forces above her thieving father-in-law's head.

"That might work," Zachary said, "but I think this will work even better." He handed her a debit card with her name embossed on the cover.

Debit card? I pondered the term. To that point I had heard of credit cards, which Deloo didn't own, but her mother used. Having heard all sorts of terrible things about credit cards, I imagined that a debit card, which sounds too much like "death card," must be worse.

Mystified, Deloo stared at the man who reminded her so much of her gentle Arthur. "What's this? I have never applied for a credit card." She lowered hazel-green eyes, thinking about her last bleak bank statement. Since Arthur's parents had insisted that she should not pay for anything, she'd been able to leave her pitiful 2,963 dollars in savings untouched. She'd forced Arthur to eat ramen noodles every night for all five months they'd been married. Once they both got jobs, both at the university, they still ate like paupers in order to put five hundred dollars into savings every two weeks. She figured that in two years they would have enough saved to buy a house. Now without Arthur, her plans had changed. All she could hope for now was to afford a very cheap car and maybe one night in a motel along the way.

Financial matters preoccupied Deloo, and now they were oppressive. From my experience in guiding widowed mortals through the grim realities of grief and loss, having the energy to think about money again showed she'd made a big step toward recovery. My job was to protect her fragile abilities to maintain focus while she imagined a new future.

However, when Mr. Goode had been explaining investment theory to her, Deloo always traipsed down her usual dithering mental path of hopelessness and drifted away. I almost followed her there, but the worrisome check she gave him weeks ago always had me seeking answers. After weeks of waiting, this old cave girl was all light wave ears. Where was my, er, I mean, Deloo's money? I had already launched into a mental tirade about the missing money when I heard Mr. Goode tell me what I needed to know.

"...ten thousand to the ten you got from the university insurance. Do you think that will help you on your big journey?" Mr. and Mrs. Goode both stared at her. Deloo gulped, realizing she had spaced out while he explained something important. From their expressions, she knew they thought it was good news.

Deloo looked at the card. I did as well and wasn't pleased with what I saw. It glowed, turned blood red and all energy in it juddered away. I didn't know enough about what it was supposed to do. Neither did Deloo. She looked at Mr. Goode, and opened her mouth, hoping something intelligent would emerge. "I..., I'm sorry. I don't understand. Could you say that again?"

Both of the Goodes burst into laughter. Mr. Goode wrapped her in a gentle bear hug and said, "I told Mrs. Goode you weren't listening to what I've been telling you these past few months about the life insurance policy Arthur and I worked out on your wedding day." The creases in Mr. Goode's face seemed to deepen and turn gray. "The insurance company came through with the final payment. Remember that form I asked you to sign a few weeks ago?"

"Yes," Deloo lied.

~No! Dotson! Liar!~ I communed to her without waiting for a response. My communes at that time always clanged against deaf mental ears. Maybe it's because I derided Raven (Dotson). Had she known, Great Aunt Pauline would have shouted hutłanee at me.

"You employed me as your financial manager with that document, remember?" Deloo remembered nodding at him at that moment. Smiling inside, she'd known then she would never allow him to manage her 2,963 dollars. She had a use for every penny of her savings.

Now, looking at the card again, Deloo shook her head. This time she attempted a laugh, but the others didn't join her. "What did you do? Sell this portrait to some foolish foreigner?" Deloo pointed to her portrait of Arthur that perched in the dining room. She spotted an annoying bit of orange that called too much attention to itself and grabbed a brush from the tool belt she always had strapped across her overalls. She picked up her ever-charged palette from nearby. Using a footstool, she stepped up to reach the canvas and communed with her painting for a while. She could feel the pressure of money-talk ease away with each stroke of the brush.

"Deloo, honey," Mrs. Goode said, her voice rich with love, "I guess you haven't listened very well to your father-in-law's financial lectures during these past months. Don't you realize that Zachary has been telling you that you became a millionaire when Arthur died? Thanks to the insurance policy that Zachary bought with Arthur for your wedding present, you have two million dollars to invest."

Deloo's knees dissolved. She fell off the footstool and onto the floor with a solid thump.

They helped her up. She felt a twinge in her left ankle, but stood without a problem. Staring at her father-in-law, Deloo murmured, "I've heard you throw around a lot of numbers, but I thought you were just making up stories like my great uncle Virgil always does. He's good at it. You should meet him sometime. He's blind, but he tells great stories."

Mr. Goode looked at Deloo with a patient smile and said, "No wonder Arthur loved you. You are worse than he was about business. I was so surprised when he followed my advice to add a Master of Business Administration to his Masters of Science in Zoology. I thought he was ready to work in the real world until he went after that PhD in Archaeology too." Zachary shook his head. Mrs. Goode patted his shoulder. "I didn't think he'd take me up on that insurance policy. I wanted to buy him something for your wedding that would go toward your future. The idea was that I would pay the first year's premium and half of the second on your first anniversary. I was sure he would let the policy go. I paid my half long before it was due. Long before his accident. It's just the way things happened.

Flowing in the air around them, I chuckled. Even though he might have made a delightful father and archaeologist had he lived, in truth, Arthur made a much better provider for my Deloo in death.

Now, a few weeks after getting the news of Arthur's insurance wealth, Deloo was on her way. As it happened, she spent a little longer with the Goodes so that she could learn the lessons about business and finance that she had ignored before. It wasn't easy for her, but she concentrated until she learned the basic concepts.

What she didn't know was that I would do my best to control all of my little mortal's ideas so that she would be independent and thus able to help Taale and a few others in typical Athabascan generosity. My beam of approval featured three fake diamond teeth of such brilliance they glittered all the way to Fairbanks. I needed Taale to tamp down Deloo's goals of giving away all of the insurance money following Athabascan notions that giving generously would lead to future generosity from others.

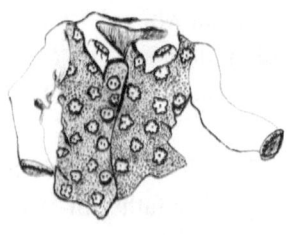

CHAPTER TEN

A photo filled a cheap frame and tilted on a shelf above the television in Fairbanks, Alaska. Deloo, hair skinned back from her face in tight braids, had been the center of Taale's universe for eleven years in the moment someone snapped the photo. Twelve, if you counted the unexpected pregnancy. Deloo was already twenty-one. Born a while after the passage of the Alaska Native Claims Settlement Act, or ANCSA, Taale had not been eligible for enrollment in their corporation, Doyon. Earlier generations did enroll. Deloo's great grandmother, Ruth, filled out all the forms for herself and her kids, since all three of her children (Pauline, Virgil, and Helen) had been born before December 18, 1971, the date President Richard M. Nixon signed the act into law. Later, thanks to newer thinking, Alaska Native corporations could vote to include all "afterborns" (as they were called in the day). Not all of them did, but Doyon voted to open shareholder rosters on a temporary basis in 1992 and then in perpetuity in 2007. Taale filled out the paperwork for herself and little Deloo, elated because Doyon gave them opportunities they couldn't have otherwise. Not much. Small scholarships or grants. It all helped but didn't make them wealthy.

Another photo caught Taale's eye. A picture of her mother, Helen, and her grandmother, Ruth. The two women leaned into each other at a family picnic. Grandmother Ruth died when Taale was six. Her mother, Helen, died later in the same year, both due to respiratory ailments thought to be related to pneumonia and possibly tuberculosis. Taale stepped over to her beading table and held a moose hide moccasin to her nose. She breathed in the smoky aroma and smiled. Her mother sewed it a few weeks before she died. Taale traced the stem of one of the flowers in the design, proud as always that even at the end, her mother's needle never faltered. The beads all lay flat against the smoke-tanned hide, perfect examples of Athabascan beading.

"Perfect as it is," Taale mused aloud, "it should be put away." Every cubic inch of Taale's petite house had a function, most of which was storage. She had designed and built a cabinet using slats of found wood and a glass door that she salvaged from an old cabinet. It held all of her beading tools and projects. The moccasins had their own cubby hole. As she closed the glass door, she noticed one of the tiny doors was ajar. She pressed it, expecting to hear a click. Nothing happened. After wrestling with it, she found the culprit: a bead.

"That's strange." she picked up the large bead that had escaped its plastic bin and stared at it. "In the first place, you are strange looking," she told the bead, "and besides, I won't have you bouncing out of your box." She examined the tan bead. It looked like wood, although it was made of plastic. She fingered the design etched into one surface. Dropping it back into its container, Taale nodded when she heard a satisfying click as the cabinet door latched.

"Got to get to work," she muttered, wondering if she should mention to her aunt Pauline her growing habit of talking to herself. "Nah, if I didn't, who would?" she laughed.

Aunt Pauline was the family boss. Grandmother Ruth had raised her two small daughters, Pauline and Helen, and infant son, Virgil, on her own. Pauline never married and lived with Ruth until both her mother and sister died. Pauline took over raising her sister's daughter, Taale, after Helen died in 1977. Pauline, Taale's aunt, known as Great Aunt Pauline by many, still lived in Ruth's old house a block away from Taale's cabin.

Deloo and her mother had lived in precarious poverty all of Deloo's life. Taale had begun to make more money because she had graduated from the university and now had a steady job as an Information Technology Specialist. She'd managed the education by getting student loans, loans for which the grace period was over and she now needed to come up with money to make the monthly payments. Taale made a steady and good income, but had very little cash to show for it.

Getting Deloo into an "outside" college like IAIA had been easy because she studied hard and made good grades. I had used spirit-guide wisdom to know she could have pursued a four-year degree, but it was too much of a financial strain on Taale, who had been working on a B.S. in Computer Science at the University of Alaska Fairbanks at the same time. Deloo finished her degree six months sooner than did Taale. And just days after Deloo graduated with an Associate of Arts degree, she met and married Arthur.

Deloo reported to Taale that she and Arthur didn't even have enough money to buy a car or a house. Once they arrived in Fairbanks, they borrowed Taale's rickety '95 Camry off and on. Arthur came to Fairbanks because he had secured a post-doctoral grant position. Deloo got a job at the university library. Arthur died so soon after starting that he never enjoyed a house or a newer vehicle—or so Deloo thought. Now, thanks to his death, Deloo could do both. The car came first.

With Zachary's help, she acquired a newish Volkswagen Passat. The price met Deloo's need for parsimony as well as Mr. Goode's qualms about used car safety. In so many ways, the Passat represented Deloo's life as an adult—a single adult. The car was solid, but had its odd moments. So did Deloo.

* * *

Static grated across Anne Murray's voice as she sang "spread your tiny wings and fly away." The radio broadcaster's cheerful voice blared into the room with a loud "Good morning Truro on this beautiful fifth day of June!" Deloo leaped out of bed, reached out to turn off the radio and knocked the sketchbook off the nightstand. Disoriented, Deloo remembered she had to pick up Arthur at the airport and she was late. She scurried around the room until I sent her a view of the casket to remind her.

Shock numbed her feet. Arthur was dead. He didn't need her any more. Deloo scooped up the sketchbook and stared without interest at the last picture she had drawn. She entered the bathroom. She put it on the vanity, still open to the sketch of me as a toddler. The shower washed away all but a vague memory of the dream. Deloo used the wispy after-thoughts of the image to take a break from grief and fear. I studied the way she worked through those intricate problems. It always helps us spirit guides. To make it even more complicated, her mourning process was unusual. She had to go through it according to rigid Athabascan standards of how to display emotion. She had to display very little emotion and yet still convey how she felt his loss.

Deloo had endured the usual twists and heaves of emotional turmoil several times. Arthur died while Deloo still thrilled with romantic fantasies about marriage, but not before coming to grips with disappointment in him. She had met nothing more than deep puddles of love pierced with shards of budding disgust. I thought she'd be over Arthur within weeks. Perhaps having to deal with being alone held her back. Studying her drawing, Deloo touched her own dimple as she brushed her teeth. Hers was on the right. The little girl in the dream (I was that adorable little girl) had a dimple on the left. The dream girl's complexion had been flawless. Deloo envied her because her formerly smooth face had developed a sun rash in the unrelenting sun of New Mexico. Arthur used to laugh at her preoccupation about her face.

"It's just a rash, Honey," he had chided her. "It will go away."

Deloo stared at her reflection. The harsh light in the hotel bathroom revealed spots that makeup and gentler lighting hid. "You're right, Arthur," she whispered. "I made too much of nothing when we were together. Who cares what I look like now?" Deloo twisted her dark hair into a towel and arranged it on top of her head. It wasn't as long as Earlene's. Her mother's best friend had hair down to her knees.

She noticed as if for the first time how dark her skin was against the bleached-white towel. She smiled. Arthur had loved finding excuses to snuggle his white face next to her darker one. A few weeks into their marriage, she realized that she was a trophy, a way for him to show off his anti-racism. At first Deloo had loved that quality in him, but noticed he nuzzled her like that more often in front of cameras than otherwise. She wondered how much he really loved her. Deloo forced herself to think of something else and looked again at the drawing. She had dark skin herself, but it was far lighter than the little girl's face.

"She was almost black," Deloo murmured. She looked at her hasty notes, found the reference to skin tone, and underscored it. "Almost black."

I flickered. It was obvious that while Deloo could pick up on my dreams, as she had done last night, she couldn't see me the way she did when she was a little tot. In those days, the two of us played often. Taale, her mother, thought it was cute for a while that her child had an imaginary friend. They both called me Bossie back then.

My disquiet today was about stalking the people who'd been at the Secret Spirit Inn. My so-called bug was too weak. Pertinent to the death or not, my bug allowed me to zoom in on one person—Prize Woman's movements and plans. While I was proud to have learned to use the tool, I didn't know why it picked up her, since I knew she hadn't been at the Secret Spirit Inn. Such bugs are tricky. Sure. You get results, but it's hard to tell it if has anything to do with what you want. Nonetheless, the bugs pick up verbal thinking. A lot more happens without words than otherwise. Oh, well. I'm still learning. It would have been ever so kind to my raw nerves if my quarry had explained in word thoughts 'we are now leaving the house, heading toward our car, and will soon move north onto the highway.'

I had to figure all of that out myself, and did after they had been on the road for ten or fifteen minutes. By then my imaginary four-inch spike heels had mashed my fake toes beyond recognition. Between watching Deloo and trying to gauge the pair's direction, and remembering how to wiggle toes, I realized that they were starting and stopping on the streets of a big city. It had to be Halifax, the biggest city for miles around. Meanwhile, Deloo got dressed and stuffed things back into her small traveling case. It was time to move.

It was time to talk to Deloo. I began with a bit of conversation about the dream. *~I was playing hide and seek with my mother. She died not long afterward.~*

"How old were you then?" Deloo asked aloud. I noticed that in her artistic frame of mind, Deloo was uninhibited. Her question thrilled me after all the animosity she'd displayed toward me the day before. I forced myself to remain calm even though I was as excited as an ancient being can be.

~I was about two.~

Deloo shivered. I was thrilled to realize she wasn't thinking about herself, but of me.

Deloo opened the sketchbook and looked at the drawing again, wishing she had paid more attention to detail. "I'm sorry she died when you were so young." She tried to think of something cheering to add. "I could try this as a watercolor if you'd like."

~Yes, but Great Aunt Pauline says you're not supposed to talk to me.~ Have I mentioned that I suffer occasional lapses in good sense? Instead of continuing a "wise and wonderful" conversation, I gave in to an irrepressible urge to joke. I do this when I know that danger is present and yet not within my range of perception.

"What?" Deloo remembered. "Oh . . . . Right. Hutłanee." She pondered the nature of her Athabascan heritage and remembered Great Aunt Pauline's instructions not to speak to spirits or else bad spirits might try to mess with you.

Disquieted about the unexplained alarms I kept getting, I floated in front of her, invisible, wilted, and edgy. *~I'm sorry. It's all right to talk* *to me. Most mortals forget how to do it when you get older. I was being mindless when I should have been telling you how proud and pleased I am to be your guide.~*

"You are?" Deloo looked around the room, trying to find me.

~I'm in front of you and a little above. Try looking for a circular shape made of golden light.~ I waited while she tried in vain to see me. After a few seconds, I continued, *~it takes a while to sort out my shape from all the other shapes in light and shadow that are around you. Let's take that part of it a little at a time.~*

Deloo stretched chapped lips and tried to remember where she'd stuffed her watercolor supplies. "Yes," she mumbled. "That would be fun." Her stomach emitted a ferocious roar and we both laughed—me in silence, Deloo a chuckle. "I'll try it after breakfast." she glowed.

I relaxed a little, but soon I would have to tell her about the innkeeper's death and my conjectures of where the killer had gone. I fluttered a few light waves to signal my pleasure at her new ability to communicate with me. I followed Deloo as she wandered down the hall to the hotel lobby's serve-yourself breakfast. I watched her inhale a bowl of cereal, four pieces of toast and a muffin spread thick with high-cholesterol cream cheese. When she was guzzling her third cup of coffee, I wished that I could do the same. I envied her ability to enjoy taking in food. It's something we spirits can't do: eat. I miss chewing and swallowing.

A television set in the dining room displayed a morning news show. I wondered if there would be information about the death already. A youngish man on the small screen blushed and stuttered while he discussed unfamiliar people and places. There was nothing about the dead innkeeper. By then someone must have found the body and called the police. Maybe the inn was too remote to make a morning newscast.

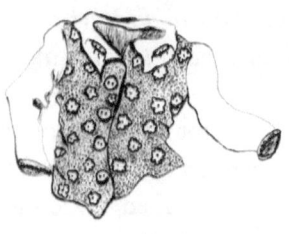

CHAPTER ELEVEN

~Take some food. You'll need it later.~

Little on the counter appealed to her as trail food, but Deloo wrapped a fresh pastry into a paper napkin for later in the day.

Now the time had come to talk to Deloo. *~Deloo, I am glad that you have slept well and now eaten well, for I have some important news for you.~*

Deloo stiffened and looked around, her large and changeable half-breed eyes, this morning greenish-blue rather than their more usual grass-green, popped open. She studied the lobby. One of the other diners stared at her until she smiled at him, turning her face to show off her dimple. It worked.

~Relax, Deloo, my charming Deloo,~ I draped her with a sense of loving comfort. *~There is no threat here. Pretend that you are watching television.~*

Deloo's shoulders aligned themselves to the TV set. Not sure of how to talk to me, she gritted her teeth and tried to create a soundless question. "What happened?"

I launched an invisible smile and plunged into it. *~As I told you yesterday, the innkeeper at the bed and breakfast called someone as soon as we-that is—you left. So, now I have to tell you she's dead because of your jacket.~*

" -y -acket?" Deloo muttered like a bad ventriloquist. She glanced around and added "-ut a-out my -acket?"

Frustrated by her amateurish effort to throw her voice from somewhere like the table top instead of her lips, I glanced at the other diner and offered, *~just THINK to me.~* I could see that she was about to repeat herself so I interjected, *~don't worry. I understood you. I don't know what's so fascinating about your jacket. It appears to be distinctive and* *like others that are "theirs." Remember? She said it was the seventeenth jacket. What do you suppose that means?~*

Deloo thought questions, and threw a dozen at me without giving me time to respond.

~Deloo, I don't know why they are so interested in beaded jackets from Alaska. Your jacket may not be what they are after. It's got to be a coincidence. However, I do know that your mother might have some-thing to do with the jacket they want.~

"Mom?!? How do they know her?"

~Sh-shh. Don't get excited. They don't know who they are looking for. They do know of a woman from Fairbanks, but they don't know much. We can ask your mother what she knows later.~

I was sorry that I hadn't paid much attention to Deloo's mother, content with following her general activities and no more. I felt inadequate having to ask, *~does your mother sell a lot of these beaded jackets?~*

"Mom?" Deloo said aloud and looked around. The other diner lifted his head and glanced at her again. When Deloo didn't say any more, he turned back to his meal. *~Sorry~,* Deloo communed as if she'd done it forever. *~Mom used to make six or seven of these jackets a year until she started taking classes for her degree. At first, she made moose hide jackets, but Great Aunt Pauline told her moose hide is for potlatches, never for tourists. After that Mom switched to town-tanned deer hide. Those sold faster than the moose hide, but it took more time than it was worth. Now she's got a regular job and doesn't need to do it any-more. She still makes one or two a year, but she sells them in Alaska, not Canada.~*

Stymied by the low number of jackets and limited range of sales, I thought about the odd telephone call. *~It is strange. The best part of it is the innkeeper didn't know what kind of car you have. The bad part is that the killer got part of your name before killing her. Someone is trying to find you.~* So much for my earlier idea of hiding the woman's death, but Deloo handled it about as well as I could hope.

"Killed her!" This time Deloo did not try to keep her voice down. The other diner glared at her and patted his lips with a paper napkin. Keeping narrowed eyes on her, he stalked out of the dining area. Deloo watched him leave, twisting her wedding ring until her left ring finger throbbed. When he was gone, she thought to me, *~what should I do?~* A spike of green from the jadeite stone split the universe in half with me on one side, Deloo on the other.

The sensible thing was to drive to the Halifax airport and catch the next plane to Fairbanks. I conveyed the idea to Deloo. Her answer proved she was a born warrior, or else stupid. She vetoed the notion without thought, typical of someone with her blended abilities.

~I am not going to abandon my car just because somebody killed a batty innkeeper.~ As she sent the thought to me, a pair of cleaning women with a laden trolley moved from the lobby to a hallway. She eyed the cleaning trolley as if the killer might pop out of it at any moment. Nothing happened and she relaxed again. *~Why not just drive back as I planned?~*

In my own way I sighed, wishing I had some assistance to back up my idea of a safe retreat. I wondered again about Grandfather Kwaikit. Instead, I offered a second idea that I thought might prevent the inn-keeper's killer from finding Deloo. After all, the killer didn't know Deloo or her car. *~There are hotels in Halifax where you can park your car out of sight for a day or so. Whoever is looking for you will expect to watch the highways, not the city. What do you think of that plan?~*

Deloo brightened. *~I'd like to get to know at least one Canadian city a little better. Let's do it.~*

I frowned. Well, of course without a mouth or eyebrows, my frown-ing days are over, so I wrinkled a few light waves. Why couldn't she be smart and follow my first and better suggestion to go straight back to Alaska? *~All right, but tuck your hair into your ball cap,~* I ordered. *~They are looking for a Native woman with long, dark hair. Be sure to pack your jacket inside the suitcase. There's no reason to invite danger.~*

Deloo nodded, got up, tossed her trash and dimpled at the cleaning crew before heading back to the room to collect her things. In less than fifteen minutes, we worked out a plan together. I was thrilled at our new partnership, but nervous because I detected a dark fury stretching to-ward Deloo from somewhere far away. In retrospect, it turned out that I was both wrong and right about hiding in Nova Scotia a little longer. In the end, I will always know that it was my own selfish desire to see what had become of my world that allowed me to forget to make sure the beaded jacket was out of Deloo's reach. She was in the habit of putting it on whether it was sunny or not outside.

While Deloo and I made our way out of the hotel northeast of Halifax, two people in a small sedan had almost reached the Secret Spirit Inn. I studied their progress. They bumped along until they crested a low rise in the road and stopped. Lights from two police cars flickered beside the inn. After a quick-fire debate in Mandarin, they decided to turn around. An ambulance with its siren piercing the air passed them just before they reached the turn off to the main road.

I sensed I had missed something important when the lid on Deloo's car ashtray burst open with a loud squeak. One of the Loonies that had landed on her Passat the day before took life and spun around before returning to nest beside its brothers in the ashtray. Just as Deloo reached out to do it herself, the lid closed of its own accord. I stared at it for a long minute, wondering if it were a car-style message of great import.

In sync with my private thoughts, Deloo touched the ashtray and whispered, "Creepy."

* * *

Miles away from Deloo at the Secret Spirit Inn, Inspector Al Beamus of the RCMP in the Special Investigation Section saw a vehicle. Observing its make, he made a mental note to find out if anyone had a record of its driver and passenger. He pulled up to the entrance of the inn and stepped out, dreading what he knew he would see inside the building. He tried to suppress the memory of the inn two-and-a-half years ago when the innkeeper, Rosemoira Keilleher, had given him a special Honeymoon Spirit rate of less than a quarter what anyone else ever paid. They discovered upon arrival that she had opened the inn just for them, as there were no other reservations that week. Rosemoira had met them at this very door and congratulated them as soon as they entered. A big basket of fruit and chocolates, their sustenance for the next two days, filled the small table next to the bed. Most of his dread had to do with telling his wife about her death. His wife and Rosemoira had formed a strong bond during that brief, fairy-tale spell.

* * *

Getting Deloo to Halifax took longer and required a lot more concentration than I expected. Traffic was unpredictable, but Deloo was a good driver. I relaxed a bit and reveled once again that I was here. I brushed aside all incoming information and bathed Deloo in gratitude. Much as I wanted to have her stop the car every twenty feet so that I could drink it all in, I didn't. I scanned Deloo's vital signs and stabilized them using basic spirit guide skills. I relaxed when her colors began to merge with the sparkling shades of Halifax in June. Like the air around her, she flowed with elements of youth and vitality. My sense of peace shattered with the first near collision between Deloo's Passat and another vehicle. I begged her to get off the streets.

"They are bad drivers! It's not me." Deloo snarled. "These streets are too narrow and crooked." She propelled the car around a corner to avoid a bicyclist. Her pulse, strong and slow five minutes ago, jigged through her arteries. I stabilized her again.

~*Turn left!*~ I communed from a position about four feet above her head. ~*There's a sign for parking over there.*~

Little as she knew me, Deloo responded at once to my command. Her heart rate slowed upon spotting a parking garage in the small downtown area.

~*Let's take a space inside where no one can see your car,*~ I suggested. Again, she obeyed without question. In a while, we were in the Public Garden and Deloo began a simple self-paced tour by walking from point to point on a tourist map. Warmed by clean sunlight, her pleasure bubbled while ancient memories tugged at me. I let myself daydream rather than keep a watchful eye on Deloo.

~*Deloo,*~ I proposed, ~*let's take a break. Why don't you sit on that bench?*~ Mind you, when I started spirit-guiding thousands of years ago, I wouldn't have been so kind to a mortal. My methods back then were uncomplicated, designed to get a young man or woman through the basic facts of life without frills or sensitivity. Most of them didn't have much affection for me after I awoke them from death. Over time, I learned to treat them with more grace and love. I realized that it was now time to kick grace into high gear. After all, today was the first anniversary of her wedding. I had expected it to be difficult, as she'd cried herself to sleep on many a night since Arthur's accidental death. Instead of pining for him on this day, she made herself comfortable on the bench by taking out a sketchbook and pen. When a pigeon approached her, she searched the pack for something with crumbs. All she had was the pastry I'd urged her to keep. The pigeon came closer.

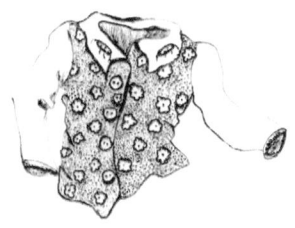

CHAPTER TWELVE

~Don't feed that bird,~ I squealed in mock, if silent, horror. *~It's a parasite-laden scavenger. You'll contribute to infection and germ production.~*

"Don't be a fool," she murmured and then looked around. No one heard her, but she remembered to think the rest, *~he's cute.~*

~She,~ I corrected, *~She's not cute. Don't feed her.~*

Deloo stared at the bird. *~How can you tell it's a female? Male and female pigeons all look alike.~*

~They look somewhat alike, but it's what's inside that counts. This one has an egg that will be ready to come out in an hour or so.~ I nudged the pigeon away with a well-shaped tendril of gentle electrical force. She hopped backward and took on the appearance of an angry dragon. My freelance artist didn't notice except the way an artist does. She had already sketched four and a half drawings of the non-descript pregnant bird. Now Deloo drew it as a lizard with a huge dragon face. I jabbed the bird again. She fluttered her feathers and did a wing hop to the other side of the path.

With her sketchbook on her lap and a pen in each hand, Deloo became a scribe of nature as well as occasional passersby. Her instructors had taught her well, and she soon had seven sheets filled with detailed drawings of the Public Garden.

My thoughts turned to her relationship with her late husband. She met Arthur during the bustle of last year's graduation in late May, each from different schools in New Mexico. They married within days and moved to Alaska. It should have been a warning to them both that one graduated with a PhD in Anthropology, the other with a two-year Associate of Arts degree from the little-known college for Native Americans. The difference in their outlooks on life was too vast for an enduring relationship. They had nothing in common other than intense,

physical attraction. I knew their marriage was doomed, but I also knew
Deloo and her immediate family would burst out of poverty thanks to
him. That's why I helped her to see all of his charms and only those
flaws that were inescapable.

All that was in the past. Today it was obvious that Deloo didn't
have a care in the world, or at least not in the Halifax Public Garden. I
punched up a wad of green and gold sparkling counter-balanced tingles
and arranged it along the veil that separated me from the top of Deloo's
head. It was my particular formula for a vibrating recliner. I flowed upward and onto it to gaze at the Halifax sky. Well, yeah. I might have
dozed off, for soon I was no longer in Blue-Sky Halifax but in Orange-
Sky Zana. My sister-in-law and I were at the well a mile or so away from
home. I helped her carry the bark water basket back to her dwelling. We
chatted, laughed, and played with her youngest baby, a little girl.

"Who is that?"

What? It was odd that I recognized the language at the same time I
knew that it didn't belong in Zana. I whipped around to find the speaker.
As I completed the turn, the sky turned blue and I toppled off my fleeting perch to enter Deloo's space via the top of her head.

~*Oof!*~ I communed. ~*That hurt!*~ Of course, nothing hurt, but it
was such a surprise that I had to complain even if I made it up.

"Who were you talking to?" Deloo asked aloud, pretending to be examining the filigree of her wedding ring.

~*Sh-h-h, not so loud. People are looking at you.*~ It was true. Two
people were staring at Deloo. I glared at them. Deloo grimaced.

~*Sorry,*~ she thought toward me. ~*I forgot.*~

I almost didn't pick up her apology. Instead, I stared at the couple
on the other side of the trail. They looked Chinese, at least he did. She
looked like a mixture of Asian and Native American. Grief or something worse entrapped her, making her face a mask without features.
Something about them seemed familiar. I communed ~*Do you know
them? Are they from Alaska?*~

Deloo looked up from her sketchbook. She had drawn an exact like-
ness of each of them. ~*No,*~ she mused to me, ~*but she looks familiar. She looks sad. My mother gets that way sometimes. You know what
I mean? When somebody will talk to me, her paler-skinned daughter,
even though she's asked them the same question or given them the same
information that I did. That half-breed business bothers her more than
it does me.*~

I was about to ask Deloo to tell me more when I picked up a meta-physical voice from somewhere in my personal space.

~Let me out! I need to be with her. Let me out! They don't know what's coming. I do!~

It was the little ghost I had captured the day before. She was savvy enough to use a spirit-to-spirit commune channel. I used mystic power to inspect her without letting her out of the darkness in which I had imprisoned her.

~What do you mean? What is coming?~ I responded in the same channel, same metaphysical language.

Silence. I waited. For us, language is done without tongues and lips. Not as sexy as what mortals do, but easier to pronounce, although not so much for the ghosts who departed less than a few decades ago.

~I don't know. I must protect her. She's all I have.~

~She's not assigned to you and I can't let you go to anyone but a ghost mentor.~

~What? No! I don't need anyone but her. Let me go.~ The last part trickled out. She'd run out of spirit power. I checked her enclosure to make sure she couldn't escape and then turned my attention back to the mortals in the park. The man was staring at Deloo. He had a gun. Not in view, of course. He simply had one with him.

I communed to Deloo, *~pretend you're feeding that ludicrous bird. They see you looking at them and want to talk to you. We need to leave now. They make me nervous.~*

"Omigod!" Deloo swore under her breath. "It's Prize Woman." Without another word, Deloo took the pastry out of its napkin wrapper and pitched big chunks at the pigeon. Three or four more pigeons soon joined the pregnant bird. One of them landed on the bench beside Deloo, who stood up, flung the rest of the pastry into the flock, and turned her back on Prize Woman. She managed to stuff the sketchbook and drawing materials into her pack before ten seconds had past.

I stayed for just a moment to put a bug on both Prize Woman and her gun-slinging companion. As I lingered, I wondered if I had forced Deloo away without cause. That's when I heard why they wanted to speak to my Deloo.

The man asked his wife, "Did you see the woman that was just here?"

"Just a glance, why?"

"She dropped this," he answered, and held it out to Prize Woman. It was a bracelet. "It's fallen apart, but I thought she might like what's left." It was a string of colorful plastic beads with two letters still on it, a K and an A.

"Just leave it on the bench. Maybe she'll come back for it," the woman said.

~Did they recognize me? ~ Deloo queried. *~Do you still think they have something to do with my jacket? I'm not wearing it.~* She touched her cap. *~I've hidden my hair.~*

I glanced rearward. They had not followed. *~I'm not sure. They found that bracelet you've been wearing. Do you still have the one your cousin made for you a few years ago?~*

Deloo checked her wrist and whispered, "Oh no. I've lost it. Kaylee made it for me when she was seven. Mom helped her with the thick elastic string."

~Didn't it have wording on it? Something that ended in K-A?~

Deloo took a sharp breath. "A-L-A-S-K-A. Kaylee was so proud of spelling the whole word." She looked down the path. "Why aren't they following?"

~The bracelet fell apart, leaving only the last two letters. Lots of words end that way, like Nebraska or parka. They left it behind. They didn't recognize you. Let's be more careful in the future. It's getting late and you have to find a place to stay.~ I drew her attention to a clock tower. It chimed the hour. *~Do you hear that? It's already noon and you need a place with off-street parking.~*

Deloo looked around to find her bearings. As luck would have it, the parking garage was in view. She strode toward it and bumped into the side of a fellow garden walker.

"Sorr..." she began. Her throat strangled the rest of the word. She swayed. I realized too late that she was about to faint.

The man reached out to right her. "I beg your pardon, Ma'am, er, Miss."

Swinging into action on the other side of the veil, I put some invisible steel into Deloo's spine and muscle into her legs. *~You'll be fine, Deloo. He's an old man—not Arthur!~*

Deloo stiffened, stared at the stranger briefly, and ducked her head before she darted into the garage. Her heart was still beating too fast when she found the Passat. "His hat. It had the UNM colors, cherry and silver. It was just like the one Arthur used to wear. A long stocking cap."

~He's also at least thirty years older than Arthur was.~ She'd been seeing Arthur for months. As in this case, there was always a mild

similarity in clothing or posture. Nothing more. *~Don't be concerned. He's gone now.~*

"But why do I keep seeing him?" she asked. She was inside the car and had it moving toward an exit.

~Half of you is still living with Arthur. Half of Arthur is still alive and well in one way or another. You'd be odd if you didn't see him for another few months. Most widows and widowers do. It's a normal phase of grief.~

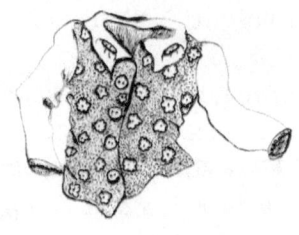

CHAPTER THIRTEEN

By the time she reached the street, Deloo's vital signs had returned to normal. Soon she drove along Spring Garden Road until it became Coburg Road. I noticed a sign to our left and recalled the name: Dalhousie University.

~Stop here,~ I urged. *~Look in your book. I remember something about this university having space for summer tourists. No one would ever expect you to hide here.~* I scrutinized the parking situation and decided it would do. While the parking area was not covered, it was behind the building and not visible except from a narrow alleyway. The car couldn't be seen from the main street by which we had come.

Deloo pulled over and rummaged in her pack to get her guidebook. Her book listed it as having inexpensive summer housing, so she went in to ask. There was a vacancy. Moreover, because a special event had drawn a crowd to the dormitory, the cafeteria would be open for all three meals this week. We could be secluded and well-fed at the same time.

Deloo opened the door to a stark dorm room, tossed her bags onto a chair, plopped onto the bed, and stared at the ceiling. It had been a year since Deloo had stayed in a dormitory. She smiled, thinking of the inane things she and her roommate had done when they lived together. Once back in that protected zone of college, she rolled over as if to chat with me, her invisible pal, and yawned. With safety came sleepiness.

"Who was that woman in your vision, Baasee'? How old were you? She looked my age." Another huge yawn muffled her voice.

With inward amusement, I searched for the quickest way to satisfy her curiosity without arousing her from what boded well to be a good sleep. *~I'll tell you if you promise to take a quick nap and not ask me any questions until after you've had a good lunch. Promise?~*

"You goof!" It was the same word she always used with Arthur except for leaving off "Sweetheart" at the end, so I knew I'd chosen the right tactic.

Deloo arranged herself in a good sleep posture on top of the blankets when I droned, ~*we were both twenty. She had a bad leg.*~ I smiled. Deloo was already sound asleep.

* * *

The pair Deloo had escaped had parked their car near the Public Gardens. Needing to calm themselves, they took a walk into the floral pathways. Although their eyes had seen Deloo, their minds had not. Prize Woman was in shock, but pulled herself together so they could return to her father's house on the outskirts of town. Once there they set up their computers and phones before going to work at her father's Halifax restaurant. He had a chain of five tiny Chinese food outlets in eastern Canada, and they had offered to fill in where needed for a few months.

The bug I'd planted on them signaled a change in their activity that affected Deloo. The woman asked someone about her by phone. I'd set up the bug to link to me if either tried to run a check on Deloo.

"I'm sorry, Ma'am, there's no one by that name in the Fairbanks area."

Keeping her temper in check, a woman murmured a polite Inuit word, 'Nakurmik' or thank you'. She ended the call with a click of a button. I tuned up the connection. Most of her thoughts were in English with occasional words from three other languages: Mandarin, French, and English. I ran her vocabulary through my data base, and discovered she spoke Inuttitut (Inuit language of northern Québec). She thought one word several times each iteration sharp with fear: Qanik.

"Qanik."

"What did you say?" her companion asked.

Every nerve in the woman's body jangled. I thought she was about to jump away when she performed the magical transformation she did in the off-road parking area. From my distant viewpoint, she formed a mask of amazing beauty and hid her fractious thoughts from the man.

"I said 'Keviuriq.' Remember that fish camp where we had our honeymoon in Northern Québec?" She sent a wistful vibe toward him. If he felt it, he didn't react.

The man and woman sat opposite each other. The woman radiated both physical discomfort and deep grief. Everything about the man basked in some smug memory. A vision came to me of their surroundings. One sat on a threadbare couch. The other sat at a small side table. I queried the Invisible Forces to find out if they were at home. Whatever the Invisible Forces are, and after all this time you'd think I'd have found out, what they are not is good at simple human communication. Even so, I get a lot of information that seems to fit my queries. In this case, I learned the couple was not at their own home, but in a house they knew well. Soon I learned more from the woman.

"Dammit, Father!" the woman muttered at a piece of paper.

"What did he do this time?"

"The usual. He includes personal expenses along with business expenses." The woman made a circle on the offending sheet. "I've told him over and over that it doesn't work. Just like I keep telling him that I'm an architect, not a bookkeeper. He never listens."

"He's an older man. Wasn't he born before the Revolution in 1949? Chinese men of that era make all the rules in the family. Besides, tax rules are different in China. Let it go. This is his house, after all."

The woman scowled, "He never paid taxes in China. He was born in Montreal, not Zhongyuan. He should know better."

My figurative purple hair stood on end. She pronounced it Joneyearn, the musical inflection of China's central plain. I leaned forward, flipping a coil of imaginary hair out of the way to hear more.

The man grunted and tapped his laptop. "I've checked with all the directories in and around Fairbanks. She's not listed."

Nothing about the man came through, but I could see a vague image of the woman. She was the woman Deloo had drawn in the Halifax Public Garden. She was, therefore, Prize Woman, as Deloo had dubbed her.

~He must be the impatient driver we saw yesterday morning,~ I conveyed in Eternalese to Grandfather Kwaikit. I wasn't prepared to get an answer from yet another spirit, but did.

~Yes. He's my brother-in-law.~

Stunned, I studied the metaphysical spot in which I'd stowed the little ghost. I asked using Eternalese. *~How did you learn to use this language?~* Unguided ghosts don't learn our fancier languages or customs without precise training.

~My sister's guide teaches me whenever she can. But I'm weak and sleep a lot.~

That made sense if she'd died by violence. It also explained why she wanted to be with her sister. *~Do you know where they are?~*

No answer. I peeked into the space I'd tucked her. Wiped out. Figures. Ghosts of just a few decades need a lot of rest. I turned my attention back to Prize woman and her husband.

"Help me figure out who that woman was." He said. "What's her name"

"Green or Gardner. She thought the first name started with a D. It could be Goodman, something with a G. She didn't write the whole name before the woman left the inn." Prize Woman chuckled. It was a pleasant gurgle.

"Yes," he said without an answering smile, "I see the problem. I'll try anyway." His fingers flew over the keyboard as he muttered, "Could it have been Goode?"

"Maybe."

He tapped his computer and waited. In a moment, he swore, waited and jotted a name into a small notebook. "That's it. Arthur Goode. It's a little article in the Fairbanks News Miner. No obituary. He was thirty. Died on Thanksgiving Day last year in a car accident."

"That's a good lead, Chuan. Who are his next of kin?"

"His parents, Zachary and Matilda, both of Boston. And a wife. No name in this paragraph for the wife, but that might be why there's no obituary: Arthur was from Boston rather than Alaska. I may as well follow up on them." Chuan provided the names in mixed English and used another language for filler words. I observed that he spoke with the comfort level of a person using a hybrid family language, a dialect of Mandarin and her languages.

"Yes," she answered in the same way. "Get as much as you can about the widow. Maybe it's all about that jacket, after all."

"The so-called fifteenth jacket, eh? Why bother?"

"Fifteenth?" The woman's heart wrenched. "I didn't know they had numbers."

"Eh?" I sensed the man tried to soothe without moving very much. "It's just what those two call them." He chuckled. "I meant seventeenth. We're on the seventeenth jacket now."

"How many of these jackets are there? I've never heard of them, numbered or not."

"Ma chère," the man placated her, "It's them—not me. They talk about them all the time."

"What about the fifteenth, then? What made you think of that one?"

"They lost it." The man laughed. "That was two years ago. Now they've lost another."

"Figures," his wife snapped. "Why did they tell us to work on it?"

"I don't know. Those jackets don't have anything to do with us. We should have been working on other projects all this time, but you know how the blonds are. They won't let go of something as useless as that jacket until they know it's useless themselves. Just like they were with Qanik. He caught a sense of her stiffening and continued in a soothing voice, "You're right. I'd better check on Mrs. D. Goode."

Just when it seemed as if my metaphysical eavesdropping was going somewhere, I felt anger rattling from beside me. It came from the field of solid darkness in which I had placed the little ghost. I peered inside. Very few ghosts of her youth were smart enough to see us ancients, and once again the little ghost surprised me by flinging herself toward me. I caught her in one of my tendrils and sent calming thoughts toward her.

~Take ... Me ... To ... Her! She ... Needs ... Me.~

I waited for more but that was all the tiny ghost could manage. Once again, she became still and silent.

CHAPTER FOURTEEN

Oh, the woes of a dazzling spirit like me. Sprouting a bright set of emerald molars to grind, I took in their words, but not why they were looking for Deloo. The tension between the unknown man in Halifax and his blended Inuit and Chinese wife might be due to his being a single-shot Mandarin man. Each of them constructed thought with numerical precision, letting their dialogue zip along with few words. Using magic, I kept up. Fending off the urge to pat my luxurious back, I forced myself to investigate them. Did one of them kill the innkeeper?

Their personal relationship was none of my business. My priority was to keep them from discovering that Mrs. D. Goode was still in Nova Scotia. How long would it take these people to find her in Halifax?

I spun around in the ethers above Deloo. Something about my agitation reached her. She stirred, rolled over, and tried to pull the blankets closer to her face.

~You are still on top of the blanket, my dear,~ I murmured.

"Whuh?" she pried open one hazel-green eye to look for me.

~Roll a little toward the edge of the bunk and lift up a corner of the top sheet.~

"Mmmph," Deloo breathed, rolled, lifted the sheet, and began rolling the wrong direction until she had mummified herself into a narrow bundle against the wall. "Thanks, Arthur," she sighed and fell asleep again. She reminded me of a three-toed sloth. I detected mouth-watering smells drifting through the halls and into Deloo's room and stimulated her into wakefulness.

Awake. Trapped. She plucked at the sheath of sheet and blanket that she had coiled around herself. Her heart reverberated and she sucked in a lungful of air in preparation to scream.

~You are safe, Deloo,~ I cautioned. *~Roll onto your back and try again.~*

Deloo hesitated and then rolled as I instructed. When the cloth loosened around her legs, she yanked herself free and sat up. She looked around the room but saw nothing. "Was that you, Great Spirit?" she whispered.

If I had mortal eyes, I would have rolled them. In the distant past, I never had to explain myself because beings like me were already a part of the system. Deloo, stuck in American history and schooling, had learned a thin element of the ancient Native American beliefs, and none of it pertains to me, the enchanting Baasee'.

~Great Spirit?~

Not bad. She communed with some success. In a wonderful mood, I answered, *~don't call me Great Spirit. Save that for the Invisible Forces, and not the likes of a simple spirit guide like me. You woke up sniffing something. What did you smell?~*

Deloo's stomach growled. She inhaled and smiled. "I guess I'll go find out."

Since she had fallen asleep with her clothes on, half of her work was done. She dragged a brush through her tangled hair and searched for the dorm room key card and her bag. Thus armed, Deloo left her room in quest of the beefy aroma that lured her. She didn't expect to enjoy dorm food and was overjoyed that a delicious meal was available after a short, winding walk through the building's maize of hallways.

The brownie following a savory shepherd's pie somehow reminded her of me, her new companion. The trust we had developed yesterday and this morning tangled with logic, a logic that warned her to get far more information about the "voice".

Deloo ventured a muted question, "Who are you?"

~I will tell you my name, but I don't think you'll understand it. Here goes: ^>^<^>~

I smiled at Deloo.

She didn't smile back.

I frowned. What did it matter? She was a moody mortal. Who needed her company after all? I had lived for centuries without a single person to talk to about my personal problems. I could spend a few more doing the same boring stuff. I hesitated for a second or two and then added, *~did you get it?~*

What Deloo felt was a sort of mental breeze where I uttered my name. Taking a deep breath, Deloo attempted to find something normal about me, the invisible. "Could you say that again … please?" she asked in a low voice.

~Remember, think words to me instead of moving your lips. People will think you are crazy,~ I quipped and regretted it. *~I'm sorry, my dear Deloo. You are not crazy, and the best way to prove it to your psycho-sensitive world is to keep your mouth shut. Just think to me. I'll get it.~*

Deloo felt a wave of humor envelop her. She smiled. *~You know Great Aunt Pauline would have words for me speaking to one of your kind!~* She waited.

~Baasee'.~ I tried again.

"What?" Deloo raked her fingers through her hair and tried to twirl around to get a full view of the dining hall without attracting undue attention.

~I'm Baasee'. I chose it because it means thank you, but when said in the mind something weird happens.~ I added, *~I'm thanking you for listening to me. Now you try.~*

Baasee' is a common Denaakk'e word. Deloo knew how to say it with her tongue but not as a commune word in her mind. *~Baazhee.~*

~See? That's what happens, but good start. Baasee'.~ I did a little jig to reward her. It would have tickled her fancy nineteen years earlier when at age two she could still see me. She didn't notice. I held back my dejection and thought in more optimistic terms, *~Remember that Baasee' sounds a lot like 'bossy' in English. Try it again.~*

Deloo's mind reeled with questions-questions about the sorrow I projected about my mother, questions about the dream girl, and questions about sanity. She forced herself to breathe and then to try the name silently again: *~Baasee'.~* Without waiting for me to correct her, she rushed on with more questions. *~What is your era? How old are you? Can you teach me to do magic?~*

I sent Deloo a grumbling frown and communed *~my era? You are very inquisitive for someone who refused to take that course in Archaeology two years ago. For your information, I'm an Ice Age cave woman with well over fourteen thousand years tucked under my aura.~*

"The Ice Age? How can you still be here?"

I could see that endless questions were going to flow without her waiting for an answer. I cut her off with an encouraging, *~when you go back to school, let's take a few courses. Archaeology, Geology, even Physics. All of them will be useful.~*

"Let's do," Deloo muttered, knowing that she'd have to take a lot of courses for a bachelor's degree; courses that she never had needed for the Associate of Fine Arts degree. Physics hadn't been one she'd thought about, but she liked the cozy phrase, 'let's take a Physics course.' Maybe she'd have a personal tutor in her head. Would that be cheating? Deloo gave a mental laugh and got up with her tray. She followed signs indicating where to deposit used trays and made her way out of the cafeteria.

On the way back to the room Deloo asked, ~*Baasee'*,~ pronouncing it my silent way ~*why are you here? Do you know what my life is going to be like? Do you do fairy-tale tricks? Can I learn them?*~

I mulled those questions over before answering. They were typical. In another time and place, I would have made short shrift of such a rude mode of interrogating me, but we had many urgent tasks to finish. I settled for giving her a companionable touch on her head with a jewel-toned fingernail.

~*Yes, Deloo, my impatient one, there should be messages in everything we do together. For instance, you forgot to take some coffee to the room with you. Do you still want it?*~

~*Coffee! Yes. I'm still sleepy. I'll go back now.*~

~*Yes. Or you could use magic.*~

We spent a solid hour on her creating first a cup, then filling it with her favorite brand and adding the cream and sugar. It didn't occur to her that she could have gone for the coffee in a quarter of that time.

"Wow." Deloo sighed after taking the first sip. "Arthur would have been impressed. Could he and I have ever learned to do it together?"

~*I'm sorry. Not your playful Arthur. You have the rare gift of making material objects out of nothing. He didn't. You can imagine things into being, like your beautiful artwork. Remember how frustrated you were when you needed a certain kind and size of paint brush in your last year at IAIA? You couldn't afford it, and the project was due that day. You tore pieces of cardboard into tiny pieces and used them instead. You'd never seen anyone do it, although your teacher said he did. Remember? You got an A for that painting.*~

"I remember. But that's being practical."

I lifted up a long lock of her hair and held it up. ~*So is doing this. Remember your friend, Sheila? She used magic on her otherwise silky hair before every class. She told you she just held it up and told it to stay. It should have fallen.*~ I let Deloo's hair drop to illustrate what

Sheila did. *~You don't have your friend's gift. I can do it for a few seconds to make a point, but it won't stay.~*

"Sheila. Yeah. She is awesome."

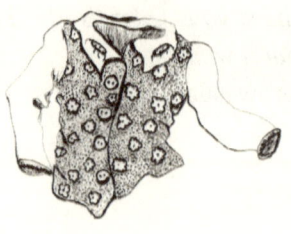

CHAPTER FIFTEEN

At a hotel at the border of Halifax and New Brunswick, Brent lounged in a wooden chair, forcing it to be a recliner by tilting it against the wall. He paused to gaze at the Harvard class ring on his right hand. He'd replaced its original synthetic ruby for a real one several years ago. He raised his hand in a mock salute to his reflection in the mirror and caught the electric blue flash of his eyes. Although he would be forty-seven in another month or two, his eyes still had the mesmerizing look of a movie star. A memory of one particular day caused his mind to drift twenty years back.

Brent enjoyed the soft crunchiness of stepping on the red and gold maple leaves. He was with Chuan Wu who came all the way from northern China. Life changed for him that day. They were waiting for Chuan's fiancée, Ming Liu, in front of Gund Hall on Quincy Street. Ming's art history class was due to end in a few minutes. Brent wasn't interested in Ming because she was half Chinese and had been born somewhere in Canada. He needed a Chinese-born contact to take him to China for archaeological field work in order to complete his dissertation. Chuan seemed motivated to introduce Brent to his homeland for just that purpose. He said his father was disappointed in his eldest son, Chuan, for not pursuing the study of ancient China. Bringing home a graduate student in archaeology would exonerate Chuan and elevate the family stature.

"There she is! My prize of a woman." Chuan waved at her.

Ming's glossy black hair flowed behind her as she ran toward them. She was one of the most beautiful women Brent had ever seen. She, by contrast, didn't see him at all. While surprised at her lack of interest in him, since most women looked at him with desire, Brent supposed that Ming might like a different kind of man. In that moment, it was obvious that Chuan fit all her standards with his Asian coloring and facial construct. A blue-eyed blond of northern European descent like Brent didn't fit Ming's sense of masculinity.

She kept her luminous black eyes focused on Chuan. Ming's father was more than satisfied that his daughter obeyed filial piety even in Canada. He had instructed his twin daughters, Ming and MoLi to find Mandarin men of northern China. If possible, he wanted men from one of the lineages that were the appropriate counterparts to his clan. Chuan matched every one of her father's instructions, and best of all, Ming found him good looking. MoLi had chosen Qanik, an Inuit man from her home village in Québec.

The three of them continued waiting on Quincy Street. Brent didn't know why and knew better than to ask. Fitting in to his new Chinese social group meant adopting their choices rather than insisting on his own. In this case, he wanted to go to Harvard Square for lunch, but smiled instead. His turn would come. His new friends had another plan that involved Howard Lee, a student whom Brent met when he first started at Harvard a couple of years earlier. Howard was tall, with dark blond hair and heavy-lidded, blue-green eyes. Like Brent, he was very Anglo in most physical matters. Brent thought about the day they met at the textbook center of the Harvard Coop. Brent couldn't afford the books, but did have a small pocket notebook and a pencil. He had just finished writing the titles, author, and year of each book for his first semester of courses. He was certain he would find most of them in one of Harvard's many libraries. When he looked up, he caught the stranger's slanted eyes studying him with interest. Brent sized him up in a single glance as rich and lifted his chin. He passed the nosey student, trying to give the impression that he was far too intellectual for undergraduates.

"Are you an Archaeology graduate student?" the stranger asked.

Brent stopped to study the other man. "How do you know that?"

Howard introduced himself, explained that it was obvious because Brent was copying titles in the section for graduate level Archaeology courses.

Brent laughed and said, "If you can tell me where I'm from, I'll be happy to call you Sherlock Holmes." He continued walking toward the stairs when he felt a touch on his arm.

"You're from Alaska."

"What?!"

"You dropped your keys. I saw the key chain," Howard smirked. "You may call me Sherlock."

Brent pulled out his keys and stared at the tiny letters spelling A-l-a-s-k-a, and chuckled. "Nice to meet you, Sherlock."

Howard cleared his throat. "May I buy you a cup of coffee?"

During that short coffee break, Brent learned that it wasn't a joke to call Howard "Sherlock," as his new friend revealed uncanny powers of observation and knowledge about others. For instance, Howard deduced within ten minutes that Brent was impoverished and that he hadn't qualified for any major fellowships. Furthermore, he guessed that Harvard had hired him as a Resident Tutor in one of the residential houses. The tutorship provided him with a free room and a limited meal plan.

After the first Sherlockian coffee break, many opportunities opened for Brent. One of them was meeting the rest of the Lee family one sunny spring day at the family mansion in Boston. It was clear that the senior Mr. Lee ran everything and that his sons obeyed their father without question.

Brent never did anything without question, but he had no objections to any of the special treats that Howard gave him, such as a summer in Uruguay twenty-two years ago or accepting his new nickname, Alaska. Why Howard took Brent under his wealthy wing remained a mystery to Brent until the day they had lunch with Chuan and Ming.

Once Howard arrived, the four set off toward Beacon Street where they found a small Asian restaurant. During lunch, Brent learned that Ming and Chuan were both twenty and both planned to graduate with baccalaureate degrees in two years. Ming was studying History of Art and Architecture and Chuan studied Computer Science and Applied Mathematics. Both of them looked at Howard, who responded to the silent prompt by saying that he had just started his MBA from the Harvard Business School. Like them, he also expected to finish in two years, and would therefore go through commencement with Ming and Chuan.

"Howard's grandfather grew up near mine. He's part of my clan," Chuan explained. "At twenty-two Howard's already planning to visit my, I mean our family in China next summer to honor his family's request. You could join us, Brent. Maybe Ming can come with us as well?" His eyes caressed his fiancée. She beamed in response. The other three stared at Ming, transfixed every time she smiled. When she widened her mouth, she seemed to send out a blast of pure light.

Brent realized that he, then twenty-years younger and more virile at twenty-six, was the senior member of the group. He told them about his PhD program and explained it would take at least three more years to finish. Everything depended on getting his research project approved by his committee. He smiled at Chuan, and accepted the invitation. It was a moment that changed them all forever.

Unseen by the younger pair, Howard met Brent's eyes, and in a split second, Brent began to piece things together. It was so obvious that Brent wondered if Howard's intuitive perceptions were rubbing off on him. Chuan's family, although in the same clan as Howard, descended from common merchants. Howard descended from the royal branch of the clan. Howard's family, as Brent already knew, descended from an imperial family whose enemies had ousted them from their palace late in the seventh century. Thus, while Chuan, a steadfast communist in the contemporary Chinese world, took it for granted that they were equals, Howard knew his father would never tolerate such contempt. The senior Mr. Lee demanded the veneration due his breeding. He also wanted the family palace restored to his ownership.

In due course, the four of them went to China together. Over time each of them built their futures based on the single opportunity provided by Chuan. For his part, Brent oversaw the graduate studies in archaeology of hundreds of northern Chinese men and women. Howard and his family contributed financial support and other kinds of assistance.

All that was unimportant compared to Brent's current mandate to find a single beaded jacket. He had spent months looking for the garment, most of that time in Alaska. The three others knew he was searching for it. So did Howard. Eventually they included Ming and Chuan in the search.

Brent pulled himself back to the present where he was still awaiting their appointed meeting time in the hotel lobby, Brent's fingers searched his pocket for a small object. He began tumbling it in the palm of his hand, occasionally looking at it with approval. It was about one inch in height and width and two inches in length. He rubbed the top side. Chuan's family owned the design and helped him produce dozens of the small cubes. They thought he used them as game pieces like they did. Brent didn't argue, since Brent felt that it represented an exciting game. He stopped playing with the object and dropped it into his pocket.

A sedan rolled into the hotel parking lot and parked near his. A man stepped out of the driver's door. Brent could see sandy blond hair and a receding hairline. A man pulled two suitcases out of the trunk and turned so that Brent could see his face.

"Howard."

Soon Brent heard footsteps in the hallway. A door squeaked open and then slammed shut. It was time. Brent pulled up his electronic contact list and highlighted Howard's mobile number.

Howard studied the display on his smart phone before accepting the call. "Yes, Alaska?"

"Greetings, Sherlock. I'm here."

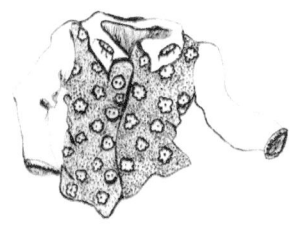

CHAPTER SIXTEEN

"I'll meet you downstairs."

"I'm in the same hall as you are, Sherlock. If you don't mind the mess, why don't you come to my room? It's private." Brent gave him the room number.

Howard entered and took the only cushioned chair. Brent attacked. "I was expecting you yesterday."

Howard shrugged. "There was a major traffic pile up, so we found a motel. It was a great, quiet week. I see Rosemoira treated you well this year."

Brent tensed. "Sure. She's a good friend."

"Was."

Suspicion intensified the prismatic blues of Brent's irises while fear expanded his pupils to their fullest extent. Had Howard not known him for over two decades, he might have assumed the other man had very round, jet black eyes. "How did you know?"

"She didn't answer either of her phones. My wife located one of them. It's in this room. Did you keep the other?" Howard remarked.

"No." Brent held his breath.

"I called the nearest neighbor, Jack Bostwick. He's always watching the inn from his front room window. He told me you were there yesterday. The cops interviewed him. He doesn't know your name, but he saw you—Blondie," Howard grinned.

Brent's pupils shrank to their normal size. "So I'm a suspect. Figures." He frowned. "I didn't do it. I thought it was you."

"You wouldn't have met us or let me into this room if that were so."

"Then who did it?"

"The list isn't long. Everyone is suspect."

"She was good to all of us."

"She kept secrets." Howard crumpled a sheet of paper.

"But she didn't have it. I searched the whole inn and all of the sheds."

"It might not have been about this year's jacket."

"What do you mean? What else is there?"

"It could have been about the fifteenth jacket that went missing a couple of years ago."

Brent scowled at Howard. "What are you saying, Sherlock?"

"Someone stole that one and it looks like this year's model is gone, too. It's got to be the same person. Do you know who took it?"

"I'm the one who sent them both. It wasn't me."

Instead of answering, Howard let his heavy-lidded, almond-shaped eyes droop.

Brent took a deep breath, stood, and snarled, "Get out."

"Take it easy. Think it through. If you didn't send it, you would have disappeared, wouldn't you?"

"You think Rosemoira knew who took it?"

"Yes. And she died because of it."

Brent's knees gave out. He dropped onto the creaky chair. "Did Bostwick, see anyone else?"

"He saw a couple of cars. Didn't get the makes, not even a color. Doesn't have a clue."

"And you believe him?"

"Yes. He's too boring to invent something."

"That leaves the other three unless you suspect your lovely wife." Brent leered.

Without warning, Howard's lean body was plastered against Brent's. After spinning Brent onto the bed, Howard stretched the older man's right arm behind him and pushed the distressed limb a little too hard.

Brent swore. "Let me up, you half-breed Chinese mutt!"

Howard released the arm and helped his mangled friend off the bed. "Yes. I believe her."

Brent eased himself back into the wooden chair. "Isn't it possible someone else did it? One of your father's ring?"

"Luisa's been working on that. It could be any of them. It could be my own father."

"How much does your father know?" Brent hissed.

"He doesn't ask how we finance the field schools. You've seen them over there every year. They want it. I've asked for a million every year. They think that's all it takes."

Brent snorted. "I meant the jackets. Do they know?"

"They must have guessed. After all, high finance is my specialty."

"So now they want a bigger cut?"

"They aren't asking for anything. They want to know what you do."

"Why?"

"I think he's got someone in mind to take over."

"He's a dreamer. North America is still a white man's world-for now. You make it work because you look white. Your father and all of your brothers look Chinese with their late mother's black hair and eyes."

Howard forced his shoulders to relax into a programmed elegance. "I realize that. They are what they are. I don't have those looks. Nonetheless, I know more about Chinese culture than any of them."

"Those jackets have paid all of my bills up until a few months ago." Brent frowned. "Hey! Did they steal the jacket and then blame it on you?"

"Like I said, they don't talk about the jackets. Besides, you haven't thought of the most obvious culprit."

"Who?"

"Someone from your own home town of Fairbanks, Alaska. Is it your girlfriend? Rosemoira met her. What was she doing here?"

Brent laughed. "No. It's not her. And don't bother to look at the small fry in Alaska. Whatever is happening here has been done. Someone we already know. Like you."

Howard shrugged, "And it's not me. My salary is great. Lots of bennies, including a ridiculous amount of paid leave time."

"It doesn't make sense," Brent swore. "They wouldn't make anything by stealing the damn jacket. Someone else must have taken it."

* * *

While Brent spoke to his long-time friend outside of my intrepid awareness, Deloo and I investigated Dalhousie University. Deloo completed a walk through several buildings on the campus. We saw a few small groups of students here and there. The students we saw were starting summer school or working on the big campus during the summer break. The university atmosphere filled Deloo with dreams of going back to school.

Out in the open air, I remembered all the malicious people who could be lurking around. I checked her hair often to make sure that she had tucked it into the ball cap. It was a warm day, so Deloo didn't miss outer covering in the least and she kept touching the cap as if to remove it.

I clenched an invisible fist around her fingers. Deloo had hidden the precious jacket in her dorm room. It was beautiful, unique, and not something that would appeal to many people. For one thing, its primary value was the beading, beading that marked its wearer as Native American in the United States or a First Nations person in Canada. Others might find it charming, different, or stylish for a while before discarding it. An indigenous owner, on the other hand, would try to keep it in the family rather than give it away.

A raven croaked from its perch above the street where Deloo walked.

"Be quiet, Dotson," Deloo quipped to the bird. She mused that Raven of Tleeyegg'e hut'aane stories was always thought of in capital letters even though capital letters were a colonialist invention.

~*Hutłanee, Deloo. You're not supposed to give orders to Raven,*~ I reprimanded with spirit guide absentmindedness. ~*Remember what your great aunt Pauline always says.*~

I wondered if there was anything to this hutłanee business. Over the years, I'd learned there is something to bad omens. If Deloo jeered at the raven on the road, she might also have forgotten to put on the beaded jacket. Who knows?

I swirled around six or seven times, hoping to clear away my guilty feelings. All right, all right. I know it has nothing to do with Deloo or those ravens. In the end, I have to take the blame for bringing her into danger. I had been yearning to go home for thousands of years, and when the way seemed clear a few weeks ago, I seized it. You'd think that I of all people would have known better. If there is anything like a single rule never to break, it is to respect the rights of the mortals to be who they are. Their lives are about themselves, their world, their responsibilities, and their desires, just as my mortal life was about me.

I've seen other spirits fall prey, just as I did, to a momentary compulsion to do something for me rather than Deloo. It's hard to keep the difference between your desires and those of the young mortal in your care in mind. I always fear repercussions by the Invisible Forces, and now strangers hunted Deloo because of my lapse. It was enough to make me want to become a clam and live in permanent hiding from everything. Thinking about these problems I fumed, I huffed, I spun around and beat smoke rings out of my invisible world. My flapping the invisible airwaves set off sparks in the hairs along her arms.

Deloo ran her fingers along her arm and cast a guarded eye upward. *~What's so funny, Baasee'? Are you the one who's making the hair on my arms move? It's not windy out here. There's no breeze whatsoever.~*

~Sorry, my dear. I was thinking of something else. Do you know anyone named Brent?~

~Brent? I do not know anyone with that name. It's not very common, is it?~

~Maybe he didn't know Arthur. It could be either a first or last name.~

Deloo thought about it and muttered an answer by voice, "There were lots of people in Arthur's lab. I didn't meet many of them. We weren't at the University long enough."

A tiny fragment of information came to me and I burst out with the commune, *~you never met him, Deloo. He was a man who had a cubicle next to Arthur. I think Arthur mentioned an unseen lab mate several times.~*

Deloo came to a full stop, "I remember. You're right. Dr. Brent Clerick. Arthur finally met the guy a day or two before the end."

Someone collided with her from behind.

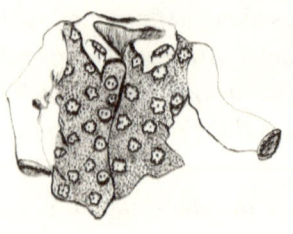

CHAPTER SEVENTEEN

"Something wrong, Miss?" A rangy young man took advantage of Deloo's confusion to offer his brawny arm.

For the first time since Arthur's death a half year ago, Deloo's hormonal system responded to a male. It pleased me to see her leave the numbing state of mourning and prodded Deloo with a light wave of amusement. I did a brief inspection. He was a blended Canadian, being partly French from the first immigration of those people, partly Abenaki, and the rest were originally British. Because he was born to a man of that first group of French people who moved to Canada and to an Abenaki woman, his father refers to their family as Acadians. Like Arthur, the stranger loomed over his target. Unlike Arthur, this Acadian, while attractive, was not the right person and this was not the right time. I had to warn her.

~Now look what you've done. He's got that look in his eye and so do you! Be careful, or you'll be taking this Acadian home with you just as you did Arthur.~

"What?" Deloo looked at the young man, unable to keep the amusement out of her face. "Are you an Acadian?" Seeing something flare in her peripheral vision. Her fingers stole toward the green stone of her wedding ring.

"Eh?" After a momentary look of surprise, the young man beamed, "As it happens, I am an Acadian. How could you tell? I'm French from the seventeenth century on my father's side. I've also got Abenaki relatives. Other Canadians who have First Nations ancestors are Métis, but Acadians have a different history. Our French ancestors came over in the first wave of French immigrants. I've got proof" With a pleased grin, he started to unbutton his outer shirt.

~There! What did I tell you?~ I communed from somewhere above Deloo.

She shook her head and furrowed her brow, "No! How dare you!" Her right hand, still hovering over her cheek, fisted and flew to her side. She turned and made a hasty dash toward the nearest dormitory door.

"No, wait, I just meant the family crest," he called after her. "See?" He pointed to an imposing design on his tee shirt.

Deloo paused, a sure sign of weakness. I swatted her with an invisible spiritual whip. She didn't notice. Her big eyes were too busy studying the stranger's well-filled tee shirt. It was adorned with a European royal crest. She snorted and stepped up to the dormitory entrance.

~Did you see his teeth?~ I remarked. *~You'd have to pay for getting them straightened. At least he has your kind of ancestry-mix. And he's proud of it. I wish more people were proud like that.~*

Deloo spotted his crooked teeth and dimpled at him. "Thanks, but not this time." She wondered if her room key would unlock the backdoor to the dormitory when a woman on its other side flung it open.

The woman gaped at Deloo in momentary surprise and then asked, "Are you staying here? Do you have your ID?"

Deloo held out the key card and her driver's license. The dormitory attendant stood aside to let her pass. With a quick nod at the dormitory attendant, Deloo marched down the hall toward her dorm room. I could have sworn I heard the clack of stiletto heels, but Deloo wore soft-soled sneakers. Thank goodness. A young widow didn't need any of that while criminals were hounding us.

~Now, back to Brent. Do you remember Arthur talking about him?~

This time Deloo gazed at a spot on the ceiling that she thought I inhabited. *~I think Arthur envied everyone who got to go for long fieldwork seasons. If I think about it, I'm sure to remember more.~* Deloo dropped her gaze and asked aloud this time, *~"Baasee', what is a half-breed? There was a lot of talk about it in college. I ended up more confused than ever before. Is there such a thing? That guy said he is an Acadian, but he has a French symbol on his tee-shirt. Is he a half-breed, too?~*

I thought for a moment. After all, she was a mere twenty-one. A dot of my age. Being way less than Tuudzaado from my mother's side and who knows what on my unknown father's side, I've pondered that issue most of my life. *~It might be best to think of a half-breed as someone who isn't. All of your short life you been told by other people that you are NOT Native because your father was white. Meanwhile, some other person will tell you to leave their presence and go somewhere else,*

*anywhere else, because you are an Alaska Native, NOT white like them.
In other words, many use the word as a way to keep people away. Being
half-breed doesn't define you. Grandfather Kwaikit always tells me that
if I can think in Tuudzaado with him, then I am a Tuudzaado person-not
half a Tuudzaado.~*

"A not? What do you mean?" Deloo pondered. "Oh, wait, I get it.
You mean Not Native or Not White."

*~Yes. But there's more. Telling someone he or she is incomplete, or
of mixed descent, is always a power-tool. It's a tool that people have
used for thousands of years to tell their enemy that he or she is inferior,
impotent, and useless. It's a negotiating device. Those who use it always
think they are right to do so if others in their group use it too.~* To give
myself a moment to think of useful examples, I did a couple of spins,
made sure the resulting wind force was strong enough to swirl her hair
around, and remembered the man who delivered me into this world and
took care of me and my mother for the next couple of years. *~There are
all combinations that feed into the "half-breed" notion. Take my Great-
Uncle Zaandan. His father and Grandfather Kwaikit's mother were full
siblings. Their biological parents were full Tuudzaado who happened to
all die by the time Grandfather Kwaikit was a nine-year-old and Great
Uncle Zaandan was a two-year-old. They had no one left. Just the two
of them. Shortly after Grandfather Kwaikit was trying to figure out how
to help his cousin, an old Hutlan woman came by. She offered to make a
deal with her tribe, the Hutlan. Her plan was to claim that Great Uncle
Zaandan was her grandchild, and therefore that he was half Hutlan.~*

*~Grandfather Kwaikit didn't have any options. He agreed as long as
he had the right to visit his cousin any time he wanted. The old woman
said he would be welcome to stay whenever he brought meat enough for
five or six people. It was a typical deal of our era.~*

*~The thing about Hutlan people is they are short, and they don't
have a mental language, just mouth-words. So Great Uncle Zaandan
was raised by them to think his mother was Hutlan. He went through
life thinking he was a half-breed. No one disagreed, although he was
two feet taller than every Hutlan he met. The Tuudzaado people were
all nearly seven feet tall. The Hutlan people were five feet tall at best.~*

Deloo's laughter tinkled. "I'd like being a half-breed that tall!"

*~Not under my watch you wouldn't and do not ever think that way
again. So, back to Arthur. Do you recall anything else about Arthur's
lab mates? What about anyone, any man trying to catch Arthur for any*

reason, ever?~ I asked. *~This guy named Brent chased Arthur on the day he was killed.~*

"What?" Deloo gasped. She dropped to the bed. "Someone was chasing Arthur that day? The police didn't tell me that. No one did."

I thought about the terrible day that Arthur died. She was right. No one had come forward with such a suggestion. I knew about it from Arthur's thoughts. Deloo's mother, Taale, was also skeptical about Arthur's accident. Taale had been on the alert as soon as she learned that Arthur had gone skiing without his wife. Taale hadn't said anything about it to anyone.

Then there was Arthur himself. He regained consciousness in the emergency room long enough to try to speak to Deloo. His muddled thoughts got in the way. He tried to convey something about his camera. No one understood him. Arthur was very clear that his camera inside its black and white striped leather case had something in it that Deloo needed. I thought he was thinking about the photo that he had taken of Deloo's sleeping face.

"Could it be the guy in the cubicle next to his? That might have been, but I doubt it." Deloo suggested. "This is unbelievable. Who could want to kill my Arthur?"

~We'll find that out together. Meanwhile, do you know a man named Howard? He is middle aged and balding. He is looking for the jacket, too.~

Deloo's fingers twitched, longing to feel the lumpy lines of beads her mother had sewn to the denim. She shook her head. "I don't remember anyone with that name, either. What about him?"

~I don't know, except he and Brent are linked together somehow. I think that Brent and Howard are together here in Nova Scotia. Also, China, the place rather than the dishes, keeps coming up. It's confusing. Howard may not have anything to do with this.~

"China?" She stood up and rummaged through her suitcase in search of the tooth paste. "I don't know anything about China."

* * *

Inspector Al Beamus was close to Dalhousie University on his way to a required training session about sexual harassment on the job. Since Al's wife gave training on the same topic for the RCMP and in his building, his supervisor directed him to take the training in another part of Halifax in order to avoid nepotistic hogwash.

"Didn't you just tell me what I need to know?" he had asked over the dinner dishes. She'd already heard his version about the behavior of one of his sergeants toward women.

She gave him a bump with her hip. "Silly! Of course, but you need to get it in an official course. Maybe he's better than me."

Al chuckled with appropriate doubt, knowing that while the other instructor might have a better lecture format, he could ask his wife as many dumb questions as needed to find out which methods might work best to deal with real-life situations.

"It pisses me off," she muttered. "Your supervisor is supposed to get this kind of training himself. It's part of his job. He has dodged all of my sessions on every topic. It's his job to handle the sergeant, not yours. If he does this to you one more time, I'm turning him in."

On his way to get official training, Al was delighted to hear his phone ring. It was the medical examiner calling about the Secret Spirit Inn case. "I'll be there in ten minutes." He left a message with his supervisor about the change in plans and drove to his new destination.

"I've already told you everything I know," the medical examiner glowered.

Al grinned. "I know, but I like to make sure I understand as much as possible. You said you haven't completed the autopsy yet. How do you know what caused her death?"

"There was food in her mouth, including the poison that killed her. Aconite." The medical examiner read his notes again. "She took a few bites. Aconite works through the lungs, soft tissues of the mouth, and the nasal passages. She must have got a little in by breathing the fumes, but that could have killed her killer as well. He knew to avoid taking in air while bending over the food itself. Since she's the dead one, I'm guessing she didn't know that. Nonetheless, she was doomed anyway. The amount in her mouth is more than enough to cause death. Aconite works on contact with any part of the body."

"How long does it take?" Al asked, hoping he would say she hadn't suffered long.

The medical examiner brightened and pawed through a clutter of paper on an otherwise tidy desk. He found what he wanted and handed it to Al. "They are copies. I keep my originals clean." He looked across the office toward his lab. "You never know what the dead can do. Sometimes they squirt things at you." He laughed.

Al felt his stomach churn. He had been planning on taking lunch afterward, but no longer had an appetite. He took the sheaf of paper. Two sets. Both were about aconite poisoning, both by the same author. Harold Johnson.

"He's not a botanist," the medical examiner remarked, "although he's written a lot about Chinese herbal medicines. He writes with such detailed knowledge that his work is approved by our peer review boards."

"What's a peer review board?" Al asked, thinking of administrative review boards.

"They are scientists who specialize in the area of any given article. They are not told who else is reviewing the material. That's to keep favoritism out of it."

"How do you know that he's not a botanist, then?"

"I called the publisher," the medical examiner grinned. "I wanted to invite him to talk at one of our conferences, but changed my mind when they told me he's not a botanist. He's well educated, but it's a degree in computer science, not biology."

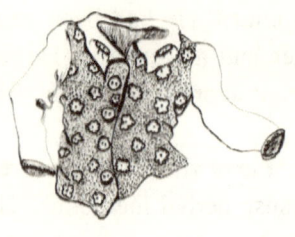

CHAPTER EIGHTEEN

Fresh from the shower, Deloo commune-sang ~*I remember who it is.*~

I cocked a non-existent, but curvaceous eyebrow on a non-existent forehead. ~*Who?*~

"Mom's friend at the bead shop. Earlene. I painted her car. She wants to go to China." I tried to remember Earlene. I recalled a woman whose thick hair was long enough to get caught in doors unless she bound it with something. Since she ran a craft shop, she had an endless supply of hair gadgets, some made by Deloo's mother. Both Earlene and Taale seemed to scrimp by on the sales of beaded goods. Suddenly I saw an image of the Goodes, Deloo's in-laws, seated beside Deloo at her mother's dining room table.

The first time I had a good look at them was after Arthur died. Taale had invited Arthur's parents to dinner the night before the funeral. Two pairs of very astute eyes had flitted to every cranny in Taale's tiny house when she told the Goodes about her tight budget and her fears of having to add student loan payments to the burden. They didn't notice such drifts in their cash flow through all of their own or Arthur's education, and had never needed to borrow money for anything. I was grateful for the opportunity they afforded Deloo, as Deloo's idea of money measured in nickels. Thanks to them, she now had to think another way. Zachary Goode was just the one to do it, since he was, according to his spirit guide, a wizard in a world of high finance.

At the end of the evening Zachary glanced at Matty, caught her nod, and asked, "Deloo, we haven't had enough time to get to know you. Could you stay with us for a while back home?"

Taale leaped at the opportunity to help her daughter and herself. Within five days Deloo was "home" in Cambridge, where she stayed in Arthur's childhood bedroom. At first Deloo had been a little uncomfortable until one day she offered to repaint the dining room while carpenters completed renovations to what would soon become their new master bedroom. The dining room needed far more than paint, and those reparations were not on their calendar of renovations. The numerous repairs on the walls, windows, and floor took several weeks for an amateur like Deloo to complete. Deloo also painted a large portrait on canvas.

I examined the painting with considerable satisfaction. Deloo had been watching for a good price on canvas at a nearby art supply store with disappointment. This was in the old days before Deloo could pick up my communes. I began looking with my psychic skill for canvas at a good price. I was excited one night when I got a mental hit on an online store. As soon as Deloo got up in the morning I made sure it occurred to her to ask the senior Mrs. Goode for permission to borrow her laptop. In a few minutes she was online. The site that had the cheap canvas was two lines from the bottom of the screen. Afterward Deloo babbled about "the miracle" that made her want to click on that particular site.

"I can't believe it," she glowed for the sixth time to her mother-in-law, "it's even bigger than I wanted, and already stretched and mounted." She danced around the room again. I jigged above her, giddy with delight. Deloo had learned to stretch canvas but her corners were always a little off square, causing the canvas to pucker.

The senior Mrs. Goode's pleased smile became an astounded gape when six days later Deloo brought her a finished painting for the dining room. That was my doing, too. No, no. Not the painting, but the prep work. I wouldn't let Deloo rest until she had blocked in the undercoat and most of the background before she went to bed on the very day the canvas arrived. I wanted Deloo's great artistic talent to show at its best, and she did it by painting a huge portrait of Arthur.

At first, I thought I had made an abysmal mistake.

That evening Deloo raged against Arthur that he had died so soon. She expressed it with a harsh underpainting in lurid purples and oranges-none of which matched the Goode's color scheme. When she finished the underpainting she glared at the canvas for a full hour until her chest stopped heaving. Hours later, she propped the canvas against a different wall and crawled into bed. I stared at the horrid ruin on the canvas, wondering what other feelings Deloo hid. At long last I realized that she had cleansed herself of much of her anger in order to express simple purity of love for the man inside Arthur Goode. The final work was a masterpiece.

Mrs. Goode stretched a hand toward the mouth-her dead son's mouth-and breathed, "Deloo, this looks just like him. I had no idea that you were such a sensitive artist."

Deloo flushed. "It's easy when you love the face you're painting."

Matty dragged her eyes away from the portrait. Tears flowed down her face as she engulfed Deloo in a tight grip. Considering that Deloo was wearing the same paint-covered overalls that she had worn since the day she began painting the dining room, Mrs. Goode's hug was quite foolhardy. Deloo's overalls did not damage the older woman's clothing. I watched the two women share their mutual love of Arthur through color and light. Both the painting and the embrace cleared away some of the biting angst they each suffered. It also opened a crack in their inter-generational disinterest in the other.

That night Deloo slept like the dead for a few hours. I did too. I am dead. In the comfort of my slumber I almost missed her strangled shouting.

"Arthur! Arthur!" Deloo screeched. A roll of sweat-drenched sheets imprisoned her. I showered her with soft shafts of love and comfort while I tore through her memory banks to find out what just happened. I shivered when I found the sacred dream.

A sacred dream is one that comes to the dreamer from the highest region of the Invisible Forces. Deloo's dream was simple: Arthur stood beside his childhood bed, the very bed that Deloo slept in at the senior Goode house. He drifted, watching Deloo. She awoke and he pointed to his camera. The camera in its black and white case floated in space above Deloo's head. Deloo reached out toward Arthur. Instead of closing on her late husband, her hand held his camera. She took her eyes off Arthur for a split second to look at the dream camera. That's all it took for both the camera and the dream to vanish. Deloo started to thrash from side to side. In her dream she was chasing him. In reality she had fallen into a feverish daze where Arthur hovered just inches away from her desperate fingers.

I helped her to come to full consciousness and encouraged her with my invisible powers to open her sketchbook to draw a picture of Arthur in the dream. She pulled off three in rapid succession, and then saw that she had to change her bedding before going back to sleep. By that time it was nearing four. Deloo stripped the bed and lay atop the bare mattress.

* * *

The phone vibrated. He clicked, groaned, and listened. After disconnecting, Chuan glanced at his watch. Five twenty-five. He grunted.

"Mmph?" Ming asked.

"Brent. We're to meet in a hotel lobby at nine. What do you have to do this morning?"

Ming spewed out a list of purchases she'd promised to make for her father's cousin. While she spoke, he realized that to make it to the New Brunswick border by nine, they had to leave in two and a half hours. He told her so.

"I can send him most of it from New Brunswick. There's always some cousin or another moving between restaurants in our family," she remarked. "That leaves the task of making our bed and then we're off."

Putting clean sheets on the bed, showering, and getting dressed took fifteen minutes. Telling her relatives she was leaving required more than two hours. When she seemed ready to go, he encircled her tiny waist to lure her toward the car.

"Wait a minute, will you? I want to say goodbye to Mother."

Chuan sucked in a bucket of air and released her. Ming rushed away, hoping that this wasn't the last time she'd get to speak with her mother. While she loved Chuan and their home in China, she missed her mother with a visceral need.

The liquid consonants of the Inuit language of northern Québec rolled between them as Ming's mother said, "Daughter, keep a smile on your face and keep your eyes on me. I have something of importance to say that I don't want everyone in our town to know."

Ming's face froze for a quarter of a beat and then glowed in a loving smile. "What is it my mother?"

"It's about Qanik. After all these years his mother and I are close friends, but I only know of her son as a little boy. Did you ever talk to him much when you were older?"

Ming frowned, then remembered to reassure her mother with a smile. "Not as much as I could have done. MoLi kept him to herself. I'm sorry my twin sister disappeared before Qanik and she got married," Ming said. "Do you know if anyone has figured out how he died?"

Her mother slid her eyes toward a visiting neighbor and flicked a smile at him. "Her mother told me the police have kept the case open because they are sure he was murdered. He would never have gone to that part of the tundra alone. Now that they have got lab results in, things will change. Maybe the police will speed up their investigation."

"Yes, Mother. I've always thought someone killed him." Ming bit her lip. "I learned something yesterday that might give us an idea of what happened. Mother, did Qanik ever talk about jackets? Beaded jackets?" She had to clarify the style, since most of their Inuit outerwear looked like jackets to average Canadians or Americans.

"No. Why?"

"It's important, Mother. Please check with his family. I want to know if he ever mentioned fifteen jackets or a fifteenth jacket. Chuan said something yesterday that reminded me of Qanik."

"There was something I heard about him showing people a bead, wondering if anyone recognized it. He died soon after. The weird thing is how he died." After a big sigh, Ming's mother whispered, "He'd been eating dry meat and margarine, and then he ended up in a tidal pool. Our village is closer to the coast than most, but it's hard to get to it from here. I just don't understand that part of his death at all."

"I agree with you, Mother." Ming shrugged with a big smile aimed toward Chuan. "Much as I love to eat dry meat and seal oil myself, I usually eat it in a house, not near a cliff."

"The margarine had wild delphinium leaves in it." Her mother's mouth seemed to dry out, as her lips no longer shaped a natural smile. "Qanik died in June before the aconite was ready to boil into rat poison. The stuff in the margarine was from plants that had already gone to seed—and become poisonous. It was an August-aged plant. In other words, someone poisoned him with their own plants. He didn't accidentally poison himself with the living plants growing around him."

Her mother stilled and waited for Ming to respond. When her daughter said nothing, Ming's mother whispered through a fractured smile, "What was it you said? Chuan said something about wolfs bane the other day?"

Through her own fence of locked teeth, Ming stuttered the words, "Yes, Mother. I found some pretty delphinium growing north of Montreal a year or two ago. Chuan told me not to touch it. He said it was wolfs bane or aconite and explained how poisonous it is."

"There's another thing you should know, then." Her mother said. "Qanik's father and mother have been singing for him. They went to the angakkuq. He's the best spiritual intermediary around. The angakkuq taught them a song." Her mother's arms stiffened around her daughter. "It's a song that will destroy the killer unless he or she knows how to make a song that breaks its power."

They stared at each other. Then, her mother gave Ming a tiny push and said, "Let me know if anything changes." She didn't look at her son-in-law.

Ming turned, captivating Chuan with a sway of her hips.

Chuan smiled, the image of graciousness. At seven-fifty-five he had loaded their bags into their sedan and waited. She emerged at eight a.m., carrying several plastic bags for delivery to other Chinese restaurants the family owned in New Brunswick and Québec. She lifted them toward him, "Each of these represents free meals in three cities."

He grimaced as he pulled out of the carport. "Right on time. He must know where we are and did the math in order to have called me when he did."

She released a long sigh and muttered something in Inuttitut, the dialect she'd been speaking with her mother. It was less well known than its northwestern dialect, Inuktitut.

"What did you say?" he queried.

"Now he knows where this part of my family lives," she sighed. "You liked seal flipper when we stayed with Mother's family last month." She quirked a smile. "Didn't you? Why don't we go back there for a while? Maybe they don't know my mother's relatives."

"We're trapped, Ming." He reached out to caress her left knee to calm her. "They'd find us no matter where we went unless we do something drastic about it."

One hour later, they neared Amherst and spotted the hotel's parking lot. The other two were waiting. Ming and Chuan smoothed their faces into well-practiced inscrutability and got out of the car. They had long since realized that their place in the team was to obey and never to reveal their active intelligence. At one time Ming would have crowed in happy innocence upon seeing the blond, blue-eyed "twins" again. After a couple of months, such jesting always ended in anger. Howard resented anyone who compared him to a white instead of to a Chinese man. Ming came to respect that being biologically three-fourths white did not mean Howard's white side meant anything to him. In his mind, he was Chinese. Over the years, Ming came to understand and then to convince her husband of how the same issue worked in her.

"Even though I am a Harvard-trained architect, no one in my father's Chinese family cares. My mother's Inuit family doesn't have a category for me as a professional woman." She shrugged, "I may as well have stayed home and taken up skin sewing."

Her father's family valued Ming's multi-cultural abilities when it came to working in their restaurant chain, however, they had no use for her architectural skills. They required her to do the most menial of tasks rather than anything to make the family restaurants look more appealing. She knew it was her father's way to remind her that no woman could appear to be better than him. She burned at the injustice. Her father had paid for her education. Why didn't he want her to use it? Over time, she realized that she would never ditch her Inuit culture to please her father or anyone else. The Inuit people she loved did not expect her to scrub pots.

She loved Chuan and liked his Chinese-born family. They were good to her. By contrast, her own Chinese family on her father's side had become difficult to tolerate. Because of their oppression, she had come to respect Howard. She told Chuan that speaking Mandarin without an accent didn't mean anything, good or bad. Ming had always told Chuan not to judge a book by its cover. Today she examined both Howard and Brent with new eyes.

Luisa loved Ming and pulled her into a tight hug. "Let's get out of here." Without waiting for a response, they left the hotel room. None of the men took notice.

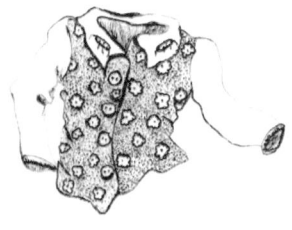

CHAPTER NINETEEN

Deloo had been up since five. She'd set up the small student desk in the Halifax dorm room as an impromptu painting studio and had strewn six or seven sheets of watercolor paper on the floor between herself and the door. She'd visualized perfectly some scenes of the Zana, my Zana. I liked the valley of blue spruce with a low range of hills in front and orange sky just beyond. Every time I tried to approach her to examine the watercolor under construction, she seemed to sense my proximity and growled. The sound reminded me of a short-faced bear about to strike.

While Deloo painted, I shaped a wad of counter-balanced quarks in hues of gold and lavender and placed it above the dormitory bed. I moved away from it by a yard or two and sprang up and forward with Olympic precision. My landing was perfect.

"So! What do you think?" Deloo asked.

I had fallen asleep. I could tell it had been a while since she'd asked. Deloo patted away tears dripping on a sheet of watercolor paper. I executed a double flip off the quarks and scooted closer to inspect her last painting. It was cave-baby me at age two. Deloo's salty tears made star-shaped white spots in the painting to add the final quality of the passage of crystalline time.

~It's the most beautiful painting I've ever seen!~ I gushed. *~It's even better than the one you did of Arthur.~*

Keeping up an enthusiastic commune-monologue, I moved around the room to see all of her work and recorded my thoughts and multiple views of it for later enjoyment.

"I… I thought you didn't like it," Deloo blubbered. "You didn't say anything for a long time." She got another tissue to mop up more tears.

It was not at all difficult to rave, *~that's what great art does to us, Deloo. You stunned me into silence with the beauty you have* *created here. Words do little to express the depth of my admiration and gratitude.~*

"I'm g-g-glad you like it," she stuttered, and put it on the floor next to the others.

There are times when an old cave woman wishes she still had big arms in order to thank her mortal with a recognizable hug as Matty had done. I had to settle for silent words to scold her into packing for the long trip back to Alaska.

Deloo had all of her gear stuffed into the Passat by a little after seven. It was cold that morning and Deloo slid into jeans and stuffed her arms into its matching denim jacket without thinking. Needing her mother, her fingers traced the beads of one of the flowers on the jacket's collar. I felt so gratified to have received her painting as a gift that I didn't process that she had donned the deadly beaded jacket. While she checked out, I overheard two people talking about a mysterious death at the Secret Spirit Inn. Deloo heard them too, and asked for more details.

"Rose worked at a B&B called the Secret Spirit Inn. I used to work there too. She was my supervisor. She was kind of mean sometimes, but most of the time I liked her."

"I'm sorry for your loss," Deloo said. At my urging she pressed on, "How did she die?"

"The paper doesn't say anything more than it's a suspicious death. I suppose it will all come out in the next few months, after everyone has forgotten her name-Rosemoira Keilleher."

Deloo said a few more words of sympathy, picked up her receipt, and got into the car. We passed by Truro and turned west toward Amherst at the border near New Brunswick.

"I'm starting to feel hungry," Deloo said. Let's stop in Amherst for breakfast."

I attempted a shrug and settled for communing agreement. We pulled off the main highway just after nine. I spotted five people standing in the parking lot of a hotel. So did Deloo.

"Hey! That's the couple from Halifax," Deloo said. She studied one of the women and muttered, "That's Prize Woman. I'm sure of it." By that time Deloo had passed the hotel parking lot and pulled up to a fast-food restaurant where she ordered a cup of coffee and an English muffin.

~I noted the three similar cars. One had a Québec license plate. You know: Je Me Souviens. I remember seeing the license plate before, but

can't place it. Je Me Souviens means "I will remember" in French. It is Québec's provincial slogan.~

Deloo, who had never taken French, gave the words a try, "Juh meh soo vee on? I've never heard of that, I just remember the cars. They might still be there. I'm going back."

The five people were not in sight. I urged Deloo to park on the far side of a tourist bus and we crept over to look.

"Look, Baasee'. There's that French phrase. It's on two of these cars."

I was about to respond to her squawk when I noticed someone emerging from a side door of the hotel. *~Quick! Get out of sight.~*

Deloo saw the door move and skittered away just before two women stepped outside.

~Prize Woman.~

They consoled each other, "What's the matter? You used to be so carefree." They walked beyond Deloo's hearing range before Ming answered.

I tried to pick out their thoughts when I felt a sharp sting from the place I'd left the little ghost.

~She ... Needs ... Me! Let ... Me ... Out.~

"Who was that?" Deloo whispered, forgetting all about the secrecy of communing.

~It's that little ghost you drew a couple of days ago when we first saw Prize Woman. They are coming this way. Get back to the car before they see you.~ I urged as I managed to get the little ghost back to her state of darkness.

"… That jacket has changed him …" floated toward us on a few molecules of air. Deloo hustled toward her car.

"What jacket?" the other asked.

"He calls it the Seventeenth Jacket. We've been clumping around Nova Scotia after a beaded …"

~There it is again-the seventeenth jacket.~ Deloo communed as she crept into her car. She left the door ajar to avoid attracting attention. The effort was unnecessary. The stranger propelled her friend to a bench at the far side of the parking lot. Their voices were inaudible.

At my urging, Deloo skulked outside of and then beside her car for a chance to hear more.

". . . I've been wondering if Chuan is going through a midlife crisis." She paused. "What do you think?"

After a while the other answered. "You've said he has complained about feeling a lot of disappointment with the field schools that Howard and Brent have run for the past two decades. Maybe you are right. Maybe he wishes he had made better choices." She made cloth rustling noises as if she had turned in her seat. "Amiga, you are sad today and I have called upon my spirit guides to tell me if this is what you face in the future. 'No!' They know your time of turmoil will be over soon."

Prize Woman squeaked a snuffling noise. "Thank you, Luisa. You've been my strength." She hesitated, then said, "My mother talked to me this morning about Qanik. Do you remember him?"

Luisa's eyes narrowed. "Of course I do. What did she say?"

"It's about our kind of spiritual ways. Mother said that Qanik's mother and father are working with an angakkuq. That's our Inuttitut word for a shaman. They want to find Qanik and his killer. They made the decision when the police said that even though they have had the body for many months and know what caused his death, they don't have enough evidence to keep working on it." Ming stopped and searched her friend's face.

"What did you tell her?"

"Nothing. I won't unless you tell me it's wise to do so."

Luisa tipped her head back. "Yes, mi amiga. You don't need my permission to do this. Maybe it's time to get rid of a big family lie."

"Speaking of finding people, has your brother, Diego, come back?"

"Yes. Like always, with his tail between his legs." Luisa sighed. "Every month is the same with them. Howard gives me a generous allowance for clothing and frills. Every month I send almost all of it to my family. Howard asks to see my new clothes." Luisa spread her long-fingered brown hands. "None. I have nothing to show him."

Ming chuckled for the first time in days. "What does he say about that?"

"Now he takes me shopping. And he still gives me an allowance. He is so good to me, Ming. I wish you the same luck as I have had."

The wind whipped through their clothing. They walked back to the hotel.

I flicked the black space in which the little ghost now resided and asked *~did you hear what those women said? ~*

~Yes.~

~Do you know Qanik?~

~Yes. He is or was my fiancé. A couple of years ago I thought he

might be dead like me. I feel him near me sometimes.~ The little ghost fell commune silent. Inside her hole of darkness she averted her light from me and wouldn't respond to more questions.

* * *

Deloo and I stopped a few minutes later at a roadside pullout to figure out the day's itinerary. Deloo picked up her atlas, twizzled her hunk of jadeite as if performing a magic trick. The ring's silver filigree caught on a corner of one map. She nodded at her ring's choice. "That should work. See? I want to drive north around New Brunswick and then aim for Québec City. There's no need to stop in Montreal at all. We'll just drive by it and on to Ontario."

Deloo was responding to my question about leaving Nova Scotia after two short days of being in Zana. Something seemed wrong with her plan but I couldn't find the error. It might have been the ring, or rather the mystical image it cast above Deloo's head: a pulsating dragon's figure. I squelched it with magical ease. Now that it was June sixth, two days after her wedding anniversary, the time had come to get on the road. ~*Let's go.*~

As our used Passat sped across the Nova Scotia/New Brunswick border again, I gazed at the surrounding world. This was the fearsome place from whence the ancient Sacred Winds had screamed into my homeland. How I wished we could have stayed for a day or two longer. I intoned a mourning song. We used to sing it to speed a person along the First Walk of the Dead.

"What is that?" Deloo's query broke through my cheerless croon. "It's beautiful. It reminds me of potlatch songs, but I don't recognize it."

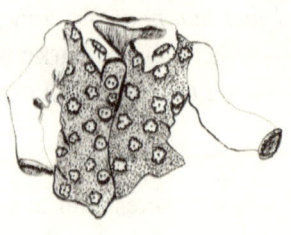

CHAPTER TWENTY

I shoved away a dark purple filament of light. ~*Yes, it is like one of your Athabascan memorial potlatch songs. It's a mourning song from my long-ago mortal life. I'll explain all of them to you another time.*~ I took a look around the New Brunswick coastline and added, ~*look where we are now. Another province!*~ In less than two hours we entered New Brunswick where we had seen Prize Woman take off a black and white dress.

Deloo mused, "Alaska is so big that it takes several hours to reach the border from almost anywhere on the road system, and days to reach the rest of the United States. So, where to now?" Deloo asked. Her stomach growled. It had been hours since she'd eaten the English muffin.

~*Let's get you something to eat. This next big town should give us what we need.*~

The signs indicated we were heading toward Moncton. Long before we began to commune with each other, I had studied the starring attraction of New Brunswick's small eastern city: Magnetic Hill. Magnetic Hill has a reputation for being able to cause heavy cars and trucks to roll uphill and backward for no discernible reason. Over time, enterprising Moncton dwellers built amusement park rides and other outlets around the hill, all in anticipation that visitors would want to test the power of their mountain. As it happened, they were right. Most people wanted to find out if the mysterious hill had the magnetic power to pull a vehicle weighing thousands of pounds both backward and upward. Adding to the mystery is that while the Hill remained successful, not one of the many electronic gadgets inside adventurous vehicles ever suffered from the intensity of the earth's pull. Detractors claimed an optical illusion duped visitors. I, with sensitivity to energetic forces beyond mortal imagination, was determined to find out more about this famous landmark.

Encouraged by my eagerness and despite her gurgling belly, Deloo went straight to Magnetic Hill. After paying a small fee, Deloo drove toward a designated sign. Someone pointed down an old dirt road and told her to put her car into neutral. Deloo and I both focused on the attendant's instructions. The car rolled backward. Maybe it rolled upward until it reached the top of the hill. Satisfied that she had navigated one of the world's great mysteries, she waved at the attendant and drove away.

"Let's eat," Deloo grinned. I observed with an inward smile that Deloo didn't want any bothersome scientific facts about Moncton's Magnetic Hill.

~*Would that I could,*~ I communed, ~*you make dead vegetables and butchered cows seem worth the effort.*~

"Don't you eat?"

~*We're in a city now. Use your commune voice. And no, I don't eat. I become quite wilted if I don't consume a little nitrogen and other fumes every day. But those are gasses, not heavy food.*~ I was about to clarify my nutritional requirements to Deloo when a vicious jolt of dark light shattered my iridescent serenity. I lashed out, giving Deloo a little shock.

"Ouch!" She looked around in surprise. "What happened?"

I couldn't answer. Something that I'd never experienced before overwhelmed me. A dense cloud of blackness had enclosed me in a smothering mass from which there seemed to be no escape. I tore through it, ~*I don't know. Deloo, dear, please search for a place to rest. I'm feeling weak. It's something about Magnetic Hill, or maybe all the effort I've been using up to help you drive.*~

"Help ME drive?" Deloo mocked. "You are a piece of air without hands and feet. Magnetic Hill has zapped all of your energy. Besides, you aren't the one who's driving. I am." We haggled over our comparative driving skills until Deloo found a small take-out Chinese restaurant in Moncton.

Deloo grabbed the most convenient outer garment to stave off the slight drop in temperature. Neither of us gave a second thought to her choosing the beaded jacket. A fresh-faced Asian teenager in a black and white dress and roller skates swooped from behind a curtain that separated the kitchen from the counter, and posed, pen to pad, for Deloo's order.

Deloo asked for steamed rice topped with a tasty looking chicken-and-broccoli combination. She paid for her food and continued to stand near the counter while waiting for her meal. She was day-dreaming when Prize Woman stepped out of the kitchen. She wore the same kind of black and white dress she had stripped off in the highway pullout. Prize Woman handed Deloo the packet without recognizing my mortal until she took a startled look at Deloo's beaded jacket. She called out something in Mandarin to the kitchen.

If I had a throat, I would have choked. The words meant 'Come here! Look at this woman's jacket!'

~*Run!*~ I commune-screamed. After Deloo ran through the door I used desperation magic. I slammed the door so hard the glass broke. Then I put a spell on the door that would fight anyone trying to get in from the inside—at least for a few seconds.

Deloo hopped into the Passat and shouted, "Which way?"

As for me, I watched Prize Woman and her male partner at the door of the take-out restaurant fighting to open the door that I had closed with tight suction force. So far, so good.

~*Just head right. We'll figure out which way to turn after you get far enough away.*~

~*Hutlanee! They're following me.*~ Deloo communed just as she turned on the car and eased it into traffic.

I looked back. Deloo was right. They were not close, but behind us. They had figured out how to release the suction on the door. Or maybe they braved the broken glass and got through it that way. Prize Woman was already in the passenger seat as an Asian man tore out of the restaurant and ran toward the driver's side.

I shivered with apprehension. ~*She's wearing the black and white dress again.*~

"It's got to be a uniform," Deloo said aloud.

~*You're right. And those coins in the pull-out must have been her tips for the day,*~ I agreed just as something clicked and a bright light flared beside Deloo. It was our car-ashtray.

We both stared at the ashtray. Its lid opened and two coins flickered in the odd light. For the first time, I felt the power of being a tuned-in spirit guide. Grandfather Kwaikit had told me it would happen one day. I was receiving explicit information about the driver in the car now less than a mile behind us. He was a diligent Chinese communist with a proud ancestral heritage. His family had always made things to sell. A parade of small tools, toys, games and other intricate goods presented themselves to my mind. The display ended with a series of ancient symbols carved into wood or something that looked like wood. They looked like the tan, plastic beads. I told Deloo. Just as I finished, I got more information about Prize Woman.

By turning right from the Chinese take-out restaurant, Deloo headed west instead of taking the scenic route toward the mouth of the Saint Lawrence River as planned. Traffic was light and no cars pulled up behind her. She was well beyond Moncton when a familiar sedan pulled to within a car's length of the Passat.

"What should I do?" Deloo asked. Ahead we saw signs for more small towns.

I rose up and reported *~There's something a mile or two away.~*

"What do you see?" Deloo kept an eye on the odometer. "We're five miles from the take-out restaurant." An odd time warp had sucked all traffic off the road except the pursuers.

When we got close to the place I had seen, I communed, *~it's time for you to become an aggressive trickster raven. Turn onto that graveled frontage road. Now! Turn left!~*

Deloo saw the sign, forced all interfering thoughts away and swerved onto the road I indicated. She found herself on a dirt road with a fresh layer of gravel spread along its surface. The car following them, while still behind, was now several car lengths back.

~Do you remember the wild driving lesson your friend Billy gave you when you were in high school? This is the time to use it! Pull a 180!~

Deloo frowned. "What? I don't drive like that."

~Yes, you still do, my secret Raven child. You learned when you were sixteen with that skinny guy who always sucked on straws.~

"You mean Frank, not Billy." Deloo almost laughed, but caught a glimpse of the car following her. "He didn't know how to spin out or do any of those tricks. I taught him how!"

~The time has come to prove you have it in you. Now!~ I had very little idea of how to pull off such a stunt in a car, but I'd done it often enough when hunting. The thing to do here is to run at top speed, keep looking for the perfect place to spin around and not get bowled over by the approaching enemy. When it's done right, they're always unprepared to stop.

Deloo did a quick check in all of the mirrors to make sure there was no other traffic and pulled her car to the left so that she was driving over the center of the road. She noted with relief that the gravel sprayed against the bottom and sides of the Passat just as she liked. Ice would be even better, but ice in Fairbanks came with frigid temperatures that caused other kinds of automobile problems. She pressed hard on the gas until the Passat zipped into action, then braked with the handbrake, spun the wheel, released the handbrake and let her car whirl 180 degrees before tapping on the regular brake. As soon as the car was half-way through the spin, she stepped on the gas and made some minor corrections. Her hands shook. She was in the other car's lane. Deloo's heart thumped so hard she was sure her rib cage had cracked. She slowed the car and began to pull into the right lane.

~*No time to be nice! Go back into their lane! Drive toward them.*~ How I wished for real hands and feet. Deloo was not a trained fighter like me.

Deloo gulped but understood the logic of my command. She stomped hard on the gas pedal. Our car hurdled toward the oncoming sedan and she got ready to pull to the right before the two vehicles collided head-on. Just when her heart felt as if it were going to explode, she imagined she could see the whites of the other driver's eyes.

At the last second, he chickened out and pulled to his right, straight into the ditch.

~*Congratulations! Deloo, you are a warrior now!*~ I crowed. ~*But, don't stop now. Move it!*~ I wished there was a way to turn up the volume on these communes. I needed to bellow at top scream level.

Deloo got into the right lane and headed back toward the hub city of New Brunswick, Moncton. The speedometer slowed to ninety miles per hour, matching Canada's one-forty-five kilometers per hour. When we were sure it was safe, I assured Deloo it was time to go slower. In a couple of minutes, Deloo spotted an exit for a main road, or at least something larger than the one we had under wheel.

Before she could form the question, I answered, ~*yes! Take it.*~

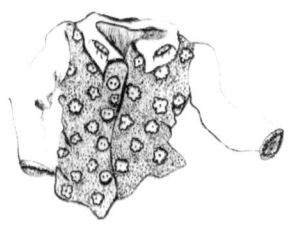

CHAPTER TWENTY-ONE

Deloo swerved onto the exit, dropping her speed to fifty-five miles an hour, and left a satisfying black streak on the asphalt. The exit took her under the TransCanada highway, giving her a little time to decide whether to go west or east. She decided to head east. As she pulled onto the highway, she slowed the Passat to the correct Canadian speed limit and looked back on the road she had just left. As far as either of us could tell, there was no sedan in sight.

~*We've lost them. You're safe for now.*~

Deloo gasped with her mouth wide open. Her heart pounded too hard and it seemed as if her lungs no longer pulled in oxygen. She was miles away from the 180 degree incident.

~*There is a little side road up ahead. Take it and find a place to stop. I want to make sure we've lost them.*~

Deloo saw an exit, took it and spotted a pullout. She nudged the Passat into the shelter of some trees. From there she had a good view of the TransCanada Highway. She sat, concentrating on being alive.

After fifteen minutes, I reassured her. ~*They didn't think a family-type car like this could move fast or that you could drive like a lunatic. Congratulations, Little Dotson.*~ I sent her a mental image of a raven with her face swooping into a daring midair rollover.

Deloo quailed. "Some Raven I am. That was sheer panic and good advice from you! Do you know why they chased me? Shouldn't I call the police?"

While I considered a reply, I added steadiness to her body rhythms. ~*As to why they chased you, look at yourself. What do you see on your bosom?*~

Deloo reached for Arthur's camera and then looked down and sucked in a shout. "My beaded jacket." She began trembling in earnest.

~And your head. You were that way in the coffee shop as well. That's where they first saw you.~

Deloo touched her exposed hair and shuddered.

I waited a few moments for Deloo to collect herself. *~We know it has to do with the dead woman at the Secret Spirit Inn and the person who killed her. Now we know that at least four, if not five others are involved.~*

~Five more? How do we know that?~ Deloo squared her shoulders.

~Think about the hotel in Nova Scotia. We saw Prize Woman and the Asian man who drove the car that tried to kill us a few minutes ago.~ I encased Deloo in a tight bond of calm and waited for it to take effect before continuing. *~There were two blond men. We might have seen one of them at that bookstore in Nova Scotia. Remember? ~*

"Yeah. The old guy with the plastic bead."

~And we saw Prize Woman walking with another woman. That makes it five that we know about so far. Plus, there's someone in Alaska.~

Deloo thought about the last unwelcome bit of news. *~What do they want?~*

~It's obvious to me they want your jacket. We need to figure out why.~

"I follow you so far, but the innkeeper didn't like the jacket, remember? Besides, there are jackets like this in plenty of stores. Why this one?"

~First and foremost, now they know what you look like and what you drive. Let's take advantage of the fact that they do not know where you are at the moment. It's time to call your mother for information. We need to know about her friend in the bead shop and more.~

"You think Mom has something to do with this, don't you?"

~Not as part of the gang who is searching for you, but she did make the jacket.~

Deloo paled and glanced at her watch. It was afternoon in New Brunswick, and late morning in Fairbanks. She touched the numbers, hoping her mother would pick up the call.

"Hello?"

"Mom!" Deloo let out a huge sigh of relief, "It's me."

"Honey, are you alright?"

Deloo looked at her phone in amazement. "How did you know? It just happened."

"Just happened?" It was Taale's turn to be puzzled. "What just happened? Yesterday was your anniversary. I expected a call. When you didn't, I hoped you were getting over it."

"It?" Deloo's eyebrows knotted. Her mouth emitted a chuckle that escalated into shrieking laughter. I knew she needed to release all the tension of these past three days and wanted to help her relax into the humor of the moment, but I could feel Taale's exasperation.

"Deloo!" Her mother's voice rang through the air and stopped another big guffaw before it started. "What is the matter with you?!"

Deloo pulled herself together and launched into a breathless description of the chase including confessing that she felt like Dotson in the way she swung the car around and drove straight at her pursuers.

Taale let her finish when she reproved Deloo. "Hutłanee! Do not call yourself Raven like that. You are asking for even worse trouble. Did you call the police?"

"No. I didn't get enough details, like make of car or license plate. But I think it has something to do with my beaded jacket-the denim one you made for me. I wore it the other day when that innkeeper was so weird. I'm wearing it now, and a different woman was eyeing it at the restaurant. She got into the car that chased me."

Taale gasped and then tried to joke. "No one ever gets so excited about my beading."

"Mom!" Deloo wailed as if she hadn't been hysterical with laughter just minutes earlier, "It's not funny. Hutłanee! Someone poisoned the first woman two days ago. They might be the people who are chasing me. I need you to tell me something."

"I'm sorry, Deloo," Taale answered, chastened. "What do you need to know?

"I think it might have something to do with the woman who runs the bead shop. The one who buys your beaded jackets."

Taale muttered, "Do you mean Earlene?"

Deloo glanced at the sky and muttered, "Yes. That's her. I spaced her name. I think she might have something to do with this because that innkeeper made some cracks about how 'I' should make them on deer hide. She liked the new style, but hated the denim."

"Denim? Oh. Yes. Earlene didn't like it either. She wanted me to make the jackets out of deer hide, too. I used denim because that's all I had. Money is tight I didn't have time to work on another deer hide jacket because of my new job. She told me she'd take it, but she must have changed her mind. She didn't even call me as usual. It was on my door-step a few days later with a note and a check."

Deloo asked, "Mom, am I wearing the jacket Earlene gave back to you?"

"Yes, Dear," Taale answered. "I had to size it down quite a bit. Earlene always ordered big men's sizes."

I demanded, *~Does Earlene work for someone who might want these jackets?~*

"No. She doesn't work for anyone," Taale responded. "She has a strange boyfriend she calls BeeGee or BeeSee. I'm not sure if those are letters or some odd name to match his personality. At least he's gone more often than he's been around."

"What color is his hair, Mom? Some guy who works in a Chinese restaurant has been following me."

Taale pondered for a moment before admitting, "I've never seen him, but she talks about him all the time."

"The woman he's with looks Native with long black hair. She's about your age. I think she's a waitress. Does that sound familiar?"

"Native women come in as many different sizes and colors as the clothes they were, Deloo." After a moment of hesitation, Taale said to her daughter, "I don't like what's happening, Deloo. You'd better go back to Boston. Let the Goodes help you."

I contemplated Taale's demand and came to a different conclusion. *~I think it's safer if we just get out of eastern Canada. Tell her you'll be all right.~*

Deloo thanked her mother for the suggestion, but declined. "Mom, don't worry about me. I'm going to drive to Alaska. I'm sure everything is fine now. I needed to hear your voice."

Even as she spoke the ashtray beside her opened briefly. I couldn't have sworn I heard it cackle at us.

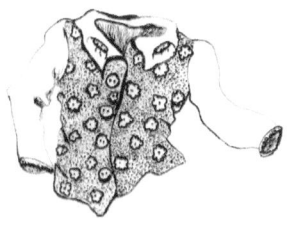

CHAPTER TWENTY-TWO

The rest of them had left the Amherst hotel. Howard sat in the hotel room's wooden chair. Luisa sat on the cushioned one. She watched him, eyes lowered, wondering what final demand the dragon fish had made. After some time had passed, Howard got to his feet in a liquid movement to reach into his small suitcase. She smiled, appreciative of his great abs.

He pulled out a sheaf of papers. "Luisa," he began, "do you ever try to envision where you will be tomorrow or next year?"

She shrugged. "Sometimes. Any envisioning I do comes from the one who taught me to think-my father. The picture doesn't change much for immigrants from Cuba. What about you?"

"It should be easier for me and both ways of thinking I got from my families, although those two ways of seeing the world often conflict with each other. You'd think all my education would change that, but all I've seen is dark, gloomy halls, sometimes with bars, sometimes worse." He handed her the papers. "I've left everything I own to you, although Father thinks that I owe him part of our property-on the Chinese side. I suppose Lydia and Mother want the money from my white side since I got so much from working with my nephew." After a lengthy pause he looked at her with implacable eyes. "You've felt it, haven't you?"

"Mi amor!" She tapped her head and chest, "I know you. The dragon fish knew you were worthy the other night. It couldn't have helped you if it saw you any other way."

"But it didn't see anything but death for me." Howard barked a mirthless sound, something like laughter. "I've felt it coming for a while. I've got to be realistic. We both have family issues. I've been talking to my mother about HayJay. He's getting more and more difficult. Mother is sure that his sense of reality is worse. You should know. Even as we solve one problem, we've got another. HayJay is determined to help me, but he doesn't know wrong from right. It is costing us money and time, so far. What about that receipt for a gun? A gun! What does a man like him want with a gun? I will talk to his caregiver."

"His caregiver you say?" Luisa rustled through a pile of bags and extracted a small pouch. "Mi Amor. You worry too much. Why don't you lie on the bed for a while? It will be all okay." Luisa used the coffee maker to heat some water. While her tea mixture brewed, she massaged his shoulder.

In a few minutes the tea was ready and she encouraged him to drink and then take a nap. After sipping the concoction, Howard flopped onto the bed. Once prone, Luisa draped a coverlet over him and watched the tension drain from his body. Howard took a deep breath and shook his head to clear his mind. "My father is bad enough. Your family is a constant drain on your time and my money. It's time for us to make our lives work. Or at least your life. You may not get the money and property soon, so I'll take care of you and your family another way that I will show you tomorrow."

She thought about the dragon fish with their spiny heads. There were several kinds. She remembered some of them fed by suction. Her husband's family, both sides of it, had sucked the life out of him for years. He worked on ways to turn against them, to sting them with the venomous spines he'd earned from two great ancestries. She waited until certain he was asleep before making arrangements, one of which was to stay at the hotel another night.

* * *

As Deloo sped down the road, I cranked up my mental gears to see if I could find our pursuers. Grandfather Kwaikit's bugging device faltered a little, then melted into benign awareness of the scene-as if I had been there in person. I sprouted apple-green hair to further my viewing and listening pleasure. Wishing for invisible popcorn, I watched passing motorists stop to help them. Blood oozed from a cut on Prize Woman's chin.

~*She's Ming. Not Pizza Womb!*~ The little ghost shouted.

What? I looked at Deloo, but she was concentrating on the road and not interested in pizza or wombs.

~*She's my twin sister, Ming. And she's in pain. That's Chuan with her.*~

I blew a kiss toward little ghost for correcting my idea of Prize Woman. Meanwhile, someone at the scene held a sanitized wipe to the wound. Ming winced, noticing the scratch for the first time. She accepted a second wipe to tamp a dribble of blood on her black and white dress. Something about the dress brought a question to my mind, but I didn't have time to investigate.

The motorist offered to call the police, but Chuan intervened.

"No, thank you." Chuan smiled at the small group of people who had gathered around them. It felt theatrical. So did his loving arm around Ming. "That driver must have been drunk. Did any of you see her?"

"I didn't notice anyone," someone answered, "not a woman driving drunk, anyway."

Another shook his head, "I didn't either. Are you sure you don't want me to call someone? How about a tow truck?"

Instead, with a little aid from two bystanders, Chuan pushed his sedan back onto the road. "Thanks for all your help," he said, guiding his wife to the passenger side. "I think we'll be okay." He noticed Ming's disheveled appearance as he closed her door. Straightening, he turned to the others and asked, "Is there a hotel near here? My wife needs to rest."

A man drove ahead of them toward a well-known hotel sign. Chuan hopped out of the sedan, forcing an artificial spring into unhappy legs and flew to the other car before its driver could get out. Reaching through the open car window, he shook the other man's hand and stopped. Too ardent.

"Thank you!" Chuan swallowed, emitting a croak instead of his usual pleasant tenor. "You've been more than kind to stop for us." He swiveled his head toward Ming and opened his eyes wide. She got the silent message and managed to show enough teeth to convince their champion.

Their benefactor blinked at the sudden beauty of Prize Woman's face, unaware of the blood he'd help to stem. He pulled himself together, tore his eyes away from hers, and remembered to be grateful that he would be able to continue his day without more time lost. Gunning his engine, he saluted and drove away.

Chuan limped to the passenger side of their car, noting with a scowl the scraped and dented right front fender. Leaning into the car he asked, "Do you want to stay here, Beautiful?"

Ming took stock of the damage with a tiny mirror. "I need to clean up, but this place is too fancy. Let's find one of those motels with individual outside doors for each guest. I don't want anyone to see me." She

tugged at the black and white fabric of her dress and added, "this is ru-
ined and I don't have another uniform with me. What were we thinking
of to leave Montreal without more clothing? Wait. I remember. This was
supposed to be simple. Just take the jacket if we got a chance. Ha-ha,
Howard. Why don't you try kissing a cougar? That would be easier."

Chuan laughed. Then he took in both the blood stains on her face
and dress, as well as the deep vertical creases that time and worry had
etched between her eyes. The gash on her chin was no longer bleeding.
"You need a bandage and antibiotic ointment to prevent scarring. No
one is going to forget you with all that blood on your clothes." He grimaced, "You're right. You need a change. I'll find a better place and get
you something while you clean up."

"That witch is crazy!" Ming cursed when he got into the car again.
"Did you see her grinning when she passed us?"

Shaking his head, Chuan pulled into the street. "She's onto us," he
snarled. "That much is clear. It would help if she were crazy because no
one would believe her side of the story."

"We don't have a 'side of the story' thanks to those two blond fools.
Neither of them ever tells us anything." Chuan hit a bump, causing her
to flinch. "So what are we supposed to do now?" Ming asked, pushing
her head into the backrest. "Can we go home yet?" She wasn't sure if
she meant the dingy condo in Montreal or their new house in China. It
took her away from the only thing that gave her joy: their private house
in China. She was so angry she'd been leaving all communication to her
husband. For Chuan's part it called for negotiating skills that he'd developed because of their odd arrangements with the two white men. He
thought back to one of the early conversations in which he tried to find
out what they were doing for such a long stint in Canada. They won the
key points about six months ago.

"Brent, you've got to tell us what is so important about that jacket.
You know that Ming's relatives aren't going to do anything for you without either a full explanation or a lot of money."

At first, Brent tried hedging, but Ming remained angry and un-
willing to help. Then he told them the truth, or at least something that
sounded like it. "It's worth millions of dollars. Hell, it's worth millions
in Euros or in dollars. I've got to find it. I'll give you fifteen percent of
its value when I get it back, but all I can do now is thirty."

Chuan reminded her of that victory and wondered if they should demand forty percent after actually tackling the woman in the denim jacket. Mrs. D. Goode was obviously a pro.

"Fifty percent," Ming snapped. "She could have killed us today. Thirty percent is not enough."

"I'll call," he growled. The swelling on his forehead surged. "We're lucky there wasn't much traffic on that frontage road, or we might have hit another car."

Ming burst into hysterical laughter. "That was her plan, you egotistical bigot! She waited to make sure no one would see her."

Chuan's jaw tightened. He looked into her eyes.

She flinched.

He searched her face, his eyes cat-like.

Ming took in a long breath and caressed him.

Preoccupied with technical problems, he ignored the amorous gesture. Grandfather's bug worked. I thought of sharing their opinion that Deloo was a professional criminal with my mortal, but she was still vibrating with terror. I stopped actively listening and merely checked on their location from time to time.

They found a suitable motel where Ming showered while Chuan went into Moncton to find a clothing store. Given the late hour and his own aches and pains, his choices were limited, but he found a dress in the right size, as well as the other things he thought they both needed for the night. Ming was asleep in the bed. He draped a black and white zigzag cotton blend dress on the bed beside her. Her family favored a different design. She didn't move, so he pulled out his phone.

Howard answered on the first ring. His voice fuzzy but audible.

"We had an accident."

"What about the woman with the beaded jacket?"

"She was the accident and she's gone." Chuan described the near head-on collision.

Ming lifted her head and whispered, "Ask him if he's seen HayJay."

Chuan nodded to her and asked, "by the way, how's HayJay today?"

"He's quiet. Brent's already headed to Montreal. I'll tell him to give you a hand." Without warning the call ended. Chuan put away the phone and crawled under the covers next to his wife.

"Thanks for reminding me to ask about HayJay. It saves a lot of time," he mumbled to Ming.

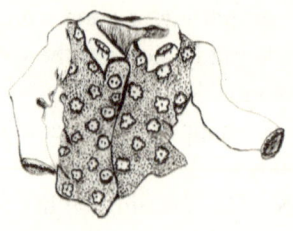

CHAPTER TWENTY-THREE

I pondered the oddness of their exchange. What I didn't pick up with the bug, but did with more ancient and reliable methods were Chuan's private thoughts. I had tuned into the bug long enough that I was able to isolate both his location and mental output. My thousands of years of practice gave me a sense of Chuan's feelings about Ming, all laced in ordeal and hopelessness.

I thought of turning the bug 'down' so the little ghost couldn't tune in to it with me. She seemed very sharp for someone so recently dead. Then I glanced at her and saw that she was once again in la-la land, or ghost-sleep. I turned back to the bug. Chuan was still tormenting himself about his wife's feelings.

Did he imagine it? Did he imagine the way she tightened whenever he touched her and then seemed to force herself to relax? Chuan couldn't remember when the first shock of separation from her occurred. He never mentioned it to Ming-afraid of her sarcasm, he supposed. After the first two-day separation, Chuan learned to shape their job assignments so that he was always with her. Ming never commented on it. More to the point, she never protested. With a grunt, he rolled onto his left side and let his right hand drop across her ribs to the place he liked the best, between her small breasts. His phone rang just as he dozed off. His hand moved so that he could see the caller ID. Brent.

"Hey."

"Are you all right? Where are you?" the other voice fuzzed.

Chuan rolled away from Ming and sat up. "Thanks for caring," he smiled. "That's more than I can say for our mutual friend." They must have thought it lent them security to speak in Mandarin. Maybe to other nosy spies, but not from me, Baasee' the Multi-lingual. They agreed to wait until the following day before making any decisions.

Chuan noticed he was still bleeding and went into the bathroom to change a bandage. An image of my precious Deloo came to him. She was in the Passat grinning as she drove away. He tipped his right hand toward the mirror in a mock salute. Shaking his head, he crawled back into the bed and was sound asleep when Ming thrust herself against his belly.

~*See? She still loves him. He's still crazy about her.*~ The little ghost gave a haunting sigh. I peeked in at her. ~*Can I come out now?*~

~*Go to sleep.*~ I closed her space.

* * *

"What shall we do now?" Deloo asked invisible me.

I took stock of her, noting that once again she was hungry. ~*You are going to open that bag of take-out food and eat your Chinese chicken for a start,*~ I answered.

Deloo couldn't help smiling as she chewed the rice and chicken with noisy gusto. "You're right. I needed that." She wiped her lips with the back of her hand and burped. "Now I need something to drink—and some chips."

I rolled a ball of lavender blue energy into the car to simulate my nonexistent eyes and gave her directions to a nearby stop-and-shop grocery. ~*Just remember that you don't like colas and prefer nutritious juices,*~ I communed into a dietary void. Once there I reversed all of my doting efforts by urging her to buy caffeinated drinks, but I knew we were in for a long drive. I watched my charge fill a basket with unwholesome food.

~*The coast is clear, my tiny glutton. They are sleeping somewhere.*~

"I'm ready," Deloo sang from the driver's seat. The soda can was empty. "Where to now, Madame Spirit Guide?"

Deloo's happy voice brought forth a memory so strong and piercing of MiMi, a long-dead mortal under my guidance who had been born with two defects: a weak heart valve and a single kidney. She was doomed from the start, and yet my little MiMi managed to live until she was thirty-two. I mourned, as I thought, in private.

~*Baasee'?*~ Deloo communed in alarm. ~*Are you... Are you crying?*~

I gathered myself together with inner chastisement for my self-pity. ~*You reminded me of one of my long-ago mortals, a dear woman. We were very close.*~

Without warning the ashtray slammed open. A spinning Loonie bounced out and landed on the top of Deloo's soda can. A shaft of light flickered toward me. Deloo picked the coin up and tucked it into the ashtray. After a moment she asked, ~*what was her name?*~

~*MiMi. I, I'm sorry I lost my grip for a moment, my dear. We have a lot to do. We have to get away from here and on a different route from the one we are using now.*~

Deloo said, "Let's go north as we planned to do earlier." Deloo made her way north toward the Saint Lawrence Seaway. There never seemed to be a place to stop except gas stations. Time dragged. When she stopped, neither of us had enough energy to ask for a hotel. Darkness fell. Deloo tried the radio with no luck, and remembered that she had a CD. She clicked it on and a sultry voice belted "Black velvet and that little boy's smile". She started to sing along.

I helped her sway in tempo. We were enjoying the serenity of our duet when a tiny spirit voice chimed in on the chorus line ~*Black velvet if you please*~ with a long riff at the end.

"Who was that? You? Was it you, Baasee'?"

~*No. That was the little ghost. She said Alannah Myles is her favorite singer. A star in the little ghost's era here in Canada.*~

"Little ghost?" Deloo looked over her shoulder into the gloom. "Oh! The little ghost from New Brunswick. Yeah. I like Myles, too, although I never heard of her before this past year. Mattie gave me the CD."

I knew she was wondering what or who the song was about. I could have filled her in about Elvis Presley, but that would have been as bad as giving her a history lesson about Zana. Meaningless at midnight after a frightful confrontation. At long last we saw signs notifying us that we were leaving New Brunswick and entering Québec.

Deloo intoned, "I'm hungry again. Very hungry. I want a big salad."

The little ghost crooned a courageous four-octave series, ~*Cheddar Cheese, if you please*~.

Deloo giggled.

I refrained from appreciating their joke and reminded Deloo about the snack bag. She opened a packet of green jelly pepper candy. Her favorite.

All of us watched the passage into Québec in a state of surreal suspension. While I wanted Deloo to be safe from the people who followed her, it was part of my curse as a spirit guide to know that she would see them again. Meanwhile, I had other problems to solve, all centering on someone Deloo did not know: HayJay.

Around nine Deloo asked a gas station attendant for directions to a hotel. He shrugged and said something in French and took her debit card with a cheerful smile. She drove on without enlightenment from him or me. She arrived in Rivière-du-Loup (Wolf River in English). Her guidebook told her the wolves were sea wolves, the seventeenth century term for seals. Deloo's mind whirled with off-balance images.

~Baasee', have you ever seen such creatures?~

While a corner of my mind noted her perfect commune, the rest of me was testy. I was still working my way through a myriad of worthless memories, and her amusement caught me unprepared and, I must add, grouchy. I deserved to be grouchy.

~No, I have never seen wolves that turn into seals. Child, it's getting late. You need to find a place to sleep and we're coming up on a town. Make sure you stop this time.~

I was about to suggest looking at the map when I had a striking vision of a giant spirit man who was working with a mortal. They were singing a very old Inuit song. It reminded me of a chant that my best friend, Tristeenin, sang often in order to lure enemies toward us. Always at night. I would hide nearby. It never took long. The enemy would find himself drawn toward her like a fly toward rotting flesh. As soon as they were close to my hiding place, Tristeenin changed the tempo to alert me. It worked every time. I was surprised to hear something so ancient being used in Deloo's world.

"What's that chanting, Baasee'? Is it the little ghost again?" Deloo's sudden intrusion stunned me.

~You could hear it?~ I knew the Inuit angakkuq or shaman was at least a hundred miles away from us. Even farther.

"No. Not with my ears. I feel it. It's kind of like a jig tune, full of energy, yet soothing at the same time-I like it. Is it the little ghost? She knows a lot of songs."

I peeped into the black space where I had tucked the little ghost. She spiraled out of the blackness and looped around my transmitter space. I pretended to flail at her. Instead of resisting, she found an indentation in my coil of tendrils and swept into a shallow cavity. Vibrating with excitement, she telepathed both of us, *~It's a shaman from my area. He's calling for my beloved Qanik.~*

I found a more comfortable position and slid a magical tether around her. To Deloo I communed ~*the chanter is not the little ghost. It's coming from a mortal shaman. Can you understand her?*~

Deloo shook her tangled hair. Like most Native American hair, it normally hung straight down because of its natural oils. Not tonight. A couple of shafts poked straight upward. "Sort of," she muttered. "I can tell two of you are talking, but not what she's saying."

The little ghost continued, oblivious of Deloo.~*I have a gift that my mother thought I could learn about. She took me to that shaman. That was a week after Ming and I graduated from the local college. Ming got accepted into Harvard and I got engaged to Qanik. Ming and I could always think to each other. I knew I was better at it than her because I could hear the thoughts of other kids. And the teachers.*~

I cocked an invisible eyebrow at her. ~*Hmmm? Does that mean you cheated on tests while your twin sister had to spend time learning?*~

The little ghost sniggered. ~*We are identical in looks, but there are some invisible differences such as thinking. I spent two weeks with the angakkuq. He taught me four chants. That's one of them. There's another for calling to ghosts. I followed the angakkuq's advice and went to China before getting married. So did Ming. All of us went on an archaeological dig. That's the last thing I remember of being alive. Afterward, I heard the chant that's for ghosts. After a while I realized that I was the ghost they were calling. It was supposed to call me to talk to the angakkuq, you know, the shaman, but I couldn't find him. I went to Ming instead.*~

~*Who is he calling?*~ I asked.

~*This song is for calling Qanik's killer. The police took a while to get back to his parents. My fiancé was poisoned, but no one has figured out who did it. My father and mother want the killer to confess. He will if he hears this chanting. If you and she can hear it, so can the guilty person.*~

I translated for Deloo, and explained what happens to mortals who hear such drumming and chanting. ~*The little ghost said if you had been the target of that chant, you would not be able to drive, let alone dance. It's a song that is designed to hypnotize the victim.*~

"Are you kidding?" Deloo swerved. The wheels roared softly as they hit gravel.

~*They are about 350 miles away, somewhere west and north.*~ I responded, ~*they are spreading a wide net for whomever they seek.*~

"So, if I were the person they wanted, what would happen to me?"

The little ghost answered, ~*You would fall into a trance. They would find a way to go to you through the mind. You would feel compelled to think about your location so they could find you. You would stay here in Rivière-du-Loup until they reached you.*~

Understanding the little ghost, Deloo sighed. "Awesome! But, if I'm not the one they are looking for, doesn't that mean that I could help find their quarry?"

Since the little ghost didn't know how to answer, I offered some wise and wonderful spirit-guide thought. ~*I don't know if you can do that yet, but I could. And I will not track them down. It's none of our business-or so I hope.*~

It was midnight when Deloo found an inexpensive hotel in Rivière-du-Loup, and neither a seal nor even a wolf was present to greet us. Nor did we find the chanting shaman. Nonetheless, the room was cozy. Worn out, Deloo crawled under the covers to sleep.

In a little while I felt like dozing as well. I sleep whenever the mortal does. However, the remark from the dorm attendant in Halifax kept me awake. "No one will remember her name in a year." When Deloo began talking in her sleep an hour or so later, I thought she was suffering from her own dreams and tried to ignore her. That's why I was out of sync with what happened next.

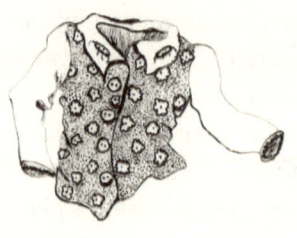

CHAPTER TWENTY-FOUR

"Get off the bed, Shattie," Deloo muttered and kicked the blankets.

Shattie? An image of a playful tabby cat came to mind. Deloo and Shattie had been inseparable until the cat died several years ago. Even alive, Shattie wasn't allowed to get into bed with Deloo.

"What you need is not what is here," someone squeaked.

"What?" Deloo quailed. She banged her wedding ring against her cheek, causing the loose ring to slide off her finger. It fell into the sheets. She found the ring but not the cat she expected to have crawled into bed with her. Shattie was not the furry thing crawling along her leg. Deloo jumped out of bed, shook out the sheets, but could not find anything that was either furry or moving in the dark. It was two in the morning.

~What happened?~ I grumbled.

"There's an animal in my bed. It might be a fox or a wolverine. It talked to me." Deloo tugged on her tee shirt and jeans. She turned on all of the lights and threw everything out of her suitcase and onto a bare spot on the floor. After shaking each item, she carried her clothing a piece at a time to the bathroom where the lights were strongest. There she repacked her suitcase, still shaking each piece before letting it rest in peace.

Tucking Arthur's camera around her neck, she announced, "Let's go!"

~It's too soon to leave.~ I complained, feeling much younger than Deloo's twenty-one years. I forced myself to think beyond myself. *~You haven't had enough sleep. You need to get more rest. Besides, a wolverine would not have allowed you to live even a second after you got into bed with it! They don't go for one-night stands. Sleep a little longer.~*

"How?" Deloo wailed.

I imagined the fun of sighing when inspiration pounced on me.

~Don't worry, Deloo. I will use my powers to vaporize the savage beast who dared to molest your sleep.~

Deloo stared at the bed while I told her I was inspecting it with my magical faculties. Soon I discovered the small mouse who had tried to cuddle against Deloo's warm body.

~I found it. It's a mouse, a spirit animal,~ I assured her. The mouse had curled into a small ball near the foot of the bed and had no intention of leaving. *~She wonders if you got her message about what you need. Do you remember hearing her?~*

Deloo's face cleared. "Something about what I need is not here. What does that mean?"

I washed a big wave of cozy warmth over her. *~We'll talk about it after you've rested. Now, just lie on top of the bed. I'll stand guard while you rest.~*

Despite herself, Deloo fell asleep and I might have taken a light nap myself.

Deloo awoke with a start.

It was the little ghost, frantic. She muttered, *~Qanik! Where's Qanik!~*

~Shhh. People search for him now.~ I sent waves of soothing calm toward the little ghost and Deloo as well. MoLi found calm. Deloo did not.

"I've slept long enough," Deloo growled. Stiff in the cold air, Deloo slipped her arms into the beaded jacket and carried her bag out to the car. She stopped at a bakery along the road. After a bagel and two cups of hot coffee, Deloo looked and felt better.

~Are you ready to travel on?~

"It's so strange-what's been happening. Why did a mouse talk to me, Baasee'?"

~It was a message from the Invisible Forces to help you stay focused. Something good will come about, but you might not like the way it happens.~

* * *

The drive from New Brunswick to their condo in Montreal was uneventful. It was their third, and least used, home. They spent most of the year at their house in Cambridge. Most of the time, Howard's mere presence calmed her, but they fell out with each other on occasion. When that happened, Luisa spent weeks at their house in Florida to visit her family. An interchangeable dozen members of her Cuban brothers, sisters, nieces, nephews, and her father, lived in the Florida house full time. Howard's father had given Luisa the house as a wedding gift, as there she could find hundreds of people she knew from her birthplace. Florida held the largest population of Cubans inside United States borders. Luisa always stayed in Florida instead of going with Howard to their fourth house in China. It was near the ruins of the seventh century palace once owned by Howard's ancestors.

Howard pulled into the garage when his phone sang. He looked at the display and murmured, "I was going to call him. He's saving me time. He accepted the call and grunted. "Yes… I know the place. I'll meet you there in a few minutes." Howard frowned at Luisa.

She shrugged. "I'll be in the condo. Go to your family. You know I always do."

Before she could get out of the car, Howard struck the steering wheel. Something slid open and he reached into a cavity.

Luisa frowned at him. "What did you do to it? Does the passenger air bag work?"

Howard laughed for the first time in weeks. "Of course it does. I would do nothing to harm you, the light of my soul." He reached into the cavity in the steering wheel and pulled out a large plastic bag. He handed it to Luisa. "This is for you. It should be two hundred fifty thousand dollars. It's my emergency stash. I don't need it anymore."

"I won't take it if you keep talking like that!"

Howard's forlorn look melted. Another kind of smile crept into his eyes. "All right. Take it as an advance payment for my demands upon you tonight."

"Está bien," Luisa grinned, "as long as you know my family will find a way to get all of this money in good time.

"I know, my love, I've always known they get everything."

Hours later, one of them slipped out of the condo for a breath of fresh air.

* * *

Inspector Al Beamus shuffled some papers together, twiddled with some pens, all in an effort to avoid looking at the latest email on his computer. Nothing serious. His supervisor outlined his assignments for the rest of the week. The mysterious death at the Secret Spirit Inn would drop off the list unless he found new evidence. His stomach burned. He rooted through his top desk for an antacid.

A sheaf of papers slid out of the drawer and spread across the floor. He stared at the mess. He spotted the author's name: H. Johnson. An idea bloomed in his mind. His stomach problems melted away as his fingers opened a search engine and typed the name. He didn't get any new contact numbers, but a glance at Johnsosn's data reminded him of someone who might be able to make the connection he needed.

A few precious minutes passed before he had the telephone number he wanted. He tapped the numbers and counted the rings at the other end.

"Hello?"

"Dr. Morrow?"

"Woodrow Morrow speaking. Who is this?

Al laughed. "It's Al. Al Beamus. It's been a while since we walked patrol, eh? I saw somewhere that you did it. Congratulations, Dr. Morrow."

After a quarter second of confusion, Dr. Morrow remembered the man who'd served with him in the RCMP. They laughed over old times. Al waited for the appropriate moment to ask if Woody had any connections at Harvard that could give him access to more information about Johnson.

"So, this guy might have killed her, hmm? Okay. Let me ask around. I have a good contact. I'm in Cambridge right now. My host graduated from Harvard. His name is Zachary Goode. He might know some people you'd like to question."

* * *

In spite of an odd sense of expectancy, everything seemed normal. Around seven that evening, Deloo stopped for gas and I spotted a Chinese eatery not far away. It didn't occur to me to inspect the restaurant for danger, forgetting yesterday's experience with Moncton's Chinese dining. Why should I? We were in Québec, not New Brunswick or Nova Scotia, a totally different Canadian province.

Deloo stuffed Arthur's camera into its black and white case under the front seat and gathered her purse to go in. She looked through the restaurant's glass door. I heard her whisper, "Oh no!" just as I saw a sedan parked beside the diner's entry.

"They're here! Right here hundreds of miles away from Moncton."

She was right. They sat at a far table. The man glanced up.

~*We have to get out of here.*~

Deloo wheeled on one foot and reached her car door in three giant steps. She turned the key when something occurred to me. ~*Write down the license plate number.*~

Deloo yanked the sketchbook from the sun visor and scribbled the letters and numbers, noting with quivering fingers, that it was a Québec plate. Without waiting for my consent, Deloo put her car in reverse and entered the slow traffic. Two hours later the traffic tangle began to dissolve and we were in Montreal.

So was the all-too-familiar sedan. Between us were four other cars.

~*We can't stop. They are a few cars back.*~

Fear inspired recklessness, and Deloo turned at the last possible second onto the off ramp leading north. Her quick action didn't help. "Look, Baasee', they are right behind us."

~*Breathe,*~ MoLi answered for me. I was surprised, but happy the little ghost was rising to new levels to help my Deloo. Suppressing an urge to gripe that she hadn't done so in Moncton, I took advantage of MoLi's new-found calming gentleness to enter my full combatant mode.

~*Look to your east. There's another off ramp up ahead. Take it. Maybe they aren't after us anymore.*~ I suggested in vain. They were still after us.

I rose up again to look for the strangers' sedan. ~*I see their car. No problem. We'll just do some old tracker dodging tricks from way back in the Ice Age era to get away.*~

"What do you mean? Ice Age tricks? What are they?" Deloo pulled into a side street.

~*Turn at the next intersection that lets you turn left. That's an Ice Age trick. There are lots of one-way streets around here. Repeat the left turns as often as you can to lose them.*~

Deloo followed my orders three times, then complained "I'm just going in circles."

~*Relax. They are beautiful, counter-clockwise circles.*~ I pulled myself up to be higher than any of the nearby buildings. I contorted my transmitter zone into a devastating smirk. ~*As usual, the right-handed world never seems to think about how sneaky the left hand is. They've lost us.*~

"Great. Let's.... Wait... Look, there's a hotel."

I had to agree that it did sport a hotel sign. It also sported a spirit sign about alternative lifestyles. Read "gay hotel" in the spirit code. I would have thought it a mansion a few thousand years ago, but not tonight and not for my tiny mortal.

Oblivious to me, Deloo swerved so hard to the left that the Passat's tires mounted the sidewalk. She slammed on the brakes and the car assumed a parking position.

"It's perfect." She jumped out of the car and trotted toward the hotel. She halted abruptly and turned around. "I should bring my bag."

~*Deloo, this hotel is not for your kind,*~ I began. A quick survey of its clientele told me it was one of the higher end gay hotels in Montreal.

"It's just right," Irritation flushed around her head in orange spillways. Deloo reached the far side and kept going. I stopped moving to locate them. They were near us.

So was Grandfather Kwaikit, who appeared out of nowhere as he often did. ~*Tell your mortal to take nothing inside.*~

I did. Deloo groused, "I need my wallet."

~*Okay. Take it,*~ I saw one of her elastic ponytail scrunchies, ~*and that hair thing.*~

"Okay." She picked up the wallet and stuffed the elastic into a pocket.

Deloo got through registration, clutching a key card as she scurried along a series of narrow hallways and up rickety stairs on the way to a miniscule room on the fourth floor.

~*Rest. You will need strength for tomorrow. We are in serious danger in this hotel.*~

"No!" I felt a tremor shoot along Deloo's spine.

~*Maybe I'm wrong about the danger,*~ I placated. ~*Braid your hair. It will help you sleep. That's why I told you to take that cute hair gadget.*~ I was getting used to lying.

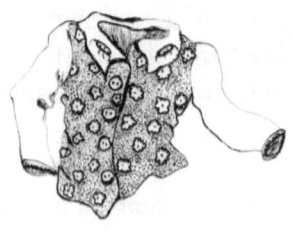

CHAPTER TWENTY-FIVE

In the predawn hours of June eighth, Ming and Chuan pulled up to their condo in Montreal. The fact that it was in the Gay Village of Montreal had appealed to all of them because of the instant camouflage. None of Ming's Canadian relatives would ever walk or drive through this sector of the city.

What they didn't guess is that a tired Alaskan woman might take the first hotel, the one across the street from their condo.

A few minutes after Deloo settled into her nearby hotel room they arrived, smarting at being foiled again by the very Alaskan woman who dozed nearby. They both agreed to get some sleep before deciding what to do next. Chuan saw a light in their front window, the one that faced Deloo's hotel. A shadow moved in the background of their condo's small window. He grumbled, "Zut! He's up there."

Ming looked up at the condo's dark window and picked out a figure near the drapes. Then she examined the alleyway near the condominium for Brent's vehicle.

"I see his car."

She opened the car door and was about to step out when Chuan barked, "Look!" He pointed at Deloo's vehicle.

Ming glanced toward her husband. He pointed at a car on the other side of the street. A grey Passat. She couldn't read the plates, but she didn't need to see them to know it was the Alaskan car.

"Omigod! It's just like yesterday. Is this a nightmare? Is she hunting us down? How'd she find us?"

Chuan shrugged. "She doesn't know us, Beautiful. She's in the hotel. I feel it."

"She'd never go to any of these hotels! This is the Gay Village. She's straight."

Chuan laughed and tapped Ming's cheek. "The sign reads "Hotel, not Gay Hotel.""

"What are we waiting for, then? Let's go get her."

They entered the lobby. They'd stayed there many times to avoid dealing with Brent, so it was easy to find out which room Deloo had taken. They talked their way past the gay man who served as the concierge, and crept down the maze of corridors Deloo had followed earlier.

Deloo, frazzled by yesterday's ever-changing field of dangers, dozed. At some point, she slept for more than an hour. I was happy that she'd got that much repose. She had flopped across the top of the bed without removing her clothing. I nudged her.

"What now?

~They're on their way to our room. You have to leave by the window.~

"The what?" She leapt off the bed and raced to the window. "This is the fourth floor. I'll break my neck."

~Take the sheets off the bed. I'll help.~

In seconds Deloo tied a timber hitch to the balcony railing and lowered herself down the side of the hotel wall to the third floor level. As a teen she'd learned an Athabascan version of rock climbing in Fairbanks when she and her buddies used to play on the tangle of wrecked cars in an empty lot. She had no fear of broken shards of glass and steel.

"Ah!" Her sneakered foot tapped along the length of a ledge before placing any weight on it. I inspected the wall below the ledge.

~Keep going. There's a lower ledge a little way from here. You can use this one for your hands and the other for your feet.~

Deloo clambered down and found the second floor ledge just as she ran out of sheet.

The ledge was wide enough to allow creeping one-foot at a time. I forced Deloo to forget to look anywhere but straight ahead so that she wouldn't get nervous.

"Now which . . . ," a male voice murmured from above.

"That's her!" The second voice was female, Inuit accent, and had a tan finger that jabbed the air so hard I could feel it penetrate my outer hide.

"Where?"

"Two floors down. Look. There are the sheets she used. I'll go after her."

~*That's Prize Woman!*~ I picked up the exchange with psychic power. ~*They made it to your room. We got out just in time. Keep moving to the right.*~

Before Prize Woman tried mounting the sheets, I snaked upward and used spirit power to unravel the knot. Just as the Inuit-Chinese woman touched the cloth, I ripped it away from her before she climbed onto it. She was lightweight enough to slide down the sheets just as had Deloo.

"Drat! We'll have to go down by the stairs."

I heard the clatter of their feet. Satisfied I had averted disaster, I returned to Deloo and began exploring the wall on her right. Sounds of two grunting men reached Deloo's sensitive ears.

~*Don't worry. It's safer than the other way.*~ I didn't want to tell her that the other way led toward the car.

Someone shouted, "She's up there!"

Another voice shouted "Look out!"

That was enough of a warning for me to tighten a molecular boundary around Deloo's head and heart. It worked. Something struck the wall instead of Deloo's head. Deloo's shoulders twitched. I muffled her with all of my force and prevented her eyes from seeing the scar a bullet had dug into the wall. I thought the shooter had finished, but I was wrong. Another shot rang out. Once again a perfectly aimed bullet flew toward my beautiful Deloo's head. There was no time for molecular boundaries. I caught it with a tendril, contemplated sending it back to its source, but the shooter had moved an inch or two. That's why I dropped the slug and wrapped Deloo in a solid force field.

"Why did you do that?" a woman rasped.

"I didn't," he answered. "See? It's cold. I haven't fired it." He held it out for her inspection.

A half block away on the ground two people scuffled for a gun. One tapped the other's ear and grabbed a weak arm. The victor muttered, "You always fall for that trick, you sucker. You should know better than this. I have told you time and again that our kind don't use firearms." The caregiver pulled out a syringe. "This will help. It's your sleeping aid."

The other mumbled, "I hear he's been asking about the ethics of causing the death of another again. Has he asked you, too?"

The first one waited for the material in the syringe to take effect and responded in kind. "It's more that he rambled about ethics. He doesn't ask me for my opinion. When I told him, and you've heard me, always heard me, that murder is wrong, he wouldn't talk to me for a week." The other shrugged and tilted his head toward a waiting car. In a few seconds they found their way inside a sedan. Even in a drugged state the drugged one recognized the gold design on the side of the red door. A dragon.

Struggling with Deloo, I heard the words, but didn't know what they meant. I missed understanding that there were four of them in separate pairs. Needing more information, I thought of calling for Grandfather Kwaikit. He waggled a 'hold on' response to me.

~Deloo, your hands are nice and grimy. Rub your face. You'll match the wall.~

Deloo rubbed grit and dust on her face. The gesture relaxed her. She lifted joyless brows in a salute. "Am I invisible now?"

I would have fluttered happy faces at her, but I was too impatient. *~Hurry up,~* I griped. *~They went back down to the street. You'll need to start climbing up.~*

Like a skilled dancer, Deloo slid her legs apart and then together again and again until she seemed to stride along the narrow ledge. Feeling an urgent need for invisibility, I blew a small hurricane of warm air around her to boil up more grey dust.

"Hey," she snapped and coughed through pinched-shut lips. *~What'd you do that for?~*

~There was a pile of it on that ledge. Sorry. You'll forgive me soon.~

Deloo reached an open sliding door that cut an angle at the corner of the building. Its narrow balcony jutted out where real walls could have been, giving the dilapidated hotel an air of tired elegance. Another balcony arched outward overhead, back on the third floor.

"Must be the fancy rooms," she muttered through dust-grey lips.

~Use your commune voice,~ I urged from above her where I could see how close she was to the roof, *~and climb up to the higher balcony.~*

Deloo stretched her fingers until they found a decorative side railing along the window's edge. Without testing her weight on it, she grabbed it and started to inch along the window ledge. The decoration gave way. Deloo started to fall. She opened her mouth to scream and I threw my biggest tendril against her spine to lend her some support. It was enough to stop the fall and her yell.

"Qui est là? Who eez dare?" The man's voice stumbled over English consonants.

Deloo froze. Recognizing signs of "Arthur" shock, I took a better look at him. As I expected, he was tall and skinny like Arthur had been. There was no other resemblance.

~It's not Arthur. Just another widow's sighting,~ I rolled soothing vibrations along her arms and back.

Deloo took a deep breath and heard sounds of feet landing on the floor and wobbling a step or two.

"Personne n'est là, Cher. Viens te coucher avec moi."

I perked up and ran a seductive sensation along the upright man's inner thigh. My efforts met those of the man's partner and both of them chuckled.

Deloo let out a soundless breath and rested her palm on the window frame. Another piece of the window edging broke and fell to the floor of the narrow balcony. The sound coincided with an amorous burst from inside the room.

I gripped Deloo. *~They're too busy to notice you anymore. With a shooter on the sidewalk, we'll have to climb. Reach up. I see something to grab.~*

Deloo stretched her right hand, found a peg extending ten or twelve inches out of the wall. She put weight on it. It held. She pulled herself up onto the window ledge while hanging onto the peg. Then her left hand found the top of the window just beyond.

~There's another one a little to the right and above the first.~

Pressing her body flat against rotting exterior siding, Deloo's right hand patted the wall. I guided her until she located it. As it happened, the pegs seemed to emerge from the wall just as she needed another hand- or foothold. We passed the fourth floor where her room was. I prompted her to keep moving. Soon she climbed up and onto the short retaining wall that surrounded the roof to its filthy surface.

I was too busy working with Deloo to see Prize Woman and her husband on the sidewalk just below us. More to the point, I didn't notice them re-enter the hotel.

Once Deloo sprawled on top of the roof, she panted, "Which way now?"

~Lie there until you feel strong enough to move,~ I communed. *~When you are ready, I want you to look over the edge of the roof.~*

Deloo rolled onto her side and crept to the short retaining wall. Gentle light bathed the side of the walls and street below. She managed to get to her knees and peer downward. "What am I looking for?"

~Look straight down. That's where you were climbing those pegs. Do you see them?~

Deloo looked downward. The wall was better lit than others, so she had a decent view. It was a good thing she was already on her knees. Her blood pressure dropped so fast that she might have fallen over the edge had she been standing. She shivered.

~You are safe, Deloo. I wanted you to know, that's all.~

Deloo blinked hard. Deloo could see the broken window molding and heard raucous sounds from inside the lovers' room.

"The pegs." She dropped back onto the roof. "Where are the pegs?"

~There are no pegs. I wanted you to know you were safe by giving you something that you were used to climbing. Remember? You used exhaust pipes that size all the time.~

"But those were real pipes. There are no pegs or pipes on that wall," Deloo jabbed a finger downward.

I shrugged a dust blossom of golden light at the wall, *~you clambered on real pipes most of the time back in Alaska, but sometimes I had to invent a pipe where you needed one to be.~* I sent her a mental image of her kicking at a mean kid.

"Fat Jake!" Deloo snarled. "He got Marlene. Almost got me too. Now she's...."

~No time for all that. We've got to get moving.~

"Afterward Willie kept showing me that side of the heap. He told everyone that it looked like I flew up to the top." Deloo swiveled her head, searching. "Baasee', it was you, wasn't it?"

~There's a stairwell over there,~ I aimed a fake saber tooth tiger claw toward it.

"It's locked," Deloo said aloud after a quick yank on the roof top door. She was about to go back to where we had climbed to the top, but I stopped her and pushed her off to one side.

~Wait. Someone is coming.~

The roof-top door rattled. A shot rang out. Deloo could see the jagged tear in the metal surrounding the now deceased lock.

"Someone offed the lock." Air rushed out of Deloo's lungs so fast she could not move. She remembered the sound of a shot, rocks flying. She gasped. "They shot at me. They want to kill me." In answer, I shoved her against the wall.

Chuan slammed the stairwell door open. He paused, seemed about to look over his shoulder toward Deloo when Prize Woman pushed him aside.

"Do you see her?" he asked.

Ming shook her head. "She's must be heading toward her car. Which way is our condo?"

Chuan pointed. They could see a small part of it.

"Okay. So when we got to her room, she was moving right from where we were. That means she moved left from where we are now. She'd have climbed up about there." He pointed straight at the place Deloo had crumpled onto the roof after making the final ascent.

They made a wild dash toward the spot. Too late.

Deloo aborted a sigh. I urged her to dash behind them and into the stairwell. Thanks to the man who had shot open the door, there was no lock to stop her. In precious seconds, we were out of the hotel and in the Passat. Deloo stepped on the gas, and shot around the corner.

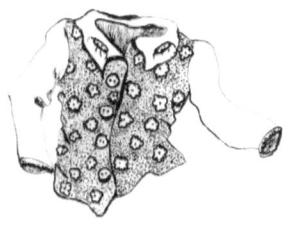

CHAPTER TWENTY-SIX

Grandfather Kwaikit blasted into my space, spluttering commands at me. ~*We need to get the slugs. They shot at her from ground level as well as into the lock at the top. Hurry. Get all of the shells and slugs.*~

Crabby, I assented, but had demands in return. ~*Okay. Since I know where we were along the wall and you don't, I'll go. You have to take care of Deloo, though. I'll get the slugs.*~

Deloo left, unaware there was a larger issue unfurling. The discussion became a short but shrill spectral fight—which I won. He doesn't know much about Deloo, but I knew where to look for the dumb shells. He caved.

~*Alright. I'll take care of the mortal. Be sure to get all three slugs and shells,*~ Grandfather growled as well as any shriveled up eternal specter can do.

It took me longer than I expected. I didn't remember which floor we were on when the first shot was fired. In fact, it took well over an hour to find both the entry hole of the bullet and then the slug from the bullet that had hit the wall and then fallen to the sidewalk below. I was tired when I started to search for spent shells on top of the building.

~*I think he stopped. Do you feel the drumbeat anymore?*~

~*What? Oh.*~ It was the little ghost. I paused a moment to find the angakkuq's chant. I didn't detect the rhythms of the drum or the voice. ~*No. Maybe they stopped to get some rest.*~

~*He had just started a new chant. Back when I was his pupil he sang it for me just to show the range of songs that could be used to catch killers. The one he just sang was to catch a spirit of the one who killed a person like me. A spirit of a man or woman who has murdered. I heard it once, but that was enough. Now he's calling Qanik, the ghost of Qanik. Chills ran through me then. Now those chills are this.*~ She illustrated her meaning by indicating a piece of herself that still vibrated. ~*When he drummed and chanted that song, I felt the touch of an evil spirit. This one was trying to kill Deloo. I don't think it was the same spirit who was after me. Did you feel it?~*

I studied the area of the little ghost and replied, *~no, I did not. Let's tell Grandfather Kwaikit about what you experienced. I'll take that vibration away from you to preserve it for him.~* I showed her what I was doing, sensing that this was part of her ongoing gift from Invisible Forces. Then I continued to look for material evidence of the shooting.

Once I located the first shell I was mystified. I don't know very much about bullets, shells, slugs, or any of that. What I do know is that there were two different shooters. That was obvious from the powerful mental energies that continued to loiter around the shells. I wondered what Grandfather would make of all this.

* * *

Deloo, hoping that Baasee' would join her again soon, turned left whenever possible instead of right. When she reached a street with obvious choices to get onto a divided highway, she chose the exit sign for the U.S.A./Sud. Having taken Spanish rather than French, she thought Sud stood for another town, and quipped "I hope someone in Sud will tell me which way will get me back home to Fairbanks." Free of fear, Deloo crowed with manic laughter. "It must be a town so clean, the people don't need soap. They are always sudsy. Right, Baasee'?" Although Baasee' neither heard nor answered, Deloo aimed the Passat with confidence onto the new highway, feeling a twinge of unease when it morphed into a country road.

"Baasee', do you think I'm going the right way?"

No answer.

"Baasee'?" *~Baasee'?~*

Minutes passed without feedback from the spirit guide who'd been with her for a week of constant uproar. Exhausted by two sleepless nights, Deloo's eyes lost focus several times. She spotted a place to pull off the road and did.

Stocked with a single trash can, the turnout was both long and wide enough to hold big transport rigs. One such truck of the size that drove the Haul Road to Deadhorse, Alaska, occupied the far end. Deloo parked as far away from it as possible.

After trying to reach Baasee' several more times, she got out of the car and wobble-trotted around it in an effort to wake up. She glanced at her watch. "Six thirty in the morning?" She poked her head into the car to verify with the Passat's clock. "Baasee', I've been driving for over an hour. Where are you?" *~Where are you, Baasee'?~*

Deloo got back into the car and started to shake. At first, she shivered. Soon the shivers increased to the body-rattling convulsions of deep shock.

* * *

Despite having helped my granddaughter with the mortal a few hours earlier, I had not taken any of the mortal's vital signs. That's what granddaughters do. Besides, it wasn't the mortal that I located. I found her by discovering signs of Baasee' in the grey car her mortal drove. Baasee' had occupied the car as much as did the mortal. Once sure that I'd found the car, I watched my granddaughter's mortal from a borrowed position in Deloo's metaphysical environment. In case you think this is Baasee' writing again, it's not. I'm Grandfather Kwaikit. It has been more than two thousand years since I'd been with a mortal. I hesitated.

~Young Female,~ I commune-announced.

Deloo swiveled her head and slid her eyes toward the backseat. She didn't answer.

~Young Female,~ I tried again, this time showering her with feelings of powerful male protectiveness.

Deloo, raised by a mother and grandmother with little or no male input, bolted out of the car and ran a half-dozen steps. I realized that I had frightened her.

~Wait, Don't be afraid. I'm your spirit guide's grandfather. I'm looking for her.~

Deloo whipped around. Her eyes searched the air around the Passat, the highway, the turnout. Nothing. Her legs dragged with leaden fatigue.

This time, prepared for her kind of need for mothering rather than fathering, I surrounded her with the best I had in a mothering grip to keep her from falling. A man might have tried to escape the smothering. Deloo relaxed a little.

"Baasee'? Is that you?"

I spotted an incipient metaphysical tendril emerge along with trust and some sort of emotional starvation. I felt the same starvation. It welled in me along with immense pride that my granddaughter could generate feelings of comfort in others all the time.

~No. I'm not the gentle guide you seek. She is my granddaughter. I am looking for her.~

Something of my fear for Baasee's safety must have crossed the barrier between the small mortal and me. Deloo turned to stare at her car. Bright green shards of nameless light shot from her eyes.

"Where is she?"

~I don't know, Young Female,~ I bathed her with a sparkle of warm feelings and added to it a touch of humor in order to reduce her fear.

Deloo responded to the humor with another frisson of fear. Fear of me. She turned toward the truck at the end of the pull out in a slow sprint.

Alarmed at the foolishness of her reaction, I communed, *~don't wake him up. He's not the rescuing type.~*

I had already ascertained that Baasee's young mortal fit the truck driver's very crude erotic fantasies. He'd picked up many women of her age and size during the previous decade. None of them survived. I must have projected a psychic clue about him, for Deloo stopped. After a shiver raced along her back, she ran back to her vehicle and got in to twiddle with something in front of her. Panting, she tried to drive the car. It didn't work and shocked me, a man five decades older than Baasee' when she leaned against the steering wheel and recalled the man in the hotel and sobbed, "I thought he was Arthur, but he's not."

Automobiles and paved highways had not been among the luxuries of my last mortal's life, however widowhood and all of its versions I'm used to dealing with. Cars not. Nonetheless, it was time to bring myself up to speed.

~Please allow me.~ I offered despite my limited knowledge of car parts.

The car lumbered forward. Then backward. Then stopped.

Deloo once again jumped out of the car. This time she ran toward the one tree that managed to survive road construction. Reaching its leafy shelter, she caved into it. Tears gushed from her eyes and nostrils, but she stayed silent and alert.

I waited until her breathing slowed and communed, *~it's this way, Young Female. I need to find my granddaughter more than you do. She's got evidence.~*

Deloo forced her shoulder muscles to relax. "What do you mean? What happened to her?"

~It's about the people who have been chasing you. I was there when someone shot at you, and later when someone shot the door beside you. I'm certain that the second shot was fired by a different person or at least a different gun. Baasee' stayed there to find the slugs. It's time for us to find her, Young Female.~

"Stop calling me 'Young Female,' like that. I'm not a dog!"

~Agreed.~

She didn't respond.

~What shall I call you?~

Deloo hesitated and then communed, *~Deloo.~*

~What happened back there at the hotel?~

The story came out in staccato phrases. "Then someone shot at me."

~Had you reached the street by then?~

"No. We were still on the wall. I had to go back up. She was amazing when that happened. She made pegs out of air."

As Deloo told the story, I filled in the blanks with what I guessed my industrious granddaughter had done. My granddaughter has developed her own signature repertoire of goofiness. And dirty fighting.

Deloo continued, "It's something about the side of the hotel where I parked. I just did what she told me to do. I was too tired to ask any questions."

~Stay here while I investigate.~

"No. You're not going without me. I'm going with you."

We argued. I'm not a professional grandfather for nothing. I tricked Deloo into driving toward Montreal. I helped her remember how tired she was. Her eyelids grew heavy. I spotted a good place to hide. A wild thicket of willows filled one side of a safe turnout. I convinced her to tuck the Passat deep into the foliage. She was asleep almost before she shut off the engine.

* * *

~Hey! What's going on? Ming's gone but I know where to find her,~ the little ghost commune-quailed.

Against my better judgment, I dawned an austere wig in shades of platinum and silver. For good measure I opted for a black and lavender false eyelash and opened the magical space in which I had enclosed her. She peered out and ducked back in when Grandfather Kwaikit called.

My eyelash fell off. *~Where is Deloo?~*

~She's safe. Did you get the evidence?~

~Yes. The slugs came from two weapons.~ We talked about the small pool of suspects, but it could have been anyone. I thanked my grandfather and relayed the little ghost's information. He gave me Deloo's coordinates and left. Minutes later I located Deloo.

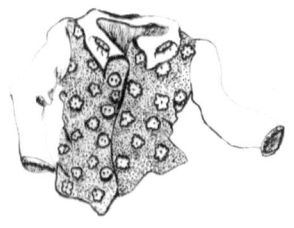

CHAPTER TWENTY-SEVEN

In another part of Canada, Howard waited for his sister, Lydia, to stop wheezing. She asked, "it's worse, isn't it?"

"Yes. The way I see it, he's going to kill someone before too long. He thinks that God comes to him to give him commands. Last night's shooting was just an example."

Lydia shook her head. "He shouted at me. Mother is too old to work with him. I told her he should be punished for his Canadian crimes."

"Good for you. Is he in jail?" Howard asked.

Lydia eyed her younger brother with curiosity. "I never know how to manage these discussions with you, Howard. No! They didn't charge any one. You know how he always comes across with sweet innocence. Mother says that it's time for me to handle the situation."

* * *

"Baasee'? Where have you been? What happened to that creepy guy? He said he was your father."

~My grandfather. Mind your tongue.~

~Is Deloo okay?~ The little ghost asked.

"Yes." Deloo answered. "I'm fine except for seeing another Arthur." She touched Arthur's camera as if to reassure herself that he was with her.

~I'm sorry. I used to see Qanik all the time. You'll stop seeing Arthur someday.~

While I helped Deloo make use of the cover of the willow branches to put on fresh clothes and clean up, I explained what had happened.

Deloo's stomach grumbled as if in agreement. She glanced at the Passat's clock, and said aloud. "It's getting late—almost nine thirty."

~Let's find you something decent to eat.~

"Anything but Chinese." She frowned at the rising sun. "I was heading for a place called Sud. I'm not sure what it is. It's got to be as big as the United States, though."

~Yes. It's time to face reality and go to safety.~ I explained to my mortal, *~In French Sud means south and South means safety to me. Let's go there.~* Deloo needed comfort and the shelter of people who could protect her and find out what was happening. Taale would protect her too, but didn't have as many resources as did the elder Mr. Goode in Cambridge. It was time for a spirit guide to make an executive decision.

"I'm not going there! I'm heading home to Mom."

~My child, we need to get help from your family in Cambridge. They'll know what to do. Your mother was right. We need to go back to the Boston area. She offered to join you, and after all the scrambling we've done since talking to her, I think we'd better find out more about the jacket. When it's a reasonable morning hour in Alaska, call her again to say you've changed your mind. Ask her to meet you in Boston. Maybe she can get there at the same time as we do.~

"You're right, Baasee'. We need to figure this out. Mom will help us, but I don't need to go back to Boston. We're hundreds of miles away from there."

The ashtray screaked open and a Loonie seemed to leap out of the bin and into her lap. A small piece of paper floated after it and also landed on Deloo's lap.

~What's that, my dear?~

Deloo glanced at the paper and tossed it to the passenger seat. "It's the credit card receipt for the hotel room."

I stared at the receipt as the metaphysical air around it burst into flames. Grandfather Kwaikit appeared before me.

~You must leave Canada now. Something about that piece of paper is going to destroy at least one life. Don't let it be hers.~ He disappeared.

~Deloo, you've got to go back to Boston. There's danger of a new and terrible kind awaiting you here.~

"Why? Because of that hotel?"

~Not the hotel exactly. It's because of that receipt. I don't know what it means, but using your debit card is going to damage someone's life. We don't have any time to waste. Drive out of Canada.~

Deloo turned right and then left, but muttered under her breath each time she turned. She kept turning until she saw a sign to the U.S. border.

~That's where we're going. Take that exit.~ I felt calm as I looked at

the sign, searched for the other car and smiled. *~You are safe for now.~*

Deloo followed signs to unknown destinations. A small town appeared with appealing signs that aimed south. I noticed, but Deloo didn't, that she kept turning into the lane on the left. Two nights with very little sleep had taken its toll on her driving ability.

~Deloo, it's time to stop and find out where we are. Take the next exit.~ I used my most authoritarian commune tone. It worked. She was getting used to being a soldier who obeys orders without argument. Soon we were driving through a pleasant town.

~I see a coffee shop on the right. Slow your vehicle now,~ I remarked.

"What? Where?" Deloo almost struck a pedestrian.

~I told you to go slow. See that parking lot on the right?~

Deloo nodded, mute and exhausted.

~Pull into it and park.~

She did as I instructed and turned off the engine.

I rose above Deloo for a look. There were lots of good prospects for a restorative breakfast. I was about to suggest that she walk along the street when I realized that she was already two doors away from me. She had spotted a tiny diner wedged between two stores and sauntered inside. I followed her, feeling foolish. After a couple of swallows of hot coffee and a bite of a bagel, she hiccoughed and sighed.

~This is what I needed.~ Deloo leaned back and smiled.

~Don't fall asleep,~ I grumbled. *~We've got a lot to do, such as finding out where we are. Could you go back to the car to look at the atlas? Or use that phone of yours? It's got maps, too.~* I wondered by I bothered with the latter. Deloo was still living in the twentieth century.

As if she heard me and finally balked at my criticism of her failure to use electronics, she pulled out her phone and dabbed at the screen with great speed. I'd watched her handling the phone a number of times with increasing envy. In short order we poured over a detailed map. A long strand of her glossy hair slid out from under her cap. She took off the cap, recoiled her hair, and sat back, leaving the cap on the table.

~You know the rules. Put on your cap.~

~Isn't this over yet? Why should I?~ She looked around the peaceable diner.

I'd been using my searching listening abilities and knew better. They were not near us, but several people were making active use of their own mortal skills to find my Deloo. *~It's not over, Deloo. We've got to keep you hidden.~*

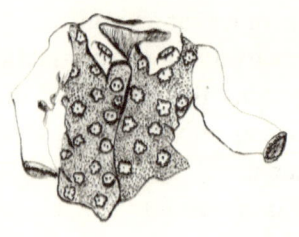

CHAPTER TWENTY-EIGHT

"We are wasting our time. I want to go home," Ming said between clenched teeth.

Chuan watched her without answering, wondering if her thoughts still moved the way his did, as they once did.

Ming swung her head toward Chuan, eyes enormous, pooled with lights he had seen in them before. "What if that Alaskan woman is after us herself? She keeps popping up all the time."

He stared at her, calculating what sort of response could bring either of them back to the old Harvard days when they still believed in Howard. He reached for her hand. She moved toward him and paused, hand poised. He closed his larger hand around it.

"That woman is part of all of this, too. Maybe she's the one who killed Rosemoira."

Ming yanked her hand back and shook her head. "No!" Ming took a deep, ragged breath, and stared at him. "She's not a killer. She's afraid of us after you shot at her. I didn't even know you had a gun, Chuan."

"Ming, ma belle, how I wish you'd never seen it. Remember what happened to Qanik? I've had the gun ever since then-for protection. He wanted out, too."

"Yes, I think about Qanik a lot." She wondered if her mother would find out something new. Ming heaved another deep sigh and straightened. "He didn't believe us when we warned him that you have to plan every detail of what you expect of them. We are, aren't we, Chuan? Planning?"

Chuan's eyes shifted to look at a building in the distance. He nodded. "Qanik didn't believe they are so focused on small details when I told him to be careful. That was a long time ago. He paid for his trust. I have gone over every penny and every move each of them makes. Howard was truthful back there in Amherst. His father keeps him in the dark about a lot of things. I am sure that I am the one who knows all of what goes on in the imperialist mind of Howard's father. We have to make sure that none of them can ever track us down the way they hunted for Qanik. I guess they didn't need to do as much work to get to Rosemoira."

Ming suppressed a shiver and sighed. "Let's go home."

"We've done all that we can tonight."

They walked back to the condo they were using for the first time in years. Their car glimmered under the street lights in its usual parking slot. Upstairs, Brent greeted them by opening the door as they mounted the last step. As with everything else about the two blond friends, Chuan discovered that if he placed anything in a different location, Brent became suspicious to the point of violence. As a result, Chuan and Ming were tidy. Likewise, Brent had locked everything he brought with him out of sight and tucked it in his bedroom. He was a large man compared to either Chuan or Ming, their dimensions came from their Chinese fathers and Inuit mother in Ming's case. Brent, by contrast, dominated the small room. In an effort to make light of his unexpected and unscheduled arrival, he made a mock bow with a big flourish. He was punctilious about who was to occupy the little condominium and precise about when any of them would arrive or depart. The quarters didn't seem to hold all of them at once.

Because Brent wanted to make sure that Howard didn't know about his secret talks with the Chinese couple, he had purchased the condo in Chuan's name and paid Chuan a generous annual maintenance fee to cover all costs, including the utilities. Since Chuan and Ming spent more and more time exclusively in China, it was a good arrangement for them all. Brent got the larger of the two bedrooms, while Ming and Chuan slept in the other. Brent always gave them a precise calendar of the days he would be there. Ming and Chuan tried to stay out of his way. When in Canada, Ming would arrange to visit her many Chinese and Inuit relatives in three provinces on his "in residence" days.

Neither Ming nor Chuan confided the location of their Chinese residence to anyone associated with Howard Lee's family. That included Brent.

"No worries. I'm awake." Brent got off his bed and walked into the narrow hall that led to their tiny bedroom. "Where've you been?"

"Chasing after that damned seventeenth jacket of yours. We almost caught her this time."

"Yeah? There's two of you and one of her. How'd she manage to get away this time?"

Chuan gave an abbreviated version.

"You'd better call Howard, then. Maybe he can trace her credit card to find out where she's gone." Ming squirmed. Brent studied her. "So, once again, no jacket and no money."

"Don't look at her, you scumbag!" Chuan shouted. "You are the one who makes twice as much as Ming and I together. You and Howard both have huge salaries while Ming and I make do by working in her father's restaurants. We might have shared a few things with each other, but you are the one who has kept my wife and me in poverty. You own this place, your home in Alaska, and two or three more houses that I don't know much about. Don't talk to me about lost money. Ming and I never got any of whatever it was you have stolen from my homeland!" He looked at Ming and nodded. Moving as one, they opened the door.

"Wait!" Brent said and then cursed. "You're right. Howard pays me a lot for what I do." He crossed the small space between himself and Chuan. "Come back in. Please."

In the first few years, the three would sit in this very room to pour over plans for their next excavation of the archaeological site in China. In those days, they would order in food and the three of them would talk long into the night. Back then they, at least Chuan and Ming did, believed that they were exploring unknown ancient ruins with Chinese graduate students who would someday carry on the excavation, leaving Brent and Howard to go back to North America with fond memories. Chuan looked at Ming and shrugged. She'd been telling him for years the dreamy days had ended. This was the first moment that Chuan felt it deep in his soul as well. Everything about the moment seemed much like the one when he spotted Howard coming out of a deteriorating building near the dig.

It happened just before the tenth archaeological field season was to begin. Howard was speaking to a man wearing a construction belt and carrying a clip board. In a few minutes, Chuan learned that Howard had just purchased the building. The man was a building contractor who had already renovated the two adjacent buildings to Howard's specifications. Both Howard and the contractor were pleased at their progress. During the afternoon of the day the scales fell away from Chuan's eyes, he learned that Howard had designated the renovated buildings to be part of the East entryway to the new palace.

"What new palace? Chuan asked, bewildered. Although he had been on the site for a decade, he'd never doubted Brent's statement that the provincial government owned their discoveries and would leave the dilapidated buildings to remind modern Chinese free men and women of the despicable era of imperial China. Howard cleared up Chuan's innocent misunderstanding by explaining that he had been buying as much of the land surrounding the ruins as possible as well as the land on which the ruins were located.

"Enemies robbed my family of their palace in the seventh century. My family and I are rebuilding the palace to honor," his smile was magnanimous, "our ancestors."

Young Chuan, the not-so-naïve Chuan stared at Howard, now aware of how the old rules of kinship had fooled him for so many years. He had ignored all of the many body signals broadcast by Howard and his family about class and rank. It made sense now: Capitalism, classism and deep-rooted issues of social politics. The Lees were living out the ideals of seventh century political schemers.

Chuan's father remained calm when he learned of the Lee family goals. Howard's father mandated the goals in a perfidious, selfish plan to rebuild the imperial palace. The elder Mr. Wu frowned and clapped a hand on his son's shoulder. "There's a reason his family was overthrown, my son. Perhaps we can find out more about those days," the older man said. "Otherwise, it's the way of our world." He gestured to the west where the coastal cities had become eyesores in obeisance to tourism. "The poor have remained poor, and the old ruling families continue to wait for their turn to come again."

* * *

A world and two decades later, Howard sat in his home office in Montreal the next morning to deal with Chuan's call. The office smelled of sandalwood, which he had been burning, hoping to restore some element of inner harmony. He felt a strong urge to sit on the floor to ground his thoughts and did. What did it all mean anymore? His slanted eyes moved around the office with the usual distaste. If it hadn't been for Luisa and everything Luisa meant to him, he would have walked out of the bank and away from his family and never returned. He wondered why he had not done so years ago, when his father asked him to find a herbal remedy for his recurring hives. Howard did so, pleased to sooth his parent. Chinese herbal medicine fulfilled his inner being. He asked for permission to seek formal education in that area, but his father refused to fund yet another degree. He lifted himself from the floor in a single fluid movement. He used to care about grace.

"Got to get to work," he muttered. Now it was time to close every other thought and concentrate on the task in front of him.

Howard spent ten minutes creating and rehearsing the story he would tell the Québec hotel manager and dialed the number. The manager's voice sounded bored, but Howard proceeded with his planned lie. His delivery was unctuous. He provided each of the few facts he knew about the grieving widow, Mrs. Goode, with an appropriate attitude of sympathy and concern for her welfare. He wanted to know if there had been any further charges to her room. As a branch bank manager and old friend of the Goode family, Howard gave them his credit card and asked them to reverse the previous charges. When asked if the hotel manager could fax him Mrs. Goode's billing information and proof that the payment was being reversed from her credit card, Howard purred his gratitude and provided a fax number. He had already rigged his equipment to make it seem as if the fax machine was located in Cambridge, Massachusetts, in his office of the bank rather than four blocks away from the gay hotel. Fifteen minutes later Howard chuckled to see Mrs. Deloo Goode's full debit card number and a home address in Cambridge, Massachusetts.

* * *

Ever since Deloo had received the debit card from her father-in-law, my sources had provided me with endless stories of graft and corruption about thieves who stole both identities and money from people with debit or credit cards. And now I received the worst possible news from the Invisible Forces. Deloo had joined the legions of such victims. I didn't waste any time. With a flicker of golden urgency, I rattled around Deloo, *~they have your debit card information. They got it from the Montreal hotel just as I thought they might. It won't take long before they track you to here. On the plus side, we are still ahead of them.~*

Agitated, Deloo stared around as if the perpetrators were in the coffee shop. Seeing no one, she muttered, "I need to get some bobby pins" The waitress came to the table and lifted an inquiring brow.

"Coffee?"

Deloo shook her head and, despite all the information supplied by her smart phone, asked, "How long does it take to drive to Vermont?"

"You are about an hour and a half from Burlington."

"Do you mean the Burlington of Burlington Coat Factory?" Deloo asked, picturing a smoke-filled industrial town.

The waitress shrugged. "I don't go there for coats. My boyfriend takes me to see the lake. It's pretty."

"Lake?" Deloo's smooth forehead wrinkled.

"Lake Champlain. It's huge. You will love it."

Deloo thanked the server, paid cash for her meal, and left the diner. In the car, she used the paper atlas to find a map of Burlington, Vermont.

I approved. *~That's ideal. It's so out of the way, no one would guess where you are.~*

~How close are they? ~ Deloo communed, fingering an invisible bump on her chin.

Unlike yesterday, when finding an answer to such questions had taken all my resources, I got answers from the Invisible Forces almost before she conceived of them. To me it was proof the situation had become deadly. *~They are still in Montreal.~*

Deloo had already pulled onto the street and soon we were on a small country road that promised to take us to the U.S. border in Vermont. "You mean we could stay in Canada instead of heading south? Let's turn around."

~It's not simply you, but the debit card receipt that forces you to leave. The pair who've been tracking you are still in Montreal. Someone else in their gang is now in Massachusetts. There are too many of them against one little you.~

"Baasee', what would you do if you were in my place right now?"

Using my ordinary emotional sensors, I detected that she felt both oppressed as well as an unexpected trust in my advice.

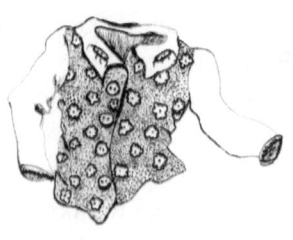

CHAPTER TWENTY-NINE

Hoping to strike the right note with Deloo, I hedged, *~are you asking what I did in similar situations when I was a mortal?~*

"Yes. Baasee' ere you ever chased by strangers when you were my age?"

If there is a way to laugh with a mortal while both invisible and silent, I managed it. Deloo smiled.

~Yes, but there is no easy way to compare your life to mine. My era was one of constant danger from both kinds of humans as well as other predators. My mother started training me to hunt as soon as I could walk. My first kill, which means I produced a dead animal or bird that I could share with other people, was an opossum that I stabbed to death when I was eighteen months old. My mother must have caught it in a snare when it was barely alive. All I had to do was poke it to finish its life.~

"Did you mean eighteen years or eighteen months?" Deloo asked in amusement.

~Months. That was a typical learning age for us. The sooner the better. Learning to hunt at a young age still happens in the wild areas of your world. People learn to take care of themselves because you never know what will happen tomorrow. Okay, back to me. My mother died when I was less than three years old. That was when my grandfather took me to a woman who lived in the southern part of Zana. She raised me. By the time I was four, my adoptive mother depended on my hunting skills for half of her rations and all of my own.~

"Wow!" No longer sleepy, Deloo's mood had changed from sullen to cheerful in less than a mile. "What about people chasing you, though? Did that ever happen to you?" Arthur's ever-present camera vibrated as if matching Deloo's curiosity.

~Yes, but I was more often the hunter than the hunted. By the time I was your age, I had killed fifteen men.~

"Fifteen?!" Deloo gaped. I could feel the thrill of movie-horror travel through her body.

~Yes, ~ I communed. *~The first time was when I was thirteen and a gang of three men tried to waylay my adoptive mother. Her name was Kesani. I was already a skilled Tuudzaado-that means Shadow People-hunter. I was less than half Tuudzaado myself. The most important of these skills was to keep a mental connection with my family. The Tuudzaado way calls for focusing on the auras around us. The writing world doesn't try to teach its young how to use aura as a learning device because many mortals don't have it. It's something like what I'm using to see you right now. As a living and breathing half-breed I did not have all the Tuudzaado skills to work with aura, but enough. My mother and grandfather could hear sounds that I couldn't. Sounds and smells were colors to them, but not me. Even so, I figured out something that worked. I always had a direct connection with both my grandfather and Kesani, my adoptive mother.~*

"That's incredible. I wish I could do that with my mother."

~Speaking of your mother, you need to call her right away.~

Deloo took a sharp breath. I knew that I had brought her back to the core of her fears. She rallied and glanced at the car's clock. "Yes, Baasee'. You're right, but it's eight o'clock in the morning here. That means it's four in the morning in Fairbanks. I'll have to wait until we've got a little farther along the way, maybe after we cross the border." She drove in silence for a few minutes, and then remembered my story. "So, what happened to your mother?"

~My own mother died after a long illness. I don't know what killed her. I was just a toddler when it happened.~ I thought about the scrapbook of metaphysical images of Mother that I have and continued, *~She would have been fifteen on her next birthday if she had lived that long. I wished I could still have the direct mental communication with my mother as I had when I was a baby, but that ended when she died.~* I stopped communing to muse about my mother's short life.

"Baasee'?" I could tell by her worried tone that she had been trying to get my attention. Her ring was fidgety, casting dozens of dragon images around me. I set off a cascade of sparks.

~I'm sorry, my dear,~ I apologized. *~I was daydreaming. What did you say?~*

"You were telling me about an attack on your adoptive mother," Deloo prompted. "What happened to her?"

~Oh, yes. Sorry. You mean Kesani. Well, it's a long story that I'll make short. Many years before I was born, my grandfather moved Kesani to the northwestern point of the catacombs that we, the Tuudzaado, occupied. We were surrounded by enemies. They knew about us but did not know the catacombs existed. They were always on the lookout for us and somehow figured out that Kesani had something to do with us.~

"Why?"

~She was born to one of their women, you see, and looked like them. She was short like they were, not tall like Grandfather. Her father was Tuudzaado. She could commune. Kesani and I were always in perfect commune mode together. We were both half-breeds. Neither one of us could see the colors that sound makes to Grandfather Kwaikit, but we could hear sounds that the Tuudzaado and others couldn't. Aura is visible to me in the ocular way now that I am a spirit. I couldn't see any of it when I was still alive As soon as she realized that I could hear what she did, even if we were a few miles away from it, she trained me to listen her way. That made her perfect as a Tuudzaado spy and perfect as my new mother. Okay, so back to the first time I killed someone. When I was thirteen, I was out hunting when Kesani communed an alarm that three men had seen her coming out of the catacombs and were chasing her. They were almost upon her.~

~My grandfather, also in commune mode, signaled to me that he was about ten kilometers away. I was two or three kilometers away-in the opposite direction from the enemies, but twice as far from Kesani as were they. I don't know how I did it, but I covered that distance in less time than it took the three men to encircle her.~

I paused to remember how it happened. *~It was the first time I ever used the warrior training that my grandfather had taught me. Before any of them touched Kesani, I was on them. One by one they lay dead on the ground. Kesani watched it all. Although I did the killing, I didn't know what I was doing. I was in a daze when it happened.~*

~Over the next three years until Kesani died, she told every single Tuudzaado person she knew about my exploits of that day. That's how I learned I bludgeoned the first one with my fists by pummeling him so fast that he fell without a struggle. The other two were more prepared. I had to hit each of them with a big stick I found nearby. Their heads were bloody and broken in.~

"Holy cow!" Deloo breathed. "Did anyone bother her after that?"

I thought about Kesani's life. Although she was very proud of me, the horror of that day seemed to drain the life-force out of her. Never again did she have enough strength to go out of the catacombs. She depended on Grandfather and me to do all the hunting.

Struggling with a tumble of memories, I communed, *~No. They left her alone after that. I made sure that they stayed away from her part of the catacombs by hanging their bodies by the feet along the way between their village and us.~*

"Shut my moose mouth! What kept them from knowing where the catacombs were?"

~For one thing, they didn't have the commune power. We were careful to stay out of sight as much as possible. We Shadow people hunted and traveled at night. It just happened that Grandfather Kwaikit and I were coming back from journeys during daylight. Our way was to stay in the shadows, but on that day, Grandfather ran all the way in plain view. I'm sure our enemies saw him, but they didn't try to follow. That's because the Tuudzaado always cut out the hearts of enemies they killed.~

~That night while I hung their bodies along the trail, Grandfather smeared the bloody pulp of their hearts on the front flaps of each man's house. Between that and their bodies hanging right outside their village compound along that trail, none of them ever strayed toward the northwest side of the catacombs again. It was gruesome, but an effective message.~

* * *

Deloo slowed the car to a crawl and said, "We're at the border already."

We had been traveling through a bird sanctuary. Deloo pulled over to get her passport ready for the U.S. Customs. She lowered the window before driving forward when the ashtray squeaked open. A large raven dropped onto the hood of the car. I could see it was a male and I used my powers to discern that he was a little older than average. The raven opened his wings and hopped closer to Deloo's side of the windshield.

"Blood, yours or his. It doesn't matter. You must fight," the raven squawked.

Talons scratching, the raven skittered backward, gave a one-eyed stare to Deloo, and lifted up and out of Deloo's line of sight. A scrap of bright fabric dropped from his talons. Deloo gaped as a tiny puff of black smoke curled out of the cloth and disappeared. The ashtray lid screaked shut.

"Am I crazy? Did that raven just talk to me?"

~Yes. He spoke in English. It was important, but no time for that now. Look sharp. The Customs agent is signaling you to come forward.~

In a few minutes, we were in the United States again and on our way toward Burlington. "Baasee', what does it mean? 'Blood, yours or his?' Is that a Dire Warning?"

I peered at her aura. It was like a small volcano of bubbling lava. Great Aunt Pauline often used the phrase, 'Dire Warning,' to explain messages from nature, such as that of a meddling raven. *~Yes. That's what it was. When a sacred warning comes to you, it's important to re-member it with precision. You left out the ending. He also said 'It doesn't matter. You must fight.'~*

"But I don't know how to fight, Baasee'. What does that mean?"

~What? Tomboy Deloo beat up just about every kid in Fairbanks. You don't need any instructions from me. If you are asking me to teach you to drive like a maniac and scare the puss out of every pimple on somebody's head, you don't need me for that either. All that raven meant is to be ready to fight to the end-and you always did that in school. You'll have to do it again. Are you ready?~

Whack! The touchy ashtray jarred the air with another of its sudden openings. This time the Loonies stayed put, but radiated a fiery burst of lights. Arthur's camera, leaning into Deloo, vibrated its agreement.

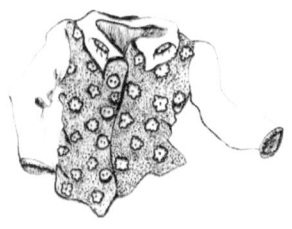

CHAPTER THIRTY

"What's the matter?" Deloo grumbled and pushed the ashtray lid closed. "Are you trying to make a Dire Warning, too?" she said with forced indifference, "Let's get out of here."

We moved toward Burlington with so little trouble that when the town came into view, both Deloo and I were surprised. "Look at this, Baasee'," Deloo glanced at the clock on the dashboard. "It's ten o'clock and we're already here."

~Is it too soon to call your mother? Ask her to meet us in Boston.~

"Mom?" She did a little mental arithmetic and said, "It's way too soon. Mom would not appreciate me calling her at six a.m., even though I am her favorite child."

I responded, *~you are her only child.~*

Deloo frowned, spun the loose wedding ring on her hand and argued, "I'm still not sure why you want her to come all the way to Boston. Why not use the phone instead?"

I wafted a series of different shades of forgiveness around Deloo, *~I didn't realize that I had forgotten to tell you why I would like your mother to meet with us in person. She's the one who made the jacket. She would know all about the little details that she put into it—things that she doesn't bother to mention. We need to know what there is about this one that doesn't show on the surface. Also, there's something interesting about the woman who owns that store. I want your mother to tell us more about her. Earlene Somebody went to see the Canadian people. Why? ~*

By the time I finished communing, Deloo arrived in the center of town and found herself plummeting toward Lake Champlain on a steep, narrow street. "I think I'll find a place to park before we do anything else," she muttered. In a few minutes, she entered a short maze of streets that ended at the verge of the lake where she found a convenient parking place. She rummaged for her smart phone and said, "I need to find a hotel."

~*You need a hotel with covered parking, just in case our pursuers ever leave Montreal and decide to come in this direction.*~

Deloo looked skyward, "We should have waited on that side of the border until we knew what they were up to and then headed up to Alaska."

I sighed-ish, once again regretting the limitations of working with such a young and irritating mortal. I regarded her with mixed emotions. ~*Just because that pair hasn't moved YET doesn't mean your troubles are over. We need to get to the bottom of this business. Now find a hotel with a covered garage!*~

Something about my outrage converted to amusement in Deloo's mind and she burst into laughter. "All right, all right. Let me take a look." She fiddled with icons on the phone for a while and showed me the one that looked the best. "How about this one?"

~*Perfect,*~ I carped, ~*call them.*~

Deloo keyed the hotel's telephone number, made a reservation and got directions. "Check-in is not for another two hours, but they said I could get in now. It's not far from here." She yawned. "I wish I could stay here a couple of days. I need to get a real night's sleep."

I did a quick mental calibration, decided not to query my higher sources on such a simple matter, and agreed. ~*You are right, Young One. It's time to rest and restore. This beautiful city is a wonderful place to do just that. Before you go anywhere, please call that hotel to see if they can give you a room for three nights.*~ I was thinking about her health when I should have been thinking about her entire situation.

Deloo didn't do any thinking other than making sure Arthur's camera was fitted safely inside her jacket. Instead, her eyes took in the lapping waves of Lake Champlain and she asked for three nights at the hotel. When she got the answer we both wanted and needed, she touched the 'end' key and smiled. "It's all set. I feel like I've won a big prize. Thanks, Baasee'!"

~*You are welcome.*~ I buffed her with a shimmer of gold energy to let her know I loved her.

As soon as Deloo dropped her suitcase onto the luggage carrier in her lake-view hotel room, sleepiness overpowered her. For my part, I needed some time to do a little research on this widespread band of scoundrels.

~My dear, why don't you lie down for a short nap before you go to lunch? It will do you a world of good.~

Deloo toppled onto the bed and tugged the bedspread over her shoulders. She was asleep before I could remind her to cover her feet. Just as well, since my efforts to find our pursuers proved successful.

* * *

Once upon a time, such as on that night back in China ten years earlier, Ming had tried to comfort her husband about Howard's wrong way of seeing the world. She failed because Canada had molded her with a very different sense of freedom and equality than Chuan's. As an art historian and architect, she was eager to see a newer model of an old imperial palace. She had no cultural place in her mind for the importance of the three Chinese revolutions of the twentieth century or of the improvements that communism promised China.

Instead, Chuan had turned to Brent, who did understand. He told Chuan the right things at the right moments in stilted Mandarin. Brent couldn't change Howard, but at least he understood what had happened to Chuan's broken ideals about clan brotherhood. Thereafter, Chuan watched Brent with mixed suspicion and admiration as the archaeologist continued to excavate the centuries old palace site. Over the ensuing years, Chuan heard many a proud northern Chinese family thank Brent for mentoring their son or daughter through the rigors of academic research and writing. No matter what else Brent might be under the surface, dozens of Chinese youth had earned all of the rights and opportunities of competitive doctoral degrees thanks to Brent's demanding standards in Archaeology. Chuan took pride in his own part in educating a new generation of northern Chinese scholars about the intricacies of computer science as well as advanced uses for ancient mathematical logic.

That was a long time before this evening in Montreal where Brent backed toward the couch and sat. "I knew you must be wondering after our meeting in Amherst the other day. Howard called for that one, by the way.

Ming relented a little and sat on the couch beside Brent while Chuan stood with his back against a wall. "Like Chuan said, Mrs. D. Goode with her hideous jacket almost killed us." She eyed Brent, wondering how she could ever have admired his electric blue eyes. "You didn't tell us about the danger of getting that damned jacket for you." She wanted to add, 'you didn't tell us someone would kill Rosemoira.'

Chuan pulled a kitchen chair from the dining area and straddled it as he usually did. "You didn't tell us that Howard had anything to do with the jacket either. What's going on?"

"Slow down," Brent complained, his face creased by sun and worry. Ming noted with mixed feelings that he was showing his age more than ever. He put an arm around her shoulders. She shrugged him off. "All right. You're right. Howard is very involved with that beaded jacket. More than that, I think he's involved with malicious death related to the jacket."

"I thought so!" Ming looked at Chuan and asked, "Did he kill our friend over a jacket?"

Brent shrugged. "Rosemoira is dead. She was my friend, too. I think Howard did it."

"Why would he kill her? It could have been you." Ming asked, keeping her mouth shut about Rosemoira calling her that afternoon, just hours before she died.

"We've all spent a fair amount of time with her at that inn," Brent agreed. "In fact, that's where I've lived most of these past months."

Chuan met Ming's eyes. "She was like family for two decades. How do you know it was Howard who killed her? Why shouldn't we think it was you?"

Brent shook his head, "I heard two people arguing. An hour or so later she was dead."

Chuan frowned. "About the jacket? Howard may be a money-grubbing capitalist, but he doesn't strike me as a killer. What could she have done to him?"

Brent looked at his old friend and said, "We've all known each other over two decades. Why wouldn't he? He's a man of many parts. Besides, I don't know if he can cook. I could smell the Chinese food all the way upstairs. Made my tonsils beg for a bite."

Ming suppressed a grin and glanced at Chuan. "We've all tasted your Kung Pao Chicken. You're the only person I know who can make everything taste like a hamburger with fries."

The three of them fell into silence. After a while Brent asked, as if to open a new line of thought, "Chuan, I have forgotten how you hooked up with Howard."

"I was one of the security guards at a credit union when I was an undergraduate. Howard was in middle management at the same place. It was a shock when one day the blond-haired American told me about his Chinese family. After a few days, Howard offered me an all-expense paid trip to China in exchange for transporting a fancy vase some rich dude bought and wanted to make sure it came to Boston in one piece. Howard was the front man with the suit. I was in a rented uniform. When we got back a week later, Howard paid me two grand extra. We did it a couple more times. We used to talk a lot together.

Ming laughed, "I came in when you and Howard were trying to figure out how to plan a small dig in a city where Chuan's family lives. It required skills in architecture."

Chuan rubbed her head. She stiffened and then leaned into him. "We were pathetic. I suppose if either Howard or I had learned architecture, we would have known to look for plumbing the way you do, my precious wife. We wouldn't have needed you."

"How did you meet Howard, Ming?" Brent asked.

"Let's see. I was fresh out of a little northern Québec town when Harvard accepted my application for an M.A. I went to a Boston temp agency looking for work with any contractor who would hire an architectural student. Howard wanted to add on a room, and a contractor hired me to design the space. Even back then Howard had fancy digs. He still lives there. One day he wanted to talk about an all-expense paid trip to China. That's when I met Chuan."

"And the rest is a story made in heaven," Brent quipped.

"Yes. Around then Howard got on with the bank he's working for now. There was another pick-up job like the first one he and I did," Chuan said. "I went with him. The thing we brought back was an ancient jade sculpture. I recognized the style as being from my father's part of China. I showed him a photo of others like it. That's when Howard said we should get an archaeologist to help find more. He started looking for a graduate student who might be looking for a leg up. He went through four others before we found you."

"I never heard that part of the story," Brent raised a quizzical brow"

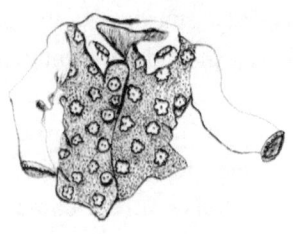

CHAPTER THIRTY-ONE

Chuan felt restraints on his arms and legs. Somewhere a man with a rich basso voice chanted, using nasalized head tones to add rhythm much like a drum. A woman sang words that sounded like bird calls. The chanting formed more bonds around him. The man's voice began to eat Chuan's heart. The woman's endless song penetrated his lungs, preventing him from shouting for help. In desperation he focused on his chi, forcing a boundary between the perverse vocals and him.

Drenched in sweat, he awoke. Ming was staring at him. Her fingers stroked his hair.

"What happened? What did you hear?"

Panting a little, Chuan told her about his dream. She asked him to describe the song. "It was like the wedding song your mother and her cousin composed for us. Sort of." Chuan pulled her onto their bed and watched his wife.

"Why are you smiling?"

"Because you want us to be the way we used to be. That's what that vision was about." Ming smiled, sighed, and got out of bed. After talking well into the late morning hours, they had run some errands and then come back to the condo.

Brent left a note on the refrigerator: "Heading out.'" She glowered at Chuan. "What does he mean?"

* * *

Deloo awoke. She lay still and asked, "Where am I?"

~You are in Vermont, safe and sound on June eighth. We are in a good hotel.~

Deloo sat on the edge of the bed and shook her head. "For a moment I thought I was with an Asian man and woman. He looked old enough to be my father. I sort of know who he is, which is impossible! I never knew my father except for what Mom told me about him. She said he was a white man from Kansas—not an Asian guy."

I knew her father's ancestry was of central Europe, not Asia, and that he had dumped her mother much as he had dumped a load of semen into her vagina, totally without a sense of commitment to her. I rolled my fabulous adorned ocular sensors and explained, *~you were not dreaming. You had a vision, and the two people in your vision are the same people who've been chasing us—Prize Woman and her husband.~*

Deloo sat up and gazed around as if hoping to get a look at me and asked in a blurry commune, *~why did I have such a vision? ~*

I had followed the vision. They were many miles to the north of us, still in Montreal. I answered her, *~it may have been another kind of Dire Warning. We'll learn more in good time.~*

Deloo stared at the wall and communed with impatience, *~why don't you know the facts of all these things? Why do you have to guess just like me? You've got all those powers. Why, Baasee'?~*

Peevish, I hesitated, remembering that I had conveyed very little about my powers or gifts since that first rush out of the Secret Spirit Inn in Nova Scotia and all that had happened since then. I began with a typical lesson, *~I am not all knowing. I'm human just as you are. I learn things one at a time just as you do. I do have powers that you don't have, and I use them well, but they are limited to where and how I direct the energy.~*

Deloo lay back on the pillow and thought about the couple in the vision. *~That woman seems familiar. It's as if I have met her somehow. She seems nice.~*

I sent a shower of sparks toward her, simulating a quirked brow. *~Even though you realize that she's Prize Woman—the one who chased you through that hotel in Montreal and may have shot at you?~*

Deloo continued, *~I mean, she's an ordinary person who wants to have a good marriage. She has nice thoughts.~*

Unobserved, the little ghost took note of the positive trend in comments about her twin sister. Having learned one of the key ways to hide her thoughts from spirits like me, she spun out of my way and continued to think about Deloo's vision.

Meanwhile, I, the lovely Baasee', thought about the woman who had been running Deloo to earth and grimaced. *~Nice thoughts? No. We have a problem to solve, and correct observation is a key part of solving the issue of why people are after you. Those two people have tracked* *you with extraordinary skill and perseverance. They are your enemies. 'Nice' is not how they have treated you.~*

Deloo whispered, "You're right, Baasee'. I didn't think of that." She sighed and fell into a deep sleep.

I communed to her sleeping mind, *~I'm not angry with you, Deloo. I want everything to work out for you.~*

The little ghost, feeling the weight of being alone, thought *~Ming is all I have.~*

* * *

The woman at the concierge desk recommended walking along Church Street to find a good Burlington lunch spot. Deloo enjoyed the walk until she reached up. *~I forgot my cap.~*

~I am sure we are safe for the moment. Don't worry. Why don't you buy a sun hat?~ Meanwhile I rose to the third story level above her on Church Street where I could almost see the University of Vermont above us.

Deloo moseyed up the busy street, picking up speed as her zeal for exploration expanded. In the next few minutes Deloo darted into several stores and stopped at one with a large array of summer hats. She picked one with bright stripes and whimsical flowers.

I floated far above her, enjoying the power of height: high enough to collide with a large raven. The raven squawked and something fell out of its beak. The bird dove after it.

So did I. Victorious, I snatched the rag from the raven's talons. The raven screeched in fury and flew at me as if to rip me to shreds. He might have been capable of doing so, since he could see me; however, I danced beyond his reach.

~Baasee'!~ Deloo communed at me. *~Are you doing something to that poor bird? Hutlanee! Shame on you.~*

I laughed and let the fabric float. It landed in Deloo's hand. *~Did you see me?~*

~No, I didn't see you,~ Deloo replied. She glanced at the wisp of cloth in her hand. *~Look! This is like the kite we saw back in Nova Scotia. This is a part of a dragon's muzzle.~* She pointed to a flared nostril and a curl of smoke just above it.

~Symbol of Chinese power,~ I mused. *~Hutlanee indeed. Now, how did you know it was me up there?~*

Deloo chuckled and looked upward. The raven was gone. *~That raven was attacking something invisible. Who else could it have been? Come on. I've got a call to make.~* As we made our way along Church Street toward the hotel, I noticed a man following us. When I swooped toward him for a closer inspection, all I regarded was a shock of blond hair on a tall body disappearing into a brick building.

~Did you see...~ I began, but by then Deloo had reached the hotel, unaware of me. When I caught up with her, she was seated in a comfy chair in our room, tapping Taale's number. After a few minutes, she glowed with contentment and disconnected.

"Mom knew I needed her. She guessed I'd do as she said: head back to the Goode's. She's already made arrangements with the university." Taale worked for the University of Alaska Fairbanks in the library building on the main campus. "She said she hoped I would call today because they approved her for two weeks off beginning next Monday. She's going to find a flight to join me in a week. By then we'll be back at the Goode's house."

Even as she spoke, I received information that would change everything. Someone named Howard had called Chuan. I recalled the raven's words: "Blood, yours or his. It doesn't matter. You must fight." Even as I recalled the raven I heard something else with my spirit-guide ears. It took me a while to understand the words from a conversation far away. Two people, maybe three, exchanged a lot of meaningless numbers about Deloo's debit card along with a good deal of extraneous information that would take a while to pull apart.

"All right," one of them said in Mandarin. "I've got what I need. We'll be ready soon." I perceived an image of a small appliance. What did he mean? What did it do?

I broke into Deloo's thoughts. *~This is important.~* I told her what I knew.

Deloo looked toward a corner of the ceiling where she thought I might be lurking. "Aren't we in the clear? They can't find us here in Vermont. They're in Canada."

I wasn't ready to agree. While I couldn't imagine how they could find us in the picturesque town of Burlington, I regretted asking Deloo to make a reservation for three nights. *~I think it's time for us to study what I just received. I know I've missed something important.~*

Something about my words hit her wrong. Deloo leaped out of the hotel chair and assumed a natural warrior stance. She looked around the hotel room with hyper-alert eyes. She startled me by saying aloud, "I think I'm going crazy. There's no one here. There's no one who can harm me in this place."

~Deloo,~ I was tentative. I knew she had to work out what was happening in her own way. On another day I would have dealt with Deloo's reaction over a few days, but we were in serious trouble now. We had minutes, maybe hours. Not days. I couldn't stop her natural human emotions. I felt waves of distrust rolling from her mind and merging with an irrepressible sadness on my part. I pushed away my emotions. Although her sudden change of mood left me feeling alone and brought out dark feelings I had long suppressed, I also sympathized with her. She had been through a lot in the past five days since the now dead innkeeper almost assaulted her over the beaded jacket. Added to that were the two inexplicable, dangerous chases in New Brunswick and Québec. It was no wonder that Deloo was reacting with so much alarms.

Deloo paused and took another deep breath before sitting again. From her silent thoughts I knew she was testing herself, half hoping that the chases had been self-induced nightmares. I sent her a subliminal reminder about the crazy way she had turned the tables on her pursuers the first time.

~They are criminals, real criminals,~ I mused. *~I am real. The danger that you are in is real. We cannot get much help from official places such as the police. Most police forces have too many cases with bloodier crimes that are visible and in a single national legal system. We are dealing with both the United States and Canadian police, and no crime has been "seen" by any of them at this time. Even the death at the Secret Spirit Inn is not our affair. We are going to have to do the work ourselves. Are you ready to deal with that?~*

Deloo examined the hotel room with great care. "I wish I could see you. I wish I had some way to know for sure that you exist, and that I haven't lost my mind."

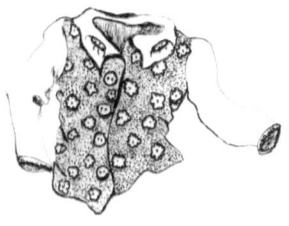

CHAPTER THIRTY-TWO

At last, Deloo made a request that I, a spirit guide, could handle. As she spoke, I willed her legs to move to the right and one step closer to the bed. When she was in the right position, I granted her wish. I'd done it countless times to other mortals, mortals who also didn't know how to give me or any other spirit credit for existing. *~As your saying goes, Beloved, be careful what you wish for.~* I nudged her along the back of her legs. The sensation, as always, made well-conditioned muscles react by bending at the knees. She stepped forward with her left foot. When she lifted the right foot, I stopped it in midair and used a puff of energy on her left shoulder. She toppled onto the bed.

Surprised, Deloo picked herself off the bed. It was enough to make her wonder. "What just happened?" She asked.

~It's what I have done with you a couple of times when you were about to take a wrong step. Remember that miraculous moment when you almost fell in front of a fast-moving car in Albuquerque? It wasn't exactly the same maneuver, but close. You would have been killed if I hadn't moved you aside—which I just did here. It's easy and foolproof. Remember?~ I sent a breeze toward her hair to lift it and keep it up.

Deloo tried to push the strand back where it belonged and thought about that day in Albuquerque. "How could I forget? I didn't see the car myself, but Arthur did. I heard him shout just as my ankle twisted on the edge of the curb. I started falling. He was too far away to catch me. But I thought he did. I felt his arms yanking me up and back to the sidewalk. The next thing I knew, there I was on a park bench with a dozen people crowded around. Afterward Arthur told everyone he met about seeing a miracle. He said an invisible something lifted me onto the sidewalk. He said it almost made him want to join a church." She patted Arthur's camera case that hung around her neck.

"It was you who lifted me, wasn't it, Baasee'?"

~Yes, it was. And you are welcome for the proof as well as for the miracle. Remember, I have to follow the rules about using mystic powers on mortals. The main one is, if the mortal can't do it herself, I can't do it for her. In other words, you could have saved your own life if I had already taught you the trick. Now, let's get busy. Here's what I've got.~ We spent the next hour going over the message that I received about someone named Howard and the man we fled in Montreal, Chuan. *~It's obvious they work together.~*

Tired, Deloo said, "I think we've done as much damage to that message as possible, but what about the people? This Howard guy—what does he do?"

~As far as I can tell, he works in a bank where he has an office. He might be an account manager. He might be the president of the bank. I get the impression that he's also a thief and that Chuan and Prize Woman are part of his ring of thieves.~

"Don't you think that calling him a thief is going too far? What evidence do we have of that?" Deloo glanced out the window. "Look, Baasee', the wind has picked up. I think it's going to rain. It's getting dark. What time is it?" She got her pajamas out to go to bed.

My view of the world is almost a mirror image of what Deloo sees. But while she sees the things that are close to her, I perceive the backsides of them as if reflected in a very unusual mirror. *~Now it's time for me to use my ancient wisdom of human nature to answer your questions. First, the weather: it's going to change. Second, I know they are thieves rather than honest people because they have followed you for little reason. Worse, I'm certain one of them caused the death the innkeeper in Nova Scotia. One of them has already shot at you. I wish I knew it if was Chuan or Prize Woman or some unrelated stranger.~*

~Those who end other people's lives operate with their own rules, rules that aren't like yours, rules that make sense to themselves. Since some of them are also people of the Chinese dragon, we have to consider that they operate with one of the many sets of Asian rules about taking human lives. Let's hope that since you don't know what happens to an ordinary person after they kill another, and that my long existence will give us enough clues to figure out who it is before he or she comes after you again.~

"Did that happen to you, Baasee'? You must have crossed that barrier yourself."

~You are very astute, Deloo. I became a different person on that day. Grandfather Kwaikit warned me to take time to pray to the Invisible Forces. He said that warriors always suffer in ways that other people cannot understand. I did both: I suffered and I prayed. In the end, I took my own life to save the lives of people I loved. I was granted the right to become a spirit guide for someone as pure as you are because I prayed to honor the suffering I face.~

Depressed, I fell silent, wanting to escape the whirl of notions that enveloped me. I watched Deloo finish bathing, checked on the little ghost and waited for answers that have never come. I always seem to have to manufacture them myself.

Long after they fell silent, the little ghost hummed a non-tune to cover her thoughts from Baasee'. Asian rules about killing Asians? I'm half Chinese. Was I murdered? Were there rules about doing in a half-breed like me?

June eighth darkened. Five days ago Deloo started communing with me. Five days and one year ago, she had been a happy bride to a man I urged her to marry. Now, she was the target of inexplicable harassment. I found myself sinking into deep depression triggered by having to reveal my ancient history to someone as young as Deloo. She couldn't understand how I could both hate the men who were intent on killing my adoptive mother as well as grieve for their immortal souls. The weight of telling her that I had killed those three men brought me straight back to that distant time. I didn't want to be with the little ghost, either.

I felt myself spiraling out of control even as Deloo went through her cleansing ritual and crawled into the comfortable hotel bed. By the time she was nesting in her sheets, I was wrestling with the demons that had tormented me since I was thirteen—the day I took three human lives. Because of my depressed condition, I did not notice the incoming alert from the Invisible Forces about the approach of Chuan and Ming.

I longed to talk to Grandfather Kwaikit who always knew how to help me through my unrest. It had been such a long time since I had killed those three men that I was unprepared for the emotions that sprang out at me: Shame, horror, fear, and hatred. Until today, my secrets had gone undisturbed for thousands of years. It occurred to me that my emotional uproar might disturb the emerging psychic, Deloo. I tried to find peace by floating away from her and toward the midnight beauty of Lake Champlain. Dozens of other spirits appeared to have had the same idea. They bobbled around me, glowing with various moods ranging from inconsolable grief to boundless effervescence. I edged away from all of them, noting that none wore the heavy cast of doom that surrounded me. After a while, I drifted back toward the hotel. As I got nearer I picked up an outpouring of frenzy. It grew more hysterical by the second. In my depressed need for solitude I tried to avoid the clamor, but discovered that it came from Deloo's room. It came from Deloo!

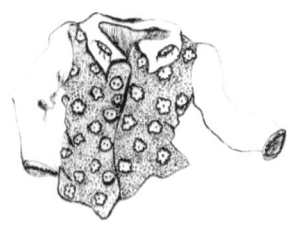

CHAPTER THIRTY-THREE

~Baasee'! Baasee'! Baasee'! Help me!~ Deloo's desperate commune was surrounded by noisy shrieks for help. Arthur's camera swung with increasing violence while Deloo thrashed the air with arms and feet at awkward angles. It looked like the camera was determined to give someone a black eye. I was not surprised to see who was its target.

So much for staying primly away in Montreal. I saw that Prize Woman and her husband had cornered Deloo. The man straddled my baby mortal on the hotel bed while he attempted to bind her wrists behind her back. Prize Woman stared from her husband to Deloo without engaging in the tussle.

"Watch me now, Raven Man!" Deloo shouted. She twisted onto her back and kicked him in the groin—or almost. Chuan dodged and tried to maneuver to the side. He was not used to fighting, and definitely not used to fighting a woman. His movements were hesitant. Deloo had fought with both boys and girls for over a decade in Fairbanks and felt his fear. She slammed into him with her entire one-hundred pounds, caught his hair in one hand while she clawed at his face. Using his natural impulse to dodge again, Deloo climbed onto his back, pummeling him with both fists and knees, Fairbanks style. He caught himself and snagged her right arm. Deloo's left elbow cracked against his chin. He still had her right arm and twisted it. Deloo blanched, but relaxed the arm while finding his shins with the heel of her sneakers.

No longer awash with foolish guilt, I didn't waste time worrying about the rights or wrongs of using ancient powers. I aimed a shard of electric current at the man's testicles. He howled, dropped Deloo's arm, and tumbled backward off the bed. Before anyone moved, I lifted Deloo up to the ceiling above the bed.

Deloo achieved a warrior stance even though she floated six feet over the pair below. Chuan flashed something that might have been a short dagger. Later I found out it was not a knife but Deloo's colored pencil case. I sent a ball of fire into it. The heat penetrated the wood and burst into flames that seared his hand. He dropped the case with a cry of pain. Although I couldn't smell the flesh burning, I could tell by the flash of red/black heat swelling out of his wrist that he wouldn't be using his right hand for a few days. Alas, Deloo would miss her pencil case.

~*Tell them to get out!* ~ I communed to Deloo as I lowered her to the bed. Even as I communed to my mortal, I was greeted by a spirit being whom I didn't know.

It announced its name in Etermalese and explained, ~*I am here in response to this small entity's request for a ghost mentor.*~ He wrapped the little ghost in a ball of golden light. ~*It's obvious that your life is in a state of chaos now, so I will not delay.*~ He then removed the little ghost from the area that had been her home for a few days.

The little ghost, MoLi, suddenly loomed out of his tendrils looking both bigger and more formal. She said, ~*Thank you, Baasee' and please thank Deloo for taking care of me. When Chuan broke in and assaulted Deloo and Ming was acting so confused, I prayed for help. At least they didn't bring weapons that could have hurt Deloo, but I didn't know that. I said it was an emergency. I hope that I will be kept close to my sister.*~

There was no time for me to respond except with a quick word with the ghost mentor. Then I returned to Deloo, who was blaring loudly, "Get out of here! Get out of here, Prize Woman!" she shouted. "I'm calling the police!"

Ming and Chuan fled into the adjacent stairwell door just as two hotel guests rushed into the hallway. Moments later uniformed men filled Deloo's room. I turned my attention to Deloo. I helped her focus while the police took her statement. Soon, they bagged the pencil case that I had thought was a knife as well as hair alleged to be that of the two suspects. Since both of the hairs were medium length, curled and brown, they didn't match either of the suspects. It would have done Deloo no good to point it out to the experts. I watched them pack their gear to leave and wondered if they would ever look for the intruders.

The hotel's night manager rushed in. He urged Deloo to move to another room. I could tell he was envisioning a room on the floor below us. He grinned. His thoughts blared that was one of the cheapest guestrooms. He reconsidered under the suspicious stares of a police officer who was waiting for Deloo's signature on her statement as well as that of a neighboring hotel guest. Sizing up the situation with spirit guide anger, I demonstrated Deloo's refusal to take a downstairs room. Once free of the flurry, he showed her to a VIP suite. The VIP suite featured a bedroom and sitting room as well as a full view of Lake Champlain. It was about four times bigger than the previous room and as big as Taale Denaa's Fairbanks house. Deloo didn't seem to notice its size. She was still in pajamas, although a hotel staff member had helped her put on a fluffy, white bathrobe to keep her warm.

The night manager waited for a porter to set her suitcase on a luggage rack before saying "I'm so sorry this has happened, Mrs. Goode. The head of security just reported that the intruders opened the lock with a duplicate electronic key. Someone with very sophisticated electronic knowledge used a combination of our computer system along with your debit card information to locate you. It was a simple matter of using the same skills to breach our security to get into your room. Rest assured that our entire security staff will be working around the clock to maintain your safety. This room doesn't have your name on it at all, so they won't be able to find you again in our hotel. You'll be safe tonight, I assure you, but I also urge you to talk to your bank in the morning."

Stunned by the information, Deloo asked, "Are you sure? They used my debit card number to get into a room? My room?"

"Yes, Mrs. Goode. I don't know how they got your bank card number, but they had it before they broke into our system." He nodded a curt goodnight.

After he closed the door Deloo latched every toggle and hasp before going into the bedroom. Once there, she locked its door as well.

To distract her mounting paranoia, I apologized for my poor showing as a spirit guide. *~I'll never let that happen again, my child.~*

"Are you kidding?" Deloo relaxed and broke into a wide grin, "You rescued me. Just like that raven said, 'Blood, yours or his. It doesn't matter. You must fight.' You rock, Baasee'. What did you do to that man? It smelled like burnt wool and singed hair. And what about Ming and her sister. Are they going to be all right? How did you find her a spirit guide so soon? Tell me everything you did." I helped her take a deep breath to slow her words and fears.

~All right, I admit that coming into their attack a trifle late made me do things that will earn me a talking-to sometime or another.~ I tried to give her a "G" rated version of my methods, but she wouldn't let up until she had the full story. I finished by communing, *~and, no, you can't learn to fly. All I did was elevate you for a minute or two. It's nothing.*

Now, before you settle down for sleep, we need to make some plans.~

"Plans?" Deloo's look of confusion transformed into sharp awareness. "Right. I won't use that debit card anymore." She looked for her wallet on the nightstand, but it wasn't there.

~It's in your blue pack. Remember? I helped you stuff it into that middle slot.~

"I remember," Deloo muffled the words as she fumbled for the wallet. "Here it is." She pulled the debit card out of its slot. "I don't know any bankers. I don't even know where Mr. Goode got this."

Deloo reached for her mobile phone when it rang. Deloo listened and said yes a few times. When she clicked off, was shaking, "that was the bank. Good thing I didn't want to use it any more. They've stopped all future use of my debit card. They will issue another one."

~No time to hold off. Now it's time to call the Goodes. They need to know what just happened and that you're coming back there. In fact, we could be there by this time tomorrow night.~ I glanced at Deloo's bedside clock. 11:35 p.m. I communed. *~After all that's happened today, it seems much later.~*

Deloo glanced at the clock and hesitated. "It's late, Baasee'. They must be asleep. I'll call in the morning."

~You're a victim of a crime. They are family, and we are going to be at their house tomorrow. You must call them now.~ I commanded, knowing that her reluctance was at least half due to the in-law intimidation factor. Either that or the 'old people are scary' element.

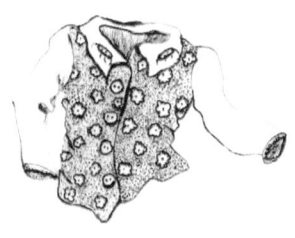

CHAPTER THIRTY-FOUR

Taking a deep breath, Deloo dug into her blue pack again to retrieve her phone. She found Matty's mobile number and tapped the small plastic screen numerous times. In a few seconds we heard Matty's voice say, "Hello, Deloo! Guess who's with me right now?"

Before Deloo could speak a male voice intervened, "Hi Deloo. It's me, Woody. It's been a while, and we just met a couple of times."

Deloo looked perplexed, so I communed, *~He's Arthur's roommate from graduate school. He was Arthur's best man in your wedding.~*

Smiling at the ceiling, alias the Great Baasee', Deloo said, "Woody! It's good to hear your voice. You're right. It was a flurry at the wedding, and you were an anchor for both of us as our best man." Arthur's black and white camera rattled against her ribs.

"I think Arthur needed me more than you did, but I was glad to be there. Um, so let me hand this gadget back to Matty."

"Deloo, dear, you must have an urgent reason for calling us this late. Have you had an accident?"

Tears started rolling down Deloo's cheeks. I used invisible tissues to dry them. *~Now is not the time to cry. She needs to know how serious this is. Ask her if Zachary is available.~*

Deloo touched her cheeks, knowing that tears had been there moments before. "I'm sorry to call you so late, Matty," she said in a normal voice. "I've had a number of problems in these past few days that have turned into major trouble about the debit card Mr. Goode—I mean Zachary got for me." Deloo took a long breath and continued, "Somebody broke into my hotel room this evening."

"What?!?" Matty gasped. We could hear her whispering to Woody, "Dear, could you get Zachary, please? He needs to hear this."

Deloo continued, "I'm not hurt. I shouted loud enough and someone called the police. The hotel manager moved me to another room. It's not under my name. They told me that someone used my debit card number to make a duplicate key for the old room. Anyway, I, I. . .." This time I couldn't hold back the floodgates. Deloo's voice quivered as she said, "Matty, could I come home for a few days?"

I glimmered with pride. Deloo had used the word "home" without any prompting from me. I knew how much Matty wanted Deloo to think of her as a mother or at least the Goode's house as her home, too.

"Deloo, Darling!" Matty gushed, "of course you have to come home. How soon can you get here?"

There was noisy shuffling in the background and Zachary's voice boomed, "Deloo, what's this about a break-in at your hotel? Are you hurt?"

Deloo repeated her story, this time with more details about the debit card's cancellation and the night manager's comments. "I need to contact my bank tomorrow, but I don't know how to do that. I was hoping you could help."

"Of course I'll help. Where are you now?"

Deloo supplied the hotel name and added, "It's in Burlington, Vermont. It's been a nightmare. This is the third time I've had trouble from the same crooks who broke into my room tonight. They tried to run me down in New Brunswick two days ago and they shot at me last night when I was in Montreal. I'll tell you more about that when I see you. I'm scared."

Deloo could hear them muttering, and I realized that they were negotiating amongst each other about who would fly to Burlington to get her. I showered Deloo with soothing vibrations while they worked their way through a maze of electronic information about flights.

"Deloo, I'll be up in the morning. Can you get me at the airport? A flight arrives a little after ten tomorrow."

"Oh, no, you don't need to come all this..." Deloo began.

"Deloo, dear, there's no use in fighting him. He's made up his mind," Matty said.

"I'll go with you, Zachary," Woody interjected. "I've just made my reservation."

Zachary laughed. "Stinker. You are just like Arthur, maybe quicker. There! I've got mine, too. Alright, Deloo, can you get both Woody and me at the airport tomorrow? Oh, and we hope we can drive back to Cambridge with you."

Deloo nodded her head and smiled into her phone. "I'll be there at ten. And, yes, you are both welcome to drive to Cambridge with me. Thank you for helping me."

Once all the Goode's final words were over and Deloo had tapped the "end" icon, I communed, ~*you've got one more call to make, Love. Please call your mother and tell her what's going on. Tell her that your jacket is now dangerous property. We need her to come to Cambridge as soon as possible to show us what could be so different about it.*~

Deloo stared at her phone without saying anything for a long moment. "Baasee', my mother didn't do anything to hurt me. I've already asked her to come all the way to the East Coast just to look at my beaded denim jacket. Putting a 'rush' on that plan is like telling her she is the master criminal behind the break in. Baasee', you are taking this too much to heart—if you have a heart. You are hysterical." Deloo stared at the wall in front of her and then lowered her head. "I just can't tell Mom anything like that."

Surprised, I mused that it had taken me centuries before I could imagine another person's perspective. Then I thought about Deloo's interpretation of a conversation that hadn't yet taken place, and things that Taale had already told us about the jacket. ~*Remember that she wanted you to go back to the Goode's. She offered to fly to Boston to help you. She's worried about you, and should be. Besides, a lot has happened since you talked to her this morning. She would be hurt if you didn't call with this latest attempt on your life.*~

"You're right, Baasee'. Mom did want to get to Boston right away." Deloo keyed the speed dial code for her mother and Taale answered on the first ring.

"Mom?" Despite her tranquil tone when telling me I was hysterical, Deloo's voice rose across the short syllable. "Mom, it's me! I'm being cyber-stalked," she shrieked the last word.

I lifted an ironic, although gossamer chin and tossed curly, golden hair to an unseeing audience. ~*Cyber-stalked? I thought it was me who's taking this too much to heart.*~ I communed my sarcasm, but Deloo's anxiety overrode her reception of my words.

Meanwhile, Taale mumbled something. Taale took the news with relative calm. Moreover, cyber-stalking was one of her specialties. After all, Taale had taken courses in computer crime and solutions for her degree. As Deloo talked to her mother, I received an emergency notification from Zephyr, Taale's spirit guide. Zephyr, an ancient bipedal primate of central Asia, and I had become close friends over the years. I decoded her brief message.

~She's in a panic about this flight because her student loan payment is due in a couple of days. She'll have to use the money for that to pay for this ticket, and changing it to an earlier flight will cost double. Can Deloo help?~

I wasn't surprised that Taale Denaa worried about the cost of the airfare on such short notice. She'd lived every day of her life without enough money to pay for frills such as monthly heating bills. She'd borrowed money to go to school, and as soon as she'd graduated and been working for six months, she received her first bill not long after Deloo had gone to Cambridge. I knew it had happened, but didn't realize how much the college loans had impacted Taale.

~Yes,~ I commune-responded without further questioning my friend.

I caught Deloo's peripheral attention. *~Deloo,~* I communed, *~your mother is avoiding telling you about a terrible financial crisis she's facing. You can help by offering to pay her back for the ticket.~*

Deloo caught my meaning and went into action. "Mom, buying the ticket to get here must be putting you in a bind. For once, I'm the one with money. Zachary will help me put the money in your account tomorrow. Arthur's insurance money will cover all the costs."

"Oh, Deloo," Taale tried to contain her relief, but it was obvious in her voice. "My student loan payments are more than I thought they would be. Thank you so much. What a blessing. I'm so glad I'll be able to be there to help. Listen to you worrying about me with all your troubles. I've got reservations already, and now I'll be able to change them with your help, Deloo. I'll try to time the arrival for midmorning the day after tomorrow," Taale said. "Oh, Deloo, what about a place to stay? We should get a hotel somewhere close to Matty and Zachary."

~No!~ I roared without a voice. *~Nothing would hurt Matty more if you didn't stay with them at a time like this. You know they have plenty of room in their house.~*

Deloo nodded at the ceiling again and said into her phone, "Don't worry about a hotel, Mom. Mrs. Goode would be devastated if we didn't stay with them. She said so just a few minutes ago. . . . No, she didn't know about you coming, but you could stay with me in Arthur's old room. They're family now, Mom. Think about how mad you got when Aunt Juliane stayed at the Regency instead of with us."

Taale laughed, "Juliane is an aunt in name only because Uncle Virgil helped her out one year. Besides, there was a little more to it than her staying at a hotel, such as her slumming with that obnoxious upriver man and being on welfare while she wasted all that money—but I get your point. Okay, my little grown up girl, I'll see you on the day after tomorrow."

Deloo slid her phone into the pack pocket and sprawled across the bed. Allowing herself to absorb the terror after the break-in as well as everything that had happened in the past few days, exhaustion penetrated her now-aching limbs. Deloo rubbed a sore elbow and smiled at the memory of the sound her skinny arm had made when she hit Chuan. After a moment of silence, she offered a sleepy mumble, "Thanks for rescuing me, Baasee'."

~You are very welcome, my stunning Deloo. Sleep well.~ I was pleased when she fell asleep, but not at all happy to know that her enemies, whoever they were, now knew a lot of details about my Deloo's identity.

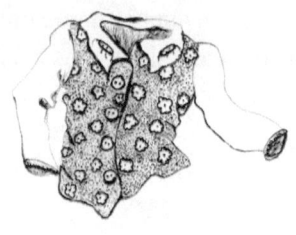

CHAPTER THIRTY-FIVE

Ming drove south on Route 89 while Chuan sagged, semi-conscious on the seat beside her. She glanced at the clock, surprised that it was already half-past one. With adrenaline still pumping through her system, she was hyper-alert. For his part, it seemed to Chuan felt deep shame. He, a Harvard graduate, had gone to school to learn to assault computers, not women. He hoped Ming would forgive him. He turned toward her to tell her how sorry he was, but she wouldn't look at him. He called quietly, "Ming."

She didn't respond. It wasn't typical of her to ignore him so long. It seemed as if something else was in the car with them. He was right. Ming's attention was caught by something well beyond his ability to apprehend. She heard, rather than saw her cherished twin sister, MoLi. Although she tried to dismiss the illusion as wishful thinking brought on by the fool they'd been chasing for days, she couldn't help trying to hear or feel MoLi's presence.

MoLi, for her part, struggled to get her twin sister's attention. *~Ming. Can you hear me? It's me, MoLi. I'm with you in spirit form. For the longest time I thought I still lived. Then I realized that I lived when you were present but not otherwise. For a while I lost you. Please let me know you hear me.~*

MoLi didn't have formal training in communing with mortals. She picked up a few tips while stuck with me, Baasee' the Kind-Hearted, and I was not with her any more. However, she and Ming used to have a spastic psychic connection. MoLi felt herself overwhelmed with exhaustion. Felt herself losing what little strength she had to keep talking.

Ming, reeling with confusion, wondered if she felt MoLi's presence or not. She murmured to Chuan, "It's like I hear my sister, and yet don't hear anything at all. Last night, for example, I dreamed about her. I thought she told me that I shouldn't have tried to hurt that Alaskan girl."

She turned large eyes toward Chuan. "I think I feel guilty about something but try to ignore it, then the spirits have a way to keep after me until I face the truth. The truth is, I was eager to kill that girl, but something happened in Montreal that changed everything for me."

"What do you mean about MoLi?" Chuan asked, the distress he'd felt seconds earlier turned to sharp interest.

"It's one of the dreams I've been having a lot about MoLi. I hear her telling me she will help me." Ming fell silent.

"That's good news, Ming" Chuan murmured. "In our old Chinese beliefs, the spirits come to us in odd ways."

Ming brightened. "That's what my mother would say, too. I mean, that's the way it is for Inuit." Ming laughed. She sounded like drizzling rain on a cluster of leaves.

"How do you talk to them? I want to talk to MoLi."

Diverted with something that called for kindness instead of brutality, as well as something he had learned from his mother decades ago, Chuan gave her some tips. "Why don't you pull off here? I'll take the wheel for a while. Maybe you'll make the connection then." What followed was a slow three-way conversation between MoLi, Ming and Chuan in which the two mortals learned that MoLi had been with the very woman they'd been chasing for days.

Using Mandarin, MoLi told Ming, *~Tell him, my sister, that Deloo doesn't know yet why you are following her. Police of two countries are involved. They'll soon find out.~*

"Am I understanding that this woman doesn't have any idea why we're after her?" Chuan asked.

Ming translated her twin's statement and added, "We should get out of this as soon as possible, Chuan. I packed everything we have and put it in the car. We're ready to go. Those two can do what they want, but they'll have to do it without me. I hope you think the same way."

Chuan gripped her hand and murmured, "I'm sorry that I've let us get dragged into this mess, my love. You're right. They don't know what they're facing. I do."

"What?" Ming asked, electrical impulses racing. "We've been whizzing around three provinces so much that we haven't had a chance to talk about your discoveries."

"If you think about it, it's obvious that they are willing to give up half of what they claim is the take on whatever is smuggled in those jackets. At a minimum, they are giving up what it's costing to fly us back and forth to China, as well as housing and food. Moreover, they've been doing this for years, as Howard said, on their own without the so-called huge grants. They said the jackets pay for everything. Well? What could each jacket be worth? I'm guessing each one has been worth over a million and probably much more." Chuan paused.

Ming mulled over his arithmetic. "That would explain why they decided to kill someone, meaning Qanik, over the fifteenth jacket."

"Sure, they've helped a lot of Chinese people get doctorates, but I think they've been pillaging that archeaology site for decades. The total value over time is likely to be well over a billion dollars. With Brent taking off so much time to look, I figure they've decided it's worth it to kill people who get in their way. They've probably already made plans to do us in."

Ming's mouth gaped, then she asked, "where do you get that number?"

"That amount is about equal to the combined salaries of you, me, and Brent. Then there are the student stipends, their housing, food, tools, and lab expenses. Considering Brent uses the lab for up to six months, holds seminars and other events at the university, the jackets are bringing in close to a couple of million dollars, minimum. If you add the desperation factor into the mess, there's got to be something in the jacket she's got now that's worth much more. Millions more."

Ming stared at him in open-mouthed horror. "They killed MoLi for whatever they're smuggling and we've been doing this for years. Did you know about the jackets before this?"

"I've known the field schools are expensive, since paying those bills is part of my job. I just accepted the cover story that they were getting big grants, and I've never had a chance to examine the receivables side. Howard does that. I never heard of the jackets until a few months ago when Brent first said something to us."

Ming's face contorted into different expressions, none of them happy. "So what shall we do now? Turn ourselves into the police? The Burlington police would jail us for breaking and entering, but smuggling? Attempted murder?" She broke down into tears.

"Let's go, Ming. No one knows about us but that woman we've been chasing. Let's go back home and forget this mess."

"No! My sister needs to be avenged. They murdered her. I want to make Brent and Howard pay for killing her."

"By doing what?"

Ming's eyes gave off two or three kinds of light as she thought. Finally she said, "Alaska. These jackets came from Fairbanks, Alaska. Brent must have been in Alaska to search for the one that woman has. Let's go to Fairbanks."

Chuan tried to laugh her out of it, but Ming was determined. It was six a.m. when he finally conceded. "Okay. Let's find an airport and head to Alaska. This is your cousin's car. What shall we do with it?"

An hour later they were on their way back to Saint John, New Brunswick on the Bay of Fundy where Ming's cousin lived. Chuan ground his teeth during the entire drive as he counted his costs in the search for a jacket that had probably been denuded of its booty.

* * *

Hours after the break in, Deloo sat up. It was dark. I awoke and took dutiful note that Deloo, although sitting, wasn't quite awake.

"What's that? Who's that?"

~*What do you see, Deloo?*~ I noted the rivulets of sweat that dripped from her hair and took her temperature my way. She had a slight fever, but nothing much. Deloo slumped back onto the pillows. I shook her. ~*Deloo, what have you seen?*~

"I don't know. It was like a kid's face. Did you see it?"

~*No. Did you recognize him?*~

"Her. It was a girl. I don't know her. A little girl. Big dark eyes."

~*Go back to sleep my child. That's what we do at night.*~

Deloo slept and awoke hours later. She slid out of bed and unlocked the bedroom door. She was not fearful. It was the other way around. I was in a dither and she was curious. Now that we were in the swamp of identity theft, I pulled myself together and started to think. An hour later Deloo had devoured the room-service breakfast she'd ordered, and was filling her cup with coffee for the second time. Between sips, she asked me more questions. "Was that man the one who did it? Stole my card?"

~*I didn't know thieves could make hotel room key cards by using a computer to read and copy their victim's credit or debit card.*~ I accused her, ~*that's your fault. If you listened to your mother, the computer geek, I would be able to keep up with that sort of thing.*~

Deloo spluttered coffee all over herself and the table. Mopping it up, she mouthed, "Now it's all my fault! How'd that happen?"

~Child! I was teasing you. Of course it's not your fault. It's what you can't do that has me worried. For starters, you as a mortal woman can't have discovered any of their names. I know parts of their names and I've shared them with you, but since I'm your invisible guide, you will not be able to back up your use of such names. You can't even tell anyone about the way I lifted you up to the ceiling without appearing to be insane.~

"I realized that last night when the police questioned me. When they asked if I knew their names, I wanted to say 'Ming and Chuan,' but I could sense their next question would be how I knew them." Deloo looked at the small table and pushed away her tray. "Saying 'Because my spirit guide told me' just doesn't work in this world. Baasee', has it ever worked?" Arthur's camera, on the night stand, seemed to vibrate in agreement.

Continuing, I answered, *~When I was a mortal, it was a world in which spirit guides were a given. In those days people knew spirit guides have useful skills. My guides were very well trained, wise, and in all ways wonderful. When I was a mortal, people hung on every word my guides said through me. In a nutshell, with so many different belief systems in the world, mortals have less and less interaction with their own spirit guides. Moreover, each religion in the world has different ways of understanding that we spirit guides can do, used to do, and want to do. So, while there are many places today where people are valued because they can communicate with the other side, my side, most police are not among such people. They require physical evidence.~*

Deloo's eyebrows knotted. "But you know so many things that could help the police and everyone else, Baasee'. Isn't there some way for me to use what you learn without the police thinking I'm nuts?"

I blew a little air toward her to let her know that I sympathized even though I was about to make things a little more complicated. *~Yes, but it will take time to figure out how. Right now I want to remind you about Arthur's friend, Woody. You and Arthur had a classic whirlwind romance, and you seemed to be blind to everything and everyone except Arthur. What do you remember about Woodrow Morrow?~*

Deloo shook her head. "I remember him a little. Dark hair and a dark complexion. He was shorter than Arthur by four or five inches. Beyond that, I can't picture him. Why?"

I smiled as I examined her memory: all visual without any words—a typical artist. *~One of the first things that Arthur said when he introduced Woody is 'here's my roommate, the ex-cop.' Remember?~*

"Ex-cop?" Deloo's eyes widened. "You're kidding. I don't remember that. When?"

~A year ago. I want you to prepare to meet a man who will behave like an old buddy, but he is and will always be a policeman. He's going to file everything you tell him about Chuan and Ming into the police evidence cabinet that used to be his brain. Where you think in pictures and emotions, he sorts the world into clues and codified legalities. It's been a short year since we've seen him. I'm sure he hasn't changed very much.~

Deloo tried to remember Woody's face, but nothing came to mind. She frowned, "did he think that way about me and Arthur getting married so soon?"

~Not at all. His mind is very tidy. He seemed to expect Arthur to want to make a big change when he graduated, such as getting married. Marriage is a big change and very predictable for young people. Far from being suspicious, Woody kept thinking with extreme sadness about a woman who seems to have dumped him a while before you and Arthur got married. Woody wanted to make the same big change himself, but it didn't happen.~

"I remember Arthur saying something about Woody and a girlfriend. I think her name is Sequin. I didn't pay much attention, since I didn't get to meet her. But, Baasee', now I'm scared of Arthur's old friend. What can we talk about?" Deloo stood up and made a tidy pile of her breakfast dishes.

That was just the opening I wanted. *~I'm glad you asked, my mortal collaborator.~*

Deloo chuckled, "When did you decide to make me your collaborator?"

~Well, I thought of it the day that you first understood my communes. It was just after we left that innkeeper. We're in the middle of a problem that's all about you! Don't you want to be my collaborator while we solve the problem of the beaded jacket? I can help you with this mortal case. You could help me with my other problems. It helps to have someone to point out what's wrong with your thinking.~

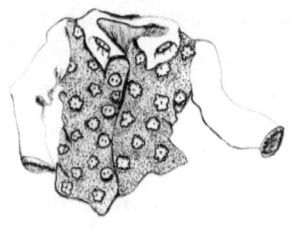

CHAPTER THIRTY-SIX

Deloo's face quirked as she held her right palm upward in the gesture I'd seen so many young people use. The delicate lacey look of the silver on her wedding band took on a deep plum color and I touched it with a gentle pod of tingles. The silver filigree cast long shots of light around the room. She tipped her hand back and stared at it. "Cool!" she murmured, and looked up at the ceiling with amused grey-green eyes. "Baasee', do you know how to make my eyes glow red?"

I blew hard enough to make her hair fly around her head. ~*Nonsense! I don't know how to do that. Now we have an hour before we leave the hotel. I want you to be ready to talk like a clear-thinking human. Not a demon.*~

Deloo laughed out right. "Okay, but one of these days, I'm hoping for demon eyes."

In an effort to move to a more practical subject I communed, ~*have you thought about who's going to drive once all three of you are in the car?*~

"What?" Deloo tipped her head to one side in puzzlement. "Oh, you mean when Woody and Mr. Goode are in the car with me."

~*Both Zachary Goode and Woody are much bigger than you are. I'm sure that even you will have trouble squeezing into your back seat.*~

"Right!" Deloo drummed her fingers on her hip. "I'll have to put something in the trunk." We headed for the garage and tackled the problem of space.

"Unless I ditch the tent, this is as good as I can do." She slammed the trunk lid shut and turned to stare at the third button of a stranger's dress shirt. He was Arthur's height.

Anticipating Deloo's panicked reaction, I surrounded her with a thick aura of calmness and communed quietly, ~*You're doing well, Deloo. He's tall, like Arthur was, but he's not Arthur.*~ Then I spotted a small pin on his lapel that featured the hotel's logo. *~See? He's with the hotel. Smile.~*

Deloo carved a smile on her lips and looked up.

"Good morning, Mrs. Goode," he murmured. "I didn't want to interrupt you. You seem to put everything in there with military precision." He gestured toward the still-full back seat, "but I could help, if you'd like some assistance."

"Who are you?" Deloo's words came out in a shout. To settle her nerves, I showered her with a mixture of soothing vibrations and thought about him not being dangerous. Or her.

"I apologize. I'm Mr. Crosby, the hotel's senior manager." He straightened his tie. "I saw you heading toward the garage and wanted to find out how you are after last night's trouble."

"Oh!" Deloo let out a big puff of air. "Yes. My father-in-law is arriving soon. His flight is due a little after ten. He said he'd like to chat with someone—I guess that would be you—about what happened to my debit card. He knows far more about identity theft than I do. I hope you don't mind."

Mr. Crosby's brow cleared. "So that explains your efforts to make room in your car." He helped her lift a heavy carton out of the back seat. With some effort they rearranged the trunk again. Several inches of back seat appeared.

Rattled, Deloo dimpled at him. "Thank you very much. I'm expecting two people. My father-in-law is bringing my late husband's best friend. I just hope that neither of them has luggage."

They both laughed and arranged to meet on her return. "Do you know how to get to the airport? Burlington is a small town with forty thousand residents, but it's still easy to get lost because of our steep inclines and narrow streets."

She took the map he offered and finished shuffling small things around in the back seat and tried it out for size. "Whew!" Her size-four rear end barely fit even with her seatbelt in place, but Mr. Crosby's instructions were perfect. In less than ten minutes Deloo found herself in the small airport's parking lot. The Burlington airport was quite a bit smaller than the one in Fairbanks. It would be simple to find them, so she hustled toward the entry to greet them. She spotted Zachary Goode just as he came around a corner. She eyed the younger man beside him without recognition.

I butted in, ~*that younger man is Woody. Look at the way his eye-brows grow. They almost meet in the center over his nose. When you met him last year he didn't wear glasses. Now he does, so his eyes and eyebrows aren't as prominent as they were at your wedding.*~

Deloo breathed a sigh of relief. ~*Thank you, Baasee'. I would pass him without a second glance.*~

~*You are welcome, my dear. I should be praising you. You have de-veloped a wonderful method of communing. You've stopped moving your lips. I'm very proud of you.*~

By that time, the two men had reached Deloo. Mr. Goode embraced her. Woody extended his hand. At my urging Deloo bypassed his hand and gave him a quick hug. "You look different with glasses, Woody. Or maybe I've just forgotten you wore them last year, too."

Woody guffawed, showing off his dazzling white teeth. "No. You're right. I had to start using them all the time this past winter when I was finishing my dissertation. It took me a year longer than Arthur. I could feel him hustle me."

"Congratulations," Deloo smiled, surprised at how good it felt to hear something about her late husband. "Arthur must have been danc-ing at your graduation." She looked at their empty hands and remarked, "Did you bring luggage?"

Both of them shook tired-looking heads. "No. It was hard to get to the airport on time as it was," Zachary said. "I wanted to drive, but Dr. Intrepid, here, told me the T would be easier."

Deloo looked confused, forgetting that Boston dwellers call the sub-way the "T".

"Alright, I admit it. I was wrong," Woody grimaced, "but I think we could have saved a little time if we had shoved other passengers out of the way to get on the Green Line. Did you ride the subway very often, Deloo?"

Deloo guided them to her car and opened the doors. She shook her head. Six months in a big city was not enough to cure her fear of two of Boston's people-moving systems: the crowded subways and the inner city highways. She feared going to the airport by car and she'd resist-ed going by the T. "Not me. I can drive on ice and snow any time, but chicken out when it comes to overpasses and underground trains." She said, "I think we all need a cup of coffee and something to munch on."

When they were about to leave, I reminded Deloo about Taale. ~*Ask Mr. Goode if they have room in their house for Taale. They took in*

Woody, so maybe there's someone else staying with them, too.~

Deloo looked at Mr. Goode with concern. "When I called last night, I forgot to mention that I invited my mother to join me. You remember my mother, don't you? Taale Denaa? I'm pretty sure she's the one who made all of the jackets those crooks want so much. Is it all right if my mother stays at your home? We could share a room. We're used to doing that. She arrives tomorrow morning."

Before Zachary had time to answer, Woody intervened, "Don't worry; we'll pick up your mother at the airport with a car." He peered into her car and added, "But maybe not yours. What do you have in here besides the kitchen sink?"

Zachary looked over Woody's shoulder, took note of the tiny space Deloo had allotted herself in the back seat, and laughed outright. "Well, my son might have fit back there once upon a time. He was scrawny as a kid, but even his rear end could not have made peace with those sharp corners." He pointed to the cardboard box that held Deloo's art supplies.

Deloo smiled at her father-in-law, and said, "I know, but it's big enough for me. I figured that you two could take the front, and I will sit back here."

"No arguments from me," Zachary said, "and by the way, I'm sure it will be fine with Matty as well about your mother staying with us. We do have more than enough bedrooms for everyone now that we've finished the renovations."

"Already! I'm looking forward to seeing what you've done. By the way, I've made an appointment with the hotel manager, Mr. Crosby. He offered to tell us what he knows about how those people got into my room last night."

The two men nodded.

"I was shocked by the little you have told us so far, Deloo," Mr. Goode said. "It will help to be briefed before we meet the hotel manager."

Deloo directed them to a coffee shop not far from the airport. While Deloo talked, the men wolfed down pastries and listened as she told them about her experiences in Nova Scotia, New Brunswick and Montreal. Deloo kept the story down to a few simple sentences that gave them plenty of detail without mystifying them with oddities like running her pursuers off the road by first pulling a 180 degree turn around. "I think that brings you up to date. I just hope we can put a stop to them."

The men squared their shoulders as if facing down a saber-tooth tiger. When they reached the hotel, they were ushered into Mr. Crosby's office where he introduced them to Jim, the hotel's head of security. After a few pleasantries, Jim told them how the suspects must have made a fake electronic hotel key.

"They had to have your credit or debit card number, your name, and some electronic information from our hotel in order for this to work. Whoever did this had all of that data." Jim paused. "All of it. What causes our staff the greatest concern is that they had our hotel's protected information that no one but me or Mr. Crosby should have."

Deloo's lower lip quivered. "The bank has called me. They've put a hold on my account because of all of this."

Mr. Crosby interjected, "Of course, our greatest concern is Mrs. Goode's safety. We thought we had vouchsafed our guests' security. Someone with superior technological skills breached our system."

"Do you know who the perpetrator is?" Woody asked.

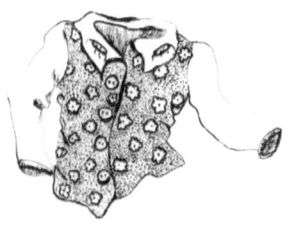

CHAPTER THIRTY-SEVEN

Mr. Crosby bowed in Woody's direction. "Yes. I worked with the Burlington Police Department to get the name of the individual. His name is Howard Lee. Do you know him?"

"I know something about him." Woody glanced at Mr. Goode. "Yesterday I had a very interesting call from an old friend of mine at the RCMP. If it's the same Howard Lee, he's a person of interest in Nova Scotia." Woody gave a brief description of his conversation with Al Beamus. "He hoped I had connections at Harvard who might help. I asked Zachary."

Zachary nodded and pulled out his cell phone. "Matty and I both know a lot of people connected to Harvard. I'll ask her to do some checking today. I'm sure she will have something for us ."

All of my circuits popped into full alert on hearing the name. *~Ask if he has something to do with the innkeeper,~* I reminded Deloo. *~Maybe he's the one who did it, especially if he's Asian.~*

Pretending that I didn't exist, Deloo shook her head at Mr. Crosby, wrote the name on a pad of paper, and then nodded to the ceiling. She burst out, "are you talking about the death of an innkeeper at a place called the Secret Spirit Inn?" She looked at Mr. Goode with a flushed face. "That's where it all started for me. I had a reservation to stay there, but the innkeeper got very pushy about my jacket. She told me I'd changed since the last time she saw me, but it was my first time in Nova Scotia."

Woody's jaw almost dropped, but instead his face closed and his eyes turned cold. "Yes. Al mentioned her, too. Deloo, could you tell us more about the innkeeper. She was killed at the inn."

Deloo stared at Woody for a long space. "I was there in the afternoon of June fourth, the day before our... my...." She stopped. Zachary patted her hand. Deloo took a deep breath and gave a slow and detailed account of her meeting with Rosemoira Keilleher. "I was so scared of her, that I avoided wearing the jacket again until I got out of Nova Scotia. I stuffed my hair inside a baseball cap so that no one would recognize me." She looked down at the table where she could see the notes and doodles the hotel manager had made. She gazed at the shapes before adding, "Now I'm sorry I didn't spend a little more time with her."

"The perpetrator might have killed you, too," Woody's grimace turned into a smile. He reached across the table to pat her hand.

An image of a Chinese dragon seemed to float out of the manager's notepad. It reminded me of the raven I played with the day before, and reminded me of the Asian possibility. *~Ask if that is a Chinese name. One of the people thinks in Mandarin.~*

"Is Lee a Chinese name? The two intruders last night looked Chinese to me," Deloo asked.

"I don't know," Mr. Crosby looked thoughtful, "although Lee is a common Asian name. He's a branch manager for a bank in Cambridge, Massachusetts." He gave the name and address of a bank near Davis Square and stared at Zachary. "Isn't that near where you live, Mr. Goode? Do you bank at Lee's branch?"

"I know of the bank," Mr. Goode answered, "but I've never done business with them. Nor do I know anyone named Howard Lee. Why does he know Deloo?"

Mr. Crosby nodded, "That's where my professional networking has paid off! We got the name of the Montreal hotel where Mrs. Goode stayed the night before last. I know one of the hotel managers there, so I called him. He was very helpful. Turns out that this Howard Lee called the hotel on the morning that Mrs. Goode checked out. He gave them a great song and dance about Mrs. Goode's debit card transaction. He claimed that you, Mr. Goode, wanted to cover the charges yourself, and that he was helping you by having them take the charges off her debit card and putting it on his own card as a personal favor. He asked key information about both of you. He got your address, Mr. Goode, and of course he already had Mrs. Arthur Goode's debit card number."

"My address?" Mr. Goode leaped to his feet in shock. "I hope that person has been fired."

"I don't know how they are going to handle it. The hotel is in Canada, after all. All too often, these matters fall through the cracks because the victims, meaning ordinary citizens like Mrs. Goode, don't know what they can do to recover from a crime. This case is different because it's international. We've alerted the authorities in Montreal as well as Cambridge. I think that you should get in contact with your police department as soon as possible to follow up on this crime." Mr. Crosby permitted himself a sneer and added, "Of course, by the same means, we have Lee's credit card number now, yet more proof of his involvement. Jim has run a check on it. It's one of those general debit cards that anyone can buy and use without identification."

Woody asked if they had any specific information about how Howard Lee made the key. "Can we find the computer he used?"

Jim handed them a sheet of paper. "This shows you the IP address of the computer someone later used to print the card key. It could be helpful to match it to the computer used to print the card, but it's easy to get throw-away machines like this one. Or steal it. It's possible he printed it from a public computer. It takes an expert to do all that."

Woody looked at Deloo with a strange expression. "What are they after, Deloo?"

Deloo looked from Woody to Mr. Goode and shook her head. "It's got to be something about my beaded jacket." She nodded toward the head of security, "I've asked my mother to come all the way from Fairbanks, Alaska to Cambridge to look over my jacket. She made it. She might know what they are after."

"Let me see if I've got this straight," Woody muttered more to himself than the others. He recited the facts that Deloo had told them. "Two people chased Deloo in New Brunswick until they went into a ditch while driving at a high rate of speed. Even if there was no damage to either vehicle, the passengers got banged up a bit. If so, maybe they turned a potential moment of immature fun into a fit of rage or vengefulness. Maybe when they saw Deloo the second time in Montreal, about six hundred miles from Moncton, they chased her again, but this time on foot through a hotel and topped it off by shooting at her. A third person was in on the third incident, that's Howard Lee, a bank branch manager in Massachusetts. Now we are looking for people who are chasing a complete stranger from Alaska. They've made a huge investment of time by three or more people and the money it costs to do it. None of it makes sense." He looked around the table and stopped when he locked eyes with Deloo. "Does it?"

~The cop has come out of hiding. So much for Dr. Morrow, the mild-mannered anthropologist,~ I jested with Deloo.

Deloo covered an irreverent snigger with a fit of coughing. I helped a few tears to glisten in her hazel-green eyes when she looked back at him. "Would anyone like to look at my jacket?" She offered.

Mr. Crosby looked at Jim and both said, "Yes!"

Deloo reached into a commodious pack and pulled out the now infamous jacket. "Here it is." She spread it across the conference table. Made of heavy, light-toned blue denim, it had darkened seams. "My mother made it for me last winter. It was my Christmas present from her." They hesitated. She added, "Go ahead. Touch it. I wear it."

Woody and the security man studied it at length. Woody surprised everyone when he brought out a folding, pocket-sized magnifying glass. "What are these odd holes, Deloo? There must be dozens of them. Did they have beads in them before?"

Surprised at his discovery, I jammed my ocular equipment next to his. He didn't notice me, but I saw what he was examining. *~He's right, Deloo. Why are these holes here?~*

Deloo studied the holes through the magnifying glass and shook her head. "I've never noticed them before. Mom will know. It looks like she tried to hide them with our family heirloom beads. She told me to cut our beads off after I've worn out the jacket so that I can sew them onto something else. She fitted our beads close to these big holes, but they don't quite cover them."

Mr. Goode studied the holes for a moment and handed the magnifying glass back. "There must have been something here that someone thinks is still attached to the jacket. We'd better put this in a safe place. How about your car?" Then he looked at his watch and patted his well-rounded belly, "it's time for lunch, and there are wonderful aromas coming from this great hotel's restaurant. Can I treat any of you to lunch?"

Woody smiled and declined. "I want to call my friend at the RCMP. He needs to know about this." Woody went to a corner of the room and after a few minutes of delay, spoke to someone with unconcealed excitement. "Right. I agree." Woody glanced at Zachary, "Yes. It's an ideal time to come to Boston. ... Right. Maybe I'll see you in a day or two." He clicked the end button on his phone, and nodded to Mr. Crosby.

"I believe the RCMP may be in contact with you and your staff. My associate is Inspector Al Beamus. We've known each other for many years. He'll be grateful to you for helping him investigate a mysterious death."

It was an obvious cue for Mr. Crosby to exchange information with Woody and then end the discussion. He did so by reassuring Deloo that there would be no charge for her stay at the hotel. Mr. Goode reiterated his invitation and made it clear that lunch was on him, but the two hotel men refused and moved toward Mr. Crosby's office door.

Once down in the garage again, Woody stated the obvious. "We need to keep that jacket safe and out of sight in the trunk. Let's get on the road as soon as possible."

"We could stop at a store to get some fruit or something," Deloo murmured as they made their way to the garage. "We'll be on the road a long time. We should eat something." She looked at Mr. Goode to get a sense of what he wanted. "That pastry is already gone, right?"

"Yes," they said in unison.

Deloo chuckled. "You are both being foolish. Let's tuck the jacket away and go find lunch. There are lots of places to eat nearby this hotel."

Mr. Goode watched Deloo put the denim jacket into the trunk of the car, and said, "Hungry as I am, Deloo, Woody is right. We should get out of Burlington and not stay here any longer than necessary. We can get something on the way."

Once on the road, none of them wanted to leave the car exposed, so they ended up going to a drive-through. They huddled in the fast-food parking lot to eat lunch and Deloo took advantage of the quiet time to call her mother. Taale was at work.

"Hi, Baby," her voice firm. "I've been approved to leave tonight. They're not going to call it 'emergency leave' so that my time off won't go on my record with a black mark, but it will be leave without pay, which I hope is better. I'm leaving tonight on a Red-Eye flight. Can you pick me up at the airport tomorrow morning?"

Deloo agreed. "I'm sure that someone will help me figure out the way to Logan, Mom. I'll be so happy to see you tomorrow morning. By the way," Deloo added, "It looks like there were some big beads attached to my jacket at one time. Were there?"

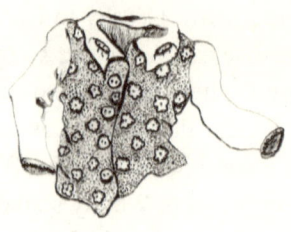

CHAPTER THIRTY-EIGHT

Deloo and Woody had finished unloading her car. I noticed Deloo flicker with irritation. Lately, I'd been watching the evolving nature of Deloo's mixed heritage in her aura. Hers was fascinating. The general aura churned vegetable green and deep azure. Woody's was not as colorful, but expansive: white and gold. I touch Deloo's dead vegetable flare to watch for odd spikes. Heh-heh. I knew she would pop again, and she did—directly into Woody's face. He blew it away. It takes so little to amuse a spirt cave woman. Sobering, I picked up the gist of the conversation.

The problem was obvious to me, the intrepid Baasee'. Woody had known Arthur for more than a decade, and he had many funny stories to tell about his closest friend. Deloo had known her husband for five short months before he died on Thanksgiving Day of the previous winter. She would never have the rich stories that Woody did. She was both angry and envious. I leaped into action. This was spirit guide work of the most typical sort. All I had to do was help Deloo realize that what she wanted so much, which was years instead of months of Arthur's time, was to treasure a quality in Arthur that only she had known as his wife. Woody and Arthur had been competitive young men. They must have hated each other at times. At least Deloo's memories were untainted. Arthur's camera moved in comforting agreement from one side of her chest to the other.

"Are you serious about giving this to Good Will?" Woody asked Deloo.

Deloo glanced at the bright blue bag that held her tent. "Yes. I couldn't have afforded any hotel without Arthur's insurance money. With money I will be much smarter to get motel rooms on route rather than try to pitch a tent in places I've never seen before. I'm not as brave as I was a week ago." While she talked, she adjusted three knapsacks on her shoulders and wheeled a suitcase behind her. "Why? Would you like it?"

"Well," Woody, looked at the almost new sack, "I don't have one and at some point I expect I'll be camping while I do more fieldwork. I've applied for grants, but haven't received word on any of them yet. With grant money I could buy camping gear."

Deloo looked around the Goode's driveway. "Do you have a car? Did you drive here?"

Woody laughed. "Yes and yes. There it is." He pointed to a rusty blue truck on the Goode's lawn. "It leaks. They want me to move it before it destroys the grass."

~Deloo, since you will fly back to Alaska with your mother, I want you to consider giving your Passat to Woody,~ I urged, keen on doing my spirit-guide duty.

Deloo nodded at my assigned spot in the sky and then chuckled, "I didn't notice it. It would blend into the Fairbanks scene. You should do your fieldwork there, and by the way, the tent is all yours. I don't want it anymore."

Woody took all three of her knapsacks from her despite her objections and smiled, "Thanks. I'll put it in the truck when I leave. I was hoping to go to Québec to do a comparative study with their rural police practices in contrast to those of New Brunswick. I used to be in the RCMP in New Brunswick."

Deloo turned a sharp eye on him. "I thought you were a traffic cop."

"Good memory," Woody told her, "I was a traffic cop. I studied law and justice at the university to try for a higher rank. When they passed me over for promotion, I decided to finish my undergrad in Boston. That's when I met Arthur. My doctoral dissertation is a cross between Anthropology and Law with a big dollop of colonialist Canadian history thrown in for good measure."

"I'm glad that I have had a chance to get to know you, Woody. You are like a second son to the Goodes—like a brother to my Arthur. Am I right?"

Woody smiled, "Sure. I've been coming and going from this house as much as I used to do at my mother's apartment in Canada. I've had my own key to the Goode's house for more than a decade." He held it out to show Deloo.

Deloo touched the key and then pointed at the Passat. "They helped me find this car. I've had it for three short weeks and done a lot of growing up in it." She felt herself tearing up and I squelched her urge to cry. "Arthur would have loved it, you know. We didn't have a car of our own in Fairbanks. We were broke, so we worked something out with one of our neighbors to get to work and sometimes borrowed my mother's car. At least, I thought we were broke." She looked at the Goode's beautiful house. "Now that I've been here for a few months, it's obvious that all he had to do was call them for some extra money and it would have been in our bank account within seconds."

Woody cocked his head and stared at her. "Are you serious? No car? What did you do for fun? Arthur was never good at buses."

Loving warmth flowed through her. "He never complained and I never guessed that he came from a background of limitless money. He ate my homemade baloney sandwiches for lunch and we had ramen noodles for supper. I was saving money for a house." She chuckled. "Now that I'm here in his home, I don't understand why he put up with all that."

Woody gazed into the sky for a long moment. "I … I…." He stopped. He choked as if covering a laugh.

Deloo stamped her foot, "It's the truth. He never complained. He never told me he went to a prep school either. Mrs. Goode had to explain what that was." Not certain whether she felt anger toward Arthur or immense sadness, she turned away.

"Wait," Woody called after her, "I'm sorry. Arthur, the Arthur that I knew would have asked his father for money to buy a car before leaving New Mexico. I just couldn't put that together with the idea of him eating baloney. He was a real picky eater."

Deloo stared at Woody in confusion. "He did, though. Every day for months."

"He loved you," Woody said, "you must have been the one woman he ever loved." He kicked a stone on the driveway. "It's my turn to say I'm glad to know you. You made a real change in my old buddy. You got it right. We were like brothers. He was the spoiled son, meaning always in trouble. I was the good son."

Deloo laughed outright. "I didn't know Arthur's spoiled side, but after living here for a little while, I believe he must have been that way."

Floating aloft, I evaluated Deloo's state of generosity, and decided she had found a way to forgive Woody for having known Arthur longer than she had. I infused her with confidence, ~*are you ready to offer him the car, Deloo?*~

"Yes," Deloo said to me. To Woody she added, "The Arthur I knew was generous to me. He gave me this. "She held up her wedding ring set. "I'm so ignorant, that I didn't know this was jade. Mrs. Goode, I mean Matty, brought our wedding rings with her to Albuquerque last year. I thought this green part was just cheap glass." She twirled the ring on her finger. They spun, showing she'd lost another pound or two.

"Mrs. Goode told me this ring was carved in China. Zachary had it done. Them, I mean. Arthur wore the one that Zachary had made for himself. Mrs. Goode said this one is worth fifteen thousand dollars." She eyed Woody. "We could have bought two used cars for that price."

"Wow!" Woody ogled the rings. "I didn't know rings cost that much."

"So, Woody, my husband's brother," she turned to face him, "I want to give you the Passat. Arthur would want me to do that."

"What?! You're crazy," Woody gaped at Deloo.

"Not crazy. Just ready," she smiled, and handed him her car key.

"Ready for what?" Woody pushed the key away.

"Ready to let Arthur," she gathered herself to say the rest, "go. I'm ready to let him be dead. Besides, lots of our stories, Athabascan as well as Lower 48 Native stories tell us not to hoard. There's one where Dotson, they call him Great Raven in the English version, demanded that a husband and wife burn all the furs that they wanted to give him as payback for saving their lives. The point of that story is to give others the kind of things they can use. Spirits can't use furs from the material world. It has to become smoke to make the transfer to Dotson."

They were silent for a long time. Then Woody said, "I'd be a fool to turn down a car. I don't have enough money to make it through the summer without begging Zachary for a loan." His mouth dipped to one side. "Besides, I can't let you burn the car just to prove a point."

Deloo patted his hand. "Then it's a done deal. The car is yours." She held out the key.

"No. The car is yours," Woody patted away the key again and grinned, "until I drive you to the airport on your way back to Fairbanks."

"Deal!" Deloo laughed as they entered the Goode's front door where the heady aroma of beef stew pulled them both into the kitchen.

Over savory smells and a musical variety of chewing sounds, Woody nodded his head. "Thanks, Zachary, for that intel about Howard Lee and another person, HayJay Johnson. That's a situation kept secret from all but a few insiders.

"What are you talking about?" Deloo asked.

Zachary shook his head. "It still amazes me on all fronts. Everything I've dug up on Howard Lee points out one key feature: he's the real deal when it comes to genius. He got an MBA from Harvard. It took him the usual two years. My anonymous source told me that during those two years he turned down every party invitation in order to spend each and every weekend in Florida with his Cuban girlfriend. The pair married and have lived in peace since then."

Matty held up a hand. "Well! My anonymous source told me that Howard Lee never left the city limits of Cambridge during those same two years. Moreover, he was already married to the Cuban girlfriend while he, Howard, earned a second degree in his nephew's name."

"What?" Deloo looked confused. "Why get a degree in someone else's name?"

"Yes, that's the crux of this data," Matty continued. "In the same week that he graduated from Harvard with a Master of Business Administration as Howard Lee, he also received a PhD from MIT in Computer Science by using his nephew's name, Harold Johnson, also known as HayJay by his friends. Hay is for Harold, Jay is for Johnson. HayJay disappeared just after completing all coursework for a PhD at MIT. He was still a teenager. No one knows what happened to him. The Johnsons have kept his disappearance a secret from outsiders."

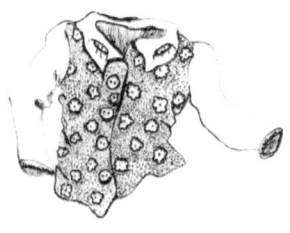

CHAPTER THIRTY-NINE

"That's crazy," Woody snapped.

Matty shook her head. "My source was willing to share her suspicions, but she doesn't have proof. She thinks they still hope that HayJay will show up some day. He was the same age as his uncle, Howard Lee. Charlotte, HayJay's grandmother, was married twice. She had a daughter, Lydia, by the first husband. Then the first husband died. Charlotte married Mr. Lee many years later and had a son, Howard. Lydia was grown by then. She married about the same time that her mother did and HayJay was born around the same time as his uncle, Howard Lee. Even as a toddler, HayJay was called a crazy genius." Matty sorted through the photos in her folder.

"Do you mean he was an idiot-savant?" asked Zachary.

Matty shook her head. "My source said he had good days and very crazy days. And he was a real genius in school, especially when it came to computers. My source thinks he died but no one talks about it."

"Perhaps they don't want to live with the truth. We looked through her old photo albums and school yearbooks, and we found lots of pictures of Howard and HayJay posing together up through age sixteen, but there weren't any of both them together afterward. What struck me about the photos was how much the boys resembled each other. Same height. Same build. Same facial features. Even though Howard's father is half Chinese and looks it, Howard's Asian heritage doesn't show very much. Howard has dark blond hair and blue-green eyes, almost like HayJay's. Likewise, HayJay doesn't have any Asian ancestry that we know of, but he sure looked like he might have. His hair was a little lighter than Howard's, and his eyes were a clear blue shade. Howard's eyes were hazel: unpredictable, sometimes green, other times plain blue." Matty reached for a folder she'd placed close to the dining table.

"I got a copy of the last photo with both of them together." She tugged a leaf out of the folder. "You can see how hard it is to tell them apart."

The photo made its way around the table. Deloo studied it for a long while. "They were used to dressing alike, just like twins often do." She jabbed a finger at the photo. "The difference between them is the tie. Each of these ties has a different design. One is dark pink and the other is red." She frowned at Matty. "Did your source explain why?"

Matty let out a satisfied breath and said, "Most of us around the table know the answer to that because this is an Ivy League town. I knew you'd be the one to see the ties, Deloo. Yes. The dark pink is known as crimson, standing for Harvard. The red tie with the grey math symbol represents the Massachusetts Institute of Technology or M.I.T. HayJay and Howard were the same age, but HayJay was accepted into M.I.T. when he was fifteen. It could be that Howard was not as smart, because he didn't get into Harvard until he was all of sixteen."

"If you look very close," Matty pointed her eyebrows toward the photo then in Deloo's hands, "you'll see that the boy with the crimson tie has very straight dark blond hair and blue-green eyes. The other has light blond, wavy hair and clear blue eyes. It's not much of a difference, but the family could tell them apart most of the time."

"I see the similarity, but so what?" Deloo asked.

Matty pulled another photo out of the folder. "This is a more recent photo of HayJay. My friend is a member of the Johnson family. She took this photo. Dr. Harold HayJay Johnson is standing next to his wife in the second row." She pulled out yet another photo. "And this is HayJay and his wife in a close up on the same day."

Everyone crowded around Matty to see the photos. The man in the close up had thinning white hair that still had some blond coloring. His slanted eyelids squinted over blue-green irises. What was left of his hair was far more curly than wavy. The tan woman next to him twisted her long dark hair into a pile on the back of her head. Her enormous black eyes seemed to be focused on HayJay.

"She looks Native. A woman with her looks would fit right into Alaska," Deloo remarked. "Is she Native American?"

Matty laughed. "In a way. My source told me that both men married Cuban women. She never saw the two women together, just as she never saw Howard with grown-up HayJay."

Woody's frown creased the sides of his face. "The man in this photo does look like the teenaged HayJay. Did all of these people call him

'HayJay' at this occasion?"

"That's what my friend told me. HayJay."

It occurred to me that it wouldn't take much to rig up a disguise for family events. *~Howard could use makeup or a wig whenever he's playing HayJay's part.~*

"You know," Deloo mused, following my lead. "Anyone can get styling gels and a curling iron. Women curl their straight hair to get a look like this. What did your friend say?"

Matty thought about the conversation. "You're right. She told me about a time when they all went swimming at a private beach on Cape Cod. I should have picked up on it then. She said, 'It's bothered me that HayJay wouldn't go swimming with us that day. Everyone else did, including his wife. But, what the heck, no one thought much about HayJay after his wife took off the see-through beach jacket that covered a bright red bikini."

Zachary grinned, "I can understand that part, but why didn't HayJay go into the water?"

"That's what my friend apologized for. She didn't ask." Matty pulled out another photo. "My friend caught a snap at that beach party. It shows HayJay leaning against his grandmother Charlotte's right shoulder and Lydia, who is both HayJay's mother as well as Howard's older sister, leaning against her mother's, Charlotte, left shoulder."

Deloo snorted. "That's hard to beat. Three identical smiles."

Matty slid a final photo showing two boys and a much younger Lydia. "Which one do you think is HayJay?"

Woody whistled. "May rigor mortis release my lungs and let me breathe! If we were trying Howard for killing his nephew, this photo would clinch it. Did HayJay have some sort of minor birth defect that made his smile droop that way?"

Matty nodded. "That crooked smile got him a lot of dates in high school. It's just enough off that it made him look shy instead of confident."

~Ask Matty how often she saw HayJay when they were in high school. I'm not getting a clear enough sense of what's going on here.~

Deloo asked, "Did you ever see Howard and HayJay together?"

Matty answered, "No. I met HayJay when he was in prep school, and I'm sure I never met Howard. My friend was a year older than Howard and HayJay. When they were toddlers, the three of them were put at the same table for dinners and required to take naps in the same room.

My friend knew both of them well until they were all about ten or eleven. Then my friend's family moved away and Howard's family began to spend time in China. It was the summer my friend turned seventeen and the two boys turned sixteen that all three were together again."

Deloo nudged Matty along. "That would have been what? Twenty-five or so years ago? So then what happened?"

"My friend said the three families went camping together one week. Each family got a cabin. On the fourth morning, Howard and his family left to go to China." Matty took a bite of stew before continuing.

"Later that day, HayJay and my friend went hiking. He was a lot better at rock climbing than she was, so she waited at the base of a treacherous incline while he kept going. She hung around for an hour, but he didn't come back. She called to him, but he never answered. She screamed. People heard her and came to find out what was wrong. Two of them climbed to where my friend said HayJay went, but they couldn't find him.'

After a round of sympathetic words and more munching, Matty resumed her story. "There was a big search and rescue effort that seemed to go on for days. His family stayed behind another few weeks to keep looking, but they never found any trace of HayJay. My source suspects the man in this photo is not HayJay, but like everyone else, she didn't say anything."

"Well, I'm stumped," Deloo said. "Why did he pretend to be his nephew?"

"I can answer that," Zachary said. "I know Charlotte and her first husband's family pretty well, but not the Lee family. Charlotte's first husband was a lot older than me and Matty, so we've never had much in common. Charlotte met her first husband in Halifax, Nova Scotia when he did a year abroad in Canada. Charlotte is from the wealthy Framboise family on Cape Breton, an island belonging to Nova Scotia. They had Lydia a couple of years before he died. After Matty got all that info, I went to visit Charlotte to learn more. Charlotte married Mr. Lee a year before Harold or HayJay was born. Howard was born a couple of months after HayJay."

"Whew!" Woody complained. "That's one of those kinship chart things that I always have trouble with." The others laughed.

Zachery coughed and said "my source told me what you will hear next in strict confidentiality. Turns out that when the Lees came back from China, Lydia called her mother. She wanted to meet with Charlotte and her half-brother, Howard. It was close to the beginning of the fall terms when both young men were due to begin new degree work at MIT and Harvard. HayJay was precocious, and started college while other kids were in elementary school. Howard must have been just as bright, but his father was determined that he learn about China as well as America, so he delayed college a few years. Howard was going to begin his undergraduate studies and HayJay was supposed to start his PhD work in computer engineering. She told them that HayJay's entire MIT education was already paid for through a family trust fund and that he and his mentoring professor had already agreed on HayJay's proposal for his doctoral project. HayJay had already worked out a detailed timeline to complete his dissertation project. He would have spent the next year implementing and testing it and then writing his dissertation. Mrs. Johnson wanted to know if Howard could pretend to be HayJay in order to earn the degree in his nephew's name. She wanted to honor her son through his uncle's efforts. That way, if HayJay reappeared, all the work for the PhD would be done and HayJay could go on with life. They said that Howard was more than competent enough to do all of it if he didn't do anything else, like have fun."

"HayJay's mother, Lydia, told her mother and brother that if he accepted her request, they both had to keep it a secret from everyone, including Howard's father." Zachary looked around the room. "Questions?"

Everyone in the room started talking at once, including me and the other spirit guides. Howard had agreed to the ruse and decided to complete both degrees at one time. And did.

Deloo pressed her hands against her forehead to signal her confusion. "Let me see if I understand this. You're saying that Howard Lee, the man who stole my identity, assumed his nephew's identity, got a Harvard MBA in his own name, and at almost the same time, got a PhD from MIT in the other name."

Woody smiled at her. "You got it."

Zachary nodded and added, "Mr. Johnson's grandmother on his father's side put money into the trust fund for HayJay. By contrast, Howard's father wouldn't go the PhD route with any of his sons, but he did give each of them a trust fund for up through the master's level."

Deloo looked around the room and said, "What a complicated way to do things. Don't you think that all of these families know the secret by now?"

Woody snarled at Zachary, "Let's hope that none of them knows as much as we do about what Howard Lee did for his nephew, but each of them knows a little. I've got to call Al Beamus on this. They could get clean away with it."

"If 'it' means killing the weirdo woman at the Secret Spirit Inn," Deloo said, "he might get away with it, but what makes you think he did it?" Her jadeite wedding ring, unseen by any of the mortals, spumed dragon smoke. I helped the smoke curl around the room.

"HayJay's mother, Lydia, maintains that HayJay is the man in all of those photos, and that he's alive. She thinks that HayJay worships his uncle, Howard, so much that he'd do anything for him. She said that if things had been different, HayJay would have done as much for Howard. Moreover, his mother Charlotte maintains that Howard has earned the honors: Howard got all those degrees and yet works at a boring bank. She thinks her grandson, HayJay, might have carried his veneration of Howard to even greater lengths. What she suggested is that her grandson, HayJay, came back to them with everything intact except a moral compass. He doesn't know wrong from right. He was always a little off. Now he's even more so."

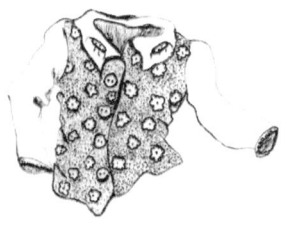

CHAPTER FORTY

They finished eating in silence. It had been a long day for Zachary, Woody and Deloo. Matty encouraged the group to get cozy around the television set in the Goode's family room.

"Cozy," described Deloo more so than it did the others. She sprawled under a warm comforter on a settee while Matty and Zachary cuddled on the couch across the room. Woody occupied a big recliner in front of the television set. I examined Deloo. Other than being sound asleep, she appeared no worse for wear for all the big changes she'd been through. An intriguing hue of carmine and ochre floated above my Deloo. In no time I spread the cloud of red across the ceiling area. I patted it into a smaller shape, tested it for durability, and pounced. It held! Satisfied that no one seemed to mind if I took a nap as well, I pressed myself into the tingling redness of it. I did so from its bottom side so that I could keep watch on my gentle Deloo. Earth's gravity, after all, has no claims on Baasee' the Feather-Weight Champion of the eternal world.

I had almost found the perfect spot when Deloo sat up and groped for the sketch pad she'd put on the sofa table behind the settee. Arthur's camera rested beside it. I yawned, wondering what Deloo had for us. Then I realized that Deloo wasn't alone.

A wraith flickered in front of her. Deloo seemed to be in conversation with it. I heaved my red cushion up and away and floated downward to find out who was pestering my precious and perfect mortal.

"Yes, Arthur," Deloo mouthed the words. She maneuvered a red pencil around on a sheet of paper with great speed, and then changed colors to a neutral shade of tan. I examined Deloo for signs of fear and wasn't surprised to note that she was not awake. She was drawing in a trance state. I turned to the wraith, not displeased to recognize it as Arthur. For someone a mere seven months deceased, her late husband was self-aware. I looked around for the spirit guide who must be marching him through his first steps toward eternity. Wouldn't you know? It was the male spirit who had been with Arthur during his short marriage to Deloo.

He greeted me.

In less time than it takes to think about it, I seized him in a harsh grip with one of my arm-like tendrils. *~You dared to place my mortal charge into a dream state without any semblance of seeking my permission. If you don't know the consequences of such a crime, you soon will. You butt head, why did you do it?~*

He writhed but couldn't escape my grip. *~I'm sorry! It won't happen again.~*

Arthur's mentoring spirit risked getting a smudge mark for making a poor choice. I spotted the smudgy black area stretched along his backside. It would disappear if he did something of great valor or kindness. Since he had quite a few such smudges, I doubt if he knew much about either courage or kindness.

Nonetheless, I answered, *~I observed you disappear many times during the five-and-a-half months that you and Arthur were with us. You need to learn something about how we, the well-educated spirit guides, keep tabs on our mortals even while taking quick breaks away. I'll give you five seconds to undo that dream state, or I'll remove it myself and leave you with a special treat.~*

Since we had a history of my version of dealing with his mischief, he backed away. I sent him a "learning" message to make my meaning clear. I'd received thousands of such "learning" messages from multiple sources over my long life. All of us in the spirit world rat on each other, just as I planned to do about Arthur's guide. The thing is, if you get enough learning messages on the same topic, you will get a visit from an Ancient Being of the Invisible Forces whose job it is to make sure you understand how to behave.

He gasped, more or less, *~I can't reverse it. He's been given a task that will earn him a higher standing with the Invisible Forces. See~* he flashed a bright prong toward Deloo. *~He's helping her draw something that will guide you through this problem.~*

I studied Deloo's drawing and realized that Arthur's guide was telling the truth. It was evidence. It looked useful. With reluctance, I loosened my grip and he wriggled free. *~Don't you ever try that again!~* I warned him.

He produced an impish gesture, *~I'll try harder to find you the next time. Any time you need to hug someone, just call on little old me!~*

I scowled and decided to add a little something tangy to soften the bite of my bad mood. All right. I goosed him. He leered. I refused to acknowledge the little kiss he blew toward me by turning my full attention onto Deloo's dazzling artwork.

Deloo's deft fingers brought to life the scene at the highway hotel in Amherst, Nova Scotia. She'd completed the images of the two people who'd broken into her hotel room. Even though she was asleep, she drew a playful circle around Chuan's crotch as if to signal where he hurt the most. The woman faced the two men who had joined them. Deloo had drawn a pair of sunglasses on Ming that snugged her hair away from her face. One figure was a slim man dressed in a three-piece suit, including a tie. I remembered seeing all of them in casual attire, perhaps a tee shirt and Dockers. I sensed the suit was a symbolic gesture. He was one of the two blond white men. Deloo had colored his hair a light ash brown rather than yellowish blond. I noted the ashy man's Asian looks. Deloo was working on the fourth man's face. Arthur was insistent that she use the closest color match to the man's striking blue eyes. His hair was a bright, white blond. She had enhanced their differences by distinguishing between shades of blond and the details of their eyes.

When she finished, she looked up at Arthur's transparent face and turned the paper toward him with a questioning look. The wraith nodded and began to float toward his mentoring guide.

"Thanks, Arthur," Deloo said aloud. She put the sketchbook back onto the sofa table and curled up under the blanket on the settee.

Woody darted to the nightstand and scrutinized the drawing. Matty dashed over to sit beside Deloo and draped her arm around her daughter-in-law's shoulders. Zachary took the other side.

"Deloo, dear, who were you talking to?" Matty asked.

Deloo, still in a daze, answered, "Arthur." She looked for him in the place she'd last seen him and blinked. "He's gone."

Zachary asked, "Whatever did he say to you, Deloo?"

"He told me to draw those people. They're in the parking lot of a hotel near the border between New Brunswick and Nova Scotia." Deloo reached for the sketchbook. Woody placed it on her lap so that everyone could see it. "He wanted me to draw that man with a suit even though he wasn't wearing a suit at the time. I think the man is Howard Lee—the man who stole my debit card number."

"What about this other guy," Woody pointed to the fourth man. "Is that the way he was dressed when you saw him?"

Deloo stared at the fourth figure with interest.

~Why does he wear a white coat? Why did you make his eyes so big?~ I, Baasee' the Subtly Wonderful, needed to know.

Deloo regarded the drawing as if for the first time. "No, he had on different clothes then. A dress shirt, the kind that Zachary wears all the time. Arthur told me to draw him with this white coat, like a doctor."

"His eyes are bigger than normal. Is that the way they were?" Matty touched the fourth figure's head.

Deloo studied her drawing—once again as if she'd never seen it before. I intervened, *~tell them that his eyes did look like that, and that you've drawn them out of proportion to his head and face because Arthur wanted us to know what color the eyes are.~*

Deloo repeated my commune almost verbatim. "They are an unusual color of blue. Hmmm. I think I know someone who has eyes just like this," She looked at the ceiling, at me, and continued, "but I can't remember his name," she handed the sketchbook to Woody, "Wait. No. I don't know him by name. He was in a bookstore in Nova Scotia. He had a bead. One like this." She pulled the plastic cubes she'd acquired on the drive toward the Secret Spirit Inn.

Deloo started shivering. Matty tugged the blanket up higher around her shoulders and told her to go to bed. "Deloo, I think it will be best if your mother sleeps with you tomorrow night. You've had too many shocks, and this impressive drawing may be the most important of them. I'll sit with you for a while tonight, but your mother needs to be with you if something else happens." She turned toward Woody and added, "By the way, Woody, did I remember to tell you to leave your bags in Arthur's room?" at this point she closed one eye toward Woody in an exaggerated wink.

Stumped, Woody shrugged at Matty, but didn't say anything. Zachary approached and whispered, "She wants to keep Deloo from sleeping with Arthur's things in case she has another ghost experience."

Understanding, Woody headed toward Arthur's old room. Matty led Deloo toward another bedroom. Matty continued, "Deloo, I made up our old bedroom for you and your mother because it has its own bathroom."

Although she had appeared to be conscious when talking to them about the drawing, in reality Deloo was just starting to awaken from the dream-state that Arthur's mentoring guide had foisted on her. Still feeling a little thick-headed, she nodded. "That's very thoughtful of you, Matty. It's a beautiful room. Your new master bedroom must be finished. When I was here a couple of weeks ago you thought it wasn't going to be ready until mid-July."

"Yes," Matty replied. "They finished in time to start another job in Framingham. They should have finished our house in March! Would you like to see it?" She led Deloo upstairs.

"Knock me over with a raven quill!" Deloo ogled the new rooms. "This is fabulous."

"Matty," Woody wolf-whistled from behind them, "you've turned that dusty old attic into a work of art. Now you'll have to keep Deloo here so that she can paint another masterpiece!"

Deloo squeezed Matty with a tight hug. "Any time! I'd love to paint for you."

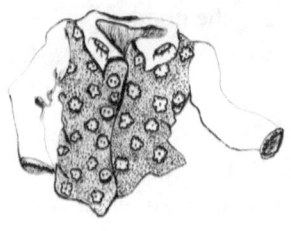

CHAPTER FORTY-ONE

Long after everyone in the Goode house was in bed and asleep, someone pried open a window on the ground floor. The alarm went off, arousing the entire household and initiating an automatic call to the security company and police department. Zachary and Woody inspected the outside of the house with the responding officers. It had rained earlier. Footprints were visible, but too waterlogged to be of use.

Back in the house, Zachary said, "We've had that security system in place for twenty years. We've paid for expensive updates every year, and every year I complain that it's a waste of money. I'm glad we have it now. The agent said someone had the right equipment to pry open a window with this kind of latch." Zachary reddened with anger. "They have our address." He turned to the cop. "I've got information to give to the police that might help explain this."

Woody cut in. "The RCMP inspector has already contacted the Burlington police. I'm sure he'll want to know about this break-in."

On advice from the police officers, Zachary Goode called the Cambridge police department at eight the following morning and spoke to the detective in charge of the case against Howard Lee. While waiting, Zachary found his hands doodling tiny dragons across the top of his notepad. He stared at the page. He hadn't drawn a dragon since he was a little boy. The last of the dragons seemed to snarl at him with fire bursting out of its mouth. Zachary tore off the page, thinking he should show it to Deloo. She knows about symbols from her art background.

The line smacked and popped. Someone gave him the name of the detective who was handling the case and then put him on hold. As it happened, he recollected the detective's father, a man he'd known since college. As his friend's son picked up the telephone receiver, someone in the police department handed the young detective information about the break-in in Vermont. "It's good to talk to you, William. I hope your father is well." After the prescribed moment of chatting, Zachary got to the main point. "The hotel in Vermont told me they would send their information to you. Have you got it, yet?"

There was a pause as William scanned the material and agreed. "Is your daughter-in-law with you?"

"Yes, she is with me now. We'll come to the station, if you'd like."

"That may not be necessary. Let's talk, first. Do you know who did this?"

Zachary supplied details. "Probably. His name is Howard Lee. He used her debit card numbers within five hours after she left Montreal. He's prepared his work with a cadre of international professionals. He works in Cambridge. He knows where I live. There was an attempted break-in last night, but not enough evidence to link it to anyone in particular. I'd like to stop this thief before he makes another move against my daughter-in-law—or anyone else in my family."

William asked a series of questions, finally ending with a question that Zachary wanted to hear.

"Yes, William, I want to file charges as soon as possible. What's the next step?" Zachary agreed to stop by the station within the hour and turned in triumph to Deloo. "My dear, I think it's time for you to take a long, slow breath. Everything is under control."

I wafted a shower of praise on Mr. Goode's head and communed, *~He's right, Deloo. Thank him and get ready to pick up your mother at the airport. Oh, and breathe!~*

Deloo released a lungful of air. "Are they going to arrest him?"

Mr. Goode shrugged. "I've known William since he was a toddler. He was one of those intense, serious children who had to be told in advance that he was going to hear a funny story. Without the warning, he'd never laugh. He is in the best profession for a man of his intelligence and disposition."

Woody, who had been leaning against the patio door during the phone call, smiled and said, "I guess that's why I didn't make it as a cop. I like jokes and pulled a number of them on Arthur."

Zachary laughed, "You two were always teasing each other. Yes, there are times when having a sense of humor can get in the way." He reached for Deloo's hand, "You two should be on your way pretty soon. The morning traffic is always the worst. By the time you get back with your mother, we might know more."

Woody and Deloo arrived at Logan airport an hour ahead of time. It was obvious he was used to the congestion, knew how to anticipate the pace of traffic by time of day and route, and best of all, he knew the local nicknames for most of the major routes. Catching a glimpse of the muscles working in Deloo's jaw, he slowed to make the correct exit for the parking garage.

"How's this for luck?" Woody beamed at the nearby walkway leading into the airport next to the parking space he'd found. "So, Deloo, which is worse? Everything that's happened to you in the past few days or Boston traffic?"

I could see that Deloo was still traumatized by the traffic, so I gave her a soft vibe of energy and suggested, ~*laugh. He's joking. Then tell him that he's not a traffic cop.*~

Deloo's laugh was at first tepid but she let it grow in volume. Grinning in genuine amusement, she shook a finger in his general direction, it being against Athabascan traditions to point at any one, and retorted, "You are not a traffic cop! You are the worst driver I've ever met. Didn't you hear all those people honking at you? You cut off two of them at that last bridge for no reason!"

Woody dropped his jaw in mock pain. "I didn't say I was a traffic cop. You did. I was on foot patrol most of the time." He opened his door, walked around to her side to open her door, and almost lost a tooth when Deloo's door swung out.

"Sorry," Deloo apologized. "Arthur used to do that, too." She dimpled at Woody. "It's one of the things Arthur would do when people were looking at us." She shrugged. "I realized that he would forget when we were alone. I would be sitting in the car and he would be halfway up the street before he thought about me and looked back."

Woody rubbed his lip around the small cut inside his mouth, "After Zigwan got used to it, she insisted that I open her door. Whenever I forgot, she'd wait." He rolled his eyes. "In hindsight I'd say that was the least of our problems."

"Zigwan. Arthur mentioned her name. Somehow I recalled her name as Sequin. Zigwan is prettier. Did I ever meet her?" Deloo asked, trying to pretend that I hadn't told her already.

Woody didn't notice the look on Deloo's expressive face. "No. She was out of my life quite a while before Arthur met you. I thought she was the one."

Deloo surprised me by quoting my sentiments from a day or two earlier, "You were doing what Arthur and I did—looking for the next important step in your life. Arthur was my next step. We just didn't know it was a step that would last five months and twenty-three days." She stopped.

As she spoke, both Deloo and I saw a vision of a little girl's face. It was very blurry. Behind her we both saw an adult woman's face. As soon as the two faces appeared, they were gone.

~Baasee', did you? ~

~Yes. I think you'll meet them soon. Pay attention to your cop. He seems distracted.~

Deloo cleared her throat and asked, "What does a Canadian cop on foot patrol do?" Deloo glanced at Woody's face and realized that he hadn't stopped thinking about Zigwan. Amused, she looked down and tried to pretend she hadn't said anything.

~Good tactic, my mortal collaborator,~ I praised her. *~When he's ready, let's find out more about the investigation into that innkeeper's death.~*

Woody murmured as if there had been no lapse in the conversation, "I was eighteen when I got hired in Fredericton in New Brunswick. That's where I grew up. I was fresh out of school. It was just my mother and me by that time. My father moved to Maine when I was fifteen, but he hadn't lived with us for six or seven years." Woody shook his head. "Now that I'm older and have had all that education, I can put it in better perspective. It was tough on him to be married to a First Nations woman in those days. His life was even more complicated because although his father was Canadian, his mother was American and insisted that her first born enter the world in the United States. I have dual citizenship: both U.S. and Canadian. I suppose that will change now that I've graduated with my final degree."

"To make things even more complicated, it was before they changed the Canadian Indian Act in 1985. My folks got married before that. My mother was forced to move off the reserve because she married out, meaning she married a non-native man. By the old law, she became a white woman as soon as they married, and my birth certificate says I'm a white man. Because of the 1985 changes, I could get federal recognition as a First Nations citizen in Canada. At first I told my mother I didn't want it, but she convinced me to get it any way."

"You're kidding," Deloo said. "I've never heard of such a thing. The way it's done in the States is by blood quantum or tribal consensus. I don't like that much either, but at least I'm called a Native even though I do have a white father. I thought Canada was the same way."

~Grandfather Kwaikit and I have followed the impact of Europe on Native Americans of North and South America for centuries. Many generations before yours legalized some predjudices even as they eradicated others. It was so easy to see other humans as non-human, that they came to believe it. As the half-millennium mark after 1492 came close in the twentieth century, there were millions of people who wanted to change such malevolent ways,~ I griped, polishing my ruby-red false eyelashes. *~Most of those changes happened before you were born.~*

Woody nodded. "That's what I thought until I studied Indian Law in Albuquerque. So my folks moved to Fredericton in New Brunswick when I was born. The paradox is that my mother and father were both raised on the reserve even though one was white and the other First Nations. That's the life they both knew. Dad's father was a teacher." Woody looked off into a world of memories. "We both learned to deal with different issues of living with the sneaky way kids can torture each other. I was tormented about being a half-breed. Dad was ridiculed because he was a white kid. Both are common stories. And so is what happened when they moved off the reserve. They were both eighteen. No college. No job training. They had to figure out how to get work the hard way. Dad got a job with a plumber who was good to him. I hear that he's doing well nowadays. My mother learned to type and landed a job with a branch of the Department of Indian Affairs in Fredericton. She's worked there ever since."

Grandfather Kwaikit suddenly appeared beside me and huffed, *~A nineteenth century mortification was to display famous Indian leaders, like the Apache chief Geronimo, at local fairs and events. Such men and women were kept prisoner. A twentieth century innovation was to hire First Nations or Native Americans, often to get tax credits. That practice is still going on.~*

Deloo nodded at Woody. By then they'd located the closest place in the airport building where passengers on Taale's flight would pass on their way to baggage claim. There was no place to sit, so the two of them leaned against a wall. "So, what made you think of . . . what's it called— the Royal Mounted Police?"

"You mean the Royal Canadian Mounted Police—the RCMP." Woody looked bemused, "Oh, right. Al, the inspector on this case, saw an ad and asked me to go with him to sign up. We both signed up and both of us got in. He's the one who made the grade for promotion, and when I didn't I went to college. I got lucky. There were scholarships at Boston University that I qualified for under the Jay Treaty—and because I had Indian status with Canada."

"Jay Treaty?" Deloo smiled. "I've heard of that one. It lets some Canadian First Nations people move back and forth between the U.S. and Canada."

"Yes," Woody grinned, "it takes educating the powers that be every time you want to exercise the right—but that's the idea."

"So that's when you met Arthur?" Deloo prompted.

"Yeah. Arthur was seven months older by age, but two years ahead of me in the university. Arthur was always testing the waters in courses that I took until his last year. By then I had taken enough extra courses each semester to catch up with students born the same year as me. Then when he decided to go for a Master's degree at UNM, I trotted right along behind him a year later."

I felt the mind and power of Taale coming toward us and urged Deloo to ask about his contacts at the RCMP. *~Keep him focused. He tends to drift off topic.~*

"So, before the innkeeper's death, did you keep in touch with Inspector Beamus or your other RCMP friends?" Deloo asked with a forced casual tone.

Woody shrugged. "Right. I've got a lot of reasons to call him. Maybe Al will come to Boston to check out Howard Lee. He ticked at his cell phone. "Al! It's Woody." He grinned at Deloo. "So how are you doing?"

"Yeah, I want to make sure you knew about the attempted break-in at my friend's house in Cambridge. I am a houseguest there. So is Deloo Goode, the woman who was chased around the Maritimes last week." Woody explained in coded police terms what had happened to Deloo.

"What's new?" Deloo asked when he ended the call.

"Al got turned down to come to Vermont, but now he might be able to swing a trip to Boston to ask us some questions and talk to Howard Lee. He said Burlington police have filed a report. I'll help him get information from the Cambridge Police Department."

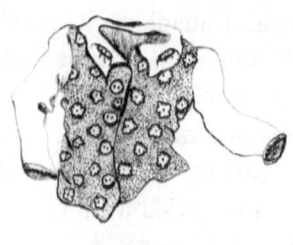

CHAPTER FORTY-TWO

"Mom!" Deloo shouted, "Over here!"

"Ha," Woody murmured, "I can tell already which one is your mother from here."

Deloo hackled up. "How? Because she's the dark-skinned person coming downstairs?"

"What?" Woody scowled, "No!" He moved a step away from Deloo. "Is that what you take me for? A racial profiler?"

Deloo flailed arms in wide swoops at her mother and hissed, "That's what Arthur did. Why would you be any different?"

"Arthur?" Woody gawked at the short woman beside him.

Floating above them, I had been busy studying Taale. She radiated good health and happiness.

Turning my sensors to Woody, it was obvious that Deloo had irritated him. Very confused, I tried to figure out what had happened to make Woody her adversary in less than thirty seconds. As if reading my mind, Woody supplied a few answers.

"Arthur wasn't a racist. I grew up around racist bigots and always knew which to avoid. Arthur wasn't like that. We were best friends from the start."

A big tour group pressed around a tall man with a placard announcing "Boston Tours". They blocked Taale's progress. Deloo stopped waving and glowered at Woody.

~Remember, he didn't know Arthur the way you did, Deloo. Besides, Arthur never said such things out loud. Instead, he thought them. You always picked up his attitude and internal thoughts without realizing it. Give yourself credit for being so psychic and credit to Arthur for keeping his thoughts to himself,~ As always, I am Baasee', the Brilliant Counsellor.

Arthur's camera rocked against Deloo's heart. She hesitated before speaking. "Now that you mention it," Deloo said to Woody, "Arthur never said anything aloud. It was always in the little things he did, like finding excuses to avoid my cousins. For instance, he wouldn't take them to his lab." Deloo shrugged, "they're in school. They wanted to know what a real scientist does."

Woody cocked his head and relaxed. "I'm sorry about that. I didn't see him around young people."

From my vantage point above his head, I knew that all of Woody's upper thoracic muscles had tightened and then I found several of his visual memories of a younger Arthur shunning Native Americans who attended classes at Boston University or later at the University of New Mexico. As Deloo said, they were inconspicuous actions that didn't impact Woody.

"I can tell the nice looking woman in the pink dress is related to you when her face softened when she spotted you. She loves you." Woody smiled, "I apologize for going cop on you. Old habits like that are hard to kick."

Icy green eyes assessed Arthur's best friend. Deloo allowed her face to open into a slow smile. "We both loved Arthur."

Taale watched her child with the piercing look that Woody had just seen in Deloo. Her daughter's face, reddened by the southwestern sun, had settled on a ruddy tan in the northeast, a signal that Deloo was more tense than usual. Taale turned her attention to the stranger who stood beside her. By the time she reached the bottom of the steps, Taale pegged him as a cop or a uniform somehow. She fixed a professional smile on tired lips and opened her arms to Deloo.

"Mama!"

Whenever Deloo slipped back into the toddler name she used to call her mother, Taale knew something bad had happened. Deloo had called her Mama for a week after Arthur died. When Taale heard Deloo say "Mom" on the seventh day, she knew her daughter had pulled herself together in the Athabascan way of emotional stoicism. Hearing Mama again spiked her maternal worry levels.

"I'm here Baby," Taale whispered into her daughter's ear. "It's good to see you."

Deloo loosened her grip on Taale's shoulders and realized that her hands were trembling. "Mama, this is Woody Morrow. He and Arthur were friends and roommates in college."

Taale extended her right hand in a firm hand shake. "It's good to meet you, Woody." She scrutinized him. "I think I met you at the wedding. Did I?"

"I remember you, Ms. Denaa," Woody shook her head. "I was the best man."

Taale laughed, "Please call me Taale."

Woody beamed, "Taale, I know you worked all day before flying to Boston. How long was the flight itself?"

"Fourteen hours," Taale answered, hoping that she had managed to comb out all signs of travel in the ladies room. She smiled. "I only had to change planes once, but that made it an all-night flight. I don't sleep well on planes. Do you?"

"Fourteen hours?" Woody shook his head. "You look fit and healthy for all that. I would be staggering by now." He stretched an arm toward the capacious bag hanging from Taale's shoulder. "May I carry that bag? It looks heavy."

Taale laughed, handed the bag to Woody, and grinned when he pretended to crumple under its weight. "I didn't have time to pack." She gestured to the bag. "I didn't check any bags, so I'm ready to go."

Woody slid Taale's carry-on bag over his shoulder and signaled for her to go ahead of him. Taale glanced at Deloo and waited for her daughter to guide them out of the terminal.

Meanwhile, I smiled a greeting to Taale's spirit guide, Zephyr. I smiled without lips or teeth. To give myself a vehicle for my dramatic urges and to explain how difficult the recent chases through Canada had been, I created a dipping movement. It was the best I could do to fake an invisible hunchbacked limp. Zephyr lent a supportive tendril to help me pretend to lurch after the mortals. I cheered up and turned my attention back to Deloo. They had already reached the Passat. Who would know it took so long to create a pathetic look in the ether world?

I hustled to catch up with their thoughts. Each had been busy assessing the others. Taale and Deloo had leaned into each other. Behind them Woody was comparing Deloo to her mother. I did the same. Taale stood at least four inches taller than Deloo, and outweighed her daughter by twenty pounds. However, since Deloo almost topped one hundred, Taale looked trim, seemed younger than forty, and was glad to be with her daughter again.

Soon they were in the Passat with Woody as driver, Taale in the front passenger seat, and Deloo in the back seat where she and Woody had carved more room. Woody opted to take a more peaceful route and drove to Cambridge the long way through Malden. Mrs. Goode greeted them all with coffee and pastries on the patio.

* * *

After the treat, everyone, including us, the spirit guides with each of the mortals, helped clear the patio table. I used a bubbling champagne mist to blow off some crumbs. Zephyr grinned and did the same with an effervescent sea-foam green. The mortals carried plates into the house, piling everything onto the counter beside the sink. All of a sudden, the kitchen was sweltering with five mortals squeezed into the awkward space.

I enjoyed the moment because I was able to confer with the other spirit guides. It took a moment to juggle for prominence and decide which of our mortals was in charge of talking about the beaded jacket. Zachary's guide, while a lot younger than some of us, pointed out that Mr. Goode was our host, therefore, Zachary was in charge by default. I simpered at him with pristine spirit manners. He and I had squared off many times during the past few months. I did it more to remind him that he had to learn to respect his elders. He didn't obey me because he was arrogant. In other words, we tolerated each other, but I acknowledged that Deloo was in his debt for many reasons. There are consequences to everything, and my antenna was flickering with mild alerts of impending trouble, but not danger.

Matty waved everyone out of the kitchen. I lounged from the top of an open window beside the sink while the ground-bound mortals collided at the entryway to the kitchen. I signaled in Eternalese to Zephyr that Deloo cleaned up after big meals, so this would be a good time to let Taale take a nap. I suggested that she encourage Taale to speak up, but Mr. Goode's guide intervened by allowing Zachary to intrude on my great plans with a more urgent request.

"Taale, it's good to see you here in Massachusetts. I wish the circumstances were a little better. At least they are not like the same sad reason that we came together last winter."

"Mr. Goode," Taale began.

Matty interrupted, "Taale, please call him Zachary and me Matty. It will make me feel more at peace with the reason that you've come to our home at this time." Since everyone had stopped moving, most were still in the narrow hallway between the kitchen and the dining area. Matty unplugged the stoppage by putting an arm around Zachary, and together they forced all mortals to move into the living room.

"Yes, of course, Matty." Taale reached for her daughter's hand and pulled Deloo close to walk toward a commodious couch just ahead. "I want to thank you for your generous hospitality to both me and Deloo. I know that Deloo needed to hang on to Arthur's memory. You gave her that." She smiled. "I wish he were here with us."

"He is," Matty began, "or at least he was here last night." She lifted her chin toward Deloo. "Show them the drawing, Dear."

Deloo swallowed. The hardwood floors seemed to reach up to grab her legs, rendering her incapable of movement. I realized that the reality of these past days was hitting her hard. I swarmed around her and helped her feet march toward the sketchpad she had used last night. As she moved, I remembered how many times I had done something similar with previous widows and widowers.

~You'll feel better in a moment, Deloo. Now is a good time to thank the Invisible Forces that you have a wonderful family, each of whom have helped you in your desperate efforts to understand what has happened to your world. Now is a good time for me to remind you that I, too, am part of that loving family. Unlike any of them, I will be with you every day for the rest of your life to help you through every single moment. I love you as much as your mother does.~

Deloo's throat tightened. She communed to me, *~Thank you so much, Baasee'.~* To Taale she said, "Last night something strange happened to me. We were all together, and Arthur was there, too. He told me to draw this picture. I saw something like this scene just before I drove out of Nova Scotia. She opened the sketchbook to the last sheet and displayed it on the table.

Hovering above Deloo, I helped her talk about each of the four people in the drawing. "This is Howard Lee," her finger singled out the man in a suit and dark blond hair. His furtive eyes were on the other white man whose hair was very light blond. "He's the branch manager of some bank. He got my debit card number and had someone make a key for my hotel room in Vermont."

"I talked to the police before lunch, Taale," Zachary exclaimed. "They told me that they had enough to arrest Mr. Lee today for identity theft."

Deloo crowed, "Thank you!"

Zachary's lips twisted. "It's just a slap on the wrist for someone like him. It's one of those things that earns him a luxury suite in some swank confinement, if that." Then he smiled at her and held something out. "I went to my bank and got this new debit card for you. It's got a different account number. You can use it right away."

Taale looked askance at Zachary. In answer to her unstated question, Zachary said, "I am a co-signer on the account. That's how I managed to get Arthur's insurance payment arranged. One of these days we'll all have to sit down again for a little chat." He looked at Deloo with arched eyebrows.

Deloo hugged him and then went back to the drawing.

At my urging, her finger moved to the other blond man. "I don't know who this is, but I saw him twice in Canada. These two," she jabbed a finger at Chuan and Ming, "broke into my hotel room in Burlington, Vermont and before that they chased me in New Brunswick and Montreal. I hope they get caught, too, or at least the man. He threatened me with a knife, only it was my own pencil case."

Zachary grunted his agreement and said, "Which brings us to the reason you are here, Taale. Deloo has already shown us the beaded jacket you made for her. Besides the break-in that endangered Deloo's life, Woody discovered something about the jacket that put more urgency on your coming to Cambridge." He nodded at Deloo and continued, "Deloo, could you show us the jacket again, please?"

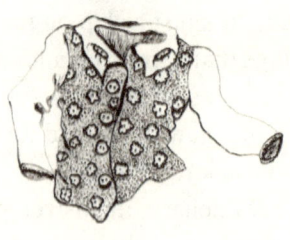

CHAPTER FORTY-THREE

They entered the living room once more. Deloo spread the denim jacket across a coffee table. Arthur's camera swung over it. Taale clutched the cardboard box in her left hand and waited from someone to ask her about the beading.

Matty supplied the necessary oohs and aahs, and fingered the blue-jean fabric, even though she had seen it countless times since Christmas. Woody produced his magnifying glass and held it over one of the pairs of empty holes he had noticed in the Burlington hotel.

"Taale," he tried not to look like a cop, "do you remember what went into these holes?

"Of course," Taale snorted. "The ugliest beads in the world. Look at them." She opened the box and sprawled them across Deloo's jacket. They counted them: fifty tan plastic beads.

"Just like the beads I found in Nova Scotia," Deloo dug into her jeans' pocket and showed off the bead the raven had pitched at her and then her encounter with a man in a bookstore in Nova Scotia. "A while later I found this one," she added the one she'd found beside the kite close to the turn off to the Secret Spirit Inn. "That's it!" Deloo dashed out of the room and brought back the sketch she'd just shown them. "That's where I've seen this guy. He was in that bookstore with a bead that looks like these two."

"These are weightless compared to mine," Taale bounced one of Deloo's in her left hand while holding one from the box in the other.

By this time, all of the spirit guides gathered around were trembling in eagerness. They had already quizzed me about the strange looking beads and could feel as well as I did the melodic sine waves sent outward by well-cut gems.

Zachary's spirit guide sidled up to me to ask, *~did you know all this time?~*

I winked at him and communed in Eternalese. *~I wish I had. It would have given me the whip I've needed to shred your fat behind!~*

He swished his nether parts. *~Mmmmm. Any time,~* he communed with a spirit purr.

I whacked him on his gossamer butt and maneuvered away from his retaliatory swat. When he missed, I blew him a kiss. He caught it and reproduced it a hundred times, and whipped it into a necklace. He arranged it around what passes for a neck in the spirit world. We ogled each other. He looked good in it.

Meanwhile the mortals below us were studying the designs on the plastic beads. Someone had etched common Asian motifs into one side of each. A loop stuck out at each end of the plastic. They all looked perplexed until Woody placed the bead in his hand between two holes near the right shoulder. It fit.

"I see," Deloo breathed. "Someone must have attached these beads to the jacket by stringing thread or wire through these holes. Right, Mom?"

"Yes, Baby," Taale responded. "I had to use wire cutters to get them off."

"That makes sense," Zachary remarked.

I communed to Deloo, *~The innkeeper heard the killer making popping sounds while examining the one they got a year or so ago. Tell them you see a seam line.~*

"A seam line?" Deloo asked aloud.

"What did you say, Deloo?" Matty queried.

"There's a seam line on this one. I think this bead is covering something else," Deloo answered. She fingered the back of her wedding ring as if seeking stability. "Could we try it?"

Woody looked at the one in his hand with the magnifying glass. Deloo and I thought at the same moment, Sherlock Holmes, thinking of the oft-brain impaired genius. I added an image of a pipe and the classic double-brimmed Sherlock hat. Deloo giggled and tried to control the sound with her hand. It didn't work. Woody scowled at her.

"She's right," he muttered. "There's a straight line all the way around. It's so indistinct I wouldn't notice it unless you said something."

"I see it," Matty crowed. "Let's pry it open."

~The innkeeper thought he popped them open, but I don't know what he used to do so,~ I offered, shaping my favorite arm-like tendril into a crow bar.

Taale examined the bead in her hand and speculated, "Do you think we could crack it open with a pair of pliers?"

Woody nodded and asked, "Zachary, do you have a tool chest?"

"I know where it is," Deloo supplied, having spent six months painting and making repairs throughout the house. "I'll get it."

The three older adults smirked at each other and waited for Deloo to return. In a few minutes, each of them held a bead and pliers. Deloo used sure-grips to squeeze her bead until the plastic made a loud "Pop".

Everyone else stopped to stare at her. Using a flathead screwdriver, she pried the incised top of the casing off and exposed a bluish, semi-firm yet pliable, plastic blob. She held it up.

"There's something inside that goo," Taale said. "Can you remove it?"

"I'll use this," Deloo whisked out a pocketknife and poked. It connected with something hard. She twisted a bit, but the blue plastic had a self-sealing personality that defied her efforts.

"Let me try with my knife," Woody said. He took the object out of Deloo's fingers and sliced a corner away. "Mine is less pointy than yours. I see how they did this," he murmured. "I learned about something like this in one of my curating classes—in the section on chemicals to use when transporting fragile items." He continued to gouge at the stiff gelatin-like plastic mold. "I don't know what this stuff is, but I'd guess they spent time learning which, if any, did not damage valuable gemstones." He caught Deloo's eye. "At least I would have." He lifted out a gem in green colors.

"It's an emerald," Matty said. "It's huge! Here, look at the one Zachary gave me for Christmas." She displayed her right hand. A much smaller, but nonetheless, expensive emerald graced her pretty hand.

"Holy Plastic Bead!" Zachary wheezed. "It must be worth twenty times what I paid for your ring, Matty." He looked at the others and said, "we'll have to get an expert to examine it—them. This one could be worth over a hundred thousand dollars."

Everyone turned to look at Taale. After a long moment of silence Woody croaked, "You carried these on board in a sack. You must have tucked the bag under the seat in front of you and slept." He tried to laugh.

Taale's knees folded under her. While Deloo revived her mother, the other three single-minded gem miners made themselves useful by opening the rest of the plastic coverings. Each of them held a gem of comparable size to the first. Zachary helped Taale stand up to look at the fifty gems that perched in four tidy rows along the bottom edge of the beaded jacket.

"Taale," Woody queried, "could you tell us how you got these stones?"

Deloo pushed a chair up behind Taale, who sat down with an unlady-like grunt. The story was businesslike. The bead store owner, Earlene, had commissioned a beaded jacket as usual Taale delivered it by November fifteenth. Earlene paid for it, but not until Thanksgiving eve. Taale opened her front door expecting to find the newspaper. "Instead, I found a big package containing the beaded jacket, a check for the usual amount that Earlene paid, and an envelope."

"Here's the envelope with the note that she wrote." Taale handed it to Deloo. Deloo handed it to Woody, who read it aloud.

Girlfriend, your jacket is beautiful, even though this jacket is made of denim and not moose or deer hide. My buyer isn't taking delivery on the jacket this year. Enclosed is a check for $2,752, our usual arrangement. You are free to keep or sell the jacket. I don't want it. If anyone asks, the number is 5472. Love, Earlene.

Woody asked, "What does she mean by the number 5472?"

Taale shook her head.

Woody held the note up to a light and asked, "What made this stain? It looks like blood."

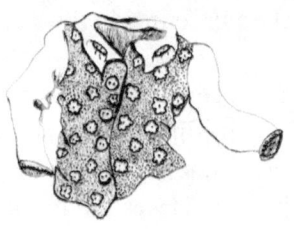

CHAPTER FORTY-FOUR

Taale nodded her head and looked at Deloo. "It is blood. Raven's blood. There was a wounded raven on the porch the night I found the package. Even though the raven was less than half the size of the box, at first I thought the raven carried the box to my doorstep. But ravens can't lift such things. Then I realized the raven must have had a fight with something just before I got home, leaving that trail of blood leading up to the box. When I turned the raven over to see if it was alive, it woke up and wobbled for two steps toward the package. When it got close it stabbed the package with its beak and keeled over, this time dead for real. I guess I must have missed Earlene when she delivered it. I told Aunt Pauline about it that evening. She said it was hutłanee, a bad omen. She said the raven was a warning about the jacket. Then Arthur died the next day. She told me to look at the jacket to see if anything was wrong with it. That's when I found all those plastic beads sewn on it. Whoever did it was a lousy bead sewer. I showed them to Aunt Pauline. She told me to take them off the jacket and put them away."

Arthur's camera rolled. Deloo's throat tightened. "You never told me about the raven or these beads, Mom."

Taale put a comforting arm around her daughter. "I didn't dare, Sweetheart. It was hutłanee. Arthur died the next day."

I'd been patient long enough. I burst in on their mother-daughter moment with a raven's squawk of my own. *~Ask if we have to give the jewels back.~* I gave Deloo a little shove.

The force of my shove took both of us by surprise. Deloo took a step forward and asked, "Do we have to give these stones back to someone?"

Five faces looked at each other in silence. I shot a query toward Woody's spirit guide, *~what does the law say?~*

His spirit guide, a woman in her mid-five thousands, answered me *~I don't know which country's law could touch this one. It's not a matter* *for Massachusetts, Vermont, or any of the Canadian provinces. She should ask someone in Alaska.~*

In the mortal realm, Zachary shifted his weight. In a quiet voice he said, "While this has never happened to me or any of my clients, I have encountered a number of somewhat similar situations." He patted the emerald, the single stone of that sort in the collection, and turned to Taale. "Since you got them with a check and a statement that you should do with it whatever you want, the jacket and its decorations are yours. As for the law, your situation is obviously life-threatening, but you didn't do anything to trigger it. Deloo, you have been chased, twice with deadly force. Now the five of us know why—or think we know why." He heaved a sigh, "whoever they are, we know that they are determined and they know I am connected to this business. I don't want any more to do with them." He gave the emerald a final pat.

There was a chorus of protests. Zachary gave a universal hand signal asking for quiet. "These gems are dangerous. We have to get rid of them."

"What?!?" protested Woody. "Why?"

"I don't mean to trash them. I mean we have to put them in a safe place as soon as possible, just not in my house." He looked at Taale. "Could we take them to a bank with a safety deposit box? My bank is right around the corner. It's very reliable, and Howard Lee doesn't work there."

Taale tittered. It was a musical sound. Woody smiled. Deloo shot a nonverbal query to invisible me.

~He's right, Deloo. Whoever wants these is criminal. They have invested a lot of savagery into finding them. Have your mother get a safe deposit box as soon as possible. You'll have to pay for it since she's broke.~

Alarmed at the last part of my commune, Deloo gave Taale a quick hug and whispered in her mother's ear, "Don't worry, I'll pay for the safe deposit box."

Taale hugged Deloo and nodded her head. "Zachary, I'll get a safe deposit box in order to protect you and Matty." Then she shook her head in silence.

~Deloo,~ I advised, *~your mother is experiencing both anger and hope. She's angry that the criminals used her jackets because they might think indigenous garments are of such low value that no one would look at them twice. It hurts her in many ways that no one here, except you,*

seems to care about how valuable such jackets are to Athabascan peo-
ple. Even though she made yours out of cloth instead of deer or moose
hide, she spent just as many hours making it. Of course she's hopeful
because she needs a lot of money to make overdue repairs to her house
and now those student loan payments.~

Deloo looked worried and hugged her mother a little tighter. *~What*
can I say that will make it better?~

I thought about it and then realized that nothing Deloo could say
would ever remove the cultural insult. *~Say nothing for now. You'll be*
able to help her later.~

Taale stood up and announced, "I need an escort."

Four people surrounded Taale as she made her way down two blocks
in one direction from the Goode's house and one more block in another.
While there, Deloo asked Mr. Goode if he could help make a transfer of
money into her mother's bank account.

"I need to help her for coming all this way. She's behind in her bills,"
Deloo whispered.

Zachary patted Deloo's shoulder and took her to see his old friend,
the bank manager. It took more time that anyone expected, but soon,
Taale had enough money to pay for her air fare and loan payment.

A half hour later everyone reconvened in the house.

As they entered, Woody's phone rang. He stayed outside while he
chatted with the caller. When he came into the house he signaled to
Deloo to come to the foyer. As customary for us spirit guides, I floated
above her.

"Al just called," he said.

"Al?" Deloo felt stupid.

I reminded Deloo, *~Al is his RCMP friend who is stationed in*
Halifax.~

"Oh, yes," Deloo continued with an apologetic smile. "Your friend
who's in the RMP. Is he going to be able to come here?"

Woody frowned. "That's RCMP, and no. Not yet. Did you know the
RCMP arrested the banker when he tried to cross the border a couple
of hours ago? He's probably out on bail by now. The American police
took over and charged him for using your debit card to make that hotel
key. Al wants to make sure the RCMP remains involved, since Lee used
information from Canada to pull it off. He's hoping to convince some
Canadian upper level officials to send him here to Boston to extradite
Lee back to Canada. I will be able to attend some of the proceedings and

they may want to talk to you, but I agree with Zachary. So does Al. This Lee character is so rich, he'll buy his way out of the mess. If he ever does jail time, it'll be in one of those ritzy joints."

Woody turned to Deloo. "I'd better catch up on email. I've applied for some positions and need to stay on top of everything. I know a lot of people with fresh PhDs like mine. All of us are job hunting—some of them have been on the market for a few years now. I don't want to let a single call or email get by me. You never know when the right one will come."

He stretched his mouth into a grin, but sitting in the living room Taale could see the stress lines on his face. She called, "don't think about us, Woody. We are an independent lot, aren't we, Deloo?"

Woody laughed. "Trying to cross the continent in a tent all by yourself qualifies for First Place in independence," he quipped. "You are so small, Deloo, last year I thought Arthur had gone crazy. He always said he wanted a strong, independent woman like his mother. When I saw the short, skinny woman he brought, I couldn't believe he'd made such a mistake." He grinned at Deloo.

I watched a parade of emotions fly across Deloo's face. *~He's teasing you. Smile.~*

Deloo glowered, then she saw him raise his arm the way Arthur used to do when he was trying to rouse her temper. She made a face and snorted, "You snot! Arthur used to say the same things to me."

Taale chuckled, "Come on, Deloo, let's talk to Matty." They turned as one, but Arthur's father appeared and asked for a private moment with Taale. He took Deloo's mother into the small guest room which he hoped would become his home office.

Woody went to Arthur's old room (now his guest room), giving Deloo a chance to chat with Matty in private. "I would like to invite you and Zachary to dinner," she said. "My treat—that is, Arthur's treat."

"Of course, Dear," Matty's eyes brightened. "There's a new French restaurant a couple of blocks from here. Shall we try that one?" Deloo agreed and they spent a few minutes admiring her portrait of Arthur. "Deloo, my dear, would you mind if I told people that you are my daughter-in-law even if you marry again?"

From my loft near the ceiling I watched the warm thrill that went through Deloo's body. *~Tell her how it works in Alaska.~*

Deloo nodded at me and said, "That makes me very happy. It would make me even happier if you called me your daughter. Tell your friends that's what we do in Alaska. Athabascans, I mean." She laughed. "I have seven grandmothers and lots of aunts. One of my cousins has three mothers; none of whom are her biological relatives. It's sort of normal for us to turn other people into our kin. I think it has to do with the old days when Alaska Native populations were very small and people didn't live as long. We keep daughter-in-laws as daughters after their husbands die. Having lots of family is better than having lots of money."

Matty's smile started to pucker. She grabbed Deloo into a tight embrace and whispered "Thank you, Daughter."

Deloo felt her own chest heaving and hugged Matty a little tighter. "I'm so glad Arthur is your son. Otherwise, we would never have met."

Taale and Zachary came out of his office. I could see that Taale was muddled about what Zachary had told her, while Zachary announced that he had a new client. He pointed to Taale.

"I heard you all talking," Woody stepped out of his bedroom and looked at Taale. "I know you seem strong, but with so much excitement combined with almost no sleep in these past few days, I wonder if you'll make it as far as Mass Ave." Massachusetts Avenue, known to locals as Mass Ave, was a block away and the place Deloo wanted to go was a long walk from there. "If you plan to see any shops, you'll be walking for a while."

Deloo nodded at him. "I know what you mean. Mom is tough, but a crash is bound to happen. When it does, we might be too far away to walk."

"Why not take the car?" Woody suggested.

"I can walk," Taale nodded, "but maybe Deloo should call you when SHE gets tired."

"Good thinking. Arthur wasn't so dumb after all!" He ducked out of reach when Deloo pretended to punch him.

From the safety of the ceiling I conveyed a little news to Deloo, ~*I know today is the day he will meet a person he must get to know. I get a hazy image of her. She's young, very young.*~

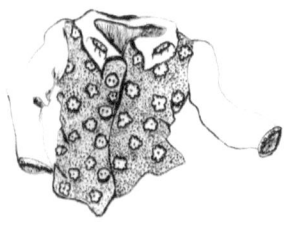

CHAPTER FORTY-FIVE

Deloo cast an intense eye at Woody.

"What?" Woody smiled peaceably at her.

I intervened, ~*don't tell him! I think you'll get to see the mystery unfold very soon.*~

Taale draped a sweater over her arm. "I'm ready, Baby. How about you?"

Deloo led her mother through the quiet neighborhood of Arthur's youth, and where Deloo had lived for six months.

"Where are we going?" Taale asked.

"It's a surprise. We have a ways to go." In a half hour they turned onto Holland Street. Deloo waited for her mother's reaction. Arthur's camera jiggled. Taale took a few more steps and saw the familiar shape of bins of beads through a window.

"Oh!" Taale skipped a little to show her reaction to the beads. "You knew I needed to see my own kind of store in this big, strange city!"

Doing big loops above the two of them, I could feel waves of renewed energy waft along Taale's body. Zephyr and I chuckled in spirit-guide style and flowed through the window of the store while the mortals took the tedious route through the door. While the mortal women moseyed down one aisle after another, I took up a place near the front door. Zephyr stayed with her charge. The store was small enough that if I felt the need to confer with Deloo, all I had to do was touch her with a long tendril. After a while Zephyr floated toward me and we caught up with each other.

"Deloo, I'd like to make a necklace for Matty as a guest-to-hostess gift. I've got a lot of ideas, and this store has just the right kind of beads," Taale held up a string of big, bright red jasper stone beads. "What do you think of that idea?"

Surprised, Deloo said aloud, "guest-to-hostess gift? I haven't given her anything either."

Taale looked askance at her daughter, "Honey, I've just seen the most beautiful portrait in the world. Your painting of Arthur is the best kind of gift a grieving mother could ever get. You don't need to give her anything else." Taale picked up a string of jade beads and sang, "ooh!" Then she looked at the price tag. "Ouch." I can't afford that much!"

Deloo took the jade beads from her mother and smiled, "Matty loves green. These are perfect, Mom." She lifted her chin toward the basket in her mother's hand. "Fill 'er up! This is my treat to the most perfect mother in the world."

Taale shook her head, "Deloo, be careful of that insurance money. I know it seems like a lot, but it will disappear in a few weeks if you aren't careful."

~She's right to caution you, Deloo,~ I communed, *~but I guarantee that this is money well spent. Please buy all the beads your mother wants.~*

"I agree with you, Mama," Deloo said, oblivious to her unconscious use of 'Mama' instead of her more mature 'Mom', "but Matty and Za-Za-Zachary," she stuttered, "have been so kind to me these past few months. I got to know more about Arthur than he ever could have told me himself. I looked at all of Matty's photo albums, heard lots of funny family stories." Deloo's smile faded as she drifted into reverie. Then she looked at her mother, "they helped me know understand why I married Arthur. Last year everything happened so fast that by the time we reached Fairbanks, I was sure I had made a mistake—that my hormones had done the talking without thinking about the consequences." She touched the basket. "Knowing that you can help give Matty such a thoughtful gift is helping me feel better."

Taale shook her head and smiled. "Okay, I guess I'll have many opportunities in the next few months or years to nag you about saving money." She reached for the jade beads in Deloo's hand. "I'll get these. We need to match them with something special. Maybe some clear round glass beads." Taale sped between bins, filling the basket with the beads, threads, and needles she needed.

A quarter of an hour later, I received the eerie alert I'd been awaiting: *~Get Woody into the store at once! ~*

Zephyr received it as well. We more or less occulated each other. What's a spirit guide to do? Then I had a flash of brilliance. I swooped toward Deloo and communed, ~*pretend you are hurt.*~ Without further ado I pressed on the backs of her knees to cause them to buckle. Then I lowered her to the floor face down.

I might as well have thrown open a theatre curtain and shouted, "Please welcome Deloo!" She flung herself into the part. "Ow! Mom! Oh! I've smashed my knee. Ooo!" She chafed her unharmed knee and aimed her most appealing look at a mystified Taale.

"Deloo, Baby, what happened? Are you alright?"

~*Call Woody to come get you. Something's up. I'll explain later.*~ I bathed Deloo with thoughts of conspiracy.

~*Cool! Could you make me float? Mom would be impressed to see that.*~

~*No,*~ I huffed, ~*she would be more upset about that than your fake wound. Could you rub one of your knees to make it look like a wound?*~

"I'm okay, but I don't want to walk anymore," she murmured while abrading her knee with a corner of her jute handbag.

Pleased at her innovation, I remarked, ~*nice work, my collaborator. Now show her your wound. I believe you've rubbed all the skin off that leg.*~

Deloo blew a puff of air to stifle a giggle, and worked the left leg of her jeans up above the knee so that Taale could see the mild abrasion her daughter had given herself. "See. Just a little scrape. But it hurts enough for me to want a ride home. I'll call Woody." She whipped out her phone and touched it. In a few seconds Woody answered and Deloo asked him for a ride.

"Sure," he responded, "Be right there."

By that time a store clerk came to their assistance. Taale followed the young woman to the checkout counter with Deloo's new debit card in hand. Deloo limped to the door, although I should have given her some pointers on how to fake an injury. She was limping on the wrong leg.

Zephyr attended Taale at the counter and encouraged Taale to ask a few questions about the store and its products.

"How long did you say you've been beading?" the clerk asked.

Taale laughed. "Longer than you've been alive, but it's been about twenty years if you're asking how long I've done it for a living." She tipped her head toward Deloo. "I needed to find a way to make money and stay at home at the same time when my daughter was a baby. Beading and skin sewing kept us alive for a long time."

The clerk nodded at Deloo and asked, "How long are you going to be here? Maybe you could offer a class. Our customers would love to meet you."

"How kind," Taale began, "but I'm just here for a couple of days."

As she spoke, the door opened beside Deloo and a little girl dashed inside. When the child realized that Deloo was holding the door open for her, she stopped and turned to stare at my mortal. Something ethereal passed between them, but was gone before I could analyze it. In a moment, a petite dark-haired woman stepped into the shop and nudged the little girl forward.

"Don't block the door, Nibuna," she rebuked the girl. "You'll let all of those street spirits in. We don't want to do that to this store, do we?"

"No Mommy," the child reached for her mother's hand.

Deloo smiled at the new arrival and was about to reassure her when she spotted the Passat pulling into a parking spot along Holland Street at that moment. "Mom, Woody's here," Deloo called out to her mother.

Taale smiled at the store clerk and said, "I guess we'd better go. You've got a lot of great beads in here. I hope I can talk my daughter into coming back before we leave."

Taale walked toward the door, Zephyr moving above her. I had already joined Deloo, so all four of us were in place when the little girl's mother whispered, "Woody?"

Woody himself strode into the store and met the young mother's eyes. They stared at each other for a long, silent moment. Woody croaked, "Zigwan?"

"Do you two know each other?" Taale asked, amused.

"Look!" Deloo burst out, "She has the same bump on her hand that you do, Woody."

All heads, including the store attendant's, swung toward the little girl, who lifted her hand up high. "Do you mean this?" She touched the tiny bump on the outside of her right hand and peered at Woody's hand. "Do you have one, too?"

Like a puppet on a string, Woody brought up his right hand and exposed a similar bump. On his adult hand, it was more obvious that it was the beginning of a sixth finger. "Yes," he murmured to the child. "I have one, too. So does my father."

"Look, Mommy," Nibuna announced. "It's just like mine!"

Woody and Zigwan resumed staring at each other.

Taale cleared her throat, "Woody, could you give the car key to Deloo? We'll drive ourselves home." She nodded with expressive eyes at her daughter. "Maybe Deloo can pick you up later."

Woody looked up with vague awareness. Deloo held out her hand and made a gesture as if turning a key in the ignition. He tossed the key at her. Deloo caught it and remembered just in time to limp out to the car.

"Dinner's at six-thirty tonight," she called over her shoulder. "Invite your friends."

Once they were both in the car, Taale opened her mouth to say something when the ashtray lid scraped open. They both stared at it in silence. Then, just as it had done before, one of the coins bounced against the side of the ashtray and spun so fast that it seemed to generate a beam of light aiming at Taale's eyes.

"Yike!" Taale exclaimed and touched an eyebrow. As she did so the coin settled down and the lid slammed shut.

"Did I just imagine that?" Taale cried out. "Deloo, did you see that coin spin?"

Deloo laughed, "it's a fairy-tale ashtray, Mom. It's been doing things like that ever since . . ." Deloo's voice faded.

"Ever since when? Deloo, you're daydreaming again," Taale said.

Deloo patted her mother's arm, "It's just that it started doing things like that ever since I saw that woman take off her dress." Before Taale could react, Deloo told her what had happened a few hours before she met the innkeeper.

"In other words, this ashtray has a spirit in it that warns you to stay sharp. I guess I'd better be alert now. So what do you make of Woody and that woman?"

Deloo maneuvered the Passat into the slow traffic on Holland Street and murmured, "If I'm right, that's Zigwan. The big love of his life. It means spring in Abenaki. She's from Maine. I sensed there was a mystery about her, but Woody and I haven't had much time to talk." Deloo reached an intersection and said, "oh-oh."

"Oh-oh?" Taale tilted her head toward Deloo. "Oh-oh about Zigwan?"

"No, oh-oh about how to find my way back to the Goode's house." She glanced in the rearview mirror and sighed. "I've never driven in this neighborhood." Gritting her teeth, she turned right without thinking.

I sailed around her with steadying force. It looked a little chaotic, but in truth, all of the cars were moving at a safe speed. Cambridge with its one hundred thousands of people was a bit larger than Fairbanks. Deloo had driven in Fairbanks, but she eyed Mass Ave as if wild-eyed monsters caroused on the sidewalks.

~*Everything is going to be fine, Deloo,* ~I reassured her. ~*I remember how to get to Matty. I'll help.*~ And did so with remarkable skill that went unacknowledged by the two women. Deloo tried to grind her teeth to powder. Taale gouged the leather of her car seat. Mortals! So untrusting.

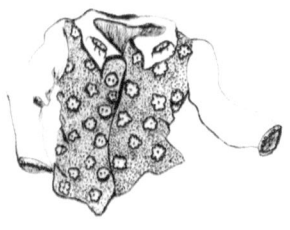

CHAPTER FORTY-SIX

"I will be so glad to get back to Fairbanks and levelheaded drivers!" Taale sighed after witnessing a car make a sudden U-turn. The driver almost battered a pedestrian. "I rarely see more than five cars on the road together except when I get off work. One good thing happened today, though."

Deloo peered at her mother. "What's that?"

"Well, between Woody and his mystery woman and Cambridge traffic, I am now wide awake. I should be good for the next seven or eight hours!"

Deloo laughed. "Me, too."

"What did you mean back there?" Taale asked.

"About what?" Deloo answered with her own question.

"About having a feeling about Woody's mysterious past."

"It's just something when we were unloading my car a couple of days ago. It wasn't anything that he said. It's just a look in his eye and an image that flashed into my mind. It was quick and blurry, but now that I've seen that child, I swear I saw Nibuna's face come into view. There was a very fuzzy female behind her." Deloo shook her head.

"You had a vision of that little girl!" Taale stared at her daughter. "Tell me more."

"I've had two visions of her. Both happened so fast, I didn't get details." I could feel Deloo shooting a mental probe toward me.

~You're doing well, my dear,~ I affirmed. *~You'll remember more as you talk. Ask yourself if it was you reaching out to Nibuna or if it was she who was reaching out to you.~*

"Reaching out to me?" Deloo murmured. "I don't remember..." The strap on Arthur's camera twitched. Struck by the implications of that possibility, Deloo turned toward her mother. "In the second vision her face floated toward me. When she found me; her face came into focus. I think she was roaming."

"Roaming? What do you mean?" Taale asked.

"Like mobile phones do," Deloo answered. "They search for the nearest satellite or whatever. It felt like she was casting around and locked in on me." She stopped to navigate around a traffic snarl. Once beyond the maze of unfamiliar signs and buildings, she recognized the Goode's street and flicked on her turn signal.

"So you think that the little girl is psychic," Taale mused. "Your great aunt Pauline told me you were psychic when you were little." Taale smiled at her daughter. "Are you?"

They removed the beads from the car and walked to the front door. Deloo smiled. She knocked on the Goode's door. "You tell me. Was I ever psychic?"

"Maybe. We all are psychic to a certain extent. For instance, I have just divined that you faked your hurt leg. You aren't limping anymore."

Deloo laughed.

Matty let them in and asked "Where's Woody?"

Four hours later Woody entered the house alone.

"Just in time for dinner," Deloo caroled.

Without accepting any of his excuses, they herded him to the French restaurant. Over an savory meal, Woody explained his relationship to Zigwan. She was a couple of years younger than he was. He met her at Boston University when classes started. Two months before his graduation, Zigwan and he had a big fight. A graduate program in New Mexico had accepted his application. He wanted to get married and move there. She didn't. She wanted to finish her degree in Boston and have her own career. She moved out that night. He tried to contact her by phone, email, talking to her friends and waiting for her to get out of classes. She dodged him. He tried to congratulate her at commencement, but she wouldn't speak with him. He spoke with her parents. At that time, they didn't know she was expecting, and they encouraged him to let her go, so he gave up and left for New Mexico.

The pregnancy had been difficult, and Nibuna was born a couple of days before her due date. Zigwan went back to Portland, Maine to live with her parents. Nibuna was frail and no one expected her to live. Together, Zigwan and her family raised Nibuna with the help of a family doctor and an older woman who knew something about old Wabanaki healing practices. The combination kept Nibuna alive.

"Nibuna is now six years old," Woody explained. "She will enter the first grade in the fall. Zigwan wants her to go to school in Boston."

At that moment, Woody's phone chirruped.

"Hello... Yes, speaking. ... Yes, I did." While the caller spoke, Woody pointed to the phone, pressed mute and said, "This is one of the federal..." He fumbled with the phone and said, "Yes, I'm still interested in the position you have to offer." He smiled at each of his friends. "Yes, I would be happy to schedule an interview." He gaped at Zachary. "Yes, I'll hold." He put the phone on mute and looked around the table in bafflement.

"Well?" Zachary cocked his head. "Who is it?"

"It's one of the federal agencies in Alaska that's looking for an anthropologist."

The phone made an odd raven-like squawk. Woody pressed a button and continued, "Tomorrow at two p.m.? Yes. I can figure it out." His eyebrows formed a thick bunch over his nose while he listened, "Thank you." He shook his head and ended the call. "I have an online interview tomorrow with a branch of the U.S. government." He looked at Deloo. "Do you know where Palmer is?"

"Your hard work is paying you back," Deloo nodded. "Yes, we know where Palmer is.

Zachary slapped Woody on the back. "Good timing. You'll be able to go to the gemologist with us tomorrow before your interview."

I would have slapped Woody as well, as I knew that this would be the single job offer he'd get. I sensed the gemologist's verdict would spell a life-changing moment for Taale Denaa's entire family and placed an invisible, faux mink stole around her shoulders. Her spirit guide, Zephyr, adorned her with an invisible traditional doyonh yoo necklace made of dentallium shells to signal a wealth-woman, hence a chief with a lot of responsibility to the tribe.

The following morning they headed to the bank where Zachary introduced Dr. Clara Morgan, a gemologist. In a few minutes all of them crowded around an oblong conference table in a comfortable meeting room. The gemologist set up some instruments and asked for an extra lamp. She asked for basic information about which part of the world the gems were from and their age. When she earned a chorus of "maybe Asia" from Deloo and Zachary, she tried for details about how they had been stored. They showed her one of the plastic casements and a piece of the blue plastic that they had pulled out of the trash.

The gemologist gaped at Zachary, "Just how did you come into possession of them?"

Between them, they gave her a jumbled account of Deloo's journey through the Canadian Maritimes, Vermont and to Cambridge, and ended by showing her the note from Earlene in Alaska.

"In other words, they might be stolen, but you didn't do the stealing, and don't know who put them onto your jacket," she said with a wry expression. She shook her head.

Zachary agreed, "these may have been stolen, but the woman who left the jacket with Taale didn't tell her anything about them. We need to find out if they are valuable and proceed from there. In other words, we need your help in order to figure out what to do next. As usual, I will pay you for your services whether or not you do anything at this time."

Clara looked at the gems and sighed. "All right. You may as well find out if they are fakes or not." She selected one of the clearest stones and went to work. "If this were a lab, I wouldn't let you stay in the room because I don't like eyes staring at every move I make." Clara glared at the windows on one side of the conference room. As it is, I'm going to request that all of you stand in front of the windows with your backs toward me, and try to close those drapes."

After drawing the drapes and arranging themselves along the length of the windows, the four tried to pretend they were fascinated with their own fingers. I reminded Deloo to wriggle to maintain her blood circulation. The older adults, however, stood like statues. Fixed on her work, the gemologist didn't notice. When Clara called them an hour later, Taale and Zachary had to hobble to her side of the room because the blood in their legs had been moving very little. Woody and Deloo, by contrast, bounded over to her.

"I could do more testing, but that can wait." She looked from face to face. "What I can tell you is that this is the most amazing set of gemstones of that size that I've ever seen—and I've had the pleasure of examining the big ones in the Harvard Mineralogical Museum. Those were much bigger than these by far."

From my guard position above Deloo I knew Clara had worked without moving her own body very much, and was stiff because of it. I ran a soft energizing tendril along her left side. Zephyr did the same on Clara's right side. Clara smiled and so did we.

"Taale," she continued, this time looking at Deloo's mother, "I agree with you. These came from Asia. I'd guess they came from multiple areas, perhaps along the path of the Silk Road trade routes. It will take a day of lab work to do a full analysis." Clara reached out to put her pale hand on Taale's brown arm, and stared at the contrast. Taale wriggled.

"Pardon me," Clara lifted her hand away, looking preoccupied. "I was absorbed by the oddness of this situation. Boston Brahmans are my usual clients."

I nudged Deloo and communed a blunt explanation, *~she put her hand on your mother for another reason, to find out if she had an aversion to touching people of another color. She's ashamed of herself now. She can't stand the truth of the racist way she is. You can help her sort through these thoughts and feelings by staying at her more neutral level. You have never heard of the Boston Brahmans and neither has your mother. Ask. It will give her a place to start thinking.~*

Deloo didn't hesitate. "What's a Boston Brahman?"

Woody, well aware of Brahman elitism, cleared his throat and lifted his eyebrows but he kept quiet.

Clara looked at my scrawny Deloo and laughed. "There you go. Asking a question that I assume everyone in the world understands. We are descendants—rich descendants—of the original colonists. We are the upper crust in this city."

Above her, I told Deloo, *~what she is not telling you that Boston Brahmans are the kind of people who always think that jewels of this quality belong to them. The Brahmans deem that they don't belong to you or anyone who is not white. She thought she had been liberated from that sort of colonialist thinking until she touched your mother's arm.~*

Deloo and Taale stared at each other while Clara began to pack her instruments into neat boxes that fit into a big, square rolling case. Woody's face surged from tan to deep maroon. Zachary cleared his throat, wondering how to redeem the explosive situation. "So, Clara," Zachary began.

"Yes," Clara said, "I will give you a full report of my analysis if you," she turned and shook Taale's hand, "will bring these gems to my lab tomorrow."

Zachary seemed to expand when he asked when they should arrive.

"Do you remember where my office is? I assume that you'll pick them up from here after the bank opens. Come to my lab at 10:30." Clara shook Zachary's hand. "I should be finished by four tomorrow afternoon."

At four the next day Clara met them in her office. She smiled and said, "Please come into my lab." She led them into her well-equipped laboratory. Two sheets of paper with Clara's tidy handwriting rested on a table.

"I'll have this typed and emailed to you as usual, but I don't think any of you would survive without bothering me at home all night." She cackled. Matty whacked the air around her. "So you will get my hand-written version today and a typed version later on this week." Clara handed the two pages to Taale and said, "Taale, they are worth at least three point one million dollars; more on the black market."

CHAPTER FORTY-SEVEN

Taale caught a glimpse of the handwritten sheet and started to tremble, forcing herself not to collapse. She smiled and thanked the gemologist for her help. The others made polite small talk, and Woody offered his arm to Taale as they all sauntered out of the tiny office. Once outside, Taale blew a noisy puff of air into the Boston summer afternoon, and looked at Zachary, "Now what?"

"Now," he smiled, "you and I will make some financial plans." He rubbed his hands together.

Woody laughed, "I'd love to be a fly on the wall when that happens. Zigwan and I will have made our own plans about marriage by then—if she doesn't chicken out again. I suppose you two will go back to Alaska, won't you?"

Taale made a small hop as she got into Zachary's car. "Yes. My tickets are already set. Deloo got the same flight. I hope you all can come up."

Hours later, they strolled the short distance back to the Goode's house from a nearby restaurant with the mortals laughing and the immortals around them teasing each other. I reveled in knowing that a few days earlier my Deloo had been driving in New Brunswick, oblivious to adorable me. Before the day we found that Canadian inn, my world had been like the weather of New England: stormy intermixed with sunshine. I gazed at the trees surrounding Deloo. Sporadic showers joined the pitch black of the Cambridge night to prevent the mortal humans from seeing beyond the glimmering street lamps. Needless to say, I, one of the dead ones, could see everything. Zachary handed Matty and Taale flashlights. The additional light encouraged them to press together. Taale, exhausted from the long days, stumbled and Woody offered her his arm again. Deloo caught a movement on the far side of the street in her peripheral vision and stopped to see what it was.

Noticing Deloo, I separated from the spirit guide group to find out what she saw. That's why not even I, Baasee' the Hyper-Vigilant, was paying attention to the man who'd tucked himself behind a big maple tree in the Goode's side yard on the near side of the street. Then he stepped out from behind it brandishing a pistol. I thought I spotted someone or something with him, but it was a blur, especially because Grandfather Kwaikit joined me.

~What brought you here, Grandfather?~

Grandfather Kwaikit tipped a tendril toward yet another figure, the one on the far side of the street, *~That.~* Then he turned and pointed to the shadows on the near side. *~And that.~*

I peered into the gloom to find the shadowy figure who jumped from the bushes beside the Goode's home to stand in front of my defenseless Deloo.

"Hand over that jacket." He pointed the gun's muzzle toward my mortal's skinny chest and Arthur's camera. It was a warm evening and Deloo wasn't wearing a sweater or a jacket and tried to say so. The gunman didn't listen for an answer. He pulled her out of the group.

Deloo screamed, "I'm not wearing a jacket. There's nothing for you here. Go away." She tried to stomp on his foot, but slid on mud instead, right into the gunman's arms.

Grandfather Kwaikit struck the man with a mild electrical shock and I commune-shouted at Deloo, *~Get away from him. Now! ~*

Deloo couldn't obey me because the villain, impervious to Grandfather Kwaikit's charge, held her tightly. I wrapped a big tendril around my little girl, trying to get her loose from the stranger. Woody, although shorter than the gunman, was younger and more muscular. He reached out to push Deloo behind him, but couldn't find a safe grip. Taale, behaving much like a mother bear, whacked the gunman with a heavy purse. It almost knocked him out. But no. The man fired a shot. His aim was erratic, the bullets went astray. Everyone stopped, then after a split second of silence, all the mortals yelled, shrieked or shouted for attention.

Just as I, Baasee' the Dutiful, tried to help Deloo escape from the throng, it seemed to me a second person separated from a dark tree across the street and rushed toward the gunman. The second person leaped on the gunman and somehow took the gun away from him. While the gun slithered across the darkened road, the gunman's attacker bent over him emanating calmness. I could make out the last three words: "I love you." I couldn't tell if it was spoken by a man or a woman.

Then one of them, perhaps the second person, released Deloo by shoving her into her mother's arms. All eyes and oculars turned to Taale and Deloo.

Grandfather Kwaikit urged me to keep my attention on the shadowy couple and not on Deloo. *~They are up to something. Watch them!~*

He was right. They exchanged something. It looked shiny, perhaps a knife or a long needle. Then the second figure slipped into the darkness and away from the crowd.

I heard a grunt and an odd gurgling sound. The mortals were busy tugging Deloo and her mother toward the street lights. A man whispered, "HayJay, can you hear me?" Deloo didn't hear it. Nor did the other mortals. I seemed to be the only one paying attention. I held an imaginary breath, wondering if there'd be an answer. It was hard to tell with all the noise from the mortals. Then I heard someone slur, "It's back. The devil is back."

Deloo looked around. "Who said that?"

Glad she heard something, I communed, *~That's Howard Lee.~* The little ghost, who had been away from us and with her official ghost mentor for days, suddenly appeared and murmured to me. *~Do you see? He's not alone. There's something with him. My mentor told me I need to find out more about these people who have dragged my sister into their wicked way.~*

Grandfather Kwaikit conveyed, *~that's what I mean. It's an incomplete spirit—the essence of someone who tried to be with this wounded man.~*

As my grandfather said, there was something unformed around the emerging shape of the spirit of Howard Lee. I took a quick peek through Deloo's eyes to find out what she could see of him. A moonless evening, it was hard for her to see beyond the shallow light of street lamps.

The dying man nodded sympathetically, and said "I'm sorry to hear that." He sighed and I could see the life force slither out of him.

Grandfather Kwaikit announced, *~I'll help separate and reformulate the two of them to get them both ready for final transformation. It's going to be difficult. I've thought all this time that you were my great transformational mess. I botched your double descent into eternity.~*

This was Grandfather Kwaikit's most common theme: mixed heritage. As if that had anything to do with these fragile mortals. I grouched,

~there is nothing wrong with me that a little less grandfather wouldn't cure. Go do your thing! ~

Meanwhile, Woody managed to call 9-1-1. In minutes the dark street was crowded with patrol cars and uniformed officers. Zachary convinced them to go into his house for a little more privacy, since most of the witnesses were in residence there. The questioning took hours. Most of our mortals had little information, and the officials didn't seem to heed them anyway.

"I heard him talking to someone," Deloo repeated two or three times. At last one of the police officers listened to her and searched the vicinity.

Speaking to the officer in charge, the policeman reported, "There are broken branches in that hedge. Most of these people are saying the dead man came from this side of the street where there's no hedge. There could have been another person across the way."

Grandfather Kwaikit had finished transforming the immortal remains of Howard Lee and what was left of the jumbled nephew, HayJay.

Glad I didn't know how to make transformations or endure my grandfather's crabbiness, I tried turning his attention to something else. *~Woody is keeping his RCMP friend up to date on the investigation on his cell phone. Listen to this.~*

Grandfather moved in on me, shoved me to a corner of my very tidy metaphysical space, and gave me a cocky smirk as he tuned in his auditory functions.

"Woody!" Al Beamus' voice brightened on hearing his friend's voice.

"Hi Al. You would love the folderol here." He spent a few minutes giving his friend the news before closing the call. "You should talk to these detectives. They think it's a suicide. I think the victim is Howard Lee. If it is, you'll find out more than they'll tell us. Looks like he stabbed himself. I'm not sure myself. Deloo thinks there was someone else out there."

"Thanks, Woody. I'll talk to your Cambridge police about it tomorrow. They've already got our files on the Keilleher case." They chatted for a bit, then Woody gloated about his own big news.

"Al, I've found Zigwan again and she's agreed to marry me. Even better, I've landed a job in Alaska in cultural resource management. I start in the fall. Zigwan and I will drive through Canada on the way to Alaska. Maybe we'll see you in a couple of weeks."

* * *

A week later, Deloo waited for her mother to come out of the ladies room at Boston's Logan Airport. Woody and Zigwan had left a couple of days earlier, saving room to visit Al Beamus in Nova Scotia on their journey to Alaska. Deloo was tired, ready, and more than eager to start life again. She glanced at the face of her smart phone. Taale was taking a long time as usual. Deloo sighed and reached into her bag for a book.

"Excuse me," an accented voice said, "I saw you go into this terminal and followed you to apologize."

"What?" Deloo whirled around to size up the woman behind her. Her looks could have placed her in Alaska but her accent sounded Hispanic. The two mortals gazed at each other. "Who are you?"

"My name is Luisa Lee. I know you because I've been following you all over Canada and New England. Now it's over. At last." She pulled a scrunched tissue from a pocket.

"I don't understand. I've been chased by two people, and I know what they look like. You aren't one of them."

Luisa slid into a seat next to Deloo. "We kept track through others. My husband was Howard Lee. I tried so hard to keep him safe, but he got …" She blew into her tissue. "I thought he was innocent after all when the scorpion fish came to him, but maybe it came to my husband's spiritual side rather than the HayJay part. Maybe it knew that he wasn't as bad as I thought. That kind of spirit never comes if the person has committed murder. Do you remember Rosemoira? She and I were friends. She ran the Secret Spirit Inn."

Deloo nodded, eyeing the stranger. "You mean, you were near the inn, but not there when I was trying to check in. You'd better go now. My mother will be here any minute."

Luisa ignored Deloo's heavy-handed hint and said, "Howard drove faster than me. I couldn't keep up with him. Then I spotted you leaving the area. When you turned back toward the Inn, I almost followed, but my spirit guide told me to wait. I had enough time to pull into a gravel patch near the main highway. I didn't want my Howard to get hurt and I tried to get there in time, but my guides told me it was too late. " Luisa dabbed her eyes with the ever more sodden tissue. "Then you came out again and I decided to tail your car. You turned off near Truro. I never made it to the Inn. There was no point. I couldn't save Rosemoira from my own husband."

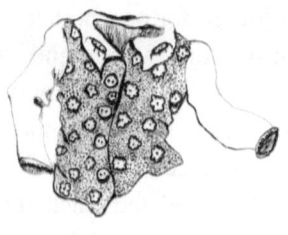

CHAPTER FORTY-EIGHT

Eyes huge, Deloo handed her a clean tissue. "I didn't see you there."

Luisa clung to her wet tissue with her left hand while taking Deloo's offering in the other. She stood up. "I'd better go. When I saw you, I followed on impulse, just as I did today." Turning, she collided with Taale, who had emerged from the bathroom in time to hear some of what Luisa said.

"Sorry," Luisa mumbled, her voice clotted with tears.

"Don't go so soon," Taale's smile was the false one she used when she sensed Deloo was spinning out a story. "I was there the night Howard Lee died. I didn't see you there. Were you?"

"This is my mother," Deloo said. "Mom, this lady just told me she was at the Secret Spirit Inn the day that woman died."

The two Alaskans wedged the Cuban woman between them on the bench. Taale said, her voice conversational, "So what about that innkeeper? Did your husband do it? If so, why?"

Luisa sagged. "Rosemoira was special to me. She was white. Most white folks treat me like dirt. His mother used to. Not anymore. Yes. I was in Nova Scotia with him, but not at the Inn. I knew he'd found out something about her. I could tell that he was caving in to the HayJay part of himself."

A spirit rose sharply. He indicated to me, Baasee' the Indignant, that I should follow him, and then he shot straight upward. Sensing that he objected to something Luisa was telling my trusting Deloo, I followed immediately.

Luisa's spirit communed, ~*the others don't want me to reveal this to you, but it will help explain things if I assure you that our Luisa was not in the car that arrived after your mortal left the Inn. Her husband was. Rosemoira Keilleher placed a call to our Luisa and one other person. Because of the call, Luisa was urged by the Invisible Forces to try to save the innkeeper from her husband. As it happened, traffic worked against both Luisa and Rosemoira that day.~*

Alarmed, I asked, ~*Why? The woman was odd, but she had done nothing to earn sudden death.~* I eyed the spirit without favor. Grandfather Kwaikit wouldn't have trusted him despite his sexy flow and blinding flares. Sure, the guy was respected by the Invisible Forces and had gossamer gewgaws to prove it, but so did I. I might have twitched a little to make sure my best one stood out a bit.

The spirit gaped at my most astonishing merit award (gewgaw to Grandfather), recovered, and said ~*Our Luisa cares for many people. So will your mortal.~* He glowed even brighter and disappeared. I returned to Deloo, seeing that she was still embroiled in a conversation with Luisa.

Deloo sat forward. "Why did he do it?" Brows knotted.

"Because she saw my Howard take those beads off the fifteenth jacket. I wondered why it took so long for her to come forward about it. When I reminded him, my Howard remembered that we got so busy over that jacket, he forgot Rosemoira was there. Until she called a few days ago, it seemed to be something Howard just forgot. It's part of what was happening to him. He was forgetting lots of things by then."

I, the clairvoyant Baasee', could tell that Luisa was engaging in a jumbled commune from her spirits while speaking to Deloo and her mother. I gathered that she told the truth.

~*What about my Qanik? Ask if he killed my fiancé, my Qanik.~* It was the little ghost. She was beside her ghost mentor.

Deloo heard MoLi without my prompting. "Did he kill that Inuit man? Qanik? Did he kill Ming's sister?"

Luisa's eyes teared up. "You know all of us, don't you? If Howard were here, he would kill you on the spot. But he's gone. He said he killed Qanik not long after he took all those gems. He was smart about it. Waited until her fiancé went back to his village and killed him there." She sighed. "At least my Howard did not kill MoLi. I don't know who did, but I do know she's not alive. My spirits tell me MoLi's with you now. Qanik was filling in for Rosemoira at the Inn the night they took all those gems. I thought Rosemoira was on vacation, but she was there, just not on duty. Howard must have thought Qanik was the only witness, but Rosemoira saw him as well. Rosemoira's call the other day changed everything for Howard."

"What about the night Howard was killed? Someone said you were there."

"Si. I just told your daughter that I followed him. It was rainy and dark and I was wearing dark clothes," she fingered her black jeans, "like these." Looking first at Taale and then Deloo, Luisa whispered, "I am a curandera. I'm a medicine woman who works with mentally ill patients. Psychiatrists work with white crazy people. I work with spirit-sick people, usually latinos. My spirits told me to leave today. That's why I'm here now. I'm leaving Boston. My flight goes in a few hours." She sighed and lapsed into silence. "When I saw it flying around outside, the spirit crow, I knew I was meant to talk to you," Luisa remarked at long last.

"You mean Dotson," Deloo and Taale said together. Deloo pushed her butt to the edge of the metal bench. Arthur's camera strap caught at Deloo's hair. She tried to loosen it.

Fascinated that Deloo could get a free lesson about how a curandera works with animal and plant spirits instead of spirit guides like me, I swooped toward them, and pressed against Luisa, flapping invisible wings. Luisa responded by seeming to stare at me, the invisible yet glorious Baasee'. In fact, I felt her mind coursing through me. Curious, I realized that was how she worked with the spirit-sick. I stayed where I was and helped her find my various edges and innards. She touched my spiritual fabric and soon gave up. It was too much and too soon. Releasing a gusty sigh, "They paid me to follow him, and later to take care of him.

"Who paid you?" Taale's voice raked the air. "Who paid you to take care of Howard?"

"His mother, his sister. I don't know which. Before that I worked for other spirit-sick people. I've worked ever since I was a teenager, but not with Howard. I didn't work with him until that time he went to Florida. When he got to Florida he had a year to go on his undergraduate degree. They'd found HayJay by then. Alive. But not well. In the end, HayJay died a few weeks before they hired me. Howard took his nephew's death hard and ran away. I think Howard must have been in a state of mental fugue. That's the psychiatrist's word. It might have been true. Maybe not. Howard was too smart for the psychiatrist to understand, or maybe too confused just as his nephew, HayJay, supposedly had been."

Luisa rested her chin on her fist. "Howard was often confused once HayJay had the initial accident. For instance, he didn't remember being in Florida at all. I don't know how he managed to get to Florida. Bus,

I guess. Maybe he hitched. I found him wandering outside the house I shared with my father in Little Havana, in Miami one night. I took him inside my father's house. He was sexy and handsome back then. He hypnotized me with his slanted eyes. And it helped that he was tall and blond. I asked him who he was and all he said was "HayJay." Luisa gazed into space for a while. "Much later I learned his real name was Howard Lee. To me as a curandera, I think that HayJay's spirit tried to possess the mind and soul of his uncle, my husband, Howard, even though Howard was way down south where I was. Maybe. Maybe that's why my Howard was so smart." She shrugged. "The psychiatrist thinks that grieving over HayJay's death forced my Howard to go crazy." She shook her head. "By that time in his treatment, Howard was good at feeding the psychiatrist answers that matched the schoolbooks. What difference does it make now? Either way, Howard did what he did, thought what he thought."

"His mother or his sister started to pay me for helping Howard stay in Florida after that. Whoever it is did it through bank transfers so that I don't know where the money comes from." Luisa murmured to no one in particular, "Howard's father doesn't know about it. He never knew about that arrangement. Howard's mother didn't want me to tell her husband. She never said anything to her husband or anyone else. A few days later Howard wanted to go back to Massachusetts. They said they would pay me to go with him and I did."

"Do you mean when he got to Florida he thought he was HayJay Johnson?" Deloo asked.

"How do you know HayJay's last name?" Luisa looked at Deloo, anger flashed in her eyes. "Did Howard tell you?"

"Not Howard. I never spoke to him until that last night. I learned bits and pieces from others. It's taken a while to get any information," Deloo supplied. "Is that who he is? HayJay, I mean."

"No, The person you met is Howard Lee, my husband. Like I said, HayJay died over twenty years ago. Howard couldn't accept his death and sometimes my Howard thought he was HayJay. Or else thought it was a good idea to think he was HayJay." Her forefinger hovered over Deloo's jadeite wedding ring. "He would like you because of this. It was made by one of his favorite jade carvers in his part of China." Luisa's throat convulsed. "Howard knew them all, and we spent time learning from this man. His signature, do you see it?"

Deloo looked at her ring as if for the first time. "I don't see any writing on it. How did he sign it?"

"No," Luisa chuckled. "I meant the dragon shape. That jade artist always managed to tease the flare of dragon's nostrils to life in every piece he made."

Deloo gawped. "I see it now, but I've never noticed it before."

"His work is subtle." Luisa squirmed as if to leave.

Taale held her in place by leaning her full weight against the Cuban woman. "Please tell us more about Howard. He is a mystery to me. Did you say they hired you to follow him to Florida?"

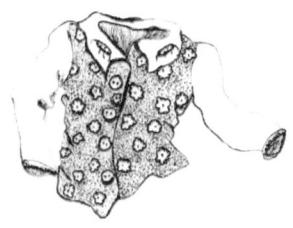

CHAPTER FORTY-NINE

"No, no." Luisa smiled at some hidden world no one else could see. "I lived in Florida at that time and I took him in out of charity. No, they hired me to stay with him up north after Howard's mind cleared and he called his mother. Once that happened, a lot of his family came down to Florida in order to bring him home: his mother, his sister, who is HayJay's mother, his father, and a couple of brothers. That's when I found out that Howard was rich. Very rich."

"Why did they hire you when you lived in Florida and they lived in the north?" Deloo persisted. "What good would you do him?"

Luisa's shoulders shifted. "Silence. They bought the brown skin of a Latina woman. They didn't want their friends and family to know—the ones who lived in New England and Canada, they didn't want anyone to know that Howard had mental issues. Being crazy is worse than being Latino."

Deloo nodded thoughtfully. "Being crazy is just as bad as being a halfbreed. Mom, do you remember how they treated that white woman, Dee? Since my name is like hers, she thought she was me. She even said she was Dena Dena and that her mother was an Indian. When they asked where she was from, she asked me where I was born."

Taale barked in horror. "I remember her. Eventually they found out her real name was Dee Douw and that she was from somewhere in Washington. She had no idea of how she got to Fairbanks. Spooky."

"Maybe she suffered from the same thing that Howard had." Luisa's face dissolved into angry tears. "I think they were sure it would ruin them even more than it would affect my Howard. They were selfish that way. A few months later Lydia, that's Howard's big sister, wanted Howard to finish her son's PhD. I thought they were the crazy ones to ask him to do it. He couldn't think straight about ordinary things. But

they were right about the degree. He had something special about thinking with a computer."

Deloo smiled, "I wish I had that kind of problem. Mom does have it.
She's great with computers."

Luisa rolled her eyes at both of them. "Then things got even stranger. They didn't want Howard's father to know about HayJay's unfinished
degree at M.I.T. because he wasn't from that side of the family. So they
cooked up another scheme. They convinced Mr. Lee to bribe me into
helping Howard by offering me money."

"My spirits told me to ignore them. Tell them no, they said to me. So
I said no. Howard's mother and sister ignored me. They told Mr. Lee it
was because Howard loved me. I loved Howard and he needed me, so I
went along with that story. Besides, years earlier my parents and I came
over to Florida without anyone to help. It was hard and we were always
afraid. My father told that to Mr. Lee. That's when Howard's father, he's
half Chinese, cooked up this harebrained scheme to bring more of my
Cuban family over to Florida to please my father and me. That's what
the father paid for. Howard's father knows a lot about immigration into
the U.S.A., Canada and the E.U."

Supported by the tight grouping of the two Alaskans, Luisa's body
seemed to become taller and more muscular. "My father made the deal.
He demanded twenty Cubanos, that's people of Cuba, with all their
housing and travel costs and fees paid for. We settled for ten people and
a big house. My father thinks we could have forced them to bring all
twenty. I ended up doing that with Howard's money. It was good for
my family for a while. But Howard was a complicated man. He looked
white to my family. They were embarrassed to be seen with him because we are all so Cuban in looks. You two know more than anyone
else, since you are Indios. Howard, for his part, thought people could
tell automatically that he wasn't all white. That he was actually both
Chinese and white American. He said he wanted to be taken as Chinese,
even though he was blond, but he also liked to stroll around the M.I.T.
campus as a white man. He got better treatment that way. Well, in the
end my family asked me not to bring him home at Christmas. He had
too many assumptions, entendéis, for everything from who should be
invited to what we should do or what we did. We, the Cubanos that they
paid to bring over, were not the hosts in our own home."

"That's a lot of money!" Deloo murmured, remembering how much
a friend of hers had forked over to bring her brother across the Mexican

border at Nogales. "He probably thought his father even paid for your smiles."

Luisa, surprised, grinned and gave Deloo a squeeze. "Si! It was more than my family ever had. And all I had to do was stay with Howard until he got over HayJay. Well, he never got over losing his best friend and nephew. He couldn't. Even though he had this thing about looking Chinese, he also had it about looking right in HayJay's white crowd. It's like the soul of HayJay came into him sometimes and stayed for a few hours or days, even weeks at a time. It didn't matter to me. By that time I was hooked on being Howard's caregiver and his wife. My father knew I would have done it all for free."

"Why?" asked Deloo.

Luisa's laugh sounded like a bird chittering in a tree. "Why? If I understood love, I would tell you. My father made the deal. I did not. He got his parents and two brothers, my mother got her parents, an older brother, and two of my cousins. I was amazed at how much clout Mr. Lee had. So did his wife, Charlotte. I was even more amazed at how willing Howard was to bend his American rules to make room for a Cuban curandera like me. It's like religion wasn't his way of understanding the world. He was much more used to the old Chinese spirit customs than into formal religions. Because of that, we got along well."

Taale mused aloud, "Sounds like there were two ways of dealing with you: Howard's way and his father's way. The one needed your love, the other needed your loyalty. So twenty years ago they bought you, your silence, and made sure the rest of your family stayed in Florida, right?"

"Si, yes. They did. I was happy until Howard told me he killed Qanik two years ago. That's when I contacted his mother. Qanik's family got help their Inuit way. It is something that my spirits and I don't work with because it's too complicated."

Taale asked "What about Howard's mother? Couldn't they help?"

Luisa jagged with anger. She shook her black hair. "No. As always, Mrs. Lee was kind but firm. She told me it was my imagination. But I told her it wasn't me who was having trouble. It was Howard. His HayJay episodes went from hours at a time to days on end. He was, I don't know the right word, something about creciente."

Taale offered, "Escalating."

Luisa nodded. "Yes. Escalating. I never took Howard's offer of going to college. I should have. He was getting worse. Charlotte Lee, that's my mother-in-law, didn't believe me at all about Howard." Luisa shrugged elegant shoulders. "She would have if I had gone to college."

"My spirits and my heart told me to cover for him one more time." She looked at Deloo. "I have spirits with me, just like you do." Luisa squeezed her way out of the hip-grip of Taale and Deloo to get to a standing position. "My father needs me to go to Florida. My work is done here in the North."

As Luisa spoke, her spirits swarmed around me, the wise and wonderful Baasee'. *~What is your attitude toward this death?~*The oldest one asked me.

I replied, *~I, that is, we already understand how the innkeeper in Nova Scotia met her end. Howard, possibly entering another HayJay fugue, was covering his trail. It was easy for Howard to kill the woman, possessed or not. If you are speaking of how she killed her own husband, the truth is foggy. Why did she do that?~*

Luisa's spirit spotted his mortal moving away. *~I must go. Her reasons are simple. She brought many relatives out of Cuba after the initial ten her father-in-law helped get into the U.S.A. All of those people cost more money both initially and afterward than any of us expected. They all need money for health care, housing, and food. She stands up for a lot of people who are almost as poor as they were in Cuba. The innkeeper knew Howard had done in Qanik and she knew he was going to kill her as well. Luisa couldn't protect Rosemoira, but tried. In the end, she realized that Howard provided more for her and dozens of others by dying. As for that last night, he'd already taken too large a dose of his medication before he went searching for Deloo. Our Luisa simply helped him to die more quickly.~*

Watching Luisa stride away, Deloo shrugged and leaned toward her mother. "Do you believe her, Mom? Do you think she killed her husband? Do you think she killed that innkeeper or did her husband do it? Do you think we should tell anyone?"

"Besides missing our flight and going through all that hassle, what would we say?" Taale shot back. "We don't have any proof of any of it. What we have is a Cuban woman who might have killed her husband—or not for good or bad reasons. Maybe to keep him from putting people in mortal danger through identity theft." She shook her head. "He did that to you, and others tried to kill you. Plus, they caught him at it. We'll do what she's doing. Go back home." Taale went to check the flight monitors again.

While she waited, Deloo muttered "I don't get it."

~What? ~ I flapped luscious spirit guide wings above her, expecting the worst. *~There's a lot to life and death that isn't for us to understand, my child. You are right to suspect Luisa of killing many people.~* I explained what I'd just learned and ended with, *~ultimately, your mother's practicality is right.~*

~That's terrible, Baasee'. Does that mean that if enough people are helped, crimes like murder are justifiable?~

~The Invisible Forces are implacable that way. So is war. Thank you, by the way, for making the effort to commune rather than speak aloud.~

~You're welcome, Baasee'. Could you help me again to understand what a half-breed is? Luisa and her talk about Howard Lee weirded me out. I get it about legal issues with different countries. Woody is a complicated Canadian/American example. But what about people like that Howard guy? Is he a half-breed because of the way his mind worked?~

I knew she'd get to this point sooner or later. *~Yes, of course. He's part Chinese. There's no point in counting microdots of genes. Genetically he was mixed, mentally he was also mixed so many ways it was hard to keep track of him, especially if by mentally you mean being crazy. Apparently he found it expedient to meld with his nephew so that he could appear to know a lot about computers while in fact he wanted to spend time with the botany of herbs. According to her spirit guide, Luisa tried to help him remove the weak HayJay semi-spirit. Perhaps she decided that it was better to keep HayJay for his amoral behavior rather than save Howard. As you will find out, we spirits have to make tough decisions outside of the laws of any mortal's legal system.~*

~What you're saying is that Howard was sort of a mental captive. Does that make him a mental half-breed?~

~Yes, and more so, because he acted the part. It was real for him to be HayJay.~

~Okay, I get that~ Deloo scuffed the floor. *~Is that what spirit possession is? Was he possessed by HayJay?~*

~Well, sort of. My grandfather showed me the little piece of HayJay that was stuck in Howard. The thing is, it wasn't much and it wasn't strong enough to commit crimes. Howard had to be motivated as well. Besides, being possessed is not about being a halfbreed. It's an honor in many parts of the world.~

Deloo braced her fingers around Arthur's camera case and whispered, ~*do you possess me, Baasee'? You do a lot of things through me that I can't do on my own.*~

She got to the big one at last. ~*Are you asking if spiritual possession makes you a half-breed?*~

"Yes, I think so."

~*Being possessed is not being a half-breed. And you are not possessed. I'm with you a lot, but I am a separate entity even when I help you out, like I did in Montreal. I made things for you to hang on to, but it was all you that did the climbing. I rarely have an opportunity to try spirit possession on anyone. It takes a specific kind of power that I don't like to use. Rather, I simply advise you. HayJay's life was cut short. Maybe he had enough power to do spirit possession. Since he was on a collision course with his uncle in terms of career and money, he could have tried spirit possession when he became a spirit himself.*~

"So what about Howard getting a PhD in computers when he's really an accountant? Seems like something helped him out a lot to do that. Arthur worked hard for his PhD. Could HayJay have done the PhD work on his own through Howard?"

I shrugged golden sparkles off a beautifully crafted lavender judge's robe. I'd made it centuries earlier to get over those rough times I often face. Like the death of someone wonderful. ~*Maybe. There has to be more to the story than we know. Luisa gave us a lot of free information, but left plenty of holes, some of which her guides explained to me. Some not. For instance, why? Why would anyone, Howard or any of them, kill that innkeeper, Rosemoira Keilleher?*~

"Yeah," Deloo muffled her words behind a yawn. "Or that other guy. Qanik. Does that little ghost think someone else did him in?"

~*She's not with us anymore, Deloo. Remember? She got her spirit mentor and will be with that guide for a long time. I understand that we might see her again in the near future as a friend and not a companion.*~ As I spoke the outer doors of the airport building opened to a family loaded with baggage. A bird flew in, flapping over their heads and toward Deloo. Then Taale appeared.

"Is that Dotson?" Deloo pointed at the door.

Taale looked around. "No, it's way too small. I think that's a crow, not a raven." Taale looked at the door and mused, "Maybe the changes crows make aren't very big or their messages are not quite the same.

Maybe it's a way of telling us that the changes Luisa has made are different than we might expect of ravens in Alaska. Dotson's changes are often dirty tricks, and once in a while they are for the good. Who can tell about what Luisa does? Not us."

ABOUT THE AUTHOR

PHYLLIS ANN FAST, winner of the North American Indian Prose Award, is an artist (painter) and a woman of mixed descent (Tleeyegg'e huͭ'aane, which is also known as Koyukon Athabascan and white American). She was born in Anchorage, Alaska in 1946 to Elsie and Oscar Fast, graduated from East Anchorage High School in the year of the 1964 Alaskan earthquake. She earned a BA in English from the University of Alaska then centered in Fairbanks, later an interdisciplinary Master of Arts from the University of Alaska Anchorage, and concluded her education with a PhD in Anthropology from Harvard University in 1998. After teaching at the University of Alaska Fairbanks and the University of Alaska Anchorage, she retired Professor Emerita in 2014, when she turned to writing fiction. She now lives in the Washington state.

Please visit her website: PhyllisFast.com

These three are also available as ebooks.

Fiction / Native American & Aboriginal

Half-Bead of Fundy

First in the Native American Mystery series

Deloo had always welcomed the pull of a myriad of oddball spirits. ~Pull a 180!~ Baasee' shouted into her head. Deloo wasn't used to spirit guides like Baasee', but the crazy people following her didn't know or care. They wanted her beaded jacket at any cost. It was up to Alaska Native, Deloo Goode, to figure out what was so important about her mother's beading— or else be killed like the innkeeper at the Secret Spirit Inn.

270 pages

ISBN 978-0-9974977-2-4 (trade paperback)

Midnight Trauma

Second in the Native American Mystery series,
sequel to *Half-Bead of Fundy*.

Someone has killed a teenager at a bead shop in remote Fairbanks, Alaska. Moreover, the owner, Earlene, is missing and the shop keeps getting broken into. Deloo Goode and her mother try to unravel the mysteries surrounding the bead shop. Luckily, Deloo has an invisible weapon: her playful spirit guide Baasee', who can see things others can't—sometimes. Will they force the murderer into the open? Can they untangle the clues and surprises before anyone else gets hurt?

250 pages

ISBN: 978-0-9974977-3-1 (trade paperback)

The Dire Wolf Alliance

A Native American Saga

Prequel to the Native American Mystery series

The prehistoric story told by her spirit guide Baasee' and her Grandfather Kwaiikit, helps Deloo, the protagonist of *Half-Bead of Fundy* and *Midnight Trauma*, come to grips with her own recent widowhood.

"Go where?" Ping asked Chebucto. "You've been banished twice. You have nowhere to go." Growing up, no matter the era or place, can be terrifying. Chebucto understood what the medicine man told him to do, but couldn't do it by himself on the ancient northeastern coast of North America. Meanwhile, adults in a local group called the Dire Wolf Alliance, tried to rescue and find homes for widows and orphans traumatized by the violent Death Runners bludgeoning their way through Zana.

260 pages

ISBN: 978-0-9974977-6-2 (trade paperback)

JUVENILE FICTION / Animals / Deer, Moose & Caribou

Tepi, the Girl Who Helped the Deer

Story and illustrations by Phyllis Ann Fast

Tepi finds herself in communication with a deer spirit who wants her to go into the forest and help an injured deer in need. This is the story of how Tepi found her calling.

66 pages, full color

Trade paperback

ISBN: 978-0-9974977-1-7

JUVENILE FICTION / Animals / Elephants

Brella and Her Umbrella, A Baby Elephant Story

Story and illustrations by Phyllis Ann Fast

Brella, the baby elephant, is so curious that she dreamily follows a pretty bird. She wanders away from her family and is suddenly LOST! Her spirit guide, Umbrella, attempts to keep Brella safe from danger.

68 pages, full color

Trade paperback

ISBN: 978-0-9974977-5-5

Available at Amazon.com and other retail outlets.

Northern Athabascan Survival
Women, Community, and the Future
(North American Indian Prose Award)

by Phyllis Ann Fast

The Northern Athabascan peoples of the Alaskan interior and the Yukon have survived centuries of contact and attempted domination by outsiders. Their lives today are rich in meaning and tradition yet are also complicated by numerous challenges such as poverty, alcoholism, domestic violence, suicide, and troubled leadership.

Combining scholarly analysis, first-person accounts, and her own experiences and insights as a Koyukon Athabascan artist and anthropologist, Phyllis Ann Fast illuminates the modern Athabascan world. Her conversations with Athabascan women offer revealing glimpses of their personal lives and a probing assessment of their professional opportunities and limitations. Also showcased is the crucial but ambiguous role of Athabascan leaders, who are needed to champion reform and social healing but are often undermined by conflicting notions of decision making, personhood, and leadership in Athabascan society.

A troubling observation of this study is the vast extent to which addiction—manifested as both substance abuse and economic dependency—pervades Northern Athabascan society and threatens to curtail its cohesion and aspirations. But Northern Athabascans are far from victims. As Fast discovers, Northern Athabascan men and women are well aware of these widespread social problems, and many have undertaken initiatives to deal with and heal them. Rigorous and compassionate, *Northern Athabascan Survival* provides an uncompromising view of a remarkable and troubled world.

When Spirits Visit
A Collection of Stories by Indigenous Authors
Compiled and Edited by MariJo Moore

WHEN SPIRITS VISIT contains stories centered on spiritual visitation – animal, bird, and people. Some are fiction, some non-fiction, and some faction. Discernment is left to each reader.

Writers included are: Susan Deer Cloud, **Phyllis A. Fast,** Gabriel Horn, Amy Krout-Horn, Evan Pritchard, Jim Stevens, MariJo Moore, Sean Milanovich, Clifford Trafzer, Dawn Karima Pettigrew, Lois Red Elk, Willliam Yellow Robe, Jr, Dean Hutchins and Denise Low—all respected published authors in the Native American realm of literature.

This book is unique in its presentation of the fact that "...many of us do believe in the mysteries of the universe, even if they cannot be 'proved' mathematically or scientifically. There are spirit beings who help us, who guide us, and there are spirit beings who can confuse us as well. Spirit beings are all around us at any given moment. These spirits have their work to do in helping us, so they need us as much as we need them."